WICKED ONYX

WICKED ONYX

DEBBIE CASSIDY

Page & Vine
An Imprint of Meredith Wild LLC

This is a work of fiction. Names, characters, places, and incidents either are the product of the author's imagination or are used fictitiously, and any resemblance to actual persons, living or dead, business establishments, events, or locales is entirely coincidental. The publisher does not assume any responsibility for third-party websites or their content.

The author acknowledges the trademarked status and trademark owners of various products referenced in this work, which have been used without permission. The publication/use of these trademarks is not authorized, associated with, or sponsored by the trademark owners.

Copyright © 2026 Debbie Cassidy
Cover Design by Covers By Christian

All Rights Reserved.
No part of this book may be reproduced, scanned, or distributed in any printed or electronic format without permission. Please do not participate in or encourage piracy of copyrighted materials in violation of the author's rights. Purchase only authorized editions.

Paperback ISBN: 978-1-964264-29-5

*To Andrea, who read the first three drafts
and to Jordyn, who read the next four.
Wicked Onyx wouldn't be the book it is without you.*

COVENS

~~Blackthorne~~
Embercrest
Evergreen
Silverthorn

HAEMATOPHAGE HOUSES

Damascus
Moon
Vayne

PACKS

Indra
Pouvoir
Thorn

SORCERER BLOODLINES

Ironhart
Onyx
Reign

> "Herbaceous magic is a most satisfying skill to master. Tricky for those not attuned to the nature threads of the Weave, but possible with tenacity and determination..."
>
> *Arcane Botany*

PROLOGUE

NIGHTSBRIDGE ACADEMY

SELINA

I'd jumped out of my fourth-floor window every night for the past week, rehearsing my escape. Slept fully clothed, just in case. But a big part of me hadn't believed the precautions necessary.

Tonight proved me wrong.

"Go," the voice inside the mirror urged. "They're coming." His misty form undulated behind silvered glass, but I caught the impression of dark, flowing locks and the flash of needle-sharp teeth.

The pulse in my throat throbbed painfully. "I'm scared."

"Good. Fear will give your feet wings. Get to the circle and stay inside it, no matter what happens. Now go!"

I shoved open the window, wincing at the creak and pop of the swollen wood, then climbed out onto the sill while maintaining a death grip on the frame. "Light as a feather, floating on a breeze, carry me safely, hold me with ease," I whispered the words into the wind before stepping into its embrace.

My scream lodged in my throat as I dropped sharply before the spell took hold and my body grew light. The ground rose to meet me, the crash and thunder of the sea a distant companion to the rapid pulse of blood in my head.

I fixed my gaze on the woodland beyond the neatly clipped quad as I drifted to the ground. Even its wild embrace couldn't protect me from *them*.

They'd follow.

They'd find me.

But not before I reached the circle.

My boots touched earth, and the essence of nature reached for me through leather and cotton, promising sanctuary.

Above me, a raven screamed.

I ran.

Don't look back. Don't slow down. Don't stop.

The air crackled with abrasive power that skimmed over my skin and clawed at my scalp, snagging in my hair as if desperate to haul me back, but the woods beckoned, and I leapt into its arms.

The shadows beneath the canopy guarded and shielded me, while the scent of nature soothed, urging me on, guiding me over bracken and tree roots to a clearing where sanctuary waited in the form of a circle made of shrubs, small white blooms, and large toadstools that gleamed silver in the moonlight.

I hurried into the circle and dropped my pack to root for the supplies needed to activate the spell I'd been working on for the past three weeks, ever since—

Crack.

No, no, no. I grabbed the pouch holding the powder and the vial filled with tincture. The hum of *their* power grew stronger, and my stomach bloomed with gnarly knots of fear.

Focus. There's time.

I drank the tincture to connect me to the circle, then sprinkled the powder all around to activate my protection spell. Quick sticks, work fast. "Hidden from every eye but mine, blessed circle, bring the enemy close and forever bind."

A calm fell over me, the thrum of panic ebbing, leaving me still and silent as shadowy robed figures drifted into the clearing, surrounding me.

"There is nowhere to run. Nowhere to hide." The voice rose and fell like the wind, the timbre unfamiliar and alien.

"What do you want? Why are you doing this to me?"

"You've never mattered to anyone. But you matter to us." One of the figures glided closer, its cloak trailing across the silver-washed blades of grass.

I wanted to see his face. Needed to know who my tormentor was, but he remained hidden in gloom.

He held out a hand encased in black leather. "Come willingly, and it will be quick."

Heat flushed through me, hugging my throat and tearing harsh words from my lips. "Fuck you. If you want me, then come and fucking get me, you bastard."

He moved so fast he was a blur—outside my circle one moment, and a foot in front of me the next.

I locked my knees and bit back a cry as my spell flared to life, silver wards flying up around us to hold him in place. I had him. I had—

The protective power surrounding me winked out, and the wind howled in mourning.

No. No, no, no...

His raspy laughter filled the space between us. "Points for effort, Selina. But your circle is useless against me."

Cold fire wrapped around my throat and squeezed until my eyes grew hot and my vision blurred.

The trees leaned toward me, branches reaching out as if they could tear me free and take me away.

The wind picked up, clawing at the figure's cloak and whipping it back and forth, then with a final burst of power, it ripped back the hood to reveal his face.

Shock punched me in the gut. No...it couldn't be...

"Goodbye, Selina."
The warm nugget of power inside me dimmed...
I didn't want to die.
I didn't—

This is forbidden. What shouldn't have happened has come to pass. My fault entirely. I should have walked away. I could have saved her...

Unnamed Journal (Vault Archives)

CHAPTER 1

CARLSTON TOWN

ANAMAYA

The tram rocked gently on a rickety track in desperate need of repairs. Everything about Carlston Town needed fixing. The houses, the businesses, the enforcement, and the people. But it was home.

The trap on the seat beside me shuffled forward, and I slammed my hand on it, drawing it back.

A low growl emanated from inside. *"Let me out. Let me go."*

"Shut up."

"Excuse me?" The woman sitting on the bench opposite glared at me, mouth pinched like she'd just sucked on a lemon.

"I wasn't speaking to you."

"Oh, really, then who were you speaking to?"

I tapped the trap. "The critter in here."

Her eyes went round. "What?" She slid along her seat. "Conductor! Conductor!"

Oh, for the love of all things dark and gory. "Shut up. And this time, I *am* speaking to you."

"Heh, heh, heh." The critter chuckled.

"What seems to be the problem here?" the conductor asked lemon lips.

"She's traveling with a critter," citrus eater said, pointing a neatly manicured finger my way. "It's against the law to bring one of those things onto public transport."

The conductor glanced at my trap which chose that moment to shuffle forward again. I scooped it into my lap and held it tightly.

"I smell your blood."

It was that time of the month, but ick.

The conductor's pencil mustache twitched. "Miss, is there a critter in the trap?"

"No."

"Liar, you said there was a critter in there," the woman said.

I smiled sweetly at her. "And I bet your hairstylist told you that bangs suited you."

"Why, you insolent little—"

"I can show you if you'd like?" I reached for the latch on the trap.

"No!" the conductor and woman cried in unison.

I bit back a smile. "In that case, I'd like to enjoy the rest of my journey in peace."

The conductor and the woman exchanged glances. "There are seats further up in the tram," he said. "I'll escort you."

The woman slid off her bench with an agitated huff, giving me a wide berth. She threw a wary glance at my trap before following the conductor down the aisle.

"I'm hungry."

I didn't bother responding.

"I have a nest. Children. They're waiting for me to bring back food."

This was not my problem.

"I never hurt a human. Only rodents and pests."

It didn't matter how innocent this critter was—I needed what the sale would bring me.

Needing a distraction from its pleading, I pulled my notepad and pencil out of my pocket and set to work sketching the *Obsidian Venenum* I'd spotted by chance earlier. A fleeting glimpse on the way to pick up my trap, but enough to capture it in graphite. I'd ink it in later. The elusive critters, commonly known as jet stingers, were highly sought after for the paralytic effects of the venom they secreted. I'd only ever come across an abandoned nest before, the eggs dull because the larvae inside were dead. Killed by another jet stinger's venom. They were a strange species, hellbent on wiping each other out... Wait, come to think of it, wasn't that exactly what humans did?

I added shading to the segmented body. The creature was a cross between a millipede and a scorpion. Its hard shell a gleaming black, with two pinpricks of red for eyes. The perfect addition to my cryptozoology codex, a leather-bound collection of sketches and information on all the critters I'd come across so far. One day I might even get it professionally printed at one of the presses in Hartwood City, or better yet, published. Maybe.

"What will happen to me? Will it hurt?"

The quiver in the critter's voice made my stomach twist. I rubbed the bandage on my hand. The psybond toxin the thing had injected into me would wear off soon enough, and it would no longer be able to speak to me. Until then, I'd ignore it.

"Please...please, I don't want to die."

It began to sob softly, and I gritted my teeth and closed my eyes. I couldn't afford to feel sorry for it.

Critters was the collective name given to all the mutated creatures that lived beneath the cities and towns of Nova Terra. The history of critter origins was somewhat murky, but the consensus was that they'd begun to evolve after The Overshadowing nearly three hundred years ago.

Some critters were dangerous, exterminated by the critter control company I worked for to cull the population, but most were harmless. Sourced and trapped so their body parts could be used in medicines, tinctures, and potions. Like the *Floramus Arachmus* I'd picked up today. They were difficult to catch, due to their nests being in the hardest to reach spots of the sewer system. Like their name suggested, they looked like a cross between a flower and a spider—eight legs and petal-like appendages sticking up from their backs, which picked up sound waves so they could see in the dark, much like bats. Fascinating little creature.

I'd gotten lucky with this one. It had been hunting for its nest. A mother trying to feed her children.

No. I couldn't allow sentimentality to color the big picture. There was a reason for what I did. A valid, vital reason, and that was all that mattered.

Pennyriff Market was one of the shadiest parts of Carlston Town, and one of my regular haunts ever since I'd taken on freelancing as a side gig six months ago. Center for Critter Control didn't pay enough for what I needed, and there was nothing in my contract stating that freelancing was prohibited. Still, I'd kept it quiet. Dabbling in critter capture for interested parties was much more lucrative, but it was also competitive. My job at the CCC provided the stability of a regular wage to cover the dry periods in freelancing.

Today, the wind had blown smog from the textile factories directly over the market. It hung low in a thick, gray cloud, the acrid stench mingling with the smell of roasting meat, ruining the usually enticing aroma. My stomach still managed a grumble, reminding me that it had been several hours since breakfast.

I wove through the crowd, trap held close to my chest, past smudged faces that looked inward. Probably lost in thoughts of their own problems. Threadbare coats, tattered scarves, fingerless gloves, and worn shoes were the dress code here. I'd done my best to emulate it, to fit in, but even then, my coat was a little too well-kept, gloves too clean, and shoes not worn enough.

I caught a few curious glances but was quickly dismissed—after all, why would anyone who didn't need to be in this part of town be here?

With no functioning telecom or radio towers, this part of town was off the grid. They'd tried to repair the towers a few times, but the fix hadn't taken. Magic was too weak here and so the magi-generators couldn't activate to power the towers.

The Overshadowing had altered Nova Terra in many ways, but the main impact lay in how technology functioned. Before The Overshadowing, magic and technology had co-existed, but afterward, the balance was disrupted. Now magic acted as a crutch for technology. Certain regions had higher magic potency than others, and it was only in those regions that magitech could function continuously. The rest of the world made do with controlled, timed surges of electricity.

Pennyriff was a low-surge area that ran on manual labor and hope. It was a place of necessity. The cheapest food and wares you'd find anywhere in Carlston, along with the kind of hole-in-the-wall places reserved for nefarious trades and deals.

I passed stalls selling fabric, bruised fruit and vegetables, knick-knacks, and old appliances in need of repair. Meat of dubious origin sizzled on a skillet to my left, and damn it smelled good.

I might grab a bite on the way back to the tram station.

The crowd thinned as I approached the edge of the market, where a row of three-story residences leaned together like conspirators, forming a barrier into what the locals called the rat run—a network of streets and alleys housing the unfortunate populace of this section of town.

It was dark in the run, claustrophobic in the narrow streets that twisted and turned, cutting slender paths between homes that were huddled together, connected by makeshift bridges made of wood and rope. Laundry hung from dark windows, and the hum of life hidden behind doors covered in peeling paint made the journey a little less creepy.

I walked faster, vigilant, because although the run was generally safe for residents, outsiders were fair game for local gangs.

My destination wasn't far now. I took a left at one of the few lampposts that illuminated the run and hurried down the alley that was one arm of a crossroads, connecting me to where I needed to be.

My scalp pricked in warning a moment before two figures stepped out of the shadows, blocking my path. The anemic lamplight illuminated them—one tall and broad, the other short and stocky. Both dressed in the gray and black overalls of the CCC.

I gripped the trap tighter. "Trent. Harry. Fancy meeting you here, in this dark alley in the middle of the afternoon, miles away from where you guys were supposed to be today." I smiled thinly. "Did you decide to take a long detour?"

Trent matched my smile with a cold one of his own, and a chill slid up my spine to hug my nape. "Cut the bullshit, Anamaya. We've been watching you."

"Well, that's not creepy at all. I'm going to have to speak to HR. I'm sure you understand."

"You always do this," Harry snapped. "Make a joke of everything. This is no joke. You're freelancing while working for the CCC, and that won't stand. Give us the critter, and we'll say no more about it." He held out his shovel-like hands, as if he expected me to simply hand over the bounty that I'd spent three days trawling through sewers to find.

"It's a good thing you're nice to look at, Harry, because you're denser than smog."

"Huh?" He looked to Trent for an explanation.

I resisted the urge to roll my eyes. "I know you're not going to take the critter back to the CCC. You're working freelance for Carlisle. I know what critters he's been after, and I know you two tossers haven't the tracking or trapping skills to nab any of them on your own. If you think I'm going to let you steal from me, then you're not only dense, you're also delusional."

Trent stepped forward, pulling himself to his full six-two height and puffing out his chest. "There are two options for you here. Give us the trap and walk away, or we beat you to a pulp and take it from you."

"I don't want to go with them. Please."

I ignored the critter, tapping my chin and feigning consideration of their proposal. "I think I'll go with the third option."

"There is no third option," Harry said, brows low in confusion.

"Shut up, H," Trent snapped. "She's being a smartass." He looked down his nose at me. "Go on then. What's the third option?"

I carefully set down the trap and dipped my gloved hands into my pocket, pulling out the case that housed my knuckle dusters. "I think I'm gonna have to kick both your asses."

They exchanged glances, then burst out laughing. I took the opportunity to bridge the distance between us and punch Harry in the face. His head whipped back, but he held his ground, blinking rapidly against the tears that filled his eyes before slowly reaching up to touch his bloody nose—blood that was already tinged blue by the toxin coating my knuckle dusters. Thumb blades would have been a better choice, but I'd used them a couple of weeks ago and hadn't had a chance to coat them again.

"Fuck!" Trent jumped back to avoid a blow, his hands coming up to fend me off.

"Wha...." Harry fell over with a thud.

The paralysis would wear off eventually.

Trent backed up, fumbling in his overall pocket, presumably for the standard issue CCC weapon.

"What's happening?"

I rushed him, not wanting to give him a chance to pull the taser free. The magitech weapon delivered enough of a shock to take down not just the hardiest critter, but humans too. He dodged so that my blow glanced off his shoulder. I spun around and tackled him, knocking the taser from his grasp. It clattered across the ground, skidding out of reach as we grappled.

Like this, one-on-one, he was stronger than me, could overpower me. But my mother had taught me that there was nothing wrong with fighting like a girl. So, I did just that—slipping under his arm to come out at his back, I delivered a sharp punch to his kidneys before kicking the back of his knee. He went down, and I grabbed him in a sleeper hold, compressing his carotid artery. He tried to stand, to lift me off my feet and take away my advantage. Like hell would I allow that.

I bit his ear hard enough to draw blood and a strangled squeal before he went limp. His body weight pulled me down, but I held fast, needing to be sure this wasn't a ploy.

"Hello? Let me out!" The trap rattled.

Long seconds passed in which the muscles in my arms began to seize, and the urge to spit had saliva pooling in my mouth—ugh. I'd bitten his ear. I released my grip a fraction, then, satisfied he wasn't faking, released him completely.

He lay crumpled on the ground, looking suddenly smaller. I turned my head and spat a few times to get the taste of sweat and blood out of my mouth. Like, seriously? Why were his ears sweaty?

I couldn't risk him waking up before I'd made it out of the run, so I grabbed his hand and ran the back of my knuckle dusters across his skin, hard enough to scrape and draw blood. Enough for the paralytic to seep into his bloodstream.

The specific neurotoxin was found in Sicut Mors—large mosquito-like bugs found in the western forestlands on the outskirts of Carlston. Nasty blighters. They stung for the fun of it, and although the bites could make you numb, the toxin wasn't strong enough to paralyze, not unless combined with several other ingredients. Bunty knew the combination and had given me a vial as a gift after the last job I worked for him.

The world was a dangerous place when you had no magic to protect you. I'd use whatever I could get my hands on in its place.

I turned down the narrow alley where Bunty & Co. was housed. A hole-in-the-wall potion emporium that doubled as a pawn shop, run by Buntington Grom, an independent incantor with nothing but nasty things to say about the Arcanus. He often spewed vitriol about the *system*, about how the covens of incantors were hoarding spells, and how sorcerers were power-hungry egomaniacs. His hatred of magic users almost matched mine.

Almost.

It was the only reason I'd trusted him with the most important job—creating healing tinctures for my mother.

The bell above the door tinkled as I entered the gloomy, slightly smelly shop and wove my way between cluttered shelves and around boxes of stuff, toward the back where Bunty held court.

A whimper emanated from the box. *"Please..."*

Dammit, when would the toxin wear off? "Bunty!" I picked up my pace, stepping over a wooden stool used to access the top shelves of his hoarder's paradise and ducking under a dream catcher to get to the counter, where Bunty was hunched over something small and mechanical.

He looked up at me with one huge, magnified eye. "Did you get it?" His impressive gray mustache moved with the words.

I held up the trap. "I got it."

"Good. Hand it over." He held out his hands, making grabby motions with his fingers.

The critter began to sob again.

"Tincture first, Bunty. You know the deal."

He wiggled his jaw, a sign of agitation, and lead bloomed in my belly. "You have made it, right?"

He plucked off his magnifying glasses and fixed dark, accusatory eyes on me. "You didn't tell me the truth, did ya?"

The leaden sensation in my belly spread. "What truth?"

"You didn't tell me who you are."

My mouth went as dry as sand. "Listen, Bunty, I—"

"No." He held up his hand. "I can't help you. You're an Onyx, not a Denton like you claimed. You've been lying to everyone."

Blood rushed to my ears, turning them hot. "How did you find out?"

"A little blood, a little spell." He shrugged.

What kind of spell could reveal my identity through a blood sample? None that I knew of. "What were you trying to do with my blood?"

He rolled his eyes. "A little persuasion to have you work for me as a favor."

The bastard had been trying to compel me.

"Oh, don't look so betrayed," he continued. "If anyone should be put out, it's me. The spell didn't work because you're not human. Got me to wondering what you were hiding and why, so I did a little digging. Rabbit holes, you know. Finally came upon an old image print in the news archives of an Ariana Onyx and her daughter after a most terrible tragedy. You look just like your mother."

"Okay, so you know. So what? You hate the Arcanus just as much as I do, so—"

"Hate them, yes, but magic is my business. I have commissions. Contacts. If anyone finds out I've been helping you, then I'm done. I'm sorry. Our business relationship is over." His gaze dropped to the trap. "Just leave the critter and go, we can keep the truth between us. No one else needs to know who you are or where you live."

Where I live? The heat from my ears cooled to ice. "Are you *threatening* me?"

"Ah, Ana, don't be so dramatic. I need the critter, and you need my silence. Think of it as a business deal. Last thing your mother needs in her condition is to be harassed."

"What my mother needs is the tincture. You don't understand how much pain she's in. It's the only thing that helps. The only thing that allows her to continue to be here for a little longer before..." My voice cracked, and a lump began to form in my throat. I was damned if I'd cry. "Bunty, she's dying, and your tincture is the only thing allowing her any quality of life in the interim."

"If I got emotionally invested in all my business transactions, I'd never make any coin." He sniffed and went back to work on whatever crap he was fixing. "Make sure you close the door firmly on the way out, you know it has a tendency to unlatch."

I wasn't surprised at his reaction to finding out my true name. That part I understood, that part had happened too many times for me to be surprised. But to deny a dying woman relief from pain? That was simply evil.

"You bastard."

His expression hardened. "Now, now, Ana, don't make me rescind my most generous offer."

There was no way out of this. I needed his silence. I set the trap on the floor.

"Please, don't. Don't leave me here."

"I'm sorry."

I turned and began to walk away.

"It's karma, you know," Bunty called out. "All the pain your mother's going through?"

I slowly turned to face him, heart pounding my ribs as heat rushed up my body. "What did you say?"

He flinched but held his ground. "I said it's karma."

"You think my mother *deserves* to die?"

"I think it's fitting that her story comes to an end."

I took a few steps toward him. A red haze filling my vision, I crouched and picked up the trap, bringing it close to my mouth and whispering. "Are you still hungry?"

"Yesss."

"What are you doing?" Bunty said, backing up a step. "Put that thing down."

My smile was a wicked, broken thing. "Happy hunting."

I opened the trap then walked away to the symphony of his

agonized screams, and the munch and crunch of a much-deserved feasting.

Karma was indeed a bitch, and some people deserved to die.

My mother was *not* one of them.

Some theorize that the advancement of technology was the cause of The Overshadowing. That in our hubris, we damaged a creation far beyond our comprehension.

History of Nightsbridge

CHAPTER 2

I'd never liked whiskey, but for some reason, it felt like a good choice of beverage for this most shitty day. Cheap, nasty stuff, but boy did it do the trick at numbing the grief that waited to tear at me.

My mother was gone. Consumed by an insidious mortal disease until she was nothing but a shadow, waiting for death to ferry her away.

That final week, she'd slept around the clock, but on the last day, she'd stayed awake, sat up even. Eaten a whole slice of pie. She'd laughed and hugged me, her body all bones—fragile and breakable. We played cards and laughed some more. That night, I stayed with her as she slept, her hand held tightly in mine, as if I could anchor her to this world. But she slipped away on a long exhale just before dawn, leaving nothing but an empty shell. Death gave us this final day, and for that small mercy, I was grateful. Grateful that her last weeks had been painless, despite Bunty's refusal to help.

With Bunty dead, I'd gone to his competition, Carlisle, for my tinctures. The smarmy weasel was twice as expensive, but he'd heard how good I was at my job. He fired Trent and Harry, who, after a warning from Carlisle, left me alone. I was worried that they'd tell my boss at the CCC about my freelance work, but I guess Carlisle had warned them against that, too. The man was dangerous, slit your throat and leave you to the rats kind of dangerous, which was why I'd avoided working with him in the first place, but desperate times called for desperate measures and all that.

It was hard to accept she was gone, even after the sorry funeral where the sky wept alongside me. The few neighbors in attendance had no clue who they were truly mourning.

Ariana Onyx had died six years ago, and today I laid to rest Ariana Denton. I couldn't even bury my mother with her real name because Onyx graves were often desecrated. The Arcanum Imperium, the governing body that was meant to protect all Arcanus, had stolen not only our power but our identities, and now... Now I was alone.

Truly and utterly fucking alone. Soon, I'd have to leave this cozy cottage we'd called home for the last six years. A place Mother had lovingly decorated with knitted throws and cushions, mismatched cutlery, plates, and cups bought from thrift stores. This place was a patchwork of antiques and color. Of love. But it was no longer safe. If Bunty had found out who I was, then others could too.

It was time to move on.

I sucked down the dregs lingering in the bottle and contemplated throwing it against the wall so I could revel in the satisfying crunch and smash, but then, who would clean up the mess?

Something clattered through the letterbox and hit the mat with a thud.

I set the bottle down on the worn coffee table and staggered to my feet. The world swayed a little, as if to remind me I was intoxicated. I shuffled out into the hall, thick socks cushioning my steps against the cold, wooden floor, and retrieved the envelope.

My name was scrawled across it in my mother's hand, along with our address, and on the back was the name of the law firm that handled the Onyx estate.

I knew what this was.

I carried it back to the sitting room and carefully opened it, tugging out the neatly folded paper that smelled like peppermint.

Mother...

My vision blurred, and I blinked away tears to read her letter.

Dear Anamaya,

If you're reading this, then I'm gone, and, honey, I'm so sorry for that. Know that if there'd been a way for me to stay, then I would have, but not even the Weave allows us to cheat death. Death... Hmm, I'm hoping he's a handsome fellow.

I choked back a laugh. She was always making jokes, even when she was in pain...especially when she was in pain, as if by doing so she could somehow lessen my agony.

I wiped my nose with my sleeve and read on.

I promised there would be no secrets between us, and for the most part, I kept that promise. But there are certain things I hid from you for your own safety. Now that I'm gone, somebody needs to hold onto these secrets in my place, and as the last Onyx, that duty falls to you.

There is a box under my bed that contains everything you need to know. What you decide to do with the knowledge inside it is up to you.

As your mother, with only the desire to protect you, I

hope you bury it and move on with your life. But if you decide to act, then, honey, I wish you the best of luck and the grandest of adventures. Know that I will be watching over you always. My big, brave girl, I'm so very proud of you.

Love eternal,

Mother x

For the first time in days, the horrible numbness that had gripped my mind abated. What secrets was she talking about? I shoved the letter into my gown pocket and headed up the narrow steps to Mother's bedchamber.

Someone had made up the bed with fresh sheets patterned with sunflowers that stood out starkly against the black-painted finish of the bed frame, as if making a statement. Probably Darla from down the road. She'd stayed the last few nights, refusing to leave me to cope alone. Then she'd asked me if I'd like her to go through Mother's things to donate them to charity, and I'd told her to go fuck herself.

Probably not my finest hour.

I grabbed the bed frame and shoved with all my might, revealing the dusty wooden floor beneath, along with a small, relatively dust-free box.

No lock.

Nothing to keep me out.

I tipped the contents onto the bed. A leather-bound book, a letter, a necklace with an oval red stone hanging off it, a silver locket, a brooch in the shape of a crescent moon, and a hairpin in the shape of a shell. I turned over the brooch to find an inscription—Bharti Onyx. The hairpin was also inscribed—Melody Onyx. The locket carried the name Irenia Onyx, but the inscription on the ruby amulet was the one that made my blood run cold—Dharma Onyx. The woman responsible for the shitstorm that had stained the Onyx bloodline.

We were sorcerers, at least we had been until Dharma committed an act so foul it forced the Arcanum Imperium to bind not just her power, but the power of our bloodline. She was responsible for the extinction of a whole incantor bloodline, and the reason why my sorcerer bloodline had been treated like pariahs for the last century.

These items were focuses belonging to the Onyx women who'd wielded our power before it had been stripped. While incantors used spells, potions, and rituals to manipulate and channel the Weave, as sorcerers, the Weave flowed directly through us. At least it had at one time, before we'd been cut off from it. Back then, these focuses had acted like conduits, a central focus for power, and a way to direct that raw magic without burning out.

We were a matriarchal family, our connection to the Weave passing from mother to daughter, regardless of whether the male sire was a sorcerer or not. But there had been no power since Dharma.

Onyx had become an Arcanus bloodline without access to the Weave, each generation of women plagued with a different curse. For my mother, it had been the curse of loss. The death of her firstborn followed by my father, then the loss of her second love, followed by the loss of quality of life, and finally, her death. Mother was right—access to our magic would not have prevented her death. But the stain on our name had kept her from getting the medical care she needed. The care she deserved. The taint on our bloodline forced her to suffer for months, because to ask for help would mean revealing her true nature, and thus, our true name. Our fake identities wouldn't have survived the scrutiny.

She'd suffered to protect what we'd built here. To protect me. I was glad I was able to ease her pain, but mine would fester until the governing body that left us to rot paid the price for their cruelty. But that would never happen. They were powerful. Untouchable. Arrogantly justified in the sentence they'd passed on my bloodline. My mother's pain was nothing to them, and I had no grounds to demand retribution, leaving me with a crushing weight of impotent rage.

I was the last Onyx. Cursed to feel neither physical pain nor pleasure. My bloodline would likely die with me, and maybe that was for the best.

I moved the focuses aside and picked up the letter. The paper was worn as if it had been opened and read many times.

My Love,

It has come to pass. The thing that we feared. They know about us, and because of that, I cannot return.

I want you to know that not a day will go by when I won't think of you. Of the way you feel in my arms, or the scent of your perfume. Not a day will pass when I won't wish to feel your soft lips against mine. I did not know it was possible to love until I met you, and the years that we shared have been the happiest of my life.

My heart breaks as I write this. I will never forget you, sweet Ariana, or my beloved stepdaughter, Anamaya. Please tell her that I will love her, always.

Goodbye, my love,

Daniel x

It took every ounce of will not to tear up the note. The bastard. The fucking gall of him. He could have stayed. But he'd chosen society over us, his secret family.

At least my real father had stuck around, leaving only because he had no choice. Death doesn't take no for an answer.

Finally, I picked up the journal. It was battered, partially burned, its pages either torn out or crumbling. I flipped through it carefully, eyes crossing at the neat, tiny script. This wasn't a job for drunk Ana.

I was about to close it when four words written in capital letters caught my eye.

IT'S ALL A LIE.

I forced my eyes to focus and read on.

I'm innocent, but they did something. They changed the truth. I know it. No one believes me, but I feel it in my bones. I'm not crazy. I'm not. I can prove it if only—

Dammit, the rest was burned away. I flipped to the front cover, searching for a clue as to who this belonged to. And there, in neat script, was her name. Dharma Onyx.

My great-great-grandaunt.

Her journal.

Her account.

How did my mother have it?

The words on the next page were blurred, as if someone had dropped water on them, leaving only a few legible lines.

Libra Veritas *is the key to the truth...*

Hidden

Lie when they say it doesn't exist.

If I can get into the vaults at Nightsbridge Academy, then...

The library is off-limits. If I'm caught, they'll kill me. But it's worth the risk to know for certain. To prove that I'm innocent. I must try...

I flipped the page, and a piece of folded-up paper fell out. This was a crisp printout. A page from a legal text, maybe?

My pulse quickened as instinct screamed that this was important.

Dammit. I was going to need coffee.

Half an hour later, I was stone-cold sober and nursing a heart that raced with possibilities. The paper *was* a legal document of sorts. It was a page from the *Arcanum Lex*. The book that set out the laws that all magic users must abide and be governed by. The laws covered both incantors and sorcerers, and any other being that drew power from the Weave. Therianthropes and Haematophages, although magical in nature, don't have access to the network of threads that comprise the Weave. So, they were governed solely by laws put in place by the Imperium Alius—a high supernal council that oversaw everything *other*, even the Arcanum Imperium. Whatever power the Therianthropes and Haematophages possessed came from Source—the mysterious well of power that created all supernal beings. Many believed it was housed in the supernal afterlife. A place called Tariffel, or Fel, as some liked to call it. Some believed the Source was a deity, and others preferred to think of it as an endless well of energy, possibly sentient. Personally, I didn't care. How we got here was inconsequential, all that mattered was how we chose to live.

I scanned the document, gaze dropping to an underlined paragraph. How my mother had gotten her hands on this, or Dharma's book for that matter, was beyond me.

While the journal suggested that Dharma was innocent of her crime, and said there might be a way to prove it, the page from the *Arcanum Lex* gave me a way to find that evidence. To find this *Libra Veritas*. The book of truth.

I read it again just to be sure.

> *No Arcanus bloodline may be allowed to be extinguished. All efforts must be made to preserve them. When in* timor exstinctionis, *channels of power must be protected and nurtured to prevent loss of connection to the Weave and destabilization.*

Timor exstinctionis... My Latin was rusty, but I was certain that meant fear of extermination. I was blocked from accessing the Weave's power but still connected to it. As the last Onyx, if I died, it would sever that connection. So, according to the *Arcanum Lex*, the Arcanum Imperium had a duty to keep the connection alive, which meant giving me the best chance at survival.

This... This was my loophole...

I could use this law to my advantage and demand to have my power restored. After all, I was vulnerable without it. I might die without access to my powers, just like my ancestors had, and the only place where it could be restored was Nightsbridge Academy, of that much I was certain. Nightsbridge was a hub of power, said to house some of the most powerful incantors and sorcerers. It was also where the block on my bloodline's power had been placed. I wasn't sure how, or by whom, but I was going to find out. Because, according to Dharma's journal, it was also where the *Libra Veritas* was housed.

Where the *truth* was hidden.

A surge of heat rushed through my veins.

I'd spent the last six years running from the Onyx name. Reinventing myself and hiding, but if Dharma had been framed and used as a scapegoat...if my bloodline was innocent, then I needed to know. If I could get proof of the Arcanum Imperium's manipulation, I could expose them to the Imperium Alius. I could demand retribution, the harshest punishment for all the pain and suffering they'd put my family through. I could finally free myself of the noose that had hung around my neck ever since birth. If I could find proof that Dharma was innocent, then I'd have revenge, not just for me and Mother, but for every Onyx that had come before. For the unnecessary curses they'd bestowed on us, for the pariahs they'd made us. For the hate and disgust and the aching loneliness. They'd pay for it all.

I set the papers down and took a deep breath. This was more than an adventure; this was a potential death sentence. At least it had been for Dharma. History was proof that she'd failed. Vanished not long after that diary entry. Presumed dead. Was I arrogant enough to think I could do better? No, I just had nothing left to lose.

My decision was made.

I was going to Nightsbridge.

It was time to become Anamaya Onyx once more.

> **It's a blessing that the event occurred on the farthest coast of Nova Terra, allowing the Imperium Alius and the Custodes Hominum to create a clear barrier between the anomaly and the rest of the world.**
>
> *The Science of Change by Bartholomew Reginald*

CHAPTER 3

Chilly air slapped me with the tang of the sea as I stepped out of the port and onto the platform of Nightsbridge Station. Weathered white stone pillars bordered the black-and-white checkered ground, housing a small redbrick guard's building. The air between me and the churning gray clouds shimmered with an electric blue glow, the wards protecting travelers from what lay beyond. The ocean on either side of the station acted as a natural barrier, rippling and rolling toward the land, lapping hungrily at the jagged beach beyond the platform.

I took a moment to drink in the sea air and serene vista while my stomach settled. I hated the aftereffects of port travel. Being magically broken down then reassembled hundreds of miles away felt downright wrong. But it was the most common form of travel for long distances, and the *only* way to get to Nightsbridge. It made sense, Nightsbridge wasn't exactly a tourist attraction, and the only people who lived there did so because they had no choice.

And here I was, hoping to become one of them.

Behind me, the glow of the port faded with a soft crackle, and I hauled my backpack onto my shoulder and strode toward the guard's office. A tram sat on the tracks beyond, its windows tinted black.

I guessed that was my ride.

The wind whistled a soft lament as I pushed open the door to the guardhouse and stepped into what looked more like a comfortable sitting room than an office. Two armchairs bordered a cheery hearth, and books were piled on a table in the corner beneath a painting of a man with a wiry beard and stern eyes set beneath bushy brows. There was only one window in the building, open despite the chill—a waste of heat if you asked me. But whatever.

A man—who looked very much like the one in the painting but without the beard—was parked behind the official desk. He nursed an impressively large mug in his hands. Tea, if the teapot beside him was anything to go by.

He took a slurp of his beverage and surveyed me from beneath his salt-and-pepper eyebrows. "If yer done gawping, I'll have yer papers."

I pulled the pass from my pocket and handed it to him. "It's sealed and everything."

"Course it is. Not every day we get a *voluntary* visitor. Especially one who's requestin' a *Perculiari Petitione*."

"News travels fast."

He tutted. "Crazy to petition to be admitted here. You do know it's a death sentence, right?"

"Surely not always."

"Optimist, huh?"

"No. A survivor."

A large bird flew in through the window behind him and landed on the top of the armchair.

A raven.

A massive one.

It preened for a moment, then cocked its head to fix me with a cold and calculating stare that was far too intelligent.

"Yes, news does travel fast around here," the man said. "I mek sure of it."

The raven cawed as if in agreement.

It had taken five weeks from my legal representative filing the necessary documents to obtain a date for this visit. I didn't want to wait around another second. "When does the tram leave?"

"As soon as you get on it," he said. "Not expectin' anyone else today, are we, Maddox?"

"We certainly aren't," the raven replied.

The raven *replied*? Out loud. Fucking hell. I'd come across critters who could communicate through psybonds, but never across an animal that could speak out loud.

The guard let out a bark of laughter and slapped his thigh. "Been a while since I saw that expression on someone's face." He turned to Maddox. "Let the border guard know that Miss Onyx is on her way."

He said *Onyx* without any inflection of disgust. *Didn't he know about the shit associated with my name?*

His eyes narrowed. "Can't have been easy for you." The kindness in his tone had unwanted heat gathering behind my eyes. No one, not in all my twenty-one years, had ever shown such consideration.

Daniel, my stepfather, had been kind, of course. But only in the confines of the estate, where he'd kept us, his secret family. He visited once or twice a week, bringing small gifts and laughter, creating an illusion of safety. But I knew now that he would have spurned us in public, because as soon as the rumors started, he'd cut and run.

"You all right, luv?" the tram guard asked.

I blinked and looked away. "I'm fine. Just eager to get going."

"Speaking of going...Maddox, why are you still here?"

"*Caw*, come on, Chester, can't a bird get warm? *Caw!*" He leapt off the chair and back out of the window, gone in a flurry of black feathers.

Chester heaved his body up from his seat and stomped past me to the door. "Come on, then let's get you off." He held the door open for me, letting in a gust of icy air. "Few rules for you." He overtook me as we stepped onto the platform, leading the way to the tram. "This here tram is warded. You stay inside, you stay safe. They can't see you, but you can see them. Ignore them. To be honest, it's been pretty quiet the past few weeks. Hunters been keeping the hot zone clean, so it should be a mundane ride. Just stay in yer carriage."

Hunters...that's what I'd be once I convinced them to remove the block on my power and let me enroll. Not that I *wanted* the damn job. If job was what you could call it. There was no pay, merely obligation and the chance to get your face ripped off by the Horrors and Echoes that were drawn to this region like moths to a flame. But if I wanted my powers—and a chance to find the *Libra Veritas*—then I'd have to submit to the process. I'd make a point to remind them of the terms of the *Arcanum Lex*—the fact that they needed me alive. Heck, I might avoid being a Hunter and land some kind of admin role instead, something that would allow me to begin my search for the book of truth... And I was getting ahead of myself. I needed admission first.

I tucked my hands into my jacket pockets to warm them. Thank Trinity for felt lining.

"Talbot'll meet you at the Border House," Chester said.

"The Border House?"

"Doubles as the end of the line. It's the messenger quarters and houses ports to the Academy buildings."

The tram door opened as we approached. "In you get," Chester said. "Do *not* disembark until you reach the Border House."

"I'm no fool, Chester." I climbed into the carriage, where it was markedly warmer.

"You should be there in just over an hour, way before the storm hits. It's not due till tonight."

"And a storm is bad why?"

"We don't run the tram during a storm—it messes with the wards. Academy is all right, though. They got the steeple that conducts and converts the lightning. Fabulous invention."

I turned to face him. "What about you? What about the guardhouse?"

He smiled. "Oh, don't you worry about me. I have me protocols. I'll see you soon, no doubt."

The doors slid shut, the tinted glass darkening the world outside. My pulse spiked at the woman staring back at me, almond eyes, sharp cheekbones, a pointed chin. Fuck, I did look like my mother.

The tram rumbled to life. We slid away from Chester and the guardhouse, pulling away from the platform and out of the wards.

Power pricked my skin—the tram wards activating, no doubt. I took a window seat and set my bag on the floor, settling down for the ride.

The beach receded, the sound of the sea fading as we slipped into forestland. Trees sprang up on either side, tall, dark, and menacing, blocking out the late afternoon sun. The tram was a lone metal snake, slithering through this deadly forest that housed all manner of monsters.

Horrors and Echoes—that's how they were classified. But the details were unknown to me, a secret that would only be revealed if the Academy accepted me. What I did know about the Academy was that it played a vital role in keeping the rest of the world safe. My home education with Mother had delved a little into the history of this place. It had been built as a bastion to house Hunters, warriors tasked with culling the Horrors that didn't belong in our world. Monsters that had come from another place. But the details of where and how were shrouded in conjecture and rumor and mystery. Maybe once I was admitted, I'd get to know the truth of it all.

There was no denying the shiver of anticipation in my belly, not all due to the verbal battle and resistance that I was certain awaited me in the *Perculiari Petitione*. Like hell would they let me into the ranks of the Arcanus without a fight, no matter what the *Lex* said. I was, after all, an Onyx.

I'd spent all my life among humans and supernals like Bunty

and Carlisle—Arcanus without affiliation to any coven—skimming the outskirts of society while the magic users who I should have been able to count on for support pretended I didn't exist. I'd worked with other kinds of supernals too, Therianthropes and Haematophages who preferred not to be drawn into the politics of shifter packs or high society.

Carlston Town had been a haven of anonymity. For a while, I'd convinced myself that my heritage didn't matter, that it was a hindrance, but now... Now it would be a hook, a weapon, an ally in getting what I needed, and no one would stand in my way.

They couldn't. Not legally. Unless there was something I'd missed.

I'd find out soon enough.

The rumble and squeak of the tram faded into background noise as I allowed myself to relax into the leather seat. This wasn't so bad.

Did the Hunters at the Academy use this tram when they went on leave? Did they get leave? Did the students training to be Hunters go home for holidays?

What would they make of me? An outsider in so many ways. Once again, the tiny voice in the back of my mind whispered that I was getting ahead of myself, but I shut it down quickly.

A flash of light split the sky, followed by an atmospheric rumble, and my stomach dipped. Chester had said the storm wasn't due until later tonight.

Another flash and rumble were followed by the hammer of rain on the roof and windows.

Shit.

We were still miles from the Border House, and if the wards went down... No, it was fine.

Chester said it had been quiet recently. Not much activity in the forest. There was nothing to worry about.

The storm intensified, a living thing fuelled by ire and intent, surrounding me in its wrathful embrace until the squeak and rumble of the tram was buried beneath its elemental voice.

Was it my imagination, or was the tram slowing down?

Long minutes passed. Wards were still holding. I'd be fine. I'd barely relaxed into my seat again when movement outside the carriage caught my eye. Before I could get a good look, the whole carriage shook violently, and I was thrown against the wall.

What the fuck?

Across the aisle, a dark shape hurtled toward the window and smashed into the wards.

Elemental beings made of earth are proof of the life that permeates nature. Sentient yet of low intelligence, mudarks seem to have only one goal. To feed.

The Compendium of Horrors

CHAPTER 4

The wards spat blue sparks as the huge rock slammed into them.

I barely had time to register what that meant before another rock hit. The wards fizzed, enraged, and the hairs on my nape stood as the temperature dropped.

So far, the windows had held, but that didn't mean that another assault wouldn't break them. I needed to know what was hurling the rocks, but the storm and the tinted windows significantly reduced visibility. Seconds dragged by before I forced myself to move closer, framing my eyes with my hands and pressing them to the glass to peer out.

Shit! What was that thing lumbering along the tree line? It was hard to make out details, but it was huge and blocky and...was it made of mud? A mud man?

The carriage rocked, and I almost lost my balance.

Another hit, farther down the tram this time. My breath plumed in front of my face.

The creatures were going to take down the wards.

Think, Ana, by the Trinity, think. There had to be a fail-safe. Some kind of alarm, *something*. I scanned the walls and the area by the door, staggering on my feet and bracing when another blow shook the carriage.

Nothing here.

I grabbed my pack and ran through to the next carriage, wildly searching, moving faster and faster through the tram, until I burst into the driver's cab, where winking buttons and flashing lights greeted me, along with what looked like a radio coms unit.

I grabbed it and pressed the button. "Hello?" I let go of the button for a beat. Static crackled. I tried again. "Can anyone hear me?"

"This is Border House Nightsbridge," a gruff male voice informed me. "Who is this?"

"My name is Anamaya. I'm on the tram, and it's under attack."

"Anamaya Onyx?"

"Yes! Please send help."

Static followed.

I pressed the button. "Hello?"

Nothing.

"Hello? Please, can you hear me?"

Static...and then, "You don't belong here, Onyx bitch."

Ice flooded my veins, quickly morphing into frostbitten rage. "Listen, you shit-stain, you best—"

The carriage jolted hard enough to throw me off my feet and into the far wall headfirst.

I came to on the ground, but the world looked odd, and it took a moment for my brain to recalibrate and adjust its perspective. I was pressed to the cabin wall, which was now flush to the ground. We'd been derailed, and the whole contraption was now on its side.

Fuck, fuck, fuck. I pushed to my feet, blinking back the blood trickling into my eye. I prodded it. Dammit, it was deep. Probably would need stitches. No way to know how bad it was without pain to guide me. My hands trembled as I pulled a roll of bandages from my pack, winding some around my head to staunch the worst of the bleeding. First aid was essential with my condition.

The Academy was another fifteen minutes by tram. I'd have to go on foot and outrun anything that came after me. Maybe I'd get lucky. Maybe the mud men were gone. Maybe they just wanted to play and knock over the tram and—

The crunch and squeal of metal told a different story. They were tearing it open like a tin can.

Shit. I had to get out, but there was nothing to break the cabin window with.

Wait. Was that a hatch? Of course, a hatch in the floor which was now facing me. I ran my fingers over the surface, searching for a latch, some way to get it open. I brushed over a hexagonal indent. The perfect fit for a metal nut? Or was it key? It had to be a key. I needed a hexagonal key!

The crunch and groan of metal was replaced by soft growls.

The mud men were inside.

Dammit, where was the damn key?

I spotted a hook by the radio with a key symbol painted above it, but the key was gone. It must have fallen when the tram derailed. It had to be here somewhere.

I fell to my knees, palms sweeping over the ground. Come on, come on. Please! My chest was too tight, my breath coming in shallow, fast gasps, and black dots danced in my vision in time to the throb of my head.

Heavy footsteps echoed toward me along with gruff grunts and growls. Rocks settled in my belly.

Please, please, please... My fingers brushed something cold and hard under the control panel. I hesitated, gripping it tighter. Could it be...? My breath hitched as I pulled it free and squinted in the dim light—yes! The key! Hands shaking, I quickly inserted it into the hatch and twisted. It turned a little, then got stuck.

Something crashed behind me, and the thud of footsteps grew louder—too close. I was moments away from discovery. I set the key back to the start position, then twisted again, hard enough to bruise my fingers. It snagged before turning all the way. The hatch popped open, and dizzy with relief, I fell out into the storm, into the sheets of rain that soaked me instantly, blinding me momentarily before I could tug up my hood.

I rushed to the front of the toppled carriage and pressed my body to it, shrinking into the growing gloom and the chaos of the storm as I studied the terrain. Any second now, the monsters would reach the control room, and once they got there, they'd discover the hatch—and come for me. I'd give anything to have my toxin-covered knuckle dusters or blades with me now. But those items had been prohibited. I'd managed to smuggle in a vial of toxin hidden in a cushioned pocket of my bag, but it was useless without a way to inject it, and who knew if it would even work on these mud men.

Fighting was not an option, not against these monsters.

Running was my only choice, but it would put me out in the open. A target. The alternative was the forest and the host of deadly things that resided there. Nope. I'd take the slow, lumbering mud men any day, and anything else that wanted me would have to break cover and come for me.

Something smashed behind me.

My cue to move.

I burst into a sprint, falling into a focused rhythm that ignored the elements, the roar of triumph from the monsters behind me, and the fact that I was now prey.

I ran—pack bumping the small of my back, legs pumping, lungs working to keep me fueled—and ate the distance, flying across the wet ground along the tracks, thankful for the grip and the stability of my boots.

This I could do all day—run without breaking much of a sweat, without tiring. I could run for miles. Not magic, not Weave power, but something else. Something innate that I'd never understood, but damn, I was grateful for it now.

The ground shook, the air trembling as the Horrors closed in.

Do not look back. Keep moving.

Lightning lit up the world with a flash that was too bright.

Too close.

Someone screamed, a desperate, wretched sound that turned my bowels liquid.

Shadows tracked me, running parallel within the cover of the woodland. If they stayed there, it would be fine. The vibration of the mud men's pursuit had faded—I'd lost them, for now.

Another flash.

The storm was closer. The lightning was almost on me, bringing with it the sharp scent of ozone.

The things running parallel to me broke cover and cut toward the track. My heart leapt into my throat, dread pushing me harder, tearing through my reserves to maintain the advantage of distance.

A rush of heat in my muscles warned me that I was testing my boundaries, that I needed to scale back, but that wasn't an option, because the things chasing me were fast and gaining ground.

Pale, humanoid, and long-limbed was all I could collate without breaking my focus, but it was enough to tease the primal part of my brain that urged me to scream in terror.

I fought the urge and won.

A fuzzy sensation filled my head for a moment, and then a voice whispered,

"*Anamaya.*"

"*Onyx.*"

"*Onyx...*"

Shit, the voice was in my head. Horror fisted my heart. "Get out! Get out of my head."

"Get out! Get out of my head," the voice mimicked, rising above the storm, outside my mind, around me, echoing over and over. "Get out! Get out of my head."

Several voices now—*my* voice screaming at *me*—spawning a vise around my lungs.

My pace faltered, slowing me down for just a beat.

But it was enough.

Hands grabbed me, then shoved me off the tracks and into

the mud.

I rolled and scrambled to my feet, surrounded by faceless, pale monsters, with arms too long and hunched backs. They circled me, screaming my words back at me until it was all I could hear, until my head pulsed, and I feared my brain would explode.

My vision blurred. No, it was them blurring. I turned this way and that, searching for escape—heart beating so hard I was afraid it would bruise—and, oh God, they were changing. Dark hair sprouted from their scalps, their skin deepening to a brown that matched mine. The blank canvas of their faces bubbled and warped until I was looking at a woman. The same woman I saw in the mirror every day. My dark brows, my sharp, angular face, my brown eyes.

Me. They were all me. "Stop it! Stop!"

"Stop it! Stop!" they mimicked, moving closer, mouths stretching in impossibly wide smiles that stole the power from my limbs, leaving me weak and trembling.

I couldn't move. What was happening?

What was this?

"*Onyx. We will crawl into your mind and eat your brain. Become Onyx. All will be Onyx. Yes, we like this. We want this.*"

The certainty that I was about to die bloomed like a wildfire inside me. As I looked into my eyes, into the faces that belonged to me and now belonged to all these others, I had no doubt that, in the next few moments, my inability to feel pain would be my greatest weapon.

"Fuck you!" I spat the words through rapidly numbing lips. "Fuck you all!"

"Fuck you!" they screamed back. "Fuck you all!"

They lunged for me as lightning brightened the world. I screamed, expecting teeth and claws. But in the darkness that followed the flare, something gleamed silver, and the two creatures in front of me lost their heads.

I stared, dumbfounded, from the headless bodies to the man swinging the sword that had decapitated them. He spun and sliced the air, taking another head, and through the barrage of rain and the whirlwind of action, I caught sight of a face, pale as the moon, hair as silver as its rays. His eyes flashed, so frosty blue they were almost white.

The other monsters screeched, their faces smoothing out into blank canvases, bodies losing their stolen forms. The world slowed, the edges of the landscape blurring. Every graceful twist and arch of my savior's body was emphasized as he spun and sliced, circling me until all the mimics were dead.

Someone screamed in the distance, forcing the world back into regular motion. The ground trembled as more figures rushed past us—men and women in black combat gear carrying silver swords.

Hunters.

The icy prick of rain ebbed as if cowed by their arrival.

I was going to be okay. Relief left me weak and cold. Thank goodness I was already on the ground. Otherwise, I was sure my legs would have buckled.

The Hunters ran at the mud men, who had finally caught up with us.

But the mammoth, earthen monsters exploded into smaller creatures, swarming the Hunters.

Several howls cut the night, and the silver-haired guy's jaw tensed. "Get up," he said to me. "Now." His tone was as cold and sharp as his blade.

I stood slowly on trembling limbs. "Thank you."

His eyes flinched, and his gaze darted over my features, leaving a scathing trail across my face and a block of ice in my belly. What was his problem?

He turned away, seemingly unconcerned by the fight going on several feet away from us. I followed his gaze to find three large beasts of fur and claw bounding toward us on all fours.

Seriously? Another attack?

I backed up, ready to run, but silver-hair grabbed my arm, his grip so tight the blood around it pulsed.

"Hey!" I tried to shake him off, but he held me tighter.

"We have it under control, Drayven!" he called out. "Take your mutts and leave."

The beasts came to a halt a few feet away, and the largest of the trio, a beast that looked like it crawled out from the pits of hell to stalk nightmares, spoke.

"Our sector," he growled, the sound like a precursor to an attack.

Drayven had to be a Therianthrope. A shifter. I hadn't met many of his kind, but I'd come across a few.

"Fine," the silver-haired guy said. "You want the kills, then you can have them, along with this." He pinched my arm harder, shaking me slightly before shoving me toward the beasts with enough force to send me falling to my knees in the mud before them.

"What the fuck?" A red wave of rage bubbled up my throat. "What is your fucking problem?" I scrambled up to face him, but his attention was fixed on the Hunters and the mud men. "Hey, I'm talking to you."

My scalp tightened.

"You're hurt," the beast behind me said. His voice was gravelly and abrasive, yet somehow managed to be soft at the same time. "Your head."

Shit, I'd forgotten about that. "It's fine. I'm fine."

Hot breath kissed my nape sending a shiver down my spine. "It's still bleeding."

I reached up to touch the wet bandages. "Shit." I turned to him. "How bad is..." Moss-green eyes flecked with gold stole my words and my breath.

He lowered his massive head and studied my head wound. "You will need stitches."

"Uh-huh..." What the fuck was wrong with me? "I mean, yes. We should do that."

He chuffed, and a warm, sweet mist coated my skin.

"Get her out of here," silver-hair snapped. "She's caused

enough chaos."

I'd almost forgotten about him, but I turned to face the fucker now. "What *is* your problem?"

His red slash of a mouth curled in a sneer, and his straight dark brows dropped low over his eyes. "If you don't know the answer to that, then you're dumber than you look, *Onyx*."

Hell no. "No dumber than a guy who makes assumptions about a person based on nothing more than their family name."

"You don't belong here, and if it wasn't my oath-given duty to save you, the stain of your bloodline would have been wiped from this world tonight."

I'd heard worse in my lifetime, but for some reason, his words stung. Like hell would I let him see it, though. "Oh, gee, well, fuck you very much."

His chest vibrated in a warning growl that made my stomach contract with fear, but I stood my ground, chin up. "Back off, Silver."

His eyes flared and he opened his mouth to speak, but the beast, Drayven, beat him to it.

"Enough. The night is young, and the forest is alive and hungry for blood, now that it's had a taste." He glanced at my head, to the wound I'd forgotten about. "I'll take Onyx to the Academy. Jay and Brek will stay and help with cleanup and neutralization."

"Good." Silver boy raked me over derisively. "The sooner this *Petitione* is over, the sooner we can throw out the trash."

"Who are you calling—"

He walked away.

"Wanker!"

"She's got that right," one of the other beasts said. He was smaller than Drayven by about half a foot, his fur a silvery gray with darker patches streaking down his face and muzzle. Spiky spines ran down his back, and his tail was a thick, hairless appendage.

"Come," Drayven said to me, his tone a soothing growl. "Climb up and hold on."

His back was five feet off the ground. "I'm good. I can walk or run. Whatever."

"Run?" Spiky beast chuckled.

"Yep. Running is my forte. How do you think I got away from the mud men?"

"Mudarks?" the other beast said. "They're not very fast." He was only a fraction smaller than Drayven, his body all sleek muscle and sinew, his fur a white gold that gleamed in the moonlight.

I was not going to allow him to belittle my escape. "Those mimics were fast, though."

"Fine, I'll give you that."

"You were lucky," Drayven said. "But I don't rely on luck, and it's not a request. Get on and ride me."

Spiky beast's snort sounded suspiciously like a laugh.

Drayven's head whipped his way, lip curling back from his fangs in a warning snarl, and the other beast quickly dropped his head.

"Sorry," he said sheepishly.

Drayven's gaze slid my way, and I quickly tucked away my smile.

"Come on, Jay," sleek boy said. "We'd better neutralize."

"Thank Luna I drank a lot earlier," Jay said.

They loped off toward silver-haired dude and the other sword-wielding Hunters, toward the mess of limbs, mud, and blood.

Drayven lowered himself, waiting for me to climb up. I did so with very little grace.

"Grab my fur and dig your thighs in to grip me," he instructed.

Oh boy, I could go in so many directions with this one, "Sounds like you get ridden often?"

His body vibrated beneath me in what sounded like a chuckle. "Not as often as I'd like," he quipped, making me warm to him even more. "Hold tight. Head down."

I barely had time to comply before Drayven lunged forward and we were in motion. Faster and faster, until the world was a blur. I closed my eyes, my heart beating in sync with the rhythm of his stride and the impact of his huge paws on the earth. Long minutes passed, but not nearly as many as expected, before a low-grade hum filled the air and my scalp prickled.

His stride slowed. "We're in a safe zone."

I slowly raised my head to the star-speckled sky peeking down at me from behind the violet haze of the wards.

The path was wider here, smooth flagstones bordered by lush woodland that echoed with the sounds of nighttime fauna. It led to a magnificent stone arch, so high it seemed to reach for the moon, the glowing runes decorating its surface winking like fallen stars. Beyond the impressive structure rose a red and gray tower, riddled with windows that watched us like a multitude of curious eyes.

"Is that the Border House?"

"Yes."

"Is that where radio messages from the tram go?"

He was silent for a beat before replying. "They do."

"Right."

Drayven's sigh vibrated through me. "I know what happened. Talbot overheard the operative on the com and questioned him, and when he realized what was happening, he alerted the on-call Hunter teams."

"And if he hadn't overheard, then I'd be dead." Saying the words out loud released a wave of horror, because now that I was safe, the enormity of what had happened, what *could* have happened, hit me. I gripped Drayven's fur tighter, waiting for the dread to pass. As much as I hated life most of the time, I hated death more and would *never* willingly embrace it.

"Are you all right?" Drayven asked softly.

I was safe. I was alive. I had hope. "I'm fine. What were those mimicking things that attacked me?"

Silence stretched for several beats. Was he going to push me on my state of mind or answer my question?

"Echoes," he said finally. "That's what attacked you. They have no identity of their own, and so they crave it. They would have stolen yours, leaving you faceless and forgotten. But their acquisitions never last, and they're soon back, craving more. But...I've never seen them attack in a pack like that before."

"Where are they from?"

"No one knows. The forest here is alive with Horrors and Echoes. A hot zone of monstrous things drawn to this land."

"Do you know *why* they're drawn here?"

"Unfortunately, no. But it makes it easier to contain and cull them, keeping the outside world safe." We continued in silence for a few seconds. "You were lucky today."

"Yeah, I'm beginning to realize just how lucky."

"I'll make sure your wound is tended to before you're sent to Bramble Tower, where you're to be housed...*if* they let you stay."

If. That was the big question. "Does everyone know about the *Perculiari Petitione*?"

He chuffed. "News is currency at Nightsbridge, and this particular snippet has been traded often the past few days."

Great. Everyone would know who I was, which meant I'd have to watch my back—just like in the old days before I'd taken on the name Denton. Mother had argued against it, of course. She'd been a proud woman, like the women before her, stubborn too. Determined to live with our name and show no shame. But pride didn't put food on the table. It didn't stop your house from being vandalized, and it certainly didn't encourage friendship. And I could be just as stubborn as her when I wanted to.

As we grew closer to the arch, I spotted several ravens flying around the top of the tower. They wove in and out of windows before vanishing into the night.

"I heard about your mother's passing. I'm sorry for your loss."

My throat tightened. "Yeah. Well, she was sick for a long time. It was a mercy."

"Maybe for her, but for you... You must miss her terribly."

I hadn't expected a Therianthrope to be so empathic. I'd learned that they were primal and gruff, both in and out of their beast forms.

"What are you?" It came out blunter than I'd planned, and he was silent for several beats before replying.

"I'm barghest."

His breed of Therianthrope was rare, only a handful of packs left in the world due to their natural habitats being sold off and built on by large Haematophage corporations.

I'd already figured out that the silver-haired dude was a Haematophage of some kind, but if I was going to add him to my shit list, then I'd need a name. "What was the silver-haired asshole's name?"

"Sterling Damascus," he said flatly. "Lead Hunter for the Haematophage teams."

He continued to speak, but the blood pounding in my ears drowned him out. I knew that name. Had dreamed of facing him one day.

"Onyx? Your pulse is racing."

I swallowed past the dryness in my throat. "I'm fine."

I was also a fabulous liar.

"No. You're not. But I understand if you don't wish to speak of it."

"Thanks." The arch grew closer as I wrangled my emotions back into the neat little boxes I'd created for them. "Why aren't you bothered that I'm an Onyx?"

"Why should I be?"

"I don't know. Most everybody else is." Aside from Chester, of course. He was the first to not give a shit.

"I'm not *most everybody else*," Drayven said gruffly.

But Sterling Damascus was.

A dhampir from the most powerful vampire bloodline.

Practically a royal.

He was also the bastard who'd murdered my father.

Built in the tenth year after The Overshadowing, the Border House is more than simply a residence for the messengers of Nightsbridge. Its secrets, however, are only disclosed to the guardians who man its many halls.

History of Nightsbridge

CHAPTER 5

I shut down the memories of my father and our final days together. Days filled with fear and sorrow until death came for him in the form of Sterling Damascus. He was one of many dhampirs—products of vampire and human procreation—bred to act as bodyguards and weapons for their pure-blood sires. But what set him apart was that his sire was a royal.

Sterling Damascus was the bastard prince and blood blade of the Damascus house.

I hadn't seen his murderous face the night he killed my father, but I'd heard his name said over and over, and I'd vowed to one day end him. He'd always been out of my reach, elusive and hidden, until now.

Now he was here.

A Hunter.

Trapped.

I could get to him. Drive a stake through his blackened heart or cut off his lying head. I could finally have my revenge—if only the option hadn't been taken from me by contracts of blood and oaths of duress.

But where there were pacts, there were loopholes, and in time I would find one. I'd get my vengeance because patience was a virtue that I'd had plenty of time to cultivate.

Serendipity, you beautiful bitch.

We passed through the stone arch into a cobbled courtyard, enclosed by towering gray stone walls crawling with flowering vines. The blue wards above shimmered in welcome, and the air pressed down on me, pregnant with power. The hum of that power was a gentle buzz in my ears and a prickle across my skin. I breathed deep, taking in the heady, electric scent of magic. This... This was my birthright, and my body seemed to know it, recognize it. Yearn for it. This...missing piece of me. They'd kept it from me. From my family. They'd left us broken and incomplete.

But soon, I'd know what it felt like to be whole, to have magic coursing through me.

The Border House loomed over me, an imposing, if not strange-looking building. It reminded me of a tower house Mother had taken me to see once. A remnant of our past, it had withstood the elements and whatever wars might have been waged upon it. The Border House was a larger, more opulent version of that. Sandstone, if I wasn't mistaken, with narrow windows looking out at the world inquisitively. What made the building truly strange were the two smaller towers bolted onto the main structure using a metal framework, so that the building looked as if it had arms.

The double doors to the tower swung open, and a tall, whip-thin man came hurrying out. His brown coat flapped about his calves as he took the steps down to us two at a time.

"How bad is it?" he demanded, gaze flying from Drayven to me.

"Mudarks attacked and derailed the tram," Drayven said. "Onyx escaped but was attacked by Echoes. She needs medical attention."

"Right," the man said. "Darla's in her lab. She'll fix you up."

Drayven lowered his body, my cue to climb off. My boots hit the ground, and the world tilted. I grabbed hold of him to steady myself.

"Anamaya, you are *not* all right," Drayven said.

I clung to him for a beat, breathing in his woodsy pine scent and stealing his body heat while the dizziness ebbed. "I'm fine." I stepped away to illustrate just how fine I was.

"Head wounds are nothing to sniff at," the Border House man said. "You tell me if you feel faint."

I wasn't used to such concern from strangers. "Honestly, I'm fine now."

"When's the last time you ate?" Drayven asked me.

"Last night. I think." Food hadn't seemed like a requirement the last few days.

"Talbot," Drayven said to the man. "Get her some dry clothes and get a raven to Vitra to make sure she's fed." Then to me, "Good luck with the Superna Coterie."

My stomach dipped at the mention of Nightsbridge's governing body. My first hurdle.

Drayven dipped his head in farewell, then bounded back through the arch, a distant speck in a second.

And I thought *I* was fast.

Now that Drayven was gone, I fully expected Talbot's attitude to shift—a curl of the lip or derision in his eyes—but he merely sighed and ushered me to follow him.

Well, that was three easy receptions so far.

Unheard of and disconcerting. Were they trying to get me to drop my guard?

Like hell was that going to happen. If they were playing nice, then I could play nice right back. If years of pretending to be someone else had taught me anything, it was never to take anything at face value.

The inside of the tower was a vast hollow space of sandstone slabs and wooden beams. A metal staircase hugged the walls, winding up but stopping at each floor to connect with a walkway before disappearing into the shadows high above. Ravens flew back and forth between floors overhead, vanishing into large holes carved into the walls.

Talbot caught me staring. "Every raven has his personal nook with an external exit. Maddox and Murder, the head ravens, have assigned each raven a tower to serve, but the Haematophages prefer to use serpentwhisper as their form of messenger."

"Snakes?" I suppressed a shudder. Snakes were not my favorite creature. "You have snakes here?"

"Don't worry. You won't see one unless it wants to be seen, and then only because it has a message for you. Come."

Did he seriously think that made me feel better?

He led me to an ancient lift in the center of the chamber, which was nothing more than a wooden box in a metal frame with a gridded concertina door. It looked battered and unstable, stretching all the way up into the shadows, connecting to each floor by a rusty-looking framework.

I hesitated, not a fan of heights on the best of days. "Is that thing safe?"

"Old Betsy here? Safe as houses," Talbot said. He hauled open the lift door with a rattle and a creak. "In you hop."

The contraption groaned and shuddered as we made our way up four flights. I caught a glimpse into a few nooks, each lined with greenery and glowing softly from within.

Betsy ground to a halt, and we stepped onto a walkway where only a thin railing kept us from a fifty-foot drop. I hurried after Talbot through an archway and into a corridor. He took a left, then a right down a second corridor, then another left.

"How big is this place?"

"Much larger than it looks from the outside."

A man dressed in brown and black hurried past carrying a sack over his shoulder. He caught my gaze briefly but quickly looked away.

Human, if I wasn't mistaken. "Who's that?"

"One of the raven keepers. They make sure the messengers are fed and watered."

"So humans work here?"

"You're full of questions, aren't you?"

"Wouldn't you be?"

"I suppose so."

I gave him a beat of silence before asking the question that burned in my chest. "What about the radio? Who mans that?"

He slowed his pace and sighed. "Ah...yes...about that...unfortunately, the Onyx name can evoke strong emotions among the Arcanus, but be assured, the culprit will be reprimanded."

Will be. Might be. I'd heard it all before, but my tormentors were never punished. Not unless I did it myself. "How? I mean, what's the punishment for attempted murder in this place?"

He cleared his throat. "That really isn't my department."

"Then whose is it?"

"You're not going to let this go, are you?"

"You're perceptive."

"You'll need to speak with Heidi Embercrest, head of the Embercrest Coven and one of the Trinity Tower Masters. Don't expect a warm welcome."

Now that was more like it. "I'd expect nothing less."

We entered a small room that smelled like incense. Shelves laden with bottles of all colors, shapes, and sizes lined the walls, and a small, silver-haired woman sat at a table, working a mortar and pestle. She looked up as we entered, tongue peeking out from the corner of her mouth.

"Darla, we have a head wound," Talbot said.

She hopped off her stool and bustled over. "Come on, lovely, take a seat." She indicated a second stool on the other side of her desk, and I slid onto it. "Goodness, look at you. Soaked through. We'll see to that in a moment." She unwound my bandage and grimaced. "Nasty." She prodded the area around the wound gently, then frowned. "That must hurt like a bunny trap."

"I have a high pain threshold." My inability to feel pain was my secret—and it might come in useful here.

She continued to examine me for a few more seconds, and I took the opportunity to study her. Her petite stature marked her as a halfling—a breed of supernal who, if my history knowledge was correct, were all but extinct.

"Hmm...just as well you do have a high pain threshold," she said, "because you're going to need a stitch or two, and I'm out of numbing agents."

"I can handle it."

Fifteen minutes later, my head wound had been cleaned, stitched, smeared with some weird-smelling gunk, and bandaged.

Darla handed me dry clothes and pulled out a screen so I could change with a little privacy. The tunic and pants she provided smelled of soap and were soft against my chilled skin, while the wool socks were a hug for my feet. I shrugged my coat back on and stepped out from behind the screen, clutching my wet clothes.

She held out her hands for them. "I'll pass them to Domestic for laundering." I handed over the bundle. "Keep that bandage on for a day. Then you'll need to clean the area and rebandage. If you're staying, Old Vitra can summon me for you," Darla said. "Now, off with you. I have work to do." She went back to her desk, to her notes and pestle and mortar, dismissing us.

I followed Talbot back into the corridor. "Who's Old Vitra?"

"Your Tower Master, and he's expecting you."

Another arch led to a flight of steps that took us to a circular room bathed in a rainbow of colors spilling from the many windows that made up the walls.

The nighttime landscape was visible through each colorful haze. Shadowy shapes jutted up in the distance—towers and, somewhere in between, a majestic castle that seemed to rise above it all, balanced on a jagged, jutting section of land.

"Impressive, isn't it?" Talbot said. "Main Building sits on an island in an inlet at sea. Only way in or out is by port or bridge. You'll need the azure window to get to Bramble Tower."

Wait a second. "You want me to step through a window?"

"No, I want you to step through a *port*, which is what the windows are."

"*That's* a port?" I pointed at the azure window through which I could clearly see the outside world. "If my gut didn't tell me otherwise, I'd think you were trying to finish the job your radio man started."

Talbot snorted. "If I wanted you dead, I wouldn't have alerted the Hunters that you were in trouble."

"Good point." I took a deep breath. I bloody hated heights, but I'd learned to keep my weaknesses and strengths close to my chest. So I shrugged, overtly unconcerned. "Okay, here goes."

I climbed the steps to the window, offered Talbot a jaunty salute, and before I could overthink it, stepped through the window.

My stomach dropped.

And I fell.

> We will rebuild and we will prevail. Our world is not broken, merely changed, and in time we will find a way to coexist with the threads of magic that have found their way into our world. Technology is malleable, and in time we will prove it.

Yuri Reginald (First Custodes Hominum Address 1 A.O.)

CHAPTER 6

The wind whistled in my ears as the world tipped topsy-turvy and inside out. A scream bubbled up my throat, rage aimed at that bastard Talbot, but before I could release it, I landed hard on the ground with a muffled *ugh*.

The ground...

Oh, thank the heavens.

I pressed my cheek against the cool wood and hugged the floor, barely registering the click of heels until a pair of shiny black boots appeared in my eyeline.

A moment later, a deep, rumbly male voice drawled, "I'm no stranger to women metaphorically falling at my feet, but this is new."

I scrambled to my feet, coming eye level with taut, brown pectorals—partially exposed because the maroon shirt he wore was too tight to do up the buttons. Normally, that would have been enough to put me off, but then I spotted the intricate ink decorating his decidedly masculine arms, also on display because his sleeves were rolled up.

My weakness for inked men kicked in, fingers itching to

investigate him.

"Have you finished taking in the view?" he asked coolly.

My gaze whipped up to the kind of face that belonged on a work of art—chiseled lovingly into planes and sharp lines, softened by pillowy lips. He arched a dark eyebrow, his tawny eyes flat and hard. Hunter's eyes. They assessed me like I was new and interesting prey, but the goosebumps that brushed over me had nothing to do with fear and everything to do with anticipation.

"Don't worry," he continued. "There'll be plenty of time for you to eye-fuck me in class if you're permitted entry to the Academy."

Perfect, he was one of *those* guys—gorgeous and completely aware of it. Totally off-putting.

My fascination with this stunning male faded. "I have a policy against *eye-fucking* arrogant assholes." I expected him to make a cutting or smart remark back, but he simply stared at me as if he could see right through me, and my stomach trembled. I didn't need this shit. "Where's Old Vitra? He's expecting me."

"Old?" His mouth twitched. "I suppose technically I am."

I am? He was Old Vitra?

This male, in his prime? Okay, so he had a streak of silver in his shoulder-length dark hair, but it was much too perfect to be natural.

The port behind me crackled and died, becoming nothing but an innocuous stone arch once more. There was another behind Vitra. This was obviously a port room, like the one at the Border House, but smaller.

He watched me process, his eyes flinching slightly as if he too was processing something. "Why are you here, Miss Onyx?"

"If you're Vitra, then you know why I'm here."

"Yes, yes. But why? Why bother coming to a place where most everyone hates you?" He sounded genuinely interested.

"Most everyone hates me wherever I go. At least here, there's a chance I might get something out of it."

"If you're expecting acceptance, you'll be sorely disappointed."

What the hell did he know about disappointment? Standing there in his expensive shirt and slacks, with his perfect hair and that sympathetic look on his beautiful face. "Fuck acceptance. I don't care what anyone thinks of me. I'm here to claim what's rightfully mine—*my* family's power back. It's been kept from my bloodline long enough." My mother's frail form filled my mind's eye, her dark eyes brimming with pain and the aching sorrow of a life saturated with loss. The Arcanum Imperium had done this to her. Punishing her for a crime committed over a century ago. A crime that was probably a lie. I swallowed the lump in my throat. "We've suffered long enough."

He looked down his nose at me, a cold, assessing gaze that made me want to curl in on myself and hide. "And what if the Coterie denies your request?"

I lifted my chin in defiance. "On what grounds?"

The corner of his mouth turned up, but there was no warmth in the half smile. In fact, if I was reading it right, it was a smile of pity. My scalp prickled with unease.

"There are *always* grounds," he said. "The *Arcanum Lex* keepers are paid handsomely to find them. And you, Miss Onyx, have given them three weeks to do so."

Well, that explained their stalling *and* his pitying smile. "I didn't *give* them anything. This was the date they provided."

"Because *they* are in control here."

"Maybe, but I can be a pain in the ass, Mr. Vitra. Trust me, I've had practice, and if you're here to feel me out and report back to the Coterie, then you can tell them to be prepared to cut the bullshit. I have enough time and funds to tie them up in legal knots for the foreseeable future."

Every coin in the Onyx wealth fund was now mine. As the last living Onyx, I was the heir to it all. I could buy an island if I wanted, but what I *wanted* was closure. What I *wanted* was justice with a hot slice of vengeance.

"I'll be sure to pass on the message." He walked off, heels clipping on wood. "Come. I'll show you to your room."

I was forced to trot to keep up with his long stride, which I was sure he was deliberately lengthening. But I'd be damned if I asked him to slow down. I could keep up just fine.

As we walked, I took in my surroundings. Whereas the Border House had been all stone and metal framework, this tower featured plastered walls and high, arched ceilings etched with intricate vine-like patterns, giving it a warmer, homey feel. The lights were low, with only every other electric wall sconce lit, leaving patches of darkness in between.

Vitra cut a regal figure. Tall. Broad-shouldered. Nice ass. The kind that begged to be cupped and squeezed. Times like this, I missed the ability to feel the pleasure of physical touch.

When my curse activated at sixteen, stealing two senses that I'd taken for granted, it hadn't immediately seemed like such a huge deal. I'd done a ton of reading to understand the parameters of my curse—how my body hadn't lost its ability to feel sensation like pressure, heat, or cold, and yet failed to translate those sensations into pain or pleasure.

The loss of pain, in many ways, was a blessing, as long as I was careful. But losing physical pleasure? Well, the enormity of *that* loss registered with my first sexual encounter. I could be drawn to someone—lured by attraction, aroused mentally and emotionally—but there would be no physical sensation of pleasure in the act of sex unless I remained mentally aroused.

So far, no male had succeeded in keeping me that way.

I'd learned to fill in the blanks, tricking my mind into believing I was feeling more than I was. It worked...sometimes. But right now, watching this fine male specimen make his way down the corridor, I was reminded that the only pleasure I'd ever experienced with a man was in my head. Thank Trinity for vivid imaginations.

We took a left onto a passage lined with vaulted windows looking out into the night, where the majestic Main Building sat on an island in the middle of the churning sea, its many windows brightly lit from within. Waves crashed and foamed against the cliffs that surrounded it, and two white bridges gleamed in the moonlight, stretching from the mainland and rising high above the waves to connect to the island. But no struts or framework were visible to explain how they were held up.

"Miss Onyx?" Vitra called from a door farther up the corridor. "I don't have all night."

I tore myself from the view and hurried to join him. "How did they build it?"

He pushed open the door and slipped through. "Build what?"

"The Main Building," I continued, "and the bridges leading to the island. I mean, it takes up the whole of that land mass...at least it looked like it from here." Once again, I had to trot to keep up.

"I'm no architect or builder." He took us up a short flight of stairs onto a carpeted corridor. "You'll be housed in the fourth-floor turret with the other Unwoven while you're with us."

"Unwoven?"

"A meal will be brought to you in an hour, and Polina will collect you at nine a.m. sharp to escort you to your meeting. You will not leave the turret tonight, is that understood?"

"Why not?"

He stopped and turned on his heel so suddenly that our bodies collided, chest to chest, long enough for me to breathe in his sandalwood scent and sip on the heat emanating from his body before I rebounded. He gripped my shoulders to steady me, and my head whipped up, gaze snapping and locking with his.

His nostrils flared, eyes narrowing slightly, and a sharp tingle rushed down my spine. I sucked in a breath. What the hell was that?

His gaze became probing, uncomfortable. "You'll stay in your quarters because *I've* asked you to. Is that clear?"

The words *you're not the boss of me* sprang to my lips, but I pressed them back. If I was going to survive here, then I'd have to defer to authority to some degree. So I arranged my face into something resembling politeness and offered him a closed-lipped smile. "Crystal."

He released me. "Good. Now, this way."

One more flight of stairs, and we entered a cozy sitting room decorated in a patchwork of colors, with several doors leading off it.

"The other Unwoven are at supper, but they'll be back soon. They'll no doubt attempt to coax you out from your quarters, but you're to say no."

"Wouldn't that be rude?" I kept my expression open and innocent. "I mean, I wouldn't want to be rude."

He gave me a flat look. "I'm sure you'll manage."

He shoved open the door to the far right. "You're in here."

The room was plain and sparse: a bed, a wardrobe, a dresser with a mirror, and a small bathroom coming off from it, and that was all.

"I'd advise you to lock your door when you sleep," he said. "You're not the most welcome guest, and I have business to attend to tonight and won't be on hand to play guard."

"I can take care of myself."

"Hmm..."

Trinity, he was annoying. "Trust me, I can take care of—"

In an instant, I was pinned to the wall, cheek to plaster, his hand on my nape. His body was a cage, powerful thigh pressed between mine, wedging me in place. Tingling heat spread out from every point of contact, bringing my body to life. What was this? What was happening to me? I twisted and bucked, but he had me trapped, his grip like steel, tightening the more I struggled, fingers pressing against my rabid pulse leaving me hollow and breathless.

A penetrating shiver awakened across my skin and gooseflesh broke out up my arms. It was a sensation I hadn't felt for years, one that bypassed the relative numbness of my senses. Trinity, how was this possible? Butterflies erupted in my belly and my eyes heated with the threat of tears. I needed it to stop. For him to stop touching me.

I relaxed against the wall. "You made your point."

His hot breath skimmed the shell of my ear, and my eyelids fluttered as a fresh wave of sensation washed over me. "I need to hear you say it, Miss Onyx."

"Fine." My voice came out as a croak. "I'll stay in the damn quarters, okay?"

"Good girl." The words vibrated through me, and another shiver skipped up my spine.

He released me, and I quickly slipped away, putting distance between us and crossing my arms to hold myself together. This... these feelings made no sense.

He watched me from hooded eyes, and silence stretched like hot toffee between us while my pulse continued to beat hard in my throat beneath the bite of phantom fingers.

I clenched my hands into fists, grounding myself, and fixed a hard glare on my face. "Was there anything else?"

"No. That's all. For now." He retreated from the room and closed the door behind him.

I curled my hand around my nape, still warm from his touch. He'd touched me and I'd felt something much more than a bland pressure. It should be impossible, but it had happened. I hadn't imagined it.

Question was, what did it mean?

A new world requires a new order. If we are to control the alien threads that are now part of our Weave, then equality cannot be the way forward. The most able must be given the greatest share of power, and if that means an amalgamation of covens, then so be it.

Griselda Blackmore (Arcanum Imperium Address, 35 A.O.)

CHAPTER 7

It didn't take long for me to conclude that my body's reaction to Vitra was in my head. I'd imagined the feelings because his presence was so potent, that was all. I was cursed and pleasure was off the table, that was a fact.

Unpacking took less than ten minutes because I'd traveled light. I'd brought only one outfit change, my comfy PJs, a small bag of toiletries, my cryptozoology journal, and the box from under Mother's bed. The voice of doubt in my head whispered that I was being premature in settling in. That I might not be allowed to stay, and as always, I told it to take a hike.

But as soon as I silenced the doubt, another part of me questioned this entire idea—what was I doing, coming here, putting my life on the line for a truth that might not even exist?

Dharma's journal entries ended after she wrote to say she was headed to the vault. Nothing but aging blank pages, which suggested that she'd never made it back.

Coming here and locking myself in these wards was more dangerous than I'd admit—but this cage was nothing compared to the one I'd lived in all my life. A cage built by a lie that the upper echelons of supernal society had woven for my family. *Why* was the biggest question. One that had burned a hole in my mind ever since I read Dharma's fractured account. And yes, she might have been mad, delusional even, but my ever-reliable gut screamed at me that she wasn't.

Now all I needed to do was gain admission and find the proof that she'd been searching for so I could expose the Arcanum Imperium and get justice. Revenge. Something for every Onyx that had come before. I could use that power to finally bring Sterling Damascus to his knees. I could demand his head as retribution.

The risk was worth the reward.

I couldn't regret coming here. I did, however, regret bringing only one change of clothes, since my traveling outfit was covered in mud. I doubted that Darla would be able to get it back to me by morning. I'd have to wear the extra outfit to the meeting tomorrow. At least the bathroom had a tub, so I could soak before bed tonight. And once they gave me official admittance, I'd see about getting hold of some more clothes.

A sharp rap sounded on the door followed by hushed, heated whispers. Were the Unwoven back? Vitra had instructed me not to leave these quarters, but he hadn't said I couldn't fraternize. Besides, I wanted to know what Unwoven were.

Another knock.

"Maybe she isn't here yet," an irritated female voice said.

"She was seen," a man replied.

"There are muddy footprints," another female voice said.

I yanked open the door, and the three whisperers jumped back. Two women and a man.

"Hi," one of the women said. "I'm Clary, and this is Dori and Benedict. We wanted to welcome you to Bramble."

There was something about her that put me immediately at ease. Maybe it was the big smile set into a heart-shaped face, or maybe it was the warmth in her big brown eyes.

Dori rolled her heavily made-up eyes. "You sound like the prima incantors. This isn't a holiday resort, and no one *wants* to be in Bramble."

Clary's eyes lit up. "But you do," she said to me. "You're here because you want to be."

"Which leaves us wondering how mad you are," Dori added.

"Dori!" Clary admonished. Then to me, "We don't think you're mad."

"Speak for yourself," Dori muttered.

While Clary was short and curvy, Dori was tall and svelte, her shoulder-length hair parted to one side, partially obscuring one eye to give her a sultry air. She had the voice to match, that slight drawl that said, *I know I'm gorgeous, so you'll stop and listen to me no matter how slowly I speak.*

"We heard the tram was attacked," Benedict said, wandering over to the sofa. "Go on, spill. What happened?" He stretched out his wiry frame on the longest sofa, tucked his arms behind his head, and surveyed me with kohl-rimmed eyes beneath messy dark hair. "Mudarks and Echoes, right?"

Three more people treating me like I didn't have the plague. Interesting.

I stepped into the sitting room. "News does travel fast here."

"You can say that again," Dori drawled. "The information mill is forever active." She threw herself into the armchair beside the empty hearth, slung both her stocking-clad legs over one arm, and flipped her sandy hair over her shoulder.

"I want to know about the attack," Benedict said. "How in Nova did you get away?"

Clary took the second armchair, leaving the two-seater free, and then they were all looking at me, a clear invitation to join them. They were acting like we were friends, like my name meant nothing to them.

Wait, maybe they didn't know who I was? "I'm an Onyx. You know that, right?"

Dori's eyes flew wide. "What? Oh. My. Trinity."

Benedict snickered.

"Shut up, you guys," Clary said before throwing a kind smile my way. "We know, and we don't care."

This was starting to get weird. "Why not?"

"Why should we?" Benedict countered. "It's not like you personally wiped out a bloodline. Kinda shitty that your whole family paid the price for one person's actions."

"It's messed up," Dori said.

"But I get it," Clary added. "Not everyone feels that way, and you've probably met your fair share of them. But we're not like that. We have our own...issues."

Now I was intrigued. "Okay." I crossed to the sofa. "You tell me yours and I'll tell you mine."

Unwoven were Arcanus whose connection to the Weave had been blocked as a disciplinary action, Clary had just finished explaining.

She pulled up her sleeve to show me a symbol that marked her as Unwoven. I'd seen it plenty of times, except on me it was faded into the skin of my thigh, a part of me because I'd been born with it.

"Once our sentence is over, they remove it," Clary said. "Then we get our familiars back and can return to Hunter duty." She wrinkled her nose. "Domestic duty sucks, and Pip is a hard taskmaster."

"And combat training hits harder when you can't throw up a shield," Dori said.

"That's not even one of your spells," Benedict replied.

"Well, it should be."

I didn't get it. "What do you mean it isn't one of her spells?"

"Dori's with the Embercrest Coven," Benedict said. "They're allocated spells at birth and aren't allowed to learn any others."

I searched the archive of my mind for that coven name. It was an ancient coven created by Embercrest, one of the oldest incantor bloodlines. They had an ancient grimoire that contained all of their powerful spells. Mother had explained that the head of the coven—always an Embercrest—was able to gift spells to its coven members, incantors from various bloodlines who'd pledged themselves to the coven. The spells were copied onto enchanted parchment before being gifted to ensure that only the new owner could read them. Mother had explained that this way, they ensured that the coven members worked together, united in power. No one incantor in the coven was more powerful than another.

"It's bullshit." Dori picked at imaginary lint on her skirt. "Especially for those of us who get the crappy spells."

"So what did you do? Steal spells? I mean, is that even possible?"

She smirked. "Nope."

"She encouraged spell sharing," Clary said, answering for her. "*Encouraged* but never forced. That point should have mattered."

"Not to my aunt it didn't," Dori said.

"Dori's aunt is the Trinity Tower Master," Benedict elaborated. "And Embercrest Coven leader."

"Which is also bullshit," Dori said. "All the other covens have senior students as leaders. We call them prima incantors. She's just a power-hungry bitch."

"But doesn't your coven have to be run by an Embercrest?" I was so confused.

She rolled her eyes. "Yes, it does, but the branch of the coven here is only a small offshoot of the main coven. Heidi can't allocate spells, only the true coven leader outside of Nightsbridge can do that. There's no reason for her to run the Nightsbridge faction. She could hand down the power, train the next generation."

"You mean like you?" I arched a brow, biting back a smile.

"I mean...yeah. But, like I said, she's a power-hungry bitch."

"She's hot, though," Benedict added. "I'd fuck her."

"You'd fuck anything," Dori replied.

"Not true," Benedict said. "I have standards."

"And nasty bitches make the cut?" Dori asked.

"I don't feel as guilty giving them a good spanking," Benedict said. "But it's the good girls that get me going the most." He winked at Clary, and her face turned red.

"You're not Clary's type," Dori said.

But the look on Clary's face, just before she hid behind the curtain bangs of her bobbed hair, said that he was *exactly* her type.

Dori and Benedict, however, seemed genuinely clueless.

So Dori's aunt was the Tower Master, which meant she was the one to ask about radio guy and his punishment. Good to know. "What about you two?" My gaze bounced between Clary and Benedict. "What covens are you from, and why did they bind your powers?"

"I'm with Evergreen," Clary said. "I refused to heal someone after they attacked another witch and got hurt. Evergreen preaches forgiveness, and I failed..."

"Oh no," Dori drawled sarcastically. "You failed at being a doormat. Seriously, Evergreen needs to sort its shit out. Three months for that? Bullshit. Benedict set someone's arm on fire and got the same. This time." She shot him a grin. "You're such a waste of space."

Benedict opened his arms and grinned. "But I'm such a sexy waste of space."

Dori threw a pillow at his face.

He caught it neatly and slipped it under his head. "I'm an Ironhart," he said to me.

My brows went up before I could school my expression. Ironharts were supposed to be huge, said to be descended from overseas invaders who claimed to have the blood of ogres in their veins. Benedict did *not* fit the profile typical for the sorcerer bloodline.

He chuckled. "I know, I know. The big guy gene skipped me."

"But you make up for it with a huge chip on your shoulder," Dori quipped.

He winked. "It is pretty impressive."

His humor was infectious, and I bit the inside of my cheek to stop myself from smiling. "And you set someone on fire?"

"It was an accident," Clary said, jumping to his defense. "It's not his fault he's attuned to Chaos Magic."

Rare for an Ironhart. They tended to do low-level telekinesis. And not many of them carried a focus because their connection to the Weave wasn't powerful enough to risk them becoming overwhelmed by it.

"He's been bound twice." Dori held up two fingers to emphasize the fact.

"I can speak for myself, you know," Benedict said, but he didn't look upset by them spilling his story. In fact, he seemed almost amused.

"Whatever," Dori said.

"We're all due to get our powers back in just over five weeks," Clary said. "Maybe if your meeting goes well, you'll be joining us."

"I doubt it will be so easy for her," Dori said. "A bloodline block is a lot harder to undo than a personal one."

Benedict eyed me from his spot on the sofa, dark eyes speculative beneath his mop of messy hair. "So, what is it? What's your curse?"

I tensed, surprised that he'd asked. The fact that the block on my bloodline had produced a curse as a side-effect was common knowledge, but it was also something people didn't directly enquire about. Arcanus were usually big on etiquette, and other supernals didn't often give a damn about what my curse was.

"Don't be so rude!" Clary admonished him, then turned a kind smile my way. "I'm sorry, sometimes Benedict has no filter."

"Like you weren't wondering the same," he muttered.

Dori shot him a glare.

"Fine, forget that," Benedict said. "Tell us about the tram attack."

One of the first lessons I'd learned out in the big wide world was to utilize all the resources available to me, and these three were the perfect resources to help me navigate Nightsbridge.

"How in the world did you survive it?" Dori asked.

It was time to make friends. I sat forward in my seat and fixed a serious expression on my face. "I ran."

I'd been running all my life, but tomorrow I'd begin the path to laying down roots.

At least for a little while.

> "We were owed a reset. I mean, how great was the world before, eh? War and famine and all sorts of stuff, weren't it? Now we have order. Sure, the supernals are mainly in charge, but they're doin' a damn better job than us humans, dontcha think?"
>
> *Miranda Star (Interview with Global Events Radio)*

CHAPTER 8

My supper arrived while I was chatting with the Unwoven, and I ate in the sitting room. A meager affair of soup and bread that barely filled my belly, but it was fine because my information meter was nicely topped up. The trio was a wealth of knowledge about the campus and the people who lived and worked here.

Hunters were trained from the age of sixteen and upward, and no one was here by choice. The Academy conscripted supernals and humans from select bloodlines to dedicate their lives to Nightsbridge.

"It's not so bad," Clary said. "Once you make friends." She smiled at Dori and Benedict.

"I don't suppose you've had many of those, have you?" Dori said bluntly to me.

"Dori!" Clary admonished. "Not everyone cares about her lineage."

Clary was either very naïve or delusional. "Dori's right. It hasn't been easy, but the last few years were good. I mean, *after* I changed my name."

"Nice," Benedict said.

"It was...while it lasted."

"I'm sorry about your mother," Clary said.

Disclosure bred familiarity and was important in making these people believe that we could be friends, but the last thing I wanted to do was talk to strangers about my mother. The last thing I needed right now was a trip into memories that would dredge up emotions I'd rather not share.

I offered her a tight smile, hoping it conveyed acceptance of her unnecessary and meaningless apology. "I should get some rest. Someone named Polina is picking me up in the morning to take me to the Main Building."

Dori made a face. "Good luck with her. Her temperament is about as sour as her face."

"Only since Vitra dumped her," Benedict said. "Before that, she was wandering the halls looking like the cat that ate the sparrow."

My interest was piqued. "Is she a student?"

"Tarrifel, no," Dori said. "She's in Domestic under Pip."

"But spent most of her time under Vitra." Benedict wiggled his eyebrows.

"It was two weeks," Clary said. "You know he doesn't keep them for long."

"Except for Mistress Selethis," Dori said. "She's his *official* girlfriend."

He had a girlfriend? Not that I cared. I sat up straighter, ignoring the sudden tightness in my chest. "And she's okay with him fucking other women?"

"Seems like it," Clary said.

What did I care about his sexual antics? "I need to get some sleep."

"Lock your door," Benedict said, suddenly all serious. "The locks here activate wards to keep unwelcome things out."

So that's why Vitra had insisted on it. "Noted. Thanks."

I left them to their conversation and headed to my room, where I closed and locked the door. I was too tired to bathe, so I stripped off and climbed into bed. I'd wake early and have a soak.

Pulling the covers up, I turned onto my side so I was facing the dresser. Sleep washed over me, and my eyes were tugging closed when something moved in the mirror. My adrenaline spiked, knocking me momentarily wide awake. But there was nothing there. Just a trick of my tired mind.

Sinking back into the mattress, I activated one of my more enviable skills.

I switched off.

Polina was at my door at eight fifty-five a.m. She was a pretty woman with the delicate features of a porcelain doll but had the expression of someone who'd smelled something off. Dori's sour face comment from last night made complete sense.

She raked me over, taking in my wide-leg gray trousers, cream blouse, fitted gray waistcoat, and calf-length brown wool coat—one of the most expensive outfits I owned. Polina sniffed derisively, then ordered me to follow her.

Was there something wrong with what I was wearing? It was the standard fare for Arcanus. Natural fabrics in neutral shades. Granted, the ensemble was a little rumpled from being tightly packed into my pack, but the coat covered most of the creases. It wasn't too bad...was it?

I hadn't bothered dressing this way in Carlston, opting to don cotton and leather to fit in with the local fashions, but was I not looking the part now?

Irritation flared in my chest. Fuck her for making me second guess myself.

We took a different route than the one I'd taken with Vitra, and once again, I was struck by the number of corridors occupying this tower. It broke the laws of physics, but then, the Weave had its own laws.

Polina ushered me through a door and out onto a stone

walkway, high above the neatly clipped grounds below that stretched away from Bramble Tower, as if reaching for the froth-coated sea beyond. The walkway ended in a stone arch.

Salt kissed my skin, and a gusty wind picked up my hair, lifting it away from my face before slapping it back against my cheeks.

Polina hurried toward the arch. "Come on."

What was it with this place and heights? I followed, veering toward the balcony so I could grip the rail for stability.

From this vantage point, the grounds were a honeycomb of grass, gravel, and cement, bordered by stretches of woodland. Several domed buildings were visible to the right of the tower. They were made of glass that glinted in the shafts of sunlight that pierced the heavy cloud cover.

The coast of the inlet was a dull gray stretch of sand in the distance, with towers rising on either side of the majestic Main Building that sat on an island in the sea. Five towers... No—six, there was one wreathed in mist far beyond the Main Building.

It looked like an optical illusion, the island that housed the Main Building couldn't possibly be large enough to house the tower wreathed in mist unless...

I hurried to catch up with Polina. "Is there another island behind the Main Building?"

She ignored the question, pressing her palm to the arch at the end of the walkway. It lit up a soft blue. A port. "There is no direct way to the Main Building from Bramble," she said, ignoring my question. "We'll take the port to the eastern bridge and go on foot over the sea. You will go first."

I didn't like the sly edge to her smile. "Why?"

"Because the port will close after me. You have not been attuned to it."

"I managed to get through the Border House port just fine."

"Yes, I delivered your sample to him yesterday morning."

"What sample?"

She stared at me as if I were stupid. "Blood. Yours, like every supernal family bound by The Covenant, is held here."

The Covenant was the agreement made by several bloodlines to work together to purge Nightsbridge of otherworldly threats. It seemed my mother had provided them with a blood sample from me at some point. I guess having our power blocked and being shunned didn't exempt us from providing DNA to these fuckers.

"Your meeting begins in half an hour," Polina reminded me.

I strode past her and through the port.

Once again, it felt as if I were falling, but this time, when the world righted itself, I was thankfully still on my feet. A white stone bridge stretched out before me, spanning what looked like maybe half a mile.

Several groups of students hurried along the bridge, which inclined gently toward the imposing tower of land that housed the Main Building.

"Hurry up!" Polina rushed past me. "Move!"

I joined her in rising above the ocean, reveling in the salty kiss of the wind as it tore at my skin and howled in my ears, competing with the crash of waves against the coast.

The Main Building grew larger as we approached—a multitude of towers and turrets, balconies, and windows...so many windows.

Young supernals, carrying bags and books, hurried passed us.

"How many students are here?"

"Too many," Polina said bitterly. "Enough to replace all those who die. Makes me glad to be human. I'd rather make beds and do laundry than go into the hot zones." She threw a sharp glance my way. "You're crazy for coming here when you didn't need to. Risking death just to get your magic back. Magic you've never had so can't possibly miss. It's greedy, and as far as I'm concerned, greedy people deserve to have bad things happen to them."

She had no fucking idea why I was here. Getting access to the Weave was a means to an end. An end to my curse, and to the stain on my family name. An end to the lie the Arcanum Imperium had woven.

Her derision meant nothing to me. "Well, aren't you a ray of sunshine."

She snorted.

God, she was a miserable cow, but that didn't mean I couldn't pump her for information. "So...the rumors about conscription are true?"

Her mouth twisted. "The Covenant families are obligated to send children here."

"You're from a Covenant family?"

"No."

"Then why are you here?"

"Because my family needed the money."

"They sold you into service?"

She snorted again. "Oh, don't sound so shocked."

I'd feel sorry for her if her attitude didn't suck.

We exited the bridge onto a wide path that wound up the side of the mountain toward the Main Building. It was steep and narrow in places, but there was a handrail built into the rock face, so that helped. The high winds did not. I hugged the wall to avoid being blown over the edge, boots slipping several times. Polina kept her distance, not bothering to help, and I thought I heard her laugh a couple of times, but it was difficult to be sure with the howl of wind in my ears.

My thighs ached by the time we reached the top. Here, the ground flattened into a vast garden dotted with stone statues of all shapes and sizes. Some grotesque winged figures, others faceless males with folded wings in various poses. They hid among flowering bushes and sat atop dried-up fountains, and several of them decorated the eaves of the mammoth building that seemed to grow with each step we took toward it.

Polina piloted me along, giving me no time to take in any more than the most basic of details. Up three steps, through double doors, past a cluster of students, and into a gloomy entranceway where vaulted windows let in meager light. Then, through an arch into a network of corridors supported by high ceilings and wooden beams, with walls lined with gilded frames depicting scenes I had no time to study.

Was the library that housed the *Libra Veritas* beneath this building, or was it on the mainland? I'd need to make discreet inquiries soon.

"In here," Polina said, shoving open a door and hurrying into a long room filled with cushioned benches. A platform housed a long judicial desk stretching along the back. Two witness boxes stood on either side of the platform.

"Seriously? I'm a criminal now?"

"You are your bloodline," Polina snapped.

"In which case, your bloodline must be filled with sour-faced bitches."

She gaped at me, and I smiled. Her cruel words were nothing compared to what I'd already been subjected to out in the big bad world.

She snapped her mouth shut, eyes narrowing to slits. "I hope they execute you."

"What? That isn't even a possibility."

An unsettling glint bloomed in her eyes. "You're so clueless, it's pathetic."

"And you like to fuck other people's boyfriends, so...yeah, whatever." It was a lame comeback, but it was all I could muster with a racing pulse and a whirring mind. What the fuck did she mean? What had I missed?

"See you around..." Polina said, smirking. "Or not." She retreated from the room, leaving me standing between the witness boxes. Like hell would I get into either. I was not a criminal on trial.

Once she was gone, the silence was intrusive. Hell, *I* felt intrusive, being here in this magnificent room, with all its polished redwood features and tall, elegantly arched windows. The view was nothing but ocean and heavy gray skies. We must be facing away from the mainland.

I crossed to the judicial desk, the top of which was a head higher than me. Deliberate, no doubt, to make me feel small. Even the witness boxes were lower than the desk, ensuring that anyone unfortunate enough to stand in them would feel small and powerless. Yeah...I'd pass.

A door behind the platform opened, and several people filed into the room. First came an older gentleman in a tweed suit and waistcoat. His wispy hair was swept over his bald spot in an attempt to hide it. Next was a rugged-looking man in a loose woolen sweater and baggy cotton trousers. He was significantly taller than the older man and had the kind of hunch to his back that suggested that he'd spent a lifetime stooping to engage with people. His short, dark hair was speckled with silver, indicating that he was probably older than he looked.

Two women followed: The first, petite and slender, sporting a pixie haircut, and the other athletic in build with an angular face that was both stern and beautiful at the same time. They both wore the neutral colors of the Arcanus, a cream blouse with a fitted waistcoat, but the petite one paired hers with an ankle-length skirt, and the athletic one sported loose cotton trousers tucked into ankle boots.

Their arrival brought a heaviness to the air, one I recognized from the Border House.

Power.

The kind that lent not only weight, but also a sharp scent to the air. Goose bumps broke out along my arms, and I resisted the urge to rub them.

The door swung shut for a beat, but opened again to admit a dark-haired woman with almond eyes and the kind of face that artists would beg to paint. She wore a long flowing black dress cinched at the waist by a wide belt. She was the first to look directly at me, and her frosty gaze took me momentarily off guard.

But my surprise was misplaced, of course these people hated me. I was an unwelcome visitor here. Asking for something they didn't want to give me. I respected the almond-eyed woman's honest reaction—easier to deal with than fake smiles and faux respect.

The Coterie members settled into their seats, and I was suddenly the focus of attention. My palms started to sweat, but I resisted the urge to wipe them on my trousers. Showing weakness in any form wouldn't help my case. This panel needed to believe I was worthy of a spot at the Academy. There was no place for the weak-willed or fragile-bodied on these grounds.

A soft vibration filled the air, and the hairs at my nape quivered as something inside me tugged with the same strange yearning that had come over me outside the Border House. The yearning to taste this power. To *feel* it rushing through me. I'd been around magic before, of course, but never this much. Never this...potent.

They sat, unspeaking. Waiting.

For what?

Was I expected to address them now? Start pleading my case?

My gaze flicked over them, one by one. The wispy-haired guy with the kind eyes looked small beside the others. There was a dullness about him, the kind often noticeable when a human was in the vicinity of a supernal, which meant he *was* probably human.

The big guy beside him, who had his attention fixed on a point over my head, looked like he worked out—a lot. With weights. He had the bulk often seen on Therianthropes, either that or he was an Ironhart.

The petite woman beside him might have been beautiful, if not for the sour twist of her mouth. She played with a ring on her middle finger. The emerald gem winked as it caught the light. A focus? It could be. Which would make her a sorcerer.

Beside her, the angular-faced woman watched me with a steady gaze that was almost unnerving. She carried no focus, but her Arcanus clothing meant she must be an incantor.

The almond-eyed beauty on the end was a mystery. She looked too regal to be a Therianthrope. Her red lips and dark eyes hinted at Haematophage, but she didn't have the telltale pallor to her skin, and her outfit wasn't what I'd expect. Haematophages favored leather in their ensembles. *Hmm...*

Five Coterie members, but six seats. They were waiting for someone.

The door opened a moment later, confirming my assessment, and Vitra stepped inside. His presence sucked some of the air out of my lungs, despite the fact that he didn't even glance my way.

He looked chic in black slacks, a turquoise shirt, and black braces clipped to his waistband. His sleeves were rolled up like last night, but half his dark hair was slicked back and secured in a bun, leaving his bone structure fully exposed to be admired.

"Are we ready to begin?" the wispy-haired man asked the others.

Murmurs of assent drifted down the line.

I forced my jaw to relax and stared up at them. Waiting.

"Miss Onyx," old wispy said. "My name is Walter Regent. My family is one of the founding families of Nightsbridge Academy. These are my colleagues and members of the Superna Coterie: Xander Crax, Tower Master for the Therianthropes. Portia Reign and Heidi Embercrest, joint Tower Masters for the Arcanus. Constance Selethis, Tower Master for the Haematophages, and Yash Vitra, Tower Master for the Unwoven.

Yash... His name was Yash... Wait...had he also said Reign? Portia Reign. Sorcerer. I knew her, or knew *of* her, because I'd been a Reign once. For a little while. This woman, Portia, was my stepfather's sister, although I'd never met her.

She knew who I was, though. Knew the truth about her brother's illicit marriage, and the curl of her lip told me that it still disgusted her. It was hard to believe she was related to my ex-stepfather. He'd been a soft-spoken, gentle man, with warm, open features, and this woman, with her pointy chin and flint eyes, didn't resemble him at all.

I offered her a closed-lipped smile, and her mouth pinched as if she'd tasted something sour. I imagined punching her in that pinched mouth of hers. Imagined the spray of blood a good, hard hit would produce. Maybe I'd knock out some of her teeth.

"We have your petition," Walter said, snapping me out of my blissful thoughts. "And the *Lex* terms by which you made it. They clearly state that bloodlines must be preserved and extinction prevented. You are the last of your bloodline, and so it may seem that you are within your rights to petition the block on your bloodline's power be removed. However, I believe you may be unaware of the full terms of the sentence passed all those years ago."

My scalp prickled, and Polina's smirking face filled my mind. *I hope they execute you.* The possibility that I'd made an oversight spawned a fist in my chest.

What had I missed? "What more is there? What are the full terms? I've checked the written accounts. I didn't see anything more than the blocking spell."

"There is more. I assure you. Papers were signed that night and—"

"Then where are they? Why aren't they in the official logs? I need to see them." I was clutching at straws now, but the bubble of panic in my chest was making it hard to breathe.

I hope they execute you.

"Of course, we can get you a copy," Walter said. "But for the purposes of this meeting, Yash Vitra will provide an eyewitness account."

Eyewitness? Wait—he'd *been* there? But that would make him...old...Old Vitra...

"Yash, if you would..." Walter gestured to Vitra to begin.

"The original punishment discussed was an eye for an eye," Vitra said. "A bloodline for a bloodline. But there'd already been so much death that we could not stomach causing any more, and so a *Tardus Mors* was agreed upon, along with a block on the Onyx power."

Tardus Mors...a slow death? A prickling sensation crawled across my scalp.

They'd sentenced my bloodline to a slow death. A sentence

that ended with me. Which meant, they had no obligation to give me my power. So why bring me here? Dark foreboding bloomed in my gut.

"And the rest of the terms?" Portia said smugly. "Remind us of those, Master Vitra, please."

Vitra exhaled through his nose, his expression flat, as if this whole thing was tedious. "A *Mortem Finalem* on the last surviving member of the bloodline, to be carried out if they have not procreated by the age of twenty-two."

Mortem Finalem...final death... A chill swept up my spine. No, that couldn't be right. I must be misunderstanding the term. "What does that mean? *Mortem Finalem*...what does it mean for me?"

"It means we can execute you," Portia said, a small smug smile curling her lips. "You're twenty-two in six months, and it's impossible for you to birth a child before then, so..." She shrugged a slender shoulder, nonchalant, as if execution were an everyday, blasé topic.

I hope they execute you.

Polina had known about this. She'd bloody known. "You can't do that. You can't just kill me." My breath came faster, panic swelling in my chest. How could I stop them? I was powerless and at their mercy. "This was a trap. You brought me here under false pretenses. You were never going to let me stay, were you?" The pity on Walter's face burned through me, and hot tears of rage pricked at my eyes. "You make me sick. The lot of you, sitting up there on your platform as if you're better than me. Fuck you. Fuck you all, and—"

My mouth snapped shut of its own volition, jaw tight as if someone were holding it closed. I tried to force it open but couldn't.

What was this? What was happening to me?

The air buzzed, pressing down on me until my legs buckled. I hit the ground on my knees, grabbing at my face, desperate to release myself from the invisible force gripping me. Terror burgeoned inside me, growing larger and larger, a desperate scream battling to free itself from my throat, heat gathering behind my eyes with the force of an impending explosion.

Was this it? Was this my execution?

Was I dying right now?

Hard to tell without pain to guide me.

Vitra's cool drawl penetrated the fog of horror clouding my mind. "I think you've made your point, Heidi."

The bonds holding me captive evaporated. I fell forward, palms pressed to the cool ground, gasping for air as if it were nectar.

"Disrespect of your superiors will not be tolerated," Heidi said coolly.

Primal instinct warned me to keep my mouth shut, that I wasn't the one in control here. But the words came anyway, because honestly, what did I have to lose at this point? "I don't see anything worthy of respect here. Besides, you're going to kill me anyway, right?" I slowly pulled myself up. "It's what your kind does. Cut down anyone who challenges you." I opened my arms, holding them out on either side. "Get it over with then. I doubt it will be the first time you've murdered an innocent."

Portia snorted. "Innocent? I highly doubt it."

"You know nothing about me, you stuck-up—"

A phantom hand wrapped around my throat, choking me until I couldn't breathe. My eyes bugged and I reached for the Coterie, my desperate gaze locking on Vitra.

He sat forward, his eyes narrowing. "Portia..."

The pressure increased, bringing tears to my eyes.

"Let her go, Portia," Vitra ordered, coming to my defense yet again.

The air spiked with an acrid stench, and the pressure vanished. I sucked in a greedy breath, swallowing hard past the lump in my throat.

Portia smirked and slowly blinked, and in that moment, I would have gladly committed murder with my bare hands.

"May I remind you all that nothing has been decided yet,"

Walter said. The knot in my stomach eased a little. "Miss Onyx, do you require a moment? Water, maybe?"

A hatchet to bury in Portia's head would be great, but I cleared the thought from my mind and shook my head.

"What do you mean, *nothing has been decided*?" Portia said. "The rules are clear."

Walter opened his mouth to reply, but the big guy, Crax, beat him to it. "A *Mortem Finalem* can be overturned." He sat forward in his seat, dark brows pinching into a frown. "Surely, we must look to the future. I, for one, do not want to be responsible for the loss of another bloodline."

"You're not seriously suggesting we disregard her crimes and admit her?" Portia countered.

"I wasn't aware that Miss Onyx had committed a crime," Vitra said smoothly.

I should keep my mouth shut. He seemed to be advocating for me, after all, but... "No Onyx aside from Dharma ever committed a crime, but that didn't stop you from punishing us all. You not only blocked our power, you cursed us too."

His eyes flinched. "The curse was an unfortunate side effect."

"Unfortunate?" I was breathless with indignant rage, eyes hot with tears of frustration, which pissed me off because the last thing I wanted to do was cry in front of these fuckers. I sucked in a breath and exhaled to calm myself. "Yes, unfortunate." I glared at them all, daring them to ask me about my curse so I could tell them where to shove it. But there was silence. Heavy, guilty silence.

Good.

Vitra was the first to break it. "The punishment was warranted at the time. But time has passed, lives have been lost. Too many lives, and now I cannot help but wonder if the sentence was too harsh."

The almond-eyed woman looked over at him in surprise, but if he sensed her regard, he didn't show it.

Portia's delicate nostrils flared. "I may be agreeable to overturning the *Mortem Finalem*, but I will *not* sanction the return of her power or admittance to this institution. She was on Nightsbridge soil for less than an hour and our tram was derailed. People could have been killed."

"Yes, that was *totally* my fault. I planned the whole damn thing."

Portia opened her mouth to respond, but Xander Crax beat her to it.

"There was no one else on the tram," he said with a sigh edged in a growl.

Portia bristled with indignation. "No, which means *she* attracted the Horrors."

This was such bullshit. "How? With what power? No, don't tell me, they liked the scent of my perfume."

"You insolent little—"

"Enough!" Vitra snapped. "Let's stay on topic, shall we?"

He looked down the table at Walter. "We should put the decision to a vote, don't you think?"

Walter Regent nodded. "Yes, indeed. I think we can all agree that the *Mortem Finalem* should be disregarded."

Crax and Vitra nodded in agreement.

"Agreed," Heidi said.

Selethis inclined her head, her expression unreadable.

Portia rolled her eyes. "Yes, yes, agreed."

"Very well," Walter said. "It's unanimous."

I sagged on my feet. The relief so acute it left me breathless.

"Now to the *Tardus Mors*," Walter said. "Should we overturn it and allow Miss Onyx admission? Bear in mind that doing so will activate the *Arcanum Lex* decree, and we *will* be obligated to return her power to her."

My gaze flitted to Vitra, finding him watching me with an intensity that made my breath stall. The contact was a zing that hit me in the solar plexus, but in the next blink the heat was gone, leaving me wondering if I'd imagined it.

"All in favor say aye," Walter said.

I resisted the urge to cross my fingers. I needed this.

Desperately needed admission.

"Aye," Crax said. "We could use all the Hunters we can get."

"You know my answer," Portia said with a sniff. "I want her gone. It's a nay."

"Vitra?" Walter prompted.

Vitra's gaze alighted on me. Unreadable. Unemotional. And if I hadn't felt his heart beating against my back last night or felt his hot breath on my cheek, I'd have thought he was made of stone. I held my breath. He seemed to have been advocating to let me live, but I couldn't be sure where his vote would land when it came to letting me stay. I couldn't read him.

"I vote aye," he said finally, his tone flat, giving nothing away.

I exhaled sharply. That was two votes in favor of me staying and one against. I might win this.

Walter leaned forward to look down the table. "Constance?"

The almond-eyed woman, who'd remained mostly silent and watchful throughout the proceedings, showing neither support nor condemnation, now fixed her dark gaze on me. "I'm sorry, I must vote no."

Who the Tarrifel was she? And was it my imagination, or did Vitra's jaw tense up at her vote?

That was two votes to let me stay and two to send me home. Only Walter and Heidi remained.

The air crackled with tension, or maybe the tension was crackling inside of me, beneath the vise that was wrapped around my chest because there was nothing I could do to influence their decision.

I needed this to be over.

Heidi's vote would be to get rid of me, that much I was sure of, so that left Walter. If he voted to let me stay, it would be a draw. Then what would happen? Maybe a draw meant I could stay? But Walter's next words dashed my hopes.

"As the spokesman, I do not get a vote," he said, "so the decision lies with you, Heidi."

My heart sank. It was over. I was out.

"The balance of power is a delicate thing," Heidi said. "Each bloodline blessed by the Trinity of Weavers plays a part in that balance. The Arcanus are connected to the Weave by threads that we cannot possibly begin to understand. The loss of the Blackthorne bloodline sent a shockwave through the fabric of power, which took decades to stabilize." She gave me a pointed look. Seriously, was she about to give me a lecture now? "Onyx may be blocked from the Weave, but they were never cut off entirely and still contribute to the balance in some way. I do not wish to see what happens if we lose this most tenuous connection."

Wait... Wait a bloody second. Was she saying what I thought she was saying?

Portia huffed. "As much as I value your insight, Heidi, I don't agree with it. The Weave is made of sturdier stuff than to be destabilized by the loss of a bloodline. If anything, it would leave more power for the rest of us."

Portia Reign was a true bitch.

"What is your vote, Heidi?" Walter asked. "So that we are clear. Nay or aye?"

Yes, please, I needed her to be clear.

She fixed dark eyes filled with indecipherable emotions on me. "I vote we let her stay. I vote aye."

Relief surged through me, leaving me dizzy.

Portia threw up her hands. "Well, in that case, *you* can mentor her when she's unbound. I *won't* have her in my tower."

"*Your* tower?" Heidi arched a brow.

"You know what I mean," Portia said. "She's not welcome in East Trinity Tower with the sorcerers."

"She can stay with the covens," Heidi said. "Once she's unbound. We can put her in an administrative position to protect the bloodline as per the *Arcanum Lex*."

"Now wait a minute," Portia said. "Surely returning her power is enough to meet the terms of the *Lex*. We are effectively giving her the means to protect herself. The rest should be up to her. If she is to be a student here, then she must be treated like everyone else."

The other Coterie members made sounds of agreement.

It was fine. I'd handle whatever was thrown at me, and I'd survive it. Portia wouldn't be getting rid of me so easily.

I understood why she didn't want me around, though. I was a reminder of what she obviously believed to be a lapse in her brother's judgment. I was certain all the Reigns hated me. All except maybe one—my stepbrother Kian.

Portia *not* wanting me around made perfect sense to me, but why did Heidi Embercrest agree to host me?

Incantors generally had very little love for sorcerers. They hated that we could tap into the Weave without having to use spells or potions. That the Weave ran through us, amplified simply by a focus object. To them, it probably sounded like anarchy. But my bloodline of sorcerer was an anathema. There were enough incantors in our family tree to have given us the ability to wield both kinds of magic. It made us an outlier, unpredictable but powerful.

Maybe she was looking to take me under her wing and use me somehow? Whatever the reason, if it kept the others off my back so that I could focus on my real purpose of finding the *Libra Veritas*, then I was good with faking being grateful to her.

Shit. Walter was talking. Focus, Anamaya.

"...Bramble under Vitra's mentorship until your power has been unbound," he said. "Heidi, can you explain what will happen next?"

"Of course." Heidi inclined her head toward him before focusing her attention on me. "The spell that blocks your access to the Weave is powerful and will need to be removed in stages. You'll see the Weave Watchers tomorrow, and they'll determine how best to unravel it." She smiled kindly. "We'll take it from there. Any questions?"

The way Dori had described her, I'd expected her to be a total harridan. But she wasn't. Not to me. Which meant she definitely wanted something. I could work with that. "I do have a question.

How will you punish the Border House radio operator who almost got me killed?"

The silence that followed was pregnant with expectation.

Portia was the first to break it. "I hardly think that's any of your concern."

I glared at her, choice words springing to my lips, but Heidi's warning earlier about respect helped me shape my response. "With all due *respect*, I wasn't speaking to you."

Beside her, Heidi bit back a smile. "The incantor responsible has been stripped of his position in the Border House and relegated to Domestic duty for the rest of the year."

Domestic duty? Seriously? "That's it? That's the punishment for attempted murder?"

Her gaze hardened. "You can trust that Domestic duty for a year is a fitting punishment for a Raichand."

Raichand were one of the highest classes of incantors and part of Embercrest Coven. To relegate him to domestic work was probably worse than making him Unwoven for a month or two.

I dropped my shoulders, conceding. "Yes, I suppose it is."

"We take transgressions seriously here, Miss Onyx, no matter the bloodline."

Walter cleared his throat to get our attention. "If that is all, let me make it official." He fixed a stern gaze on me. "Anamaya Onyx, welcome to Nightsbridge."

> "The Supernal have lived among us for centuries. Keeping their own rules, their own counsel, hidden from the vast majority of humans, but there is no denying that humanity would have been wiped out without their aid."
>
> *Excerpt from Triton County Debate*

CHAPTER 9

The judgment panel disbanded, but Vitra looked over and held up a finger, motioning for me to wait before leaning in to speak to Constance Selethis.

She tipped her face up to his and placed her hand on his arm, stroking almost absentmindedly. Wait a minute. Selethis...she was his girlfriend. His *official* woman, and I could see why.

She was gorgeous, and they made a beautiful couple. Right now, standing face-to-face, leaning in toward each other, they created the perfect romantic scene. If I were an artist, I'd be scrambling for paint and canvas.

But I wasn't.

I was a woman on a mission, and I'd just overcome my first hurdle toward my goal. Excitement fizzed in my belly, undiluted by how badly things could have gone today.

But they hadn't.

I was safe and officially a student, on my way to having my power restored, and once I was whole, I could use the Weave to find the book that would prove my family's innocence.

I couldn't wait for the meeting with the Weave Watchers—

whoever they were— and to finally get started.

Constance glanced my way, then nodded up at Vitra before following the others through the door at the back of the room.

Vitra tucked his hands into his pockets and ambled over. "It looks like you'll be staying."

I'd forgotten how tall he was. How I had to tip my chin up to maintain eye contact. "Thanks to you."

"I wasn't the only vote in your favor."

"I know, but you advocated for me, so...thank you." He'd been there to decide Dharma's punishment. How much did he know about the crime? About the *Libra Veritas*? The temptation to pump him for information was almost too much, but it was too soon.

If the notes I'd found in Dharma's diary were true, if the truth of what happened had somehow been hidden, then he might know, and if I started digging, then who knew how he'd react? Disclosure such as that required a little more familiarity. It required time and trust. I needed to take it slow. Now that Walter Regent had assigned Vitra as my mentor, I needed to get to know him. Build a connection and trust then pick my moment.

We headed out of the room, into corridors bustling with students who instinctively parted to let Vitra pass. I stayed close, taking advantage of the break in the wave of bodies.

Someone accidentally bumped me into Vitra, and his arm went out to steady me, fingers curling around my waist briefly. My body flared with sensation, shivering tingles radiating out from where his hand lay on my waist.

I pulled away from him sharply, heart drumming against my ribs.

"Are you all right?" he asked.

"I'm fine."

His eyes narrowed a fraction, dropping to my mouth as if he could see the lie on my lips. And I felt the touch of his regard there, like a physical pressure.

Blood rushing in my ears, I ducked my head and hurried toward the main doors, the echo of his touch still resonating through my body. I'd felt him. Again. What the Fel was happening to me? It had to be this place. The magic here...maybe it was messing with my curse somehow? Yeah...that had to be it.

I passed a group of fresh-faced teens, sitting on the steps outside the main doors, poring over textbooks. One of them looked no older than twelve or thirteen.

I sensed Vitra behind me and scrambled for something to say, anything to hide my fluster. "Some of the students look too young to be here."

"Admission starts at sixteen," he said, leading the way down the steps. "But some are sent younger. Not often but...it happens. This will be their life now." He sounded almost sorry for them.

"Because of some agreement made between the bloodlines?"

"Yes."

"Why?"

"Someone had to take responsibility for keeping our world safe from the Horrors and Echoes spawned by this land."

Stepping out from beneath the porch with no cover from the elements, an icy breeze trickled over my skin. I buttoned up my wool coat.

Vitra seemed unbothered by the chill, ambling along as if it were a summer day.

"Spawned? You make it sound as if the earth itself creates them."

"Maybe it does. The forest is a beast unlike any other."

"There has to be more to it than that."

"Oh yes, much more, and you'll learn all about it in History of Nightsbridge."

He swerved away from the path that led down the mountain, taking me toward an ivy-covered arch.

"Why can't *you* tell me?"

"And risk the wrath of Mistress Selethis? No, thank you." He glanced down at me. "History is her forte, and you'll learn everything you need in her class."

"Wait a second, didn't you just get assigned to me as a

mentor?"

He smiled. "I did, which makes you a very lucky woman." Was he flirting with me? "I am an excellent mentor," he continued. "But it isn't my job to educate you on history. My job is to help you settle in at Nightsbridge and provide guidance should you have any problems."

Okay, so he wasn't flirting, and why was I disappointed about that? I cleared my throat. "Does everyone get a mentor or am I special?"

He slid a tawny-eyed glance my way. "You're the last of your bloodline, Miss Onyx. Of course, you're special."

The narrow, cobbled path twisted ahead. I wanted to ask where we were going, but when I opened my mouth, that wasn't the question that spilled out. "How long have you two been together?"

The corner of his mouth lifted in a half-smile. "Almost two years." He didn't sound surprised that I knew, but then, like everyone kept telling me, news was currency.

"She's not Arcanus, is she?"

"No."

I waited for him to elaborate, but he didn't. "What is she?"

He chuckled. "Constance is a lamia." I opened my mouth to ask him what that was, but he cut me off and continued. "And if you want to know what that is, you'll have to find out for yourself."

A squat brick building with lime-green shutters and a shiny gold weathervane on the roof came into view.

"What is that place?"

"Port station," Vitra said. "There are a few scattered around campus."

There were crystals embedded in the wall, and he tapped them quickly in a combination that I barely managed to catch and file away.

The door clicked open, and I followed him inside.

The room was empty, its walls lined with arches of various colors.

He led me to a bronze arch. "Your signature will be added

to the Academy ports by tomorrow. Meanwhile, you'll need another student to activate them for you. Polina will deliver your admission packet this afternoon." He pressed his palm to the arch, activating it. "This will take you back to Bramble Tower. Use the rest of the day to get acclimated. Everyone else has had years to adjust to living in Nightsbridge, but as of tomorrow, you'll be on the fast-track route."

"I can handle it." I made to step forward, but he gently gripped my arm to stall me.

Once again, his touch spawned delicious shivers. I could no longer convince myself that the sensations were in my head, and as his tawny gaze filled with shadows, my stomach dipped.

"Admission doesn't mean acceptance," he said. "Violence between students is prohibited, but accidents happen all the time. If you're going to survive here, find people you can trust and surround yourself with them. Make friends, Anamaya."

"Friends?" I stared up at him, shivers forgotten. Was he seriously that clueless? "There's no such thing as *friends* for an Onyx. Friends betray and lie and pretend not to know you when others find out about the *friendship*." I'd succeeded in making friends as a Denton, but friendships built on lies weren't real. "I learned a long time ago that an Onyx can only ever trust another Onyx."

"But you're the last Onyx," he said.

"Yep. And trust me, I've got my back."

The Unwoven would be my buffer and Vitra my mentor—until I had my magic and the *Libra Veritas*. Then I was out of here, truth in hand, ready to tell the world about the lies the Arcanum Imperium had spun.

"See you around." I gave him a mock salute and stepped into the port.

Damn, I couldn't wait to get started.

What do we truly know about The Overshadowing? About the cause and the origin? How can we be sure it was caused by humans at all?

Excerpt from Triton County Debate

CHAPTER 10

Bramble Tower wasn't just home to the Unwoven—it also housed the Domestic team that kept Nightsbridge Academy functional. I discovered as much when I walked into the sitting room to find the door to my bedroom open, sheets flying about on their own as they laid themselves on the bed and neatly tucked themselves in.

"Miss Onyx?"

I spun to face the young man standing in the sitting room doorway. He wore a flat cap that made his ears stick out, and the cuffs of his button-down shirt left his bony wrists exposed. His trousers were too short, leaving his patterned socks on display, but his shoes were clean and buffed to a shine.

"Me name's Pip," he said. "Head of Domestic. We'll have yer room spic and span in no time. Uniforms have been ordered and will be with you by this evening, along with casual wear and undergarments."

"Don't you need my size?"

He gave me a once-over. "No worries, miss, I have a good eye for sizing." He glanced over my shoulder into my room. "Wipe down the window, Mildred. I want no streaks."

A cloth materialized from thin air and glided over the window in my room. "Ghosts?"

"We call ourselves Spectral Domestic Assistants—SDA for short."

"We...? Are you—"

"Dead? A long time ago. Now, if you require anything—anything at all—you can ask for me at the SDA office on the second floor. There's always someone on duty, whether you can see them or not."

Wait a second. "You live in this tower? All of you...specters? Watching us whenever you want?"

The twinkle in his eyes died. "I assure you, madam, we do not spy. An SDA agent will always announce his presence."

Shit, I'd offended him. "I'm sorry. This is all new to me."

His face relaxed, and a hint of a smile returned. "Of course. Understandable. The second and third floors are our residences. Fourth and fifth are for the Unwoven. You'll find ports on those levels. The rest of the tower, sixth floor upward, belongs to Master Vitra."

Cold fingers of air brushed past me, and I sensed several presences.

"All done," Pip said. "A late breakfast will be brought to you as you missed the official meal due to your meeting this morning. It will be left on your desk."

Desk? There hadn't been a desk in my room. I turned to look, and sure enough, there was now a desk pushed up against the wall on the windowless side of my room, along with a stack of books filed neatly in a small bookcase.

"Thanks. I—"

But the doorway where Pip had been standing was empty.

He and his specters were gone.

⁓

I leaned against the dresser positioned against the wall to the right of the door and took in the space that would be mine for the next few weeks. The surfaces gleamed, and the air smelled like lemons. A small double bed, facing the door, was dressed in fresh white sheets, with a dark blue comforter folded neatly at the bottom. To my left, scented candles decorated the empty spots on my new bookcase, which stood beside the bathroom door. My desk, snug between my bed and the window to its right, now housed notebooks, pens, and academic textbooks. The titles were all in Latin, but I recognized a few from my studies with Mother. *Just because we don't have access to our power doesn't mean we can't understand who we are by learning about the Arcanus...*

God, I missed her.

But God was a human deity. The Arcanus worshipped the Trinity—the three daughters of the ancient gods, born to manage and protect the Weave of magic that spawned from the essence of all gods. According to the Arcanus beliefs, gods didn't die—they transformed into something else. So the Weave, magic, everything we thrived on, came from the essence of gods.

I wasn't sure I believed it, but maybe that was because I'd never been allowed to connect to it. But Mother had believed, calling on the Trinity in times of need rather than the human God. Not that they ever answered. I'd been careful not to call on the Trinity out loud, using the human God in my exclamations to help hide my identity as Arcanus. But now that I was here among supernals that knew who I was, there was no longer a need to hide.

Someone knocked on the door. "One second!"

A breakfast tray rested on the ground. There was no sign of who'd left it. Probably a member of the SDA.

Back in my room, I ate at my desk, barely tasting anything. The heightened sense of alert I'd been running on the past few weeks had dipped, and exhaustion had me in its snare. I didn't even have the energy to riddle over how Vitra seemed to be bypassing my curse. How was it that his touch could evoke physical pleasure?

Was it this place? Was it messing with my curse somehow?

I stabbed my hand with my fork, drawing a little blood but

feeling no pain.

The curse was still active. So what was happening?

Ugh. I needed sleep. The conundrum would have to wait.

Food done with, I stretched out on the crisp white sheets and passed out.

I woke to the whisper of a name that wasn't mine.

"Selina? Is that you? Selina?"

"What the..." I forced my eyes open to gloom and shadow. The mirror on the dresser glinted oddly, then something moved across its surface.

My pulse spiked, and I sat bolt upright, heart hammering with that awful sensation of threat. But the moment passed.

The mirror was simply a mirror, the shadows a reflection of the clouds passing by my window. I slumped back against the pillows and stared at a crack in the ceiling until my pulse slowed.

How long had I slept? The clock on the bedside table answered that question.

I'd been out like a wick for six hours.

Ugh. I dragged myself out of bed and cracked open the window to let in some air. The frame creaked and groaned in protest where the wood was slightly swollen. What was that... Something etched into the wood? *S.E.* Initials? Probably belonged to the previous occupant of this room.

Ah, the cool air felt nice. I shoved the window wider and poked my head out. The woods below were wreathed in mist that left only the canopy visible. The quad was split into hexagonal sections, bordered by bushes and small hedges. A pavilion stood to the right of the tower, partially obscured by more mist. The haze parted to reveal a woman, standing so still that if not for her silvery hair moving in the breeze, I would have mistaken her for a statue. What was she doing alone out there?

A knock sounded on my door.

I pulled the window closed and hurried to answer. "Coming!"

Clary waited on the other side, arms weighed down with bags. She was dressed in the Nightsbridge uniform—black slim-fitting trousers and a mid-thigh blazer in a brown so dark it was almost black. The blouse beneath was a deep mossy green. It wasn't the most appealing ensemble, but it looked comfortable.

"Your stuff is here." She held up the bags. "The SDA must have dropped it off while you were sleeping and not wanted to disturb you."

"*You* didn't have a problem disturbing me."

"Oh no, did I wake you?" She blinked sharply, lips parting, clearly horrified by the thought, and I instantly felt a pang of regret.

"No. I was already up. I'm glad you knocked."

"Oh, good." Her shoulders dropped in relief. "You want to take these?" She passed me the bags.

I carried them over to my unmade bed. Clothes, uniforms, casual outfits, PJs, and...undergarments. I checked the labels on the underwear, then the bras. My size. "What do you know, Pip *can* tell size just by looking."

"What?" Clary asked from the threshold.

"You can come in, you know."

"Oh...thanks."

I pulled out the final set of clothes. Black breeches and a fitted tunic, knees and elbows padded with leather. "What's this for?"

"Training clothes. You want help putting stuff away?"

There wasn't much to put away, but if I was going to make fake friends, then... "Sure, that would be great."

It took less than five minutes to shove the clothes in the dresser and hang up the uniforms.

"Oh, one second." Clary ducked out, returning with a thick envelope. "Your admission paperwork. You'll have a schedule in there too."

"Fabulous." I chucked it onto my bed.

Clary's gaze flicked from the envelope back to me. "Aren't you going to check it?"

Damn, I was rusty with this whole buddy-making malarkey. "Sure..." I ripped it open and tipped out the contents. Paperwork... whoop-de-doo.

"That's the schedule." Clary pointed at a cream sheet of paper. "Ooh, you have Combat 101 with us next week."

"Isn't that a beginner's class?"

"Kinda, but when you're Unwoven, you have to retake them—basically as punching bags for the other students." She shrugged. "It's not too bad. Most of the students don't even know how to land a punch."

"Sounds wonderful."

My dry tone had her chuckling. "It can be fun. The younger students are all in awe of us more advanced ones, and being Unwoven gives us an edge of danger." Her eyes lit up. "We've been encouraging speculation about our crimes. Some of the theories are wild. *You'll* need to pass the class, though, because essentially, you're a beginner."

"I took defense classes for years. I can handle myself."

She gave me an indulgent smile. "It's all about the *offense* here and weapon use. You'll need to learn how to wield swords and daggers."

I scanned the rest of the schedule. There wasn't anything on my rota for this week aside from History of Nightsbridge, but we're coming to the end of the week, so that made sense. Next week I had Combat 101, more History of Nightsbridge, and Horror 101, along with counseling. The next four weeks were variations of the same until something marked *grading*.

"What's grading?"

"That's the culmination of Combat 101."

"Like an exam?"

"Yes. You need to pass to move to Advanced Combat—and be eligible for the hunt." Her eyes lit up. "Hunters are respected highly here."

"And if I fail?"

"You could retake it or accept a post in another role like ward keepers, border watchers, domestic..." She winced.

The roles she mentioned would be safer and allow me to work on finding the *Libra Veritas*, but I got the impression that being on the hunt came with status, which would open doors.

Failure was not an option. "What about these counseling slots? I don't need those."

"Sorry, but those are mandatory. Life can be isolating here—surrounded by death. Miss Snap is amazing, though. You'll love her."

The last thing I wanted to do was lie on a couch and talk about my feelings, but if I had to, then I'd make some shit up.

"Hellooo!" Dori called out from the sitting room. "I heard that we have a new admission." She popped her head around the door. "I see the SDA kitted you out. Wait...are those scented candles?"

"Yeah."

She pouted. "*I* didn't get any scented candles."

"You can have them."

"Really?" She was already across the room gathering them up.

A shadow washed over the room as a massive bird landed on the windowsill.

I jumped, bumping into Clary, who put her arm around me. "It's okay," she said. "It's just a raven." She hurried over and slid the window open. "Hi." She beamed at the bird. "You have a message?"

The raven dipped its head and fixed its beady eyes on me. "Message for Onyx from Heidi Embercrest," it said in a croaky voice, then... "Good afternoon, Miss Onyx." Heidi's voice drifted from the raven's beak. "I will escort you to your meeting with the Weave Watchers tomorrow. Meet me in Trinity Hall at nine a.m. sharp—do not eat breakfast beforehand." The raven cawed. "Would you like me to repeat the message?"

"No thanks." Once was creepy enough.

The raven flew off, and I crossed the room to close the

window.

"You're seeing the Weave Watchers?" Dori asked.

"Yeah, apparently they need to figure out how to remove the block on my power." They watched me, looking slightly paler than usual, if I wasn't mistaken. "Okay, what is it now?"

Clary answered, eyebrows pinching in a frown. "The Weave Watchers are the boogeymen of Nightsbridge, said to be more dangerous than a Horror and more powerful than any coven or Arcanus bloodline. There are stories of students being sent to see them but never returning."

"Not just any students," Dori jumped in. "Students who prove to be dangerous. Who can't control their power, who cause consistent harm—who prove to be unworthy of it."

"Yeah, well, I haven't committed any crimes or caused any harm, and I haven't had a chance to demonstrate how worthy I am because I haven't had access to my power."

"Good point." Clary's frown cleared. "But this means you'll be able to tell us what *they're* like and what it's like down in the catacombs."

"Claustrophobic, no doubt," Dori said with a shudder.

My stomach growled. "I need food."

"Just as well that it's suppertime," Dori said. "Time to introduce you to the food pit."

"Aren't meals in the Main Building?"

"Yep," Dori said.

I glanced out into the night. "I don't much fancy climbing up the side of the mountain in the dark. Once today was enough. Can't we get food somewhere else?" They both stared at me in confusion, eyebrows furrowed, heads tipped to one side. "What?"

"Polina took you up the mountain trail?" Clary asked.

Dori's mouth tightened. "That bitch."

Realization dawned. "There's another way up, isn't there?"

"Yeah, there is," Dori replied. "A lift up the side of the mountain. The footpath is only for emergencies, like if a storm knocks out the magi-generator tower or something."

Now it made sense why no one else had been on the path when so many had crossed the bridge with us. Why hadn't I picked up on that at the time? Oh yes, because I'd been too busy trying to stay alive.

"I'm sorry," Clary said softly.

I blinked and fixed a smile on my face. "It's fine. I'm used to it, but this..." I pointed between the two of them. "Arcanus being nice to me? That I am *not* used to." I narrowed my eyes, injecting a playful tone into my voice before asking a very real question. "What do you both want from me?"

Clary balked, but Dori rolled her eyes.

"I told you she'd think we were playing her," Dori said to Clary.

"We're not," Clary said. "Honest."

"We're just not assholes—unlike some of the people you've met."

Everyone had an agenda, even if they didn't consciously know it, but I needed these women on my side if I was going to survive—and get to the book.

"We just want to be friends," Clary said.

Friends...that loaded word again. "Fine. Okay. Friends, it is." I grabbed my coat. "Let's go get some food."

> **I want her to walk the halls of Aakash Ghar. To be by my side. Mine to claim. To love. But it can never be, and that tears me up inside. When this is all done, how will I leave her?**
>
> *Unnamed Journal (Vault Archives)*

CHAPTER 11

The lift ride up the side of the mountain offered a sweeping view of the coast and the five towers that made up the Academy residences. But as we neared the top, the elevator took a curve around the mountain, revealing a tower isolated on an island out at sea.

"What's that?"

"Coral Isle," Clary said. "It's where we go to blow off steam—and have a little fun."

"There are a few places to eat, a market, and some night lounges," Dori added.

"And the tower?"

"It's been sealed for a long time," Dori said. "Rumor is that it belonged to the Blackthorne bloodline."

"They had a whole tower to themselves?"

"I guess so."

Now that was interesting. The Blackthornes had been powerful enough to claim an entire tower on their own island—yet Dharma had supposedly wiped them out single-handedly?

"I know what you're thinking," Clary said.

"No. You don't."

"You're wondering how one sorcerer could have exterminated a whole bloodline as powerful as Blackthorne."

"Okay, so you do know what I'm thinking. Please don't tell me you can read minds." Shit, what if she could?

"No. I just... I've often wondered the same."

"It doesn't help that the details are classified," Dori said.

They had no idea. "Imagine being punished for a crime, not being given the details of said crime, and being forced to simply accept that the punishment is just."

We fell into silence, watching the sea shift beneath the night sky as Coral Isle flickered to life with twinkling lights. A boat bobbed across the waves toward it, two figures silhouetted in the moonlight.

The lift came to a halt against a platform jutting out of the mountain. A short flight of steps took us onto a dusty path that carved its way through stone-figure littered grounds toward the Main Building.

In the daytime, with the gray sky hanging low and heavy, the sprawling four-story castle looked large and imposing. But at night, bathed in the silver glow of a crescent moon, it seemed to stretch out forever, held in place by shadows that dominated every crevice and corner of the statuesque structure. The path melted into shrubs and brush, a wild landscape of flora and stone. It would be easy to get lost here at night, but the lights of the Main Building acted as a guide.

A group of students came up behind us, dressed in casual wear of loose trousers, cream tunics, and long wool coats, too engaged in their conversation to give us a second glance. They seemed young, maybe fifteen or sixteen. Arcanus, if the neutral colors of their clothes were anything to go by.

A huge shadow darted across our path and into the brush on our left. Clary let out a yelp, barely dodging it in time.

I froze, body on high alert. "What was that?"

"Nothing," Dori said quickly.

Clary nodded, hand on her chest. "Let's just keep going."

"That was *not* nothing." I followed the thing's trail, spotting dark splodges on the ground where it had passed. Blood? "It's bleeding."

"Sounds about right," Dori muttered.

"What?"

Clary hugged herself, eyes darting this way and that. "We should go."

"Come on." Dori urged us to continue, but a mournful whimper stopped me in my tracks once more.

"Ignore it," Dori said, grabbing my arm and forcing me to pick up the pace.

A pained whine trailed after us.

A cry for help.

How could they urge me to walk away? Their actions made no sense. What did make sense, what felt right, was stopping to help. I dug in my heels. "Something's hurt."

"We can't help him," Clary said.

"Him?"

Dori shot her a glare.

The whine came again, thick with pain, dejected and despondent. I moved toward the sound instinctively, stepping off the path and into the brush.

"Ana, don't!" Dori made a grab for me, but I shook her off, diving deeper, past a gargoyle with outstretched wings and another sporting a vicious sneer.

Another whimper, followed by panting—the kind that spoke of a desperate attempt to manage pain.

"Anamaya?" Clary's voice wavered. "Stop."

"I need to see."

Dori caught up with me. "Trust me, you don't, because you can't help him. No one can."

I rounded a cracked, dried-up fountain, where a large hound-like beast lay panting on his side. The scent of blood coated the air, seeping from the many wounds scoring his body, and my skin pricked with the heat of rage.

The wounds were deep lacerations, dragging through flesh but jagged in places, as if hooks had caught the skin. If I had to guess the weapon used, I'd say a barbed whip.

Behind me, Clary let out a strangled cry, and the creature's eyes rolled in our direction. He snarled, attempting to sound menacing but failed when the sound dissolved into a whimper.

He was too hurt to protect himself. "It's okay." I held up my hands. "I'm not going to hurt you."

"Ana..." Dori reached for me again, but I shot her a warning glare, and she backed off.

I tugged off my coat and approached the hound. He attempted another growl, but it was a half-hearted attempt, tempered by his agony. "Hush... I just want to help." I kept my voice soft and low so as not to spook the creature. "We need to stop the bleeding."

His lips fell back over his teeth, and his head dropped to the ground in defeat, almost as if it understood me. And hell, this was Nightsbridge; he probably did. I fell to my knees beside him and pressed my coat to his blood-soaked flank, wincing when he yelped.

Oh, this was bad. The wounds were deep. "Clary, can you heal it?"

"I'm Unwoven, remember? No access to magic, but even if I had my power, I couldn't help him. No one can."

"What do you mean?"

"Ruspin has been claimed as a blood debt," Dori said. "He's off-limits to everyone except his owner."

"What the fuck is a blood debt?" I shook my head. "You know what? I don't care what it is. This is *not* okay." I stroked the creature's head, and he closed his beautiful brown eyes for a beat. "Ruspin, right? Hey, I'm going to help you." I glanced up at Dori and Clary. "We have to get him to a medical room. That woman—Darla, the halfling—she can help, right?"

"You don't understand," Dori said. "No one can help him. It's forbidden by—"

"Forbidden?" I stared at her, incredulous. "It's forbidden to help a wounded creature, but it's okay to beat him until he's bleeding out? What the fuck kind of place is this?"

"I know it sounds crazy to you," Clary said. "But the law is clear on interfering with a blood debt. We have to go. Now. Before someone sees us and—"

"What do we have here?" A woman stepped into the clearing with us. "Are you attempting to soothe my pet?" The icy glint in her eye contradicted the sweet childish pitch of her voice.

Dressed in fitted black breeches, a high-necked white shirt beneath a crimson waistcoat, and a long leather jacket, she presented a sophisticated picture. She couldn't be more than five feet in height. But her golden, intricate topknot added an extra three inches to her stature. Her eyes were so dark they swallowed the light, and her alabaster skin gleamed in the moonlight. I'd bet my left boob this bitch was a Haematophage.

Her dark eyes bore into me, the hard look in them contradicting the smile on her painted lips. "Well?"

"You did this?" I gestured toward Ruspin.

"Not my finest work, but yes. Why? Do you not like it?" She smirked.

"You sadistic little—"

"She's new, Tamina," Dori said quickly. "She doesn't know the rules. We were just explaining them to her." She threw a warning look my way.

Tamina's gaze flicked above my head to Dori. "How considerate of you. But then, you were *always* so very sweet."

Dori's jaw tightened. "It's an honest mistake. No retribution required."

"Oh?" Tamina said. "But retribution is my *favorite* pastime..." She pouted and tapped her chin. "But, since it's you, how about we make a deal? Spend the night with me, and I'll forget this little infraction."

Clary gasped, but Dori didn't even flinch.

"Now you just sound desperate," she said.

Tamina's eyes flashed dangerously. "Oh, sweetheart, you have no idea what desperate truly means. You, in my bed, or I'll claim my pound of flesh from your new little friend."

I pulled myself to my full five-seven height and looked down on her. "I think your perception is a little skewed, don't you?"

She arched an appreciative brow. "Wait...you're the Onyx, aren't you? Of course..." Her gaze flicked back to Dori, and a dirty smirk played on her crimson mouth. "You always did like the bad girls."

Dori rolled her eyes. "Whatever. I'll be at yours later. No need for drama." She grabbed my arm. "We're leaving."

A flash of something sharp and ancient flitted behind Tamina's eyes. "Maybe I've changed my mind. Maybe I want my pound of flesh after all."

Dori's grip on my arm flexed once before she released me and sauntered over to Tamina, coming to stand mere inches from her petite form. "Have you? Changed your mind?"

Tamina swayed toward Dori inhaling deeply. "Oh...how I have missed that scent."

Dori stiffened but held her ground as Tamina leaned closer, pushing up on her toes to brush her nose against Dori's neck.

Dori's hands curled into fists. "Well?" she snapped. "Do you want me, or do you want her?"

Tamina sat back on her heels. "There is no competition, you know that. I want you, of course, my sweetling. Always you."

"Then we have a deal. Say it."

Tamina sighed and shrugged a leather-clad shoulder. "I forgo the right of retribution in this instance." She narrowed her eyes my way. "But touch what's mine again, and you *will* pay the price."

I had no doubt she wasn't just referring to Ruspin.

The hound watched me with dull eyes, resigned to his fate, and my stomach twisted. I didn't want to leave him with the crazy bitch, but I'd come here for the *Libra Veritas*, and the best way to get to it was to fly beneath the radar. I couldn't afford to get into a fight.

This couldn't be my problem.

Even though it seemed I'd made a problem for Dori. Fuck...

Tamina plucked my jacket off Ruspin and threw it at me. "You can keep the blood. A gift from me." She snapped her fingers at Ruspin. "Up! Now."

The silver collar around his neck gleamed, and he jolted like he'd been shocked.

She turned on her heel and strode off, the tail of her long coat flapping about her calves.

Ruspin dragged himself upright, his breath shallow and fast, his brown eyes filled with absolution, as if to say, *you tried your best, thank you.* Then he turned and followed Tamina through the brush and toward the castle.

Clary exhaled shakily. "Wow, that was close."

I bunched my jacket under my arm; it was too blood-soaked to wear now. "Who the fuck was that, and what exactly just happened?"

"That was Tamina Vayne," Dori said wearily. "She's Baobhan Sith royalty."

I rifled through what I knew about her kind. Blood-drinking, matriarchal society with roots buried in folklore tied to a species called the Shining Ones. The Baobhan Sith were known for their heightened sexuality and lack of empathy. They took several lovers at a time to satiate their hunger for blood and sex, and from the sound of it, Dori had just agreed to be this bitch's next meal.

I couldn't let her do this. "Dori, I'll speak to her and take the retribution."

"No. You won't," Dori said. "I can handle Tamina. She won't hurt me."

"I can't let you do that. What's the retribution?" Whatever it was, I'd take that rather than let Dori go into the bloodsucker's boudoir. I wouldn't sleep tonight otherwise.

"The retribution can be anything that Tamina wants it to be," Clary said. "And trust me, she's inventive when it comes to inflicting pain."

"Pain, I can handle. I have a high threshold."

"Higher than a Therianthrope?" Dori asked with an incredulous snort.

I was about to say yes, because even though Therianthropes were renowned for their high pain tolerance, it was nothing compared to feeling no pain at all, but I bit back the admission. "Maybe not *that* high."

"She's brought them to their knees," Clary said.

I could fake being in pain, pretend to pass out—let the bitch get her kicks—if it meant Dori didn't have to sleep with her. "I want to try. I'll speak to her and—"

"It's done," Dori said firmly. "The deal is made and cannot be unmade."

"As much as I hate that Dori has to do this, it's better than the alternative," Clary said. "Besides, I have an excellent tincture to aid sleep." She dimpled in Dori's direction. "Trust me, she'll have the sweetest dreams."

"Oh, I remember, and I was banking on it." The two women bumped shoulders and set off toward the path.

Unease bloomed in my chest. "Why would you do this?" I jogged to catch up with them. "Why did you offer yourself to her for me? You barely know me, and I *blatantly* disregarded your warning about not touching the hound."

She smiled and shook her head. "You'd do the same for me."

Guilt pricked my cheeks—I was pretty sure I wouldn't have. Thankfully, the darkness hid my shame.

She slung an arm around my shoulder. "Besides, us Unwoven, we got to stick together, right?"

The unease grew. "Yeah...right."

"Dark skies, you're freezing!"

Her words acted like a trigger, prompting me to register the chill seeping through the thin material of my blouse. My teeth immediately began to chatter.

"Take my coat." Clary slung it over my shoulders, enveloping me in her warmth. "I have a wool undershirt on."

Keeping my guard up around these two was going to be harder than anticipated.

The supernals have their own hierarchies of power, and at the top of the Haematophage pyramid are the Vayne and Damascus houses. Bonded through blood and marriage for centuries, these two houses are rooted in ancient traditions that are beyond human comprehension.

A Study of the Others

CHAPTER 12

Wall sconces bathed the Main Building in warm light, and this time I was able to take in more of the details as we made our way to the dining hall. Ornate molded ceilings loomed above, so high they were shrouded in shadows, so it was difficult to make out the intricate swirls and circles etched across their surface, but when I squinted and focused, they looked like painted cogs. Thick beams crisscrossed above, providing a framework with which to hold up the impressive roof. Tapestries and mirrors of all shapes and sizes lined the walls, ensuring there was always a looking glass to peer into.

My step faltered as we passed a wall decorated with portraits of men and women set in gilded frames.

"This is the gallery," Clary explained. "Every influential member of the Superna Coterie from the last few centuries is here."

I spotted Vitra's portrait right away. He gazed off into the distance with a slight smile that practically said, *admire me if you want. I get it. I'm fucking hot.*

Portia and Heidi were a row below him, looking stern and forbidding. But further up were faces I didn't recognize. Then there was a gap marked by an oval of light-colored paint. "There's a painting missing."

"Where?" Dori asked.

"Up there." I pointed to a blank space several feet up.

"I noticed that when we got here a few years ago," Clary said. "I asked around, and I found out that spot used to belong to Dharma Onyx."

What the fuck? Dharma had been part of the Coterie? She'd been one of the few in charge here, so this place had obviously been important to her. Why would she have risked it all to commit a heinous crime? It made no sense to me.

"Come on," Dori said. "Benedict will be holding our table, and I'm not sure he'll have the willpower to stave off the silvers without us."

They ushered me through a vaulted arch and down another passage that split into two. One route was brightly lit, the other was shrouded in shadows, but I could make out a door at the end.

The group veered toward the lit corridor, but I found myself gravitating to the shadows.

"Ana, this way," Clary said.

I took another step toward the gloomy passage. "What's down there?"

She huffed slightly. "It's restricted."

"Why?"

"Something to do with structural stability. They've been meaning to work on the wing for ages."

"Come on," Dori said. "We need to get to Benedict."

They hurried off, and with a final glance at the dark passage, I followed.

A couple more turns led us to a huge room dotted with plush booths occupied by students. One side of the room was all windows, offering a grand view of the epic ocean, so from this vantage point, it looked like we were riding the waves. A sense of calm fell over me, but the next moment, the hum of conversation and the aroma of various dishes hit me. My stomach tightened with nerves as memories I'd strived to bury surged up, pricking at my conscious mind.

What are you eating, Onyx? The dried-up hearts of long-dead Blackthornes?

Don't touch her. You might catch something.

Then there were the shoves and the tripping, and the lonely corner table where I'd eaten lunch every day. I could have skipped it. Saved myself the grief, but no. I'd gone. Every fucking day. I'd gone, and I'd endured. And thank Trinity I had, because it had built my armor, showing me that the old adage was true: sticks and stones, baby. Sticks and fucking stones.

But this dining hall was nothing like the ones I'd frequented. It was grand and opulent, with a checked tile floor of cream and silver. Chandeliers hung from wide beams above us, and beyond that, hidden in the gloom, was another domed ceiling painted with golden cogs and silver swirls. Mirrors on the far wall created an illusion of space, and for a moment, it looked like shadows moved within. But on closer inspection, all I saw was a mirror image of this room—and my face staring back at me. The face of a grown woman, not the young girl from six years ago.

My anxiety melted away. I was no longer afraid or ashamed.

"Oh shit," Dori said. "The silvers have Benedict." She set off quickly toward a booth in the far-right corner of the vast room, where Benedict sat with three women with long silver hair.

Clary and I hurried to catch up.

"Dori." Benedict grinned up at her, a goofy smile on his face. "Have you met my friends?" He indicated the three women squished onto the bench opposite him, identical except for eye color. "They want to take me for a schwim... Schwim... Swim!" He beamed at us when he finally nailed the word. The women nodded in unison, and he sighed. "Of course I would."

"Piss off, you three," Dori snapped at the women. "How many times, eh? He's not interested."

The middle one with violet eyes glared at Dori.

"Yeah? You can glower at me all you want, fish-breath, but

you can't get in my head. So go on, fuck off, before I call Master Trax."

The trio hissed in unison, baring a mass of needle-long teeth that transformed their beautiful faces into something hideous and terrifying.

Across from them, Benedict jolted back in his seat. "Argh!"

"Go on, get!" Dori shooed at them.

The silvers slipped from the bench and glided out of the room, the hems of their long dresses sweeping the floor behind them.

Benedict ran a hand down his face and shuddered. "What took you so long?"

"Sorry," Clary replied. "Anamaya met Tamina." She took the space beside him, and Dori and I sat opposite on the bench vacated by the silvers.

Benedict grimaced. "You saw Ruspin, huh?"

I nodded. "I did. But first, who were they?"

"The silvers?" Benedict shuddered again. "They want my body. Literally." He made a chomping motion with his mouth.

"What the fuck?"

"They're sirens," Dori said. "You know your sea folklore."

"Not really." Sea lore wasn't something Mother had thought I needed to learn growing up.

"Clary, you do the honors," Dori said. "I'm gonna order our meals. What do you guys want?"

"I'll have a pot roast," Benedict said.

"Lamb shank for me," Clary replied.

Everyone looked at me. "Um...what are the options?"

"Whatever you want," Clary said.

"*Whatever* I want?"

"Yep. You order it, and it'll be created."

"You want last night's spaghetti? You got it," Dori said. "You want the meal you had on your sixteenth birthday? The kitchen will whip it up."

"How is that possible?"

Dori shrugged. "Don't know. Don't care."

"So what will it be?" Clary asked.

There was one thing I wanted to eat really badly, something I'd thought I'd never get to taste again. If what they said was true, then... "My mother's belly-warming hot pot."

Their eyes softened at my request, and I wanted to kick myself. I might as well have rolled over and shown them my belly. It was suddenly a little harder to breathe. "You know what, forget it. I—"

"Too late." Dori strode off.

"Wait!" Clary called after her. "I changed my mind. I want to try Ana's mother's belly-warming hot pot too."

"Make that three," Benedict added.

Dori dropped us a jaunty salute. "Four Onyx hot pots coming up."

The tightness in my lungs eased, replaced by that strange bubble of emotion again. But I ducked my head, breathing through it. "So...the silvers and sea folklore?"

"Oh yes," Clary said, eyes lighting up. "There is a ton of it—about the alliance between land and sea after The Overshadowing, and—"

"She hasn't taken Selethis's class yet, so she probably only knows what the outsiders do," Benedict reminded her. "Look, all you need to know is that sirens can get into a human's head, and they have a taste for male flesh. The Land-Sea Pact prevents them from attacking pure humans, but"—he jerked a thumb at his chest— "I'm part human on my mother's side. I was raised by my father after she abandoned me." He spoke of abandonment as if it didn't bother him. Maybe it didn't. Maybe he'd never known her. I wasn't about to pry.

"Which is why they keep trying to lure him into the sea," Clary said. "He's the only human male at Nightsbridge they can snack on."

"Part human," Benedict corrected.

"Ugh, Evergreen Coven just strolled in," Clary said.

"I spot a few Silverthorn and Embercrest too," Benedict said. "I'm so glad my lot eats much later."

The incantors occupied the area closest to the windows. They all sported the green and brown Nightsbridge uniforms, but some also wore scarves of different colors: metallic gray, orange, or lime green. Their coven colors, no doubt, but being from different covens shouldn't stop them from mingling—covens often worked together. Sorcerers, however, kept to themselves, as evidenced by their two-booth separation from the incantors. Their scarves were royal blue. The Reign colors.

They ate together, but whereas the incantors chatted amiably with one another, the sorcerers ate in silence.

No Arcanus glanced our way, which was good. Being invisible here, as much as possible, would be a bonus.

If I kept my head down, I could claim my power, find the book, and—

"Oh great," Benedict muttered. "She just had to bring him in here, didn't she?"

"Right by the Therianthrope booths, too," Clary added.

I followed the direction of their gaze to where Tamina was settling into a booth in the center of the room with three other Haematophages. Beyond them were the booths occupied by large males, who, from all the obvious muscle, had to be Therianthropes.

They either turned their backs on the Haematophage or looked away.

"What's happening?"

"Tamina is about to put on a show," Clary said dryly. "She does this every so often. Ignore her. Don't watch." She gnawed on her bottom lip, her gaze darting to me. "Actually, maybe we should just go."

Ruspin hobbled into the room. The wounds on his side had begun to clot, but his eyes were bloodshot from pain, his tail tucked between his legs.

Tamina beckoned him to approach, and he obeyed, each step labored and slow.

She stood and slipped off her jacket before carefully laying it on the bench behind her, a small smile playing on her crimson mouth. She waited patiently for him to get close, cooing words of encouragement softly to him, but as soon as he was within touching range, she stepped back and kicked him in the face with enough force to send him toppling onto his wounded side.

His yowl of pain shot straight through me.

I bolted to my feet, but Clary pulled me back down.

"You can't. Please..." Her words were buried beneath the raucous laughter of Tamina's sucker crew.

My nails bit into my palms as I looked to the Thropes, trying to catch an eye, to see a reaction. But there was none. They continued with their meals in silence. Practiced and schooled. How often had Tamina put on such a display?

Ruspin shook his head then stared up at his mistress with a resigned expression, waiting for her next move.

She beckoned him closer, and once again he obeyed. This time, she punched him in the head, rallying another round of laughter from her cronies.

My gums pulsed from how hard I was clenching my teeth. "If the Thropes can't do anything, why don't they leave? Why give her an audience?"

"Solidarity," Benedict said softly. "They bear witness, and through that, they offer Ruspin strength."

"That's all well and good when *they're* not getting their heads kicked in—"

Another blow landed on the hound, this one sending him flying back, his head whipping our way. He blinked blearily, the look in his eyes dead and empty. A look of learned helplessness that I'd seen in the mirror too many times in the past.

Tamina crooned his name, summoning him once more as one of her companions handed her a coiled whip.

No...

"Maybe we *should* leave," Clary said.

Ruspin's body heaved with panicked breaths. He knew what

was coming, but he didn't run. He waited to receive the blows.

Waited for a punishment he didn't deserve.

Tamina raised the whip, pulling it back, ready to strike.

Heat flooded my limbs, and before I could think it through, I was out of my seat and across the room, a red haze of rage clouding my vision.

The whip lashed down, curling around my hand, its bite nothing more than an uncomfortable pressure.

The shock on the bitch's face was priceless.

My rage cooled to something cold and hard as I held her gaze. "Do you think hitting someone who can't fight back makes you powerful?"

She recovered quickly, eyes narrowing to slits. "I warned you not to interfere with my pet, didn't I?"

"You did." I yanked on the whip, and she staggered forward a step before catching herself. "But I don't take orders from psycho bitches." I yanked again, but this time she held her ground, and the whip dug harder into my palm.

Her gaze dropped to my hand. "You're bleeding."

"Yeah. I know."

She arched a brow. "You like pain?"

"Not as much as you enjoy inflicting it."

She smirked and released the whip handle. "How about this... you last three minutes in the arena with me and I'll stop hurting the hound."

Behind me, Ruspin whimpered, the sound not one of pain but one of hope, and suddenly, stopping her from hurting him wasn't enough. "How about this? I last three minutes in the arena with you, and you let Ruspin go. You set him free." Her eyes flared, gaze flicking from side to side as if she were having doubts. It was my turn to smirk. "What? You afraid you'll lose?"

She lifted her chin and matched my smirk. "Oh, sweetie, I never lose, but I think we should sweeten the pot. If I win, you're mine for a week. *My* pet to do with as I please."

"Ana, don't," Dori said from somewhere behind me.

I kept my gaze locked with Tamina. "You have a deal."

An uproar rose behind her—the Thropes buzzing among themselves.

"Keep the whip," Tamina said. "A pre-fight gift. It's been a long time since someone stood up to me. How exciting." She clasped her hands together beneath her chin. "I do hope you don't crumble too soon..."

"You can count on it."

"Next week, arena day. Seven sharp. Don't be late." She singsonged her last words, blew me a kiss, then clipped toward the exit. "Ruspin, come."

Ruspin lingered a moment, his huge brown eyes filled with words he couldn't say.

"Ruspin!" Tamina snapped.

I smiled down at him. "Go."

He padded close and bumped me with his snout before following his mistress from the room.

As soon as they were gone, the chamber erupted in a cacophony of sound.

Clary rushed over and took my bloody hand. "Dark skies, that's deep. We need to get you to Darla. Now. Oh, Trinity..." She carefully unwound the whip from my hand.

"That's gotta hurt like a hex," Benedict said.

I winced and let out a groan, an expert in faking it. "The adrenaline helped. I'll be okay."

Clary pulled a handkerchief from her pocket and wrapped it around my palm.

"You idiot," Dori muttered, pacing back and forth. "I'll speak to her. I'll fix this. It'll be okay."

But I didn't need her to fix anything. "I want to do it. Just le—"

"The muscles are coming over," Benedict whisper-hissed.

Four males ambled over, dressed in undershirts that hugged their pectorals, leaving their epic biceps on display to be admired. Trousers hanging low on their hips left no doubt that the rumors of Therianthrope *size* were real.

The one leading the group had spiky dark hair streaked with silver highlights. "You're chaos, Onyx," he said.

There was something eerily familiar about his smiling brown eyes. "Chaos?"

Benedict leaned in, speaking from the side of his mouth. "It means insane, crazy, delusional, psycho."

"Ah, well, the only way to fight psycho is with psycho."

"She'll turn you inside out," one of the other males with white gold hair said. "Trust me, we've all tried to free Ruspin."

"Well, anyone who can survive a mudark and Echo attack has my vote," spiky hair said.

Dammit, that voice... "Have we...met?"

He offered me a lopsided smile. "Is that a pickup line?"

"What? No!"

He chuckled. "Yeah, it's Jay, from the other night on the road."

Of course it was, and white gold dude had to be Brek. "You're Brek, right?"

"In the humanoid flesh," Brek said. I scanned the other two males. "Drayven isn't here," Brek said. "He doesn't come to the canteen anymore."

I didn't bother denying that I'd been looking for the barghest. "Yeah? Well, say hi from me."

"We need to get you to Darla," Clary said. "Your hand is bleeding." She shook her head, her brows drawing together as if struggling to make sense of my calm.

I forced a pained look and nursed my hand to my chest. "Yeah, it really hurts."

"Nothing compared to what next week will bring," Jay said, all somber now. "Look, no one will think less of you if you drop out. Get Trax to talk to her. He's the Hall Master, and he runs the Main Building. She has enough infractions pending. Get him to add the pressure."

There was no way I was letting Tamina walk away from our bet. "I appreciate it, but no. I can handle her."

The Thropes exchanged glances, then Brek nodded. "In that case, best of luck."

"You've bled through the handkerchief," Clary chided. "Come on."

I allowed her to lead me from the room, aware of the many Arcanus eyes on me.

So much for staying invisible.

The Shining Ones: Unknown species named for the ethereal glow emanating from their bodies. They occupied Nightsbridge between 1 A.O. and 10 A.O., then vanished. The only evidence of their existence are the Baobhan Sith and halfling, the latter a hybrid species which is now hurtling toward extinction.

The Evolution of the Supernal

CHAPTER 13

"Oh dear. Well now, this is nasty, isn't it? Hmm?" Darla examined my hand. "Luckily for you, there won't be any stitches required, and I have just the ticket to speed up the healing."

She bustled across the small medical room to a cabinet filled with jars of gunk in various colors. Her braid swayed to and fro as she moved about, so long it passed her bottom. She was adorable with her trouser cuffs rolled up to account for her small stature, and a tunic that fell to her knees, topped with a green apron, its pockets bulging with items.

The room was down the corridor from our quarters, empty unless she was summoned by a student, which Clary had done by pressing her palm to the crystal on the desk.

Clary stood close by, wringing her hands. "I'm sorry," she said again. "I wish I could heal you."

I waved her off with my good hand. "It's okay. I'm fine."

"Yes, she'll be right as rain," Darla said. "This will numb the pain *and* heal." She scooped some green ointment from a jar and lathered it onto my hand before wrapping a bandage around it. "Palm injuries are the worst. So many nerves and things. But this will set you right in a couple of days." She handed me the jar. "Take this and make sure to reapply it morning and night. Clary, dear, grab some bandages, would you?" She gently gripped my chin and peeled off the bandage on my head. "Let's get this one cleaned up, too."

She was finishing up when Vitra walked into the room. The space seemed to shrink around him. He stood by the door, his golden gaze tracking Darla's movements as she taped gauze over my head wound.

"You want to speak with Miss Onyx, I assume?" Darla said once she was done.

"I do."

Trinity save me. His voice did strange things to my insides, and when his gaze landed on me, trapping me in warm honey, breaking contact became an exercise in will. Fortunately, will was something I had in abundance. I dropped my gaze to his mouth, to the knowing smile that played there, then away, anywhere else to give my pulse a moment to settle.

Darla grabbed a couple of jars and popped them into her apron pockets. "Come on, Clary. You can help me back at Border House. I have some tinctures to finish."

Clary chewed her cheeks, gaze flicking from me to Vitra and back again. "Ana?"

"She'll be fine," Vitra said. "I'll escort her to her room personally."

Did I want to be alone with him?

Darla took Clary's hand, and they both vanished into thin air with a soft pop, leaving me with no choice in the matter.

Vitra dragged a stool over, parking it so close that when he sat, his knee brushed mine.

I resisted the urge to pull away and instead looked him dead in the eyes. "What? Have I done something wrong? Broken a rule? Or is this a check-in visit?"

The corner of his luscious mouth lifted. "So abrasive," he drawled.

No, abrasive was the way his voice teased my senses.

"I heard what happened in the dining hall," he continued.

"And?"

"It's a bad idea."

"You know what's a bad idea? Letting someone like Tamina into this Academy. The fact that you'd train Phages like her to be Hunters says a lot about this place."

His expression pinched. "I don't disagree. But all establishments require funds to operate."

"Oh, I get it. Say no more. That makes the abuse of innocent creatures okay, then."

"You have every right to feel that way. And you're not the only one. But rules and covenants exist for a reason, and blood debts are never paid lightly. We have no idea what Ruspin did to be bound to Tamina like that."

"Whatever it was, it can't possibly warrant being humiliated and beaten daily. No one has the right to own someone else."

"Are you sure your personal experiences aren't coloring your judgment?"

Heat rushed to my cheeks, stinging as if he'd slapped me. "You don't know me, Master Vitra, so please keep your assumptions to yourself."

"I see I've touched a nerve."

"No, you're simply *getting* on my nerves."

He tipped his head to the side, that enigmatic smile back on his luscious lips. "Are you always this argumentative?"

"Are you always this attentive to new students?"

His eyes narrowed. "As your mentor, it's my job to make sure you're safe."

The mentor I was supposed to be cultivating a relationship with, the one that I needed to use at some point, and dammit, I was blowing it. I ducked my head and exhaled. "I'm sorry. It's been a long day."

He sat up straight and looked down his nose at me, as if he was trying to decide what to do with me, as if I were a problem.

I'd seen that look too many times for it to bother me, but for some reason, right now it did. And I had to bite my tongue to stop myself from saying something I'd regret.

He sucked in his cheeks, his eyes lighting up. "So you do have some self-control."

"What?"

"I can speak to Tamina and dissolve your deal."

The sudden twist in topic threw me for a moment, but I recovered fast. "No! I'm not backing down on this. And if that's the only reason you wanted to see me, then we're done." I made to stand, but he placed his hand on my thigh, holding me in place. Heat spread beneath my skin, and I bit back a gasp. There was no more denying that this man was somehow bypassing my curse. No denying that I liked it either.

"I don't recall dismissing you, Miss Onyx."

The command in his tone both repelled and excited me, leaving me momentarily flustered. And he was *still* touching me. Surely that was inappropriate. I should point that out, right?

Yeah. I should definitely point it out.

I arched a brow, gaze dipping to his hand on my thigh, then rising to his face.

He slow-blinked and withdrew his hand, leaving me hollow.

"You should reconsider your deal with Miss Vayne. Once you step onto Coral Isle, you are no longer under Nightsbridge protection. I will not be able to help you."

"The arena is on Coral Isle?"

I'd been so caught up in playing the part of someone in pain that I'd neglected to ask for details about my upcoming rendezvous with psycho bitch.

"Yes. Coral Isle is free land. A place where the students can... be themselves, without academic repercussions."

It made sense. Thropes and Phages were both bloodthirsty in different ways. Working together wasn't a natural state for them, and they needed some place where they could expel their rage. Clary and Dori had explained as much on the lift ride up to the

Main Building. I should have realized that the fight would take place there. *Outside* the confines of the no-aggression rules.

Vitra crossed his arms, distracting me with the inked patterns on his skin. Gorgeous whorls and unfamiliar writing in a language that I didn't recognize.

"Miss Onyx?"

Shit. "I'll be fine. I can handle my..." I trailed off, recalling the last time I'd said those words to him—how it had felt to be pressed to the wall, his thigh between mine. An air bubble formed in my throat, and I swallowed it down. "I'll be fine."

A ghost of a smile played on his luscious lips. "Good girl." He stood in one fluid motion and headed for the door. "Come now. I'll walk you back."

I didn't want to walk back with him. I wanted to put distance between us so I could figure out why he affected me in such a strange way. What was so special about him that he could bypass my curse?

"I don't have all night, Miss Onyx."

"Why, Master Vitra? You got a date?" Why had I said that?

His brows lifted. "As a matter of fact, I do."

Selethis, the lucky bitch. "In that case, we'd better not keep her waiting." I hopped off the stool. "Lead the way." So that I can ogle your butt.

He glanced over his shoulder. "What did you say?"

"I said, *lead the way.*"

"No, after that."

Wait... Had I said the last part out loud? No. No, I hadn't. I was sure of it. "I didn't say anything else."

"Hmm..." He continued down the corridor, and I followed, leaving enough room for a good view of his ass.

Not all Horrors must be extinguished, for there are those that can be tamed.

Anonymous

CHAPTER 14

Dori insisted on walking me to Trinity the next morning—a walk that took almost half an hour, driving home just how large the Nightsbridge campus was. We passed the barracks, a sprawling structure with a central tower, spokes jutting off it and connecting to two smaller towers.

"The Phage and Thrope Hunter teams have separate sleeping quarters," Dori explained.

Figures dressed in the Hunter garb of black on black moved about at the base of the main tower, probably heading to the training grounds behind it. There was a garden somewhere back there, too. I had a mental schematic now, thanks to the map in my admissions pack.

The location of the library housing the *Libra Veritas* wasn't on the map—because that would have been too easy. It was clearly a secret library—hidden, forbidden, or both.

I'd find it, though. In time. "What about the Arcanus Hunters? Where do they sleep?"

"They bunk with whichever team they happen to be on."

"How many Hunters do we have here?"

"Most everyone above the age of eighteen is a Hunter, but there are thirty *active* Hunters at any time, living in the barracks. The teams cycle every year to give everyone a respite, and the non-active Hunters get the option to leave Nightsbridge for a few months. When they return, if they're not a seasoned Hunter, they'll take classes and prep to go back on active duty."

Smart to keep the teams fresh and revitalized. "And how long does it take to become seasoned?" Not that I cared, but she'd expect me to ask questions and be interested.

"It's not about time served, it's about kills. More than twenty-five kills and you're a Gold Stripe and officially seasoned. Five kills make you a Brown Stripe, and ten gets you a Silver Stripe."

"So you can come here and shoot straight up to seasoned status over another Hunter just by getting more kills? No real experience or time on the job required?"

She chuckled. "Making plans, are we?"

"Hardly, just... It seems unfair."

"Kills are everything here," Dori said.

"Oh? And how many do you have?"

"One." Her eyes darkened, and she shook her head. "I'm more of a backup gal. But Sterling Damascus...he's a different story."

His name set my teeth on edge. "Really?"

"He wasn't sent here at sixteen like the rest of us. Got here a year ago. That should give you something in common." She had no idea how much we had in common. I gave her a close-lipped smile, and she continued. "Anyway, he flew through classes, aced his grading and combat trials, and made the active Hunter unit within three months. Two months later, he had his twenty-fifth kill, and *bam*, he's now in charge of the Phage unit. Caused some disruption from what I've heard."

What had the perfect little blood blade done to get sentenced to Nightsbridge? I should feel satisfaction that his freedom had been taken, but it wasn't enough. Not for what he'd done.

"Have you worked with him?"

"No. I'm assigned to the Thrope unit."

"Drayven's unit?"

"Yeah. The guy is terrifying—and a hardass."

I hadn't found him terrifying. "He seemed okay to me."

Her brows shot up. "Are we talking about the same Thrope?"

"Unless there's another Drayven here."

"No, just the one."

We continued in silence for a minute, in which I gathered the courage to ask the question that had been burning a hole in my mind since I'd woken up this morning. "Are you okay, Dori? The Tamina thing...did the tincture to put her to sleep work?"

"I'm fine. Everything was fine," she said quickly. "Oh look, here we are. Trinity Tower."

Dammit. She obviously didn't want to discuss it, which meant things hadn't gone to plan. My gut twisted as I warred with keeping my mouth shut or pushing. Fuck it. "Dori, I'm so sorry, I—"

"Don't." Dori gripped my hand. "Please. It's fine. Being with Tamina is never awful, I just... I know she's not good for me. I don't like her, but..."

Comprehension dawned. "You like the way she makes you feel."

Her cheeks reddened. "Can we agree not to talk about this again?"

"Sure."

We approached Trinity Tower in silence. It was a beast of a building, comprised of a blue and gray central tower with shuttered windows. Passages jutted off it to connect to three smaller towers.

Dori's chin lifted in pride, a slight smile curled her lips as she drank it in. Pride and nostalgia.

I nudged her with my shoulder. "Hey, you'll be back here soon enough."

"Yeah, not sure how welcome I'll be, though."

"So you tried to incite a revolution. Big deal."

She laughed. "If only Arcanus didn't walk around with sticks up their asses, eh?"

The door to the main tower opened, and two women and a man stepped out.

"Speaking of sticks up asses," Dori muttered, her expression darkening.

"Embercrest," the guy said. "Don't tell me your sentence is over already."

"I won't," Dori said.

"Then why are you here?" one of the women asked. Her gaze flicked to me. "There is no way *she's* coming inside."

"*She's* been invited here by Heidi, so back off."

"I didn't get a memo," the other woman said. "And as prima incantor, I would have been informed."

Dori's lips pinched. "I see you got what you wanted, then, Viola."

Viola smiled and shrugged. "Don't I always?" She slid a glance up at the guy, who quickly looked away.

Undertones and tension thickened the air. "Well, if you're done blocking the doorway, I have an appointment to get to." I strode toward them, expecting them to move, but they held their ground. "Seriously?"

"I need to see some evidence of this *appointment*," Viola said.

"It came by raven," Dori bit out.

"Shame," Viola said. "I'll have to ask you to leave."

"Since when do prima duties extend to monitoring the tower entrance?"

"Since we had a change in coven management," Viola said. "The other primas and I have agreed on it. No outsiders without a pass."

The bitch was clearly on some kind of power trip, and the only way to deal with someone like her was to give her what she wanted—with a side of repercussion of course.

I crossed my arms and shrugged. "Fine, I'll just wait right here. The poor new student with no family, simply trying to fit in while fighting prejudice from the very leaders that are supposed to be setting an example."

"What are you talking about?"

"You *are* supposed to be setting an example, right? For the younger incantors and sorcerers inside?" I indicated the tower. "Isn't that what people in authority do?" I looked to Dori wide-eyed. "Isn't that part of what a prima incantor is meant to do?"

"Totally," Dori said, biting back a smile.

I nodded slowly. "I thought so. And I'm sure Heidi will come looking for me soon enough and be interested to know why I'm standing out here, teary-eyed and flustered." I blinked a few times, summoning tears. "And when she asks, I'll be sure to tell her about your *policy* and how you called me a filthy, dirty, Onyx bitch."

Viola stared at me wide-eyed.

"She won't believe that," the other woman snapped.

I allowed my eyes to fill with tears, then blinked, releasing fat droplets down my cheek.

Viola swallowed hard.

"You're chaos," the man said in a tone that was more awe than disgust.

I beamed up at him through my tears. "Isn't it wonderful?"

"This is a waste of time," Viola said. "*You're* a waste of my time." She lifted her chin. "Enjoy your short visit. Come on, Tristian." She grabbed the man's arm and yanked him aside. "Freak." She spat the word at me as if it were a weapon.

I blew her a kiss as I walked through the door into a small redbrick entranceway. A second door opened into a cozy room lined with bookshelves and dotted with a variety of seating, ranging from armchairs to stools. A fire burned low in the hearth at the back of the room, barely embers now, and a staircase wound up to the first-floor balcony overlooking the sitting room and library area.

"Wow," Dori said. "That was...wow..." A slight frown marred her forehead, and it didn't take a genius to figure out what she was thinking.

That if I could act that well, summon tears on demand, then could I be trusted? I *needed* her to trust me, and that meant giving her a crumb of the truth. "Look, life was hard for me out there, so I learned how to cope the best I could, and putting on a front was my strongest defense. Attack them before they can attack you."

She was silent for several beats, mulling over my words. "You don't have to be that way anymore, though. You have me, Clary, and Benedict now. You *never* have to pretend with us." She cupped my shoulder and squeezed. The bubble returned to my chest, inflating, and making it a little hard to breathe. Her words were sweet, but I'd heard sweet words before. Words followed by a long visit to the hollow pit of betrayal.

I plastered a smile on my face, forcing it to reach my eyes. "Thanks, I appreciate it."

A crow circled the tower above us before diving out of sight, and a moment later, a tabby cat padded down the steps, caught sight of us, then bolted back up again.

"Good, Libby has spotted us," Dori said. "Which means that Heidi will be down soon."

"Libby?"

"The cat. She's Heidi's familiar. The crow belongs to Arthur Mort. He helps run the tower with my aunt and Portia Reign. Poor guy's the buffer between those two."

A necessary one if the dynamic between them at my *Perculiari Petitione* was anything to go by. "What's your familiar?"

Her expression softened. "His name is Mr. Twiggins. He's a cat, stodgy old fellow with a superiority complex, but I love him."

I'd learned about familiars. Spiritual entities that took the form of animals, bonded to an incantor, able to communicate with their bonded telepathically or out loud. A familiar provided insight and protection, along with a connection to the spiritual realm—a gateway to the Weave. At puberty, incantors went through a ritual to summon a familiar, as their power was limited without one. Sorcerers, however, didn't have familiars. Our direct connection to the Weave meant that all we required was a focus. Not even the Onyx bloodline, riddled with incantors, had ever produced an Arcanus who'd required a familiar. Other bloodlines and species that had joined with ours had always been overshadowed by the Onyx genes.

My family's connection to the Weave had been strong once.

The sharp clip of heels signaled Heidi's arrival. Libby, her familiar, trotted along beside her, wide gray eyes assessing us as her mistress made her way down the stairs.

Today, the Tower Master was dressed in a buff-colored calf-length wool skirt, cream blouse, and chocolate waistcoat that emphasized her athletic form. It was obvious that she did some kind of physical training. Her hair was down, golden locks sitting about her shoulders in gentle waves, softening the harsh planes of her striking face. She stopped on the second-to-last step, clasped her hands in front of her, and peered down at us.

"Good. You're punctual. You may go now, Dori. I'll make sure Miss Onyx gets to class on time."

Dori's shoulders dropped. "Yes, Aunt. I'll meet you in the lunch hall after morning classes, Ana." She slipped out of the room, closing the door softly behind her.

What was the deal with those two? It didn't matter, but I made a mental note to ask Dori about it anyway. After all, it's what a real friend would do, and I needed to maintain the façade of being one.

"Well," Heidi said. "Are you ready?"

Ready to go into the catacombs where students reportedly never return from? "Do I have a choice?"

"No."

"In that case, I'm ready."

She crossed the room to the hearth, but Libby remained at the foot of the stairs. "Solaris, I beseech thee, guardian of the flame, arise." She muttered something else I didn't catch, words that were rough and guttural.

The embers glowed bright, flames erupting upward and deepening to a vibrant orange before turning purple.

A voice made from the crackle and pop of flame eating wood filled the room. "Embercrest, you call my name, and I answer."

"I require passage for myself and one other."

"You are expected, and so is the one who follows. Therefore, you may pass."

The flames flared, the deep purple fading to a lilac shade.

Heidi beckoned. "Come, we must hold hands to pass."

I eyed the flames. "*Through* the fire?"

"Yes. Solaris is the gatekeeper of the catacombs. The only way in is through him."

I'd heard stranger things. I took her hand, and together we stepped into the purple flames.

Darkness stole my vision. When it returned, we stood in an underground chamber lit by wall sconces. Several passages veered off from the chamber, each one pitch black and forbidding.

Heidi released my hand. "This is the antechamber," she explained. "Every entrance from above leads here."

"There is more than one entrance in Trinity?"

"Solaris is the flame in every hearth, so every hearth is a gateway, if he allows it to be."

"Okay, so we're here. Now what?"

"Now, we wait. No one is permitted to go farther than this room. The catacombs are ever-shifting; only the Weave Watchers can navigate them."

Images of scuttling, burrowing creatures filled my mind, along with a reminder that no student who'd seen these Weave Watchers had returned to tell the tale. "What are they? The Weave Watchers?"

She shook her head slightly, her gaze flicking from tunnel to tunnel in a way that made me more nervous than I already was. The way she stiffened, the tension in her jaw—everything about her body language screamed fear.

"Heidi? Hey?"

She licked her lips and shook her head once more. "No one knows for sure. They simply...are. But we know what they do. They protect the sanctity of the Weave and act as intermediaries between the mortal realm and the Trinity, so..." She trailed off, head tilting to one side, listening to the silence. "They're coming."

I felt it then, the strange shift in atmosphere. The air thinned, charged with an unnatural energy that pricked at my skin, and goose bumps crawled up my arms.

The primal instinct to run rushed through me, but I locked my knees and swallowed past the sudden dryness in my throat. "Where... Where are—"

The lights went out, and when they flashed back on, we were no longer alone in the chamber.

This plane of existence is simply one of an infinite number. Pockets between life and death are passages between worlds where up is down and down is up, and the rules that we cling to matter not at all.

A Theory of Everything by Theodore Regent

CHAPTER 15

Five hooded figures floated a foot above the floor surrounding us, their presence bringing a fresh chill to the chamber, which intensified the power of my primal fear. I breathed through it, reminding myself that they weren't here to hurt me, that I hadn't committed any crimes. Yet.

"By the Trinity, we are blessed," Heidi said, her voice coming out smooth and confident—completely at odds with her tense form. "And by the Trinity, I beseech you to aid this woman in reclaiming her connection to the Weave."

"We know what you want," they said in unison. Their words echoed through the chamber with an otherworldly timbre that made my stomach hurt. "We know why you are here. We remember what was done. But can it be undone?" They floated back a few steps, and shadows rushed forward to cover them as a strange green light bloomed around me.

Where was Heidi? I couldn't see her anymore. Couldn't see anything beyond the blinding green light.

"Anamaya Onyx, daughter of Ariana Onyx, blood of Dharma Onyx, the chosen betrayer. You seek to be blessed?"

"Yes. I do."

"You deem yourself worthy?"

"I do."

"Liar," they hissed. "You do not feel worthy. You deem yourself as broken. Undeserving."

Phantom fingers gripped the back of my skull, and a strange pressure resonated through my head. They were trying to get inside. To read me.

No. "No!"

The pressure released.

"*Why* not? What are you hiding, *hmm*?"

"I'm not the one floating around in a hooded cloak." Fuck, fuck, fuck. What was I doing? Shut your mouth, Ana.

"You're afraid, and so you lash out."

I took a slow, steady breath, then spoke, keeping my tone even. "I'm not afraid of you."

"No?" The lights died again, and when they flashed back on, a horrific, elongated face loomed inches from mine—lips peeled back from blackened gums and inch-long, yellowing teeth. An aged, browning blindfold covered its eyes, below which rested two crimson slits for a nose.

Those slits widened and contracted as the thing inhaled. A fist of terror formed in my belly, stealing my bravado and leaving me limp and weak-kneed.

The lights flashed off, and when they turned back on, the face was gone.

My chest trembled, but I held my ground. "You're not that scary."

Raspy and chilling laughter surrounded me. "We like you. You have backbone. But we can tear that backbone from your body if we wish. We can strip your skin from your bones and use your essence to feed the glorious Weave.

"We can do all those things. But not today. Today, we grant you clemency... a reprieve from carrying the burden of the chosen betrayer. You will taste the power of the Weave."

A strange sensation spread across my thigh, tingling and jarring. I slapped a hand to it. The sensation almost echoed what I remembered of pain. It was gone too soon for me to examine closely.

"The mark has been lifted," they said. "But the veil remains—for now. A precaution while the Weave tests how you will fit into its web. It may grant you protection in this time, or it may not. Your connection will be fully restored in two blessings. You will take the first blessing with the Unwoven, and *if* you prove yourself thereafter and pass all classes, you can return to us on the Weaver Moon, to be made whole. Fail, and forfeit your chance to be restored."

The light dimmed, and icy fingers ran up my arms and along the back of my neck. "But be wary. Be aware. Be vigilant," they whispered. "The earth senses all but cannot speak. Much is hidden in memories lost, but eyes born of ancient power can see."

"What? What does that mean?"

"We have said more than we should. More than is permitted. Go now."

The lights went out completely, and when they came back on, I was standing by the hearth in Trinity Tower.

Heidi leapt up from her armchair, her gaze sweeping over me. "You're all right?" she said in a rush.

All right, but bloody disoriented. "Yeah...I'm... I'm good."

"They let you return," she said softly, giving me the impression she was speaking more to herself than to me.

From what the Unwoven had told me, there were rumors of students going to see the Weavers and not returning. Mainly students who'd transgressed in some way. But considering they'd sent me down there to find out what could be done to lift the ban on my power, I hadn't expected my survival to be in question.

"Are you saying there was a chance that the Weave Watchers *wouldn't* have let me come back?"

"Who knows? But they found you worthy, and you're here. Although I must admit, I panicked a little when I was ejected without you."

I swallowed past the thrumming pulse in my throat. It was over. I was fine. "When were you ejected? When the lights went green?"

"The lights went green?" She frowned. "Not to my knowledge. You stood beside me while they spoke through the tunnels and told us how to restore your power."

"That's all you heard?"

"There was more?"

The rest had been for my ears only. A riddle that I needed to file away for later examination. "Nothing. It was all just so strange." She continued to look probingly at me. "So, how many times have you been down to see them?"

She blinked sharply and looked away. "A few."

"But this is the first time a student has returned," another voice said.

"Libby!" Heidi snapped.

"What? It's true." Libby flicked her tail, peering up at Heidi. "It makes you sad, and I don't like it when you're sad."

Heidi sighed, then crouched to stroke her cat. "I was worried about how this meeting would go, but all is well."

"So, the whole feeding students to the Weave Watchers thing is true, then?"

"Most rumors have some element of truth to them."

Her words hung between us, leaving me to wonder how much truth was in the rumors surrounding Dharma. I'd find out soon enough.

"When's the Weaver Moon?" I needed to know when I'd be fully restored.

"A little over three months. It's a powerful time for Arcanus and Therianthropes." She smiled tightly. "But you'll learn all about that once you begin your classes at Trinity next month."

"I'll have classes here?"

"You're Arcanus, so of course you will join us for classes once a part of your power is restored. You'll begin with Arcane Botany and Mental Defense Against the Echoes, among other things. But for now, we should get you to class. Mistress Selethis does not tolerate tardiness."

"It's fine, I can find my own way. The ports should have my signature by now."

"Are you sure?"

Her concern unsettled me. Especially since she'd had no qualms about using her magic to choke me during the *Perculiari Petitione*. "Why are you being so nice to me?"

She blinked sharply. "Excuse me?"

"You're an Embercrest. A coven leader. Most high-level Arcanus hate everything associated with the Onyx name." I arched a brow.

She pressed her lips together. "Truth be told, if we were anywhere but Nightsbridge, I would never associate with you. But Nightsbridge is its own ecosystem, its own little world, and we do what we must to maintain balance. Like it or not, *you* are part of that balance."

"Not everyone feels that way."

"Then they are fools. Bigoted and small-minded. Give it time. Meanwhile, be wary."

The Weave Watchers' words filled my mind. *But be wary. Be aware. Be vigilant...*

"You can use the port on the first floor," Heidi said. "It will take you to the bridge." She headed for the exit. "I'll see you soon, no doubt."

I took the stairs two at a time, eager to be out of the tower and as far away from the hearth and catacombs as possible.

The port on the first floor was an arch built into the wall with several colored crystals embedded into the stone beside it. Which did I press? Ah, there was a plaque with codes printed on it: Solarium, the East and West Quads, the bridge, and the North and South Borders.

I tapped the sequence for the bridge, but nothing happened. I tried again. Still nothing. Dammit, had they not added me to their database yet? Or was I doing it wrong?

I went to try again, and a hand clamped down over my mouth. "Let's see you talk your way out of this one." Viola rasped in my ear.

I twisted, trying to gain leverage to elbow her in the gut, but invisible bands held me firm, locking me in place, making it impossible to break free. The bitch was using a spell to immobilize me.

Tristen rushed forward and tapped the crystals, lighting up the port.

"Enjoy playing with the ratakan." She shoved me into the blue haze.

The world tipped, and power fizzed over my skin. I landed on my hands and knees, sinking into something cold and wet. Icy wind slapped my cheeks as I raised my head to face the biting swirl of a bitter wind that cut through my wool coat and blazer and swept under my blouse to frost my skin.

The portal crackled behind me, still active.

I scrambled up and ran toward the blue haze, but it winked out before I could reach it, leaving a free-standing stone arch in the snow-covered clearing.

"Shit!" I pressed my palm to the single crystal embedded into it. Nothing. "Fuck!" They hadn't added me, and Viola had taken advantage of that. Had the attack been opportunistic, or had they known I wasn't in the system and waited for a chance to ambush me?

It didn't matter. They'd pay for this regardless. But first, I needed to get back to campus.

I couldn't see the Academy from here. Just snow-covered land and trees in the distance. I rubbed my arms and stamped my feet to generate heat.

What crystal combination had Tristen pressed on the port? If I could remember, then I may be able to figure out where they'd sent me, which would help me work out which way to head. It was still early morning, and the sun was making its ascent. Rising in the east, so west would be—

A dark shape bounded out of the tree line—then another. And another. Three hulking forms charging at me.

I caught the glint of red eyes and the flash of brown fur, and as they grew closer, the gleam of elongated yellow front teeth.

Enjoy playing with the ratakan...

My heart swelled and slammed into my chest because I knew what they were.

Humongous rats.

Biology determines connection to Source, therefore, a biological comprehension of the threat is essential in neutralization.

Initiative Manual

CHAPTER 16

I bolted.

Through the dead port arch and toward the tree line behind it.

Could rats climb trees?

It wouldn't matter if I didn't make it to cover.

The ratakan screeched with excitement behind me, and I didn't need to look back to know they were gaining.

Come on, Ana! I pushed harder, faster, using the ball of anger inside me as fuel. Viola's smug face filled my mind, and I imagined busting it open with my fists the moment I got out of this mess. No way was I getting chowed down by rats on my third day in Nightsbridge.

I hit the tree line and dove into the forest, leaping over a fallen tree and crushing bracken as I wove between slender trunks. The woodland closed around me, reaching for me with spindly evergreen branches, as if imploring me to stay.

The screeches grew louder.

I ducked my head, driving forward, pushing my limbs to the limit. I burst from the forest onto a stretch of unfrozen land—and

Trinity be blessed, was that a tower in the distance?

A rush of relief filled my chest. The Academy was visible beyond another stretch of forestland. If I could get to—

I slammed into an invisible barrier. The impact sent a vibration through my whole body, gripping and shaking me until my teeth chattered. It released me suddenly, and I hit the ground, limp and unable to move.

What... Oh...wards. I was outside the damn wards. I pushed up on shaky palms, every hair on my body standing to attention.

A low-grade hum filled the air—a warning growl on the verge of menace. Breath coming in shallow gasps, I slowly raised my head. Three ratakan surrounded me, caging me in. They had the heads of rats, but quills ran down their backs, and their front legs were tipped with powerful paws and claws perfect for slashing and tearing.

They closed in, growls deepening, frothy white drool bubbling from their mouths, hitting the ground where it fizzed and smoked.

Shit. My stomach dipped, and a weight settled on my chest. There was no way out of this one.

Damn Viola. Damn my lack of power.

I'd failed my mother. Failed myself.

The ratakan pounced.

Heat surged through me, and I screamed, piercing the air with the full force of my horror and rage. The ratakan snapped their teeth mere inches from my body before being hurled back, their bodies twisting unnaturally, slamming into the ground several yards away.

What. The. Fuck?

They sprang to their feet, and one of them sprayed green gunk. I dove to avoid it too late. Warmth seeped through my pant leg, and the world wobbled as I staggered to my feet.

The ratakan rushed me.

I screamed again, but this time the sound was eclipsed by a shrill whistle.

The ratakan ground to a halt, their beady red eyes now fixed on something behind me.

I didn't want to take my eyes off them—but I needed to see what was coming.

I risked a glance, locking my knees when they threatened to buckle.

A hulking figure ran toward me.

Another whistle sounded, and the ratakan backed up a few steps.

The wards behind me crackled and fizzed.

My head grew suddenly light and floaty.

"Anamaya?" A large hand closed around my arm. "It's okay, they won't hurt you now."

The voice was familiar, but I'd never seen this man before. Tall and built with biceps to spare, his strong facial features were framed by a neatly clipped beard. His long, dark hair was tied in a knot, leaving the short back and buzzed sides on display. Oh, he had a pretty mouth...

"How did you get out here?" he asked.

Several figures dressed in black and gray rushed by in my periphery, and another shrill whistle sounded.

"Border clear!" someone called.

I stared up into moss-green eyes flecked with yellow. The same eyes as the barghest who'd carried me to safety... "Drayven?"

His beautiful eyes warmed. "That's right."

"You look good." My words came out oddly slurred. Ooo... sparkles.

"Shit, they sprayed you."

"Huh?" My knees finally lost the will to hold me, and I buckled.

He snagged me around the waist and hauled me against his body. I grabbed hold of him on instinct, my palms coming to rest on his silken, taut skin. "Nice." I gripped his biceps. "Big." A pleasant tingle rushed up my arms.

Someone snickered.

Drayven glared over my head, and the laughter died instantly. "Anamaya, how did you get out here?"

His skin was so soft. I rubbed my cheek against his arm. "You feel so good."

"Anamaya?" He gently pushed me away. "How did you get here?"

Oh...yes. I was in danger. Had been in danger because of Viola. "That bitch shoved me through a portal. I'm going to have to break her face."

"The border portal?" someone said. "She outran the ratakan?"

"Jay?" I tried to turn my head to find him, but the world swam.

Drayven cupped the back of my head. "Hey, keep your eyes on me. No sudden movements, or it will disorient you. Why didn't you use the portal to get back?"

He had such a nice voice, and the vibration of his chest against me when he spoke was soothing. What would he taste like?

"Anamaya. Focus." The snap to his tone cleared a little of the fog clouding my mind.

"Oh...I—uh. I tried, but I don't think I'm in the system. The portals didn't recognize me. And the wards knocked me back."

"Which means they forgot to add her to these border wards," Jay said.

"I'll take her through the portal," Drayven said. "Get back to the Academy and speak to Milanthra. I want to know why the fuck Onyx isn't in our systems yet." He scooped me into his arms.

"Whoa..." I squeezed my eyes shut against a wave of dizziness.

"Lean your head on my shoulder," he said. "I've got you."

I inhaled him greedily. "You smell so good."

His chest rumbled. "You're not yourself right now."

I sniffed him again. "Good. I don't want to be myself. I hate myself."

He pulled me closer, a sigh rattling through him. "Oh, Anamaya..."

His tone had a grounding effect, and the world grew less

distant, leaving my words hanging between us like a dirty confession. My chest tightened. I wanted to take them back, to say I hadn't meant them, but that would be a lie.

Damn the ratakan spray. Tension flooded my limbs—those creatures were still on the loose. "Drayven, the ratakan are still out there."

"Don't worry. They won't hurt you, not while you're with me." He set off at a brisk stride.

I let my head fall to his shoulder, suddenly bone-achingly weary. From the run, from my loss, from my fucking life.

"Are you all right?" Drayven asked softly.

I didn't want to talk about my feelings. Not now. Probably not ever. "I'm fine. What are the ratakan?"

He was silent for a moment, and I sensed him wavering between answering my question or pressing me about my mental state. I held still, barely breathing as I waited.

"Ratakan are border guards," he said finally. "Created to act as sentries to keep Horrors from getting too close to the wards." I relaxed against him, and he continued. "A decade ago, we had a minor breach—the ward was overwhelmed by a horde of Horrors. The Carvers stepped up and created the ratakan to prevent that from happening again. They're fed Hunter blood every month, so they recognize not to harm us. You were lucky we reached you before they could attack."

But the ratakan *had* attacked—and then been repelled. My scalp prickled, and something the Weavers had said about the Weave came to mind.

It may grant you protection in this time, or it may not.

They'd also said a veil still existed between me and the Weave. That I needed two more sessions to be fully restored, but... "I think the Weave protected me against the ratakan." I quickly explained what happened.

"That's encouraging. It means the Weave deems you worthy."

Wings of hope fluttered in my chest.

"The northern border can get icy," he continued. "Let me

know if you get too cold."

"Coming from someone wearing only an undershirt."

"I'm always hot."

"Damn straight you are."

He chuckled, and my cheeks burned.

"I'm not sure why I said that."

"You mean you didn't mean it?" he teased.

I grinned up at him. "I'm obviously heavily under the influence right now."

His face fell in mock disappointment. "Well, there goes my ego."

"You have a mirror in your room, I assume."

"Of course."

"I'm sure that's all the ego boost you need." Oh Trinity. Shut up, Ana!

"I could say the same to you, pretty girl."

He thought I was pretty? That wasn't the word men used for me. Striking or interesting were the usual. My features were too sharp, even harsh in some lights. But it felt nice to hear him say it.

"Thank you."

"You're welcome." We entered the gloom of the forest. "You ran a long way and maintained your speed. It's an asset that saved you again today. The ratakan would have torn you to shreds."

A shiver passed over me, and I snuggled closer to Drayven. "I know." Goose bumps pricked my skin. "It's definitely colder here."

He hugged me tighter, and the heat from his body seemed to go up a notch. "As the ratakan spray wears off, you'll feel the cold more acutely. The Carvers created it to incapacitate prey and allow an easier kill."

"Who are these, Carvers?"

"Evil geniuses," Drayven said dryly. "I don't agree with their practices, but without them, we'd be playing a guessing game when it comes to the Horrors surrounding us."

"What do you mean?"

"As Hunters, part of our job is catching Horrors for the

Initiative—a program run by the Carvers. They take them apart to figure out how they tick. Horrors are constantly evolving, and what works one decade might not in the next, so the more we know about them, the easier they are to kill. You'll see when you take the Anatomy of Horrors."

"That's not on my schedule."

"It will be soon. You've been fast-tracked. Your name is on the Hunter orientation schedule for next month. All you need to do is pass grading."

"Will I be with you?" I sounded a little too hopeful. Dial it down, Onyx.

He peered down at me, his mouth mere inches from mine. "Trust me, you don't want to be on my team."

His breath fanned across my lips, warm and sweet like honey. If I lifted my chin a little more, I could taste him. Would the contact make my mouth tingle? Was this real or an effect of the ratakan spray?

His eyes darkened. "Yes, you definitely don't want to be on my team."

"Why not?" My question was a whisper.

"Because if you're on my team, I won't get to be Mr. Nice Guy."

"I'd rather be with you than with Damascus."

The ghost of a smile hovering on his lips died, and his jaw tensed. The moment between us lost.

Was he grinding his teeth?

"Drayven?"

He exhaled sharply through his nose. "Sterling is a good hunt leader."

"He's also a murderer." Dammit. The spray obviously hadn't worn off yet. "Forget I said that."

The crunch of bracken beneath his boots was too loud in the silence.

His heartbeat quickened against me. "I know of his life before coming here," he said finally. "I'm sorry if his actions touched your life in a negative way."

There was something in his tone, an understanding, a sadness that spoke of true empathy. "What did he do to you?"

"Nothing that I wish to revisit right now."

"Got it."

He carried me out of the forest in silence, stepping onto the snow-covered stretch of land where the portal arch waited in the distance. How far had I run to reach the Academy's border wards?

The wind whistled, plucking at my hair as the final effects of the spray evaporated completely, leaving my head clear and my thoughts sharp. But the pleasant hum that danced beneath my skin remained. Unrelated to the spray and everything to do with him. First Vitra, now Drayven. The curse must be unraveling. It was the only explanation. If that was the case, I'd milk it for every ounce of pleasure I could—starting with staying in his arms for a couple more minutes.

But a couple of minutes turned into three, then four, and before I knew it, we were at the port.

"How are you feeling now?" Drayven asked. "Do you think you can stand? Walk?"

Heat rose to my cheeks. I should have said something sooner. "I feel better. I can walk."

He lowered me carefully, holding on to me until he was sure I was steady on my feet. "The portal opens at the barracks. Each tower has access to the border portals, but students know better than to use them unless they're on the active hunt team. Outside of that, they're for emergencies only." He pressed his palm to the crystal, and the portal flared bright blue. He pressed his hand to the small of my back to guide me through.

We emerged in a stone room filled with weapon racks hung with swords, daggers, shields, and axes. A forge burned at the back of the room, and a giant, half-naked male slammed a hammer against an anvil to render some kind of blade.

He looked up and wiped sweat from his brow with the back of his wrist, which was wrapped in a cloth band.

"New recruit?" His voice boomed across the room.

"Yes and no," Drayven said. "Frederick, this is Anamaya Onyx."

His brows flicked up slightly. "Ah, the subject of much discussion. At least in Trinity Tower. My boy Benedict has only good things to say about you. You have my assurance that the Ironharts hold no ill will toward you."

This was Benedict's dad? The man was a monolith of muscle, his body stocky, his face rugged with a heavy jaw. I searched for Benedict in his features and failed.

I fixed a smile on my face to hide my confusion. "It's nice to meet you."

"Likewise."

"Let's get you to the infirmary," Drayven said.

I glanced at the clock behind Frederick and let out a yelp. "Shit, class started five minutes ago. Can you open a portal to the bridge?"

"You should get checked out first."

"No. I'm fine, I just can't be too late."

He chewed the inside of his cheek for a moment. "Fine. But I'm coming with you."

I was already late. I just hoped Selethis didn't give me too much of a hard time about it.

Were they demons or angels? I found them to be neither. They were something else. Something more than we could have ever imagined...

First Contact Memorandum (Vault Archives)

CHAPTER 17

The Main Building halls were quiet as we made our way to the first floor, where History of Nightsbridge was taught. The place was a maze of corridors and smaller rooms, and although I had a pretty good sense of direction, I was soon overwhelmed.

I'd need help making my way out. Hopefully, another student, or maybe a map of the building. Either would work.

"Don't be nervous," Drayven said, mistaking my silence for apprehension. "Constance is a ball-breaker, but once she hears what happened—"

"No. I don't want everyone knowing what Viola did."

"Fine, I'll ask Selethis if we can speak in private. But there should be repercussions for what Viola did."

"Oh, believe me, there will be." I preferred to serve my revenge over several courses, with a little added garnish for presentation.

He eyed me warily, and I realized I was wearing what my mother liked to call my murder grin. I quickly rearranged my features into a relatively normal expression and shrugged. "Karma, you know."

"Yes...of course." But he didn't look convinced. Smart guy.

We stopped at a set of wooden doors carved with an ornate pattern of roses and thorns, the red wood gleaming from frequent polishing.

"This is it," Drayven said. "Wait here."

He ducked into the room, and my stomach twisted. Damn, I hated this feeling. The nerves that dragged me back to my student days. I shouldn't be feeling them now. None of this mattered. Not in the grand scheme of things. Not when it came to my true goal for being here. I didn't need Constance or anyone in this twisted place to like me.

But the nerves didn't seem to understand this and continued to tie knots in my belly.

Drayven returned with Mistress Selethis in tow.

She closed the door and peered down at me over her perfect nose. She couldn't be more than half a head taller than me, but in that moment, as she looked me over, I felt much smaller.

Her dark hair was pinned in a chic twist, and the navy skirt and blazer she wore over her cream blouse gave her a professional air while accentuating her slender curves.

She was too gorgeous to be real. Why would Vitra want to sleep with anyone else?

"You're twenty minutes late," she said. Trinity save me, even her voice was beautiful. Soft and sultry, but not overly so. I bet she could turn up the allure if she wanted to. Damn it, she was speaking. Focus. "I'm assuming you've convinced Mr. Thorn to advocate for you?" She arched a brow at Drayven. "You should know better, Mr. Thorn. You took my class, albeit a few years ago, but you know the rules."

"I do," Drayven said. "But I also know there are exceptions. Miss Onyx was pushed through a portal that took her outside our wards into the northern borderlands." Her brows lifted slightly, the only indication that she was perturbed by that information. "She isn't in the system yet," Drayven continued, "even though she should be, and so was unable to return to the Academy. She succeeded in evading the ratakan and reached the wards. They repelled her—but also alerted us to a presence. We were able to get to her just in time to save her life."

"Well..." Mistress Selethis said, pursing her lips. "That *is* an exception. You're a very lucky woman."

"You don't need to tell me twice."

"I'll need the name of the student who pushed you."

I'd learned a long time ago that ratting got me nowhere. Administration liked to pretend it cared, but nothing ever changed. The only result was that the bullies got more creative. Best way to handle a bully was to deal with them myself.

"I didn't see who it was. I'm truly gutted about that."

Beside me, Drayven tensed but didn't correct me.

Selethis arched a brow. "I see."

She totally didn't believe me. "I really don't want to miss the lesson."

"You're now thirty minutes late, but I will make an exception on this occasion. I'm sure your fellow students will understand—considering the circumstances."

"I'd rather they didn't know...the circumstances."

"Oh?" Her perfectly plucked brow arched once more.

I shrugged. "Wouldn't want anyone else to get ideas."

The corner of her mouth twitched. "Very well." She nodded at Drayven. "I can take it from here, Mr. Thorn."

Drayven's gaze dropped to me, warm and concerned. "Stay out of trouble."

"I'll do my best."

Selethis pushed open the door. "Welcome to History of Nightsbridge."

The lecture hall was packed with students, rows of elevated seats rising before me in a sweeping arc. Thick drapes covered what must be floor-to-ceiling windows. A couple of wall lamps at the back of the hall cast a weak amber glow, leaving the room in relative gloom, but even the dim lighting couldn't hide the ornate wooden moldings that braced the ceiling.

None of the students looked over the age of seventeen. At almost twenty-two, I was the oldest of the bunch, which made sense, considering this was an introductory class.

But still, it was bloody embarrassing.

I took a spot at the front, closest to the exit. As Selethis fiddled with the slide projector, and the class waited for her to resume the lesson, it hit me—I'd forgotten to grab my bag this morning. Just as well, it would probably have gotten lost or damaged out in the borderlands. But now I had nothing to take notes with.

Someone tapped me on the shoulder and passed me a notepad with an ink pen clipped to it.

"You can keep them." The girl behind me pushed her glasses up her nose and smiled. With her wild, curly chestnut hair and round face, she looked too young to be here.

"Thanks." I took the items.

The room went dark, and the wall at the front lit up, along with the white crystal embedded in the projector. It pulsed slowly, siphoning magic from the air to power the machine. Machines usually needed to be connected to a grid powered by magi-generators, but now, new inventions with built-in crystal siphons were being developed. They were pricey though, but from the looks of it, Nightsbridge could afford them.

"As you all know, we have a new student with us today," Selethis announced. "Let's take this opportunity to briefly review the pertinent facts that we've learned over the past few weeks. Who would like to explain The Overshadowing?"

Hands shot up, and Selethis pointed to a boy in the back. "Mr. Robin."

"The Overshadowing was an event that occurred three hundred years ago. Resulting in the barriers between worlds thinning, causing a merger of worlds. This allowed Horrors and Echoes into *our* world. No one knows exactly what caused it, though."

I knew this much already. How The Overshadowing had warped technology and mutated certain creatures and insects. I needed to know more.

"And how did we stop it?" Selethis asked another student.

"*We* didn't stop it," the girl said. "The daeva did. Beings from another world. Guardians of sorts. They helped the humans and supernals of Nova Terra seal the breaches and restore balance. But the Horrors and Echoes—creatures from other worlds—bred, evolved, and took over the land. It's why the Covenant is so important."

"You're jumping too far ahead," Robin said. "You haven't explained the Covenant yet."

The girl drew back her lips, baring her fangs to hiss at him.

"Enough." Selethis didn't raise her voice, but her command echoed throughout the chamber. The silence that followed rang in my ears.

Fang girl dropped her lips back over her teeth and fixed her gaze on her desk.

"Miss Pouvoir," Selethis called on another student. "Explain the Covenant."

A pale girl with bright purple hair sat up straighter. "The Covenant was a pact formed by several supernal bloodlines and covens. The same bloodlines and covens who fought at the Apex Breach, working together to seal it. When they succeeded in closing it, they vowed to provide adolescents from their own bloodlines to cull the threats spawned by The Overshadowing. Thus, the Covenant was formed."

Selethis gave her a nod. "Good. And what was the location of the Apex Breach?" Selethis asked.

"Here," Pouvoir said. "In what is now known as Nightsbridge. It's why the Horrors and Echoes remain. The daeva were able to draw them here with their otherworldly power, but failed to eject them all from this world before the breach was closed. So, the Arcanus built wards to keep them penned in."

There was no mention of daeva in any of the history books

that spoke of The Overshadowing. The public accounts focused on the event's impact on our world's technology and infrastructure, skimping on the details of what had occurred *during* the event. And when it came to the question of what caused The Overshadowing, all we had was conjecture.

"Carter, name the houses, covens, and packs," Selethis asked, moving on.

A girl with a sleek bob rattled off a list of names. "The Haematophage houses of Damascus, Vayne, and Moon. The sorcerer bloodlines of Reign, Ironhart, and Onyx," Her gaze slid my way briefly before she continued. "Packs are Thorn, Indra, and Pouvoir, and covens are Embercrest, Silverthorn, and Evergreen." She sat back with a smug smile.

"You forgot Blackthorne," a voice piped up from across the room.

All eyes turned to me—descendant of the Blackthorne exterminator. Great.

"All right," Selethis said. "Good." Her gaze landed on me. "We've covered a lot in the past few weeks, but you should have been provided all the textbooks you need to catch up. The history of each bloodline and coven is detailed, and you will learn it. Understanding each other is key to a unified front against a common threat. All animosity and conflict must be left outside of Nightsbridge. If we cannot work together, the Horrors will prevail." She paused and ran her gaze up and down the rows of students. Silence stretched for several seconds as students exchanged glances and hesitant smiles. "There will be a test at the end of the month. Going forward, we will be learning about the pact between land and sea."

She pressed the clicker in her hand, and an image of a ship appeared on the wall. "Before the pact, we were forced to hunt the undersea Horrors from above the waves. No easy feat, as you can imagine."

"What kind of undersea Horrors?" someone asked.

"That is a question for Horror 101," Selethis said. She clicked again and showcased an illustration of a man leaning over the side of a small boat, talking to another man, who was partially submerged in the water. "Alfred Regent was the human emissary who first made contact with the seafolk and brokered the deal that led to them working with us to keep the sea around Nightsbridge free of threat."

"What kind of deal?" Pouvoir asked.

Selethis's lips curved into a bitter smile. "Read pages 221 to 300 in *Above and Beyond the Waves* before your next lesson. There will be a quiz." She clapped her hands sharply. "You're dismissed."

The students were quick to fly off their seats and out the door.

I lingered as the last students cleared out. It was almost lunchtime, and my stomach was growly. Dori and the others would be in the dining hall, and if I followed the crowd, then I'd find it easy enough, but by the time I got out of the room, the corridor was empty. "Damn, things move fast here." My stomach grumbled. "Don't worry. We'll get some food."

"Hey." I turned to find the wild-haired girl from earlier standing in the doorway behind me. "I'm Cami. Jay's cousin. He mentioned you." She smiled shyly and nudged her glasses up her nose. "You want me to walk you to the dining hall? I'm headed there anyway."

Now that we were out of the gloomy lecture hall, the similarities in their features were obvious. "Meeting friends?"

She ducked her head. "Not really." We set off down the hall. "I haven't made any friends yet. I'm sure I will, though. Soon. I mean, I have Jay and the pack so..." She shrugged. "But they're older so..." Her throat bobbed, her gaze darting away, clearly embarrassed.

I knew what it was like to be lonely, better than most, but telling her to learn to love her own company probably wasn't what she needed to hear right now. "Friends come in all ages."

Her smile returned. "That's what Jay says."

We took a left into a wide hall that I recognized because of all the vaulted windows looking out toward Coral Isle.

"This way." Cami led me through an arch and into a huge

common room area.

It was the most modern room I'd come across since getting to Nightsbridge. The standard redwood of this place was offset with lighter, brighter colors in an attempt to create a welcoming atmosphere. There was a variety of seating options, ranging from chairs to armchairs to squishy sofas decorated with throws and patterned cushions. Books sat higgledy-piggledy on a bookcase built into the far wall, next to a large ornate mirror—the only old-fashioned item in this room. There was a coffee station with a huge silver machine, the kind found at the bistros back in the nicer parts of Carlston, and several students stood around it, nursing cups of coffee and chatting.

The machine stood out like a beacon. "You must have some powerful magi-generators here."

"We'd be lost without them. The ports rely on them. There's a master generator and several smaller ones, all connected by a network of underground cables. They all link to the lightning rod, so we get extra energy from the storms. We get plenty of those here." We passed students playing billiards. "Through here."

She led me beneath another arch and into a familiar passage. If I wasn't mistaken, the dining hall came off here. "I know where we are now."

"Good. The common room is kinda central to this floor. I call it the anchor room."

"Good to know. But what would be better is if I had a map of this place. Do you know where I can get one?"

"Oh, there are no maps," she said. "We just have to...figure it out."

I lengthened my stride to catch up to her. She walked fast for someone so small. "Wait, are you saying that no one has a map of the Main Building?"

She shook her head. "Not as far as I'm aware."

"Don't you think that's strange?"

"I mean...I did...at first, but it's such an old building, and there are off-limit zones, so..." She shrugged. "Administration probably thought it best to leave us to map out the routes we needed, and there's always someone to show you around if you get stuck. And here we are."

The dining room doors were open, welcoming us into a room buzzing with activity and filled with delicious aromas. The midday sun streamed in through the wall of windows across from us, bathing the room in honey tones.

My altercation with Tamina meant we hadn't eaten our meal here last night. Pip had been kind enough to provide a light supper at Bramble, but I was determined to taste my mother's hot pot today. There were a lot of younger students about, but no sign of any older ones. No Arcanus or hulking Therianthropes. The Hunters were probably training or on duty. I spotted a couple of boys who had the pallor associated with sith or dhampir, but it was impossible to be certain without asking.

But Dori was here, as promised, along with Benedict, at the same table we'd shared yesterday. They waved me over.

"Okay, well…I'll see you." Cami backed away, her smile still in place, but her eyes dull.

I knew that look. And the feeling associated with it. "Do you want to join us?"

She blinked. "Really?"

"Of course." I offered her a smile of encouragement.

I'd say it wasn't a big deal, but I knew how much of a big deal it could be. I'd been her all my life—lonely, friendless, eating my packed lunch in the washroom to avoid Veronica Blastenbury, the Arcanus bitch and self-proclaimed queen bee of the school. I'd have happily drowned her in honey if I could.

Uncertainty flitted across Cami's face. "Are you okay?"

Dammit, I had my murder smile on again. "I'm fine. Come on."

She hesitated, shuffling from foot to foot. "They might mind."

"If they do, then they're dicks. But I don't think they are."

Cami trailed behind me.

Dori beamed up at me as we approached. "How was class?"

"Good." I slipped into the seat opposite her, my back to the exit so that I was facing the epic windows. Cami dithered and I scooted over, indicating for her to join us. "This is Cami. She adopted me in class today."

"Hi," Benedict said. "I'm Benedict, and this is Dori."

Dori lifted her chin in greeting, her gaze assessing. "You're Jay's cousin, aren't you?"

"Yes," Cami said. "I've seen you at the barracks. Before you got in trouble."

Dori snorted. "Shit happens. But I'll be back. Trust me."

"How did things go with the Weave Watchers?" Benedict asked.

Dori elbowed him, her gaze darting to Cami.

Cami ducked her head. "Maybe I should go..."

"It's fine." I sat back in my seat. "It was weird..." I filled them in on my visit to the catacombs, leaving out the strange riddle. I wanted to think on that myself for a bit. "And then I got shoved through a portal and ended up outside the wards in the north border."

"What!" they said in unison.

I filled them in on the ratakan and the chase, how the wards repelled me, and how I'd repelled the ratakan in turn. "But then they sprayed me, and if Drayven hadn't shown up, I'd be ratakan food."

Benedict and Dori sat back in stunned silence.

"*That's* why you were late for class," Cami said.

"Yeah, but don't tell anyone, okay?"

She made a mouth zipping motion.

"Food will be here soon," Clary said, joining us. "Onyx hot pot, since we didn't get to eat it last night."

"Who pushed you?" Benedict's eyes narrowed to slits.

"Pushed who?" Clary asked.

Dori replied, "Someone pushed Ana through a port and into the north borderland."

"What?" Clary's eyes went round. "What happened?"

"Ugh, bitch patrol is here," Dori groaned.

I twisted in my seat to see who she was referring to, a wicked smile curling my lips at the sight of the prima incantors. Viola caught sight of me first, her mouth falling open in shock, arm whipping out to halt her companions. The trio stared at me, clearly stunned at seeing me alive and unscathed.

I wiggled my fingers in a mock wave, then blew them a kiss.

Viola snapped her mouth closed and leaned over to whisper something to Tristen, then the three of them turned on their heels and left.

They were probably worried I'd tattled on them, worried they were going to get some kind of reprimand, and when none came, then they'd wonder why. Oh, how I loved mind games.

"Viola did it, didn't she?" Dori asked, eyes flicking between me and the retreating trio.

"Bitch!" Benedict said.

"Wait till my aunt finds out," Dori added.

I shook my head. "I'm not reporting it." The room dimmed as the sun hid behind a cloud.

"Looks like a storm's brewing," Cami said. "Strange. The weather reports that came in said it would be clear today."

"Forget the weather," Benedict said. "I want to know why Ana won't report Viola. That bitch needs to be put in her place."

I snorted. "Then what? She comes at me again, thinking that I can't fight my own battles? No. I'll deal with her myself in my own time, and—"

The shrill sound of a siren split the air, battering my eardrums and drowning out my voice.

"Emergency drill!" someone yelled over the wailing alarm.

Dori rolled her eyes and grabbed her bag, ushering for me to follow suit.

Looked like I was going to miss out on that hot pot once again.

I grabbed my notebook and slid out of my seat, the siren still blaring and covering the sound of the many boots shuffling toward the exit. There was no urgency in anyone's stride. Looked like drills happened often here for there to be—

All thoughts stopped as an icy, phantom hand gripped the back of my neck, and my knees buckled. I grabbed hold of Benedict, who was closest to me in that moment.

"Ana, what is it?" he asked.

A prickling sensation crawled across my scalp. "Something's wrong..."

Whump, whump, whump.

"What is that?" Clary turned to the window.

Whump, whump, whump...

"Trinity save us." Someone cried.

Shadows swallowed the room, as something huge, scaly, and blue filled the windows. My warning cry locked in my throat as it crashed through the floor-to-ceiling glass, bringing the salty spray of the sea with it—icy and sharp as it pricked my skin.

I hit the ground, shielding my head with my arms to protect my face from flying glass. Ears ringing and heart thudding in my throat, I slowly raised my head to the sight of wings, talons, and a serpentine body eating up the space.

My astounded brain finally registered what I was seeing.

A dragon...

I was looking at a fucking dragon.

The tithe must be paid century on century. Land and Sea must remain united if the pact is to continue.

Extract from The Land-Sea Pact (Vault Archives)

CHAPTER 18

The dragon shook its head, dislodging a shower of sea spray. Its scales glistened, coated in foam, as if it had sprung from the ocean itself.

A gleam of milky white eyes flashed, a moment before it opened its mouth and roared, spewing a jet of purple flame, drowning out the screams and bellows of alarm as students rushed for the exit. But the rush of bodies created a bottleneck, trapping us all.

Steam streamed from the beast's nostrils, its slanted apertures flaring and snapping shut in rapid succession.

The beast sniffed, head swiveling as if hunting.

Searching.

My stomach grew rock hard with dark foreboding.

"The kitchens!" Clary grabbed my arm, and the creature's head whipped our way. The milky film over its eyes snapped back, revealing bright emerald irises. It drew one deep, intentional inhalation—then froze, horizontal pupils dilating and locking onto me.

Seriously? Again? What the Fel was wrong with this place?

"Oh shit," Dori's voice trembled. "Run!"

We bolted across the room in the direction of the kitchens, but a wave of other students had the same idea. They cut across the chamber, inadvertently blocking us off.

They were so young. Terrified children bound to be here by an ancient covenant, and now facing a fucking dragon. There was no option but to attempt escape, their powers would be no match for this creature. Where were the Hunters?

"This way!" Benedict veered left, toward the now-clearing main exit.

The air thinned then crackled, as if whispering a warning. Instinct had me turning back toward the beast, just in time to see its throat light up, flames churning their way upward, moments from eruption.

It was about to spew.

I should have ground to a halt, should have turned and run the other way, but instead, I bolted toward Benedict. "Watch out!" I grabbed him, yanking him back toward the rest of the group, as a terrifying roar rocked the room.

Clary screamed, high-pitched and horrible, as purple flame enveloped us. But there was no smell of burned flesh. The flames raged around us, battering at the invisible force that held it at bay.

Was this me? Was *I* holding the flames back?

The fire dissipated with a hiss, unsated and unsatisfied.

The dragon roared and charged at us.

Instinct took over. I slammed into Benedict, using all my body weight to fling us to one side, narrowly escaping the snap of lethal teeth.

A gust of air hit us as the beast swung our way again, determination blazing in its emerald eyes, smoke billowing around it like an epic backdrop of doom.

"Ana! Benedict!" Dori shouted from the now-empty kitchen doorway.

We scrambled up and broke into a sprint toward them.

The air crackled in warning of another blast of fire.

Benedict shoved me aside, diving in the opposite direction. Heat seared my face, hot air tearing at my hair, whipping it over my shoulders as flames devoured the spot where we'd been a moment ago.

I pulled myself up, each breath a battle, and hurled myself toward the kitchen exit where Dori and Clary jumped up and down with urgency. Benedict ran parallel to me on the other side of the room.

We were almost there, but the dragon couldn't be far behind. Like hell would I break stride to check though.

"Ana, look out!" Dori yelled.

Something hit my legs, sweeping me off my feet. I hit the ground on my back, head slamming against tile. Darkness edged my vision, but I gritted my teeth and fought against unconsciousness, forcing my unsteady limbs to sit me up.

Someone screamed my name, but the ringing in my ears overshadowed the sound.

"Ana, move! You have to—"

A primal growl rumbled around me, and something blue and scaly moved in my periphery two feet off the ground, then three. It took a moment to identify it as the dragon's tail.

Fuck, the dragon's tail was around me!

The acrid scent of sulfur and brimstone stung my nose, making my eyes water. I looked up through a haze of tears at the dragon, looming majestic and lethal over me.

I was trapped.

About to die a crispy fried kind of death. Or maybe it would burn me to ash. I wasn't afraid of the pain—there would be none, and death had only frightened me when it meant I'd be leaving Mother behind. In truth, I'd craved the oblivion, the freedom from my shitty life, at least I'd always thought so. But now, as I stared it in the face, there was no way I'd be going quietly. No way I'd go down without a fight.

I'd been targeted and attacked constantly since coming to Nightsbridge, and I was fucking done with it.

The heat of purpose surging through my limbs, I took a deep breath, then released my frustration and rage in a bloodcurdling roar that propelled me onto the beast's tail and up into the air. "Agh!" I drew back my fist and punched the dragon in the face.

Crunch.

The impact reverberated up my arm, but did nothing to move the beast, which made sense because it was a fucking dragon, but a part of me had hoped that maybe... Maybe the Weave would have helped me again, twisting defense into offense.

Obviously not.

I expected retaliation. A snap of teeth, or a blast of flame to end me, but the dragon merely tipped its head to one side, horizontal pupils dilating to drink me in. Its regard held a human-like awareness and intelligence that made my pulse quicken with unease, my skin prickling with a subliminal awareness.

I cradled my rapidly swelling hand and took a tentative step back. "Sorry?"

A blast of wet, hot steam hit my face, and my bladder twinged despite my bravado. The dragon's lips pulled back, baring teeth as thick and long as my forearm, and the air vibrated with a snarl. Pressure filled my head. Clawing. Whispering.

"I...see...you..."

The voice slithered into my mind. Deep and resonant, the tone like rolling rubble and gravel. It burrowed, insidious, intrusive and—

"No!" a male voice boomed.

Cold water speckled my skin, jolting me free of whatever power had me in its grip. The dragon's eyes flew wide before a powerful jet of water propelled it away from me and across the room toward the windows.

The beast twisted midair, shrieking with rage and baring its teeth at its attacker.

Vitra stood with one hand out, commanding a swirling sphere of water. His dark hair was unbound, floating about his head in a phantom breeze, and his eyes blazed neon blue.

The air fizzed with power, raising goose bumps up my arms. Power that came from Vitra, larger than life somehow as he faced off against the dragon. There was no fear on his face, no hint of doubt as he locked gazes with the beast, if anything, he looked downright annoyed that the creature dared to be here—and boy was that sexy as fuck.

"Return!" he ordered the beast.

The dragon recoiled, its serpentine body trembling as if trying to resist the command.

I held my breath, gaze flicking between the dragon and Vitra.

Vitra spoke in a language I didn't understand, yet something about its cadence felt familiar. A strange conviction took root—if I just focused a little harder, if I listened a little longer, then—

"Now!" Vitra thundered, done with the foreign words.

The dragon twisted toward the windows and smashed through the remaining glass panes, leaping out into the afternoon sun.

I rushed to the windows, but the dragon was gone, leaving nothing but sea foam in its wake.

Vitra appeared beside me. "It won't be back."

The swirling water sphere he'd been projecting was gone, and his eyes were back to their normal tawny shade. And when had he tied his hair back up?

He arched a brow when he caught me staring. "You're in shock. It will wear off soon enough."

Shock was an understatement. "That was a dragon. And it came out of the sea. What the hell?" My pulse throbbed hard in my throat, my voice barely a whisper. I sucked in a breath to calm my nerves. "Dragons are real?"

"Evidently." He slipped his hands into his trouser pockets, cool and collected, as if he hadn't just jet-streamed a monster into the sea. "They're also classified as Horrors. Ones the seafolk should have in check. We haven't had a sea Horror attack since the Land-Sea Pact was put in place."

"Then maybe someone should speak to them?" Dori said,

joining us.

The others were close behind.

"Oh, Trinity." Clary gently gripped my wrist, bringing my swollen hand up for all to see. "It's broken."

"I can't believe you punched it in the face." Benedict stared at me with wide, kohl-rimmed eyes. He reminded me of a marsupial I'd seen in an old picture book. I couldn't recall its name.

"You did what?" Vitra demanded, his gaze sharpening.

"She punched the dragon," Benedict repeated. "In the face."

Vitra's nostrils flared. "I would ask what you were thinking if I suspected you'd been thinking much at all. You're lucky to be alive, Miss Onyx."

"So everyone keeps telling me. It came for me. *Directly* for me. Just like the mudarks."

"I very much doubt that the Horror leapt from the ocean specifically to accost you, more likely that you were the closest, easiest target."

But it hadn't been like that—I was ready to argue, but my words wilted on my lips when his long fingers curled around my wrist, branding me with pleasant heat.

"Your hand does look broken," he said. "But Darla will have something to speed up the healing." He canted his head, his gaze shrewd and probing. "It must hurt."

Shit. With all the chaos, I'd forgotten to keep up my act when it came to pain. "Now that you mention it, yeah, it fucking kills. The adrenaline must be wearing off."

"Yes," Vitra agreed, his eyes narrowing slightly as his grip on my wrist tightened a fraction.

I was quick to let out a pained gasp.

"Apologies." He released my wrist. You should get to the infirmary." His smile didn't reach his eyes and my pulse fluttered in my throat. Had the wrist squeeze been a test? Was he suspicious? Had he guessed the truth?

Vitra released me from his dark regard, gaze flicking to the ocean once more. "It seems that the ocean patrol needs a reminder of the terms of our agreement."

I swallowed my sigh of relief. I wanted to keep control of when and with whom I shared the details of my curse. Having someone deduce it and corner me into revealing it wasn't ideal. The longer I kept it to myself, the more useful it could be.

Students filtered back into the room, taking in the carnage with wide-eyed shock.

Vitra sighed and broke away from us, crossing the room toward them. "Nothing more to see here. Get back to your classes." He threw a look my way. "You escaped death twice in one day. I'm not sure if that's luck or talent—so do the wise thing and don't test it." He ushered the students from the room, leaving me wondering when Selethis had shared the ratakan information with him. A little lunchtime tryst, maybe?

Pip hurried into the ruined dining hall followed by several sweeping brushes. "Everybody out. We have cleanup to do."

Seriously? "That's it? Cleanup? Get on with classes? We were just attacked by a water-Horror-dragon thing."

"It almost burned me to a crisp," Benedict said. "But you stopped it." He was doing that wide-eyed marsupial look again.

It made me uncomfortable.

"I didn't *do* anything...at least not consciously."

"I've never seen a reflexive defense response like that," Dori said. "Using the Weave, whether as an incantor or a sorcerer, always involves intent."

"I don't know. I have no idea how it works, or even if it's consistent, but I'm sure that dragon was after me."

"It attacked everyone," Dori said. "Maybe you just pissed it off when you threw up a shield."

"I did that *after* it gunned for me..." Hadn't I? The whole incident felt like a blur now. Had I imagined the Horrors' focus on me? Did I have some kind of victim complex? It wouldn't be surprising considering all the shit I'd been through.

"If Vitra hadn't shown up in time..." Clary hugged herself. "The Hunters are on a recon excursion for the Carvers today. We'd have been toast."

But the dragon hadn't made a move to attack once it had me trapped. Not even when I punched it. Instead, it looked at me with eyes that held thoughts. Feelings. There'd been a presence in my mind. Words that I couldn't recall now. Had the dragon been trying to communicate with me?

Clary interrupted my thoughts. "I didn't know nagas could manipulate water like that."

Vitra was a snake shifter? Those were rare, like one in a million rare.

"I doubt anyone does," Dori said. "I've never heard of him using his power before."

"I heard he's a royal," Benedict said.

"Yeah, he is," Dori confirmed. "The last of his bloodline."

Brooms wielded by invisible specters converged on us, scraping broken glass into dustpans held steady by phantom hands.

"Out," Pip snapped.

"We didn't get any lunch," Clary grumbled as we made our way out of the dining hall.

Our boots crunched on broken crockery as we dodged spilled spaghetti and sauce, stepping onto the scorched part of the floor where the purple flames had cracked the tiles.

How Pip was going to fix this mess was beyond me. My stomach growled, reminding me that I'd missed out on the Onyx hot pot once again. But there was a new hunger inside me now, a hunger to know more about the magnificent Tower Master with the ability to single-handedly subdue a sea dragon.

Power comes in many forms and can be converted or subverted using the appropriate mechanisms.

Notation on Nightsbridge Academy schematics

CHAPTER 19

I woke up the next morning to a growling stomach and no idea how I'd gotten to bed...fully clothed.

I lay under the duvet for long seconds. Gray morning light filtering in from between my drapes, slowly lighting up the room. Images trickled up to fill the gaps in my memory—Darla examining my hand and telling me it was fractured, not broken, much to everyone's surprise. Benedict saying something about having strong bones. Darla tutting and smearing healing ointment over the swelling before wrapping it firmly. And then... Then she'd insisted I take a tincture for the pain, watching as I drained the vial before telling me that it would make me sleepy.

Everything was a little fuzzy after that.

I guess when she said that the tincture would make me sleepy, she'd actually meant it would knock me out.

The insistent throb in my hand told me that whatever pain relief I'd been given had worn off, and if I could feel it, I'd be in agony. I'd have to be careful and try not to injure it any further.

There was a gentle rap on my door before it opened a crack and Clary popped her head in. Her bangs were pushed back by a headband today, giving her a fresh-faced, youthful look. "Good, you're awake. Pip delivered breakfast."

My stomach growled again. "Thank fuck, I'm ravenous."

I shoved off the duvet and padded into the sitting room after her, breathing in the delicious aroma of coffee and bacon. Benedict and Dori knelt around the coffee table, busy lifting metal domes off plates of toast and bowls of bacon and scrambled eggs. They looked up as I joined them.

"Ah, sleeping beauty awakens." Benedict handed me a cup of coffee, and I took a spot on the floor opposite him.

"I'm assuming I passed out?" I took a sip of my beverage, sweet and strong, just the way I preferred it.

"You keeled over like a log," Dori said. "We thought you were dead."

"You should have seen Darla's face," Benedict chuckled. "Thought she was about to have a coronary."

Clary elbowed him. "That's not funny."

He sobered quickly, shaking his head. "So not funny."

I set my cup on the coffee table. "What happened to me?"

"Adverse reaction to the tincture, it seems," Clary said. "Like an allergic reaction, at least that's what Darla thinks. Although it's never happened before. She checked in on you several times until she was satisfied that your pulse and heart rate were normal, and that you weren't going to suddenly stop breathing."

"Vitra was pissed," Dori said, eyes going round. "You should have heard him telling Darla off. It was kinda terrifying, and poor Darla looked as if she were going to cry."

That hardly seemed fair to Darla. "It's not her fault. How was she to know how I'd react?"

"Right?" Dori agreed. "That's what we said. But he refused to leave until Darla assured him your vitals were steady."

He'd come back to check on me and stayed, huh? Did it matter that much to him if I lived or died? Or maybe there was a penalty if I died on his watch. "Good to see that he's taking his mentoring role seriously."

Clary buttered a slice of toast and took a huge bite, and my stomach reminded me once again that I'd missed lunch and supper yesterday.

I grabbed a plate and began loading it up with toast, bacon, and eggs. "Why can't we eat here all the time instead of trekking to the Main Building?"

"I dunno," Benedict answered around a mouthful of food. "Rules are that meals are to be taken in the Main Building unless we're sick or the weather is too bad to make the trip."

"I'm assuming breakfast has been provided because I fall under the sick category?"

"Must be so," Dori said. "This wonderful spread was here when we woke a little while ago."

Benedict raised a slice of toast and winked a kohl-rimmed eye. "Thanks for that."

We ate in silence for several minutes, and I lost myself in the simple pleasure of a cooked meal. The bacon was crispy, the toast thick and delicious when lathered with butter, and the scrambled eggs were fluffy and flavorsome.

The gnawing in my stomach ebbed.

"So, what are you going to do today?" Clary asked me. "You have a free day, don't you?"

My unexpectedly long sleep had stolen my chance to plan. I shrugged. "No idea."

"How about you come to class with us?" Clary clapped her hands together as if it were the most exciting idea ever.

I stared at her, deadpan. "How about no."

Benedict snorted into his coffee cup.

Clary's face fell, and I immediately felt like a bitch. She was trying to be nice after all. "I'm sorry, that came out wrong. I must still be under the effects of the tincture."

"Nice save," Benedict muttered.

I ignored him and continued. "I don't want to come to classes, but I *will* come to the Main Building with you guys. I could do with exploring to get my bearings."

"And tonight, we can take you to Coral Isle!" Benedict said. "You can get a look at the arena before your date with Tamina." He arched a brow, a slight smirk on his lips.

Was he hoping that I'd see a few fights and get put off? "Sounds lovely."

Dori drained her cup. "We've got to leave in fifteen. Can you be ready, Ana?"

I looked down at my rumpled uniform. I did have another to alternate, but I'd rather get this one washed and pressed before I risked the spare set. With the shitty luck I'd been having since getting here, I wouldn't be surprised if I was targeted again and ended up bloody, muddy, or both.

"I don't have to wear a uniform on my day off, do I?"

"Nope," Clary said. "You can pop the clothes you want washed down the laundry chute in the hall. I'll show you."

We gathered up the plates, popping them onto the trays they'd been delivered on, ready for the SDA to collect, before dispersing to our bedrooms to get ready.

I quickly washed, then changed into wide-legged trousers and a thick tunic top with a wide belt. My wool coat went nicely with the outfit, and my ankle boots finished off the ensemble.

I grabbed my bag, tipped out the books, and replaced them with my cryptozoology journal and sketch pencils. Maybe I'd find a quiet nook to draw in. Goodness knows I had plenty of updates to add. Critters had evolved after The Overshadowing, and the Horrors and Echoes had entered Nova Terra *because* of the event, so maybe there were commonalities between the two.

My stomach fizzed with excitement, but I quickly tempered my enthusiasm. I wasn't here to further my knowledge on cryptozoology, I was here to find the *Libra Veritas*. Nothing could come between me and my goal.

I could still sketch, though.

We ran a little late because I insisted on dropping in on Darla, just to let her know I was fine and that I didn't blame her for what had happened. The relief on her sweet face made the few minutes we spent on the detour worth it.

Outside, the sky was heavy with gray clouds, and the air was misty and wet where it touched my skin. A sharp, cold wind cut through my wool coat, eager to chill me. It was a relief to get into the Main Building.

"Meet for lunch?" Clary asked as we hurried past the vaulted windows and toward the stairs to the first floor.

"Sounds good." We parted in the corridor above and they rushed to make their lessons on time, while I slowed to an amble, stepping to one side to let several students pass.

It wasn't long before the passages were silent, and I was the only one walking them. I stopped at the arched windows to look out at the tumultuous ocean and beyond to Coral Isle. It would be an interesting evening, followed by a weekend where I could get to know my tower mates a little better, and maybe do a little more sleuthing about campus. But for now, I needed to make a mental map of the Main Building as best I could. I didn't want to rely on other students to get me from A to B. It would be hard to snoop if I needed someone to accompany me everywhere.

I left the window and headed back down the corridor, taking turns at random and making mental notes of landmarks—various landscapes that filled the space between classrooms, or the intricate tapestries hanging between sconces. My explorations took me past the common room and into an area I recognized. The dining room doors were shut, a notice pinned to the wood stating that the room was out of order.

Looked like we'd be lunching back at Bramble.

I dove deeper into the building, away from any windows and natural light. The passages were lit solely by the anemic glow of wall sconces and seemed a little narrower, but there was something familiar about this area. I'd been here before, coming from a different direction. I realized why a moment later when I spotted a vaulted arch leading to an intersection. One corridor was brightly lit, the other was shrouded in shadow.

I'd definitely been this way, but Dori and Clary had led me away because it was restricted.

Restricted, what a deliciously dirty word. I glanced quickly around to make sure I was alone, then ventured into the shadows.

The walls here were gray stone, and the wooden floor looked scuffed and old. A dark wooden door, set in a vaulted arch, sat at the end of the passage. The wood looked solid—thick and heavy. There were intricate patterns carved into it, but not enough light to make them out clearly.

The desire to know what lay beyond was an insistent tugging in my chest. A quick peek couldn't hurt, could it?

There was no door handle, so I pressed my palm to the wood and pushed. It didn't budge, which made sense. Restricted usually meant locked, but there was no denying the flare of disappointment in my chest.

"Hey! What are you doing?"

I spun away from the door, hand going to my chest as a stocky figure barged toward me. "You. Come 'ere."

Shit. "I'm sorry. I'm new. I got lost." I hurried toward him, an apologetic smile on my face.

Up close, the man looked to be in his late twenties or early thirties, his hard, blocky features further accentuated by a buzz cut. The dark blue overalls he wore set him apart from the teachers here. Could this be Master Trax, the man who took care of the Main Building?

He jerked his chin up and looked down his nose at me. "Onyx, right?"

"News sure travels fast around here."

He pressed his lips together, nostrils flaring. "Hmmm. I'm Master Trax, grounds watchman, and this area is restricted."

"Oh?" I plastered an innocent look on my face. "I'm sorry, I didn't know."

"Hmmm..." He looked over my head and down the dark hall. "You'd best get going to class."

"I don't have class. I was exploring."

He dropped his gaze to me, his eyes narrowing slightly. "Explore somewhere else."

"Right." I ducked around him. "I'll be off then."

I walked quickly toward the light and glanced back once I reached the intersection.

Trax was gone.

I spent the next half hour retracing my steps to familiarize myself with the overall layout of the building. The place was a maze, and it would take more than a morning of exploration to memorize the many paths, nooks, and alcoves of this place.

I found a window seat on the first floor, close to the dining hall, and killed an hour sketching the long-limbed, eerie Echoes that had attacked me my first day here. The blank faces, the thin fingers with too many joints—all of it went onto paper. These faceless creatures could morph into any person they wanted to. Change form at will... Wait, there was a critter that could do that, too. I flipped pages until I found the one I was looking for. The *Chamaeleontis Vermis*, the chameleon worm. It couldn't make itself look like another insect completely, but it could change color and texture to mimic aspects of other insects and critters. Was there a connection there? I was probably reaching, but I made a note beside my Echo sketch anyway.

I was about to start on a sketch of the mudark when the corridors erupted with the sound of bootfalls and chatter.

Looked like classes were over.

I tucked my journal into my pack and left my cozy spot to head to the dining hall. It was closed, but the Unwoven probably didn't know that and would be headed there like all the other students.

I hoisted my pack onto my shoulders and joined the flood of bodies.

The storm broke just after lunch. Rain hammered at the windows, falling in sheets that blurred the outside world.

"Looks like classes are canceled for the rest of the day," Clary said, flopping down on the sofa, paperback in hand.

I settled in one of the armchairs and tucked my feet beneath me. "Because of the weather?"

"Storms mean no port travel," Dori said from her spot by the hearth. She teased the flames with an iron poker, nudging the fire to burn brighter. "Storms tend to mess with the ports."

Benedict stretched and yawned. "I might take a nap." He wriggled, getting comfortable in the larger armchair, and closed his eyes.

A languid silence settled over us. Dori stretched out on the rug by the fire, arms behind her head, and Benedict's breathing slowed and deepened as he drifted off.

I considered getting up to grab my journal, but moving felt like too much of an effort. I peered across at Clary, trying to catch the title of her book. Her gaze shifted off the page and to me.

"*Tower of Midnight* by Delila Trust," she said. "It's my comfort read. Have you read it?"

"I'm not much of a fiction reader."

"We should do something," Dori said.

"Oh, I know," Clary said. "We could do face masks. I made a mixture that will cleanse and brighten our skin."

"No," Benedict mumbled. "Sleeping."

Dori sat up. "I'm in, and you should be too, Benedict. Your skin's been looking a little dry."

His eyes snapped open. "Excuse me? I have excellent skin."

"There's always room for improvement," Clary said. "Ana, you in?"

I wasn't too sure I wanted to put on a face mask, but Clary looked so excited I didn't have the heart to turn her down. "Sure. I could do with a little pampering."

"Ooh, we should dye our nails too!" Dori pulled herself to her feet. "I'll get my dyes."

The women hurried to their respective rooms.

Benedict groaned, but there was a twinkle in his eyes. "It never stops at masks and nail dye, you know."

"No?"

"Last time, they made up my whole face—lip stain, rouge, eye powder, the lot."

"Nice to see a man who's comfortable enough in his skin to allow that."

He gave me a sheepish smile. "I was asleep at the time."

Dori and Clary returned, carrying boxes and bags.

"See," Benedict said to me before turning to the women. "Anamaya says she'd like you to make her up."

Dori's eyes lit up like beacons of hope, and dread pooled in my belly.

"Wait. I didn't—"

"No." Dori held up her hand. "You can't take it back. This is happening."

Benedict snickered, and I shot him a glare.

"You can look glamorous for your first trip to Coral Isle tonight," Dori said. "Providing the storm stops."

"You're going to look beautiful," Clary added.

I had no intention of leaving the tower with a made-up face, but I could burst their bubble later.

I sat back in my seat with a sigh. "Fine. Let's do this."

I studied my made-up face in the bathroom mirror. Smudgy dark eyes, pouty berry lips, and contoured cheeks. I looked like a stranger. A stunning stranger.

Dori had done a great job, but my skin felt stiff and itchy.

I gathered my hair into a knot, then washed my face clean. Cards was next on the menu, and I was already socially drained, but I'd be lying if I said I hated spending time with the trio.

I exited the bathroom to a flash of bright light, followed by a deep rumbling.

"Ana!" Clary popped her head around my door. "Come, quick. You have to see this."

She ushered me into Dori's room, a haven of knitted throws and scented candles. Dori and Benedict stood at the window, beckoning me to join them, moving aside so I could look out.

Dori's room afforded a view of the inlet and the landmass housing the Main Building. "Okay, what are we looking at?"

"Just watch," Benedict said.

Lightning lanced from the sky and shot toward the Main Building, latching onto a tall rod projecting from a southern tower turret. The building lit up bright for a moment, each dark window screaming into the night as the rod held the lightning in its grip for long seconds.

My breath snagged in my throat at the raw power of this moment. The lightning broke free, and I imagined I heard the snap and sizzle of its escape. The Main Building fell into darkness once more.

We waited long seconds and the sky lit up again, another bolt, another connection with the rod.

"It's amazing, right?" Benedict said. "I always wonder what it would feel like to be inside the building or on the grounds. The sheer power being harnessed right now…"

Chester had mentioned the steeple that conducted lightning. "What do they do with the power?"

"Reserves, I think," Dori said. "Who knows. We have magi-generators, so maybe they use the power in conjunction with those somehow."

Or maybe it was used for some other purpose...

We stayed to watch the lightning for a little longer. The companiable silence settling around me like a hug.

"Looks like Coral Isle is definitely off the agenda for tonight," Benedict said. "Might be off the agenda all weekend. Storms like this won't pass quickly."

"We'll just have to make our own fun," Clary said with a little too much enthusiasm.

I stifled a groan. It was going to be a long weekend.

Pipers: Rare breed of Horrors known to occupy the marshlands of Nightsbridge. They lure their prey with high frequency sound waves, then incapacitate them with a neurotoxin so that they may consume them alive.

The Compendium of Horrors

CHAPTER 20

The storm did indeed last all weekend. But time passed quickly, mainly because the Unwoven were so determined to make my first weekend at Nightsbridge fun. I wasn't used to spending so much leisure time with people, and I expected to hate it, but...it wasn't so bad.

Monday dawned bright and clear, as if the storm had been nothing but a dream. I'd have been more excited to get out of the tower if my first class hadn't been Combat 101 with Sterling Damascus.

The only good news was that the swelling in my hand had all but disappeared. I could even move my fingers. My gut warned me to keep this information to myself. Rapid healing wasn't normal for an Arcanus. Fel, it had never been normal for me either. But being on Nightsbridge soil was changing me in ways I didn't understand. Until I figured it out, I'd keep schtum.

I doubted an injury would prevent Sterling from putting me through my paces. I'd hoped for a little more time to wrestle my emotions into the neat little boxes I'd learned to house them in before facing him again. Boxes labeled *anxiety*, *rage*, and *murderous intentions*. The murderous intentions box was the largest because it housed all the ways I'd imagined ending his life.

One day soon, I'd unpack that box and pick a method. Or maybe two or three to make it interesting.

The training grounds were on the other side of the barracks, and beyond that were some pretty gardens, not that I'd had the chance to explore them yet. But as we rounded the barracks tower, I spotted a guy standing by the gated entrance. He clutched a book to his chest, looking wistfully in our direction.

I raised a hand in greeting, and he blinked sharply before tentatively lifting his hand in return. His attention shifted to Dori, who was walking ahead of me. He waved, but she didn't notice.

"Hey, Dori, there's a guy waving at you over... Oh, he's gone."

"What did he look like?" she asked.

"Messy, blond hair and glasses. Tall, I guess."

She shook her head. "No idea who that is."

The clang of wood on wood grew louder as we crossed the running track that surrounded the oval training area. It contained an obstacle course and an area for combat, which was taking place right now as paired-up students clashed with wooden swords and fists.

"If they pair me with that sadistic turd Tyler, I will break his teeth," Dori said.

"Who's Tyler?"

"A Damascus," Clary provided. "Thinks he's untouchable because his brother is a hunt leader."

Sterling had a brother? Interesting. And there he was, the bastard himself, standing with his back to us, arms crossed, assessing his students.

As we approached, he turned his head, zeroing in on me with his eerie pale-blue eyes that I was certain would look better on the end of toothpicks. I'd scoop them out of his head first, of course, careful not to damage them, while I reveled in his agonized screams.

Oh, and there it was—the lip curl, the nostril flare—as if he was looking at a pile of shit.

I gritted my teeth, keeping my expression neutral.

"He looks pissed," Benedict muttered.

"Nothing new," Clary said through the smile fixed on her face.

"Someone get him a blood bag." Dori didn't bother to lower her tone.

Sterling's brow lifted slightly.

"I think he heard you," Clary whisper-hissed.

"Like I give a shit." Dori shrugged.

Sterling broke away from the students and walked over to us. Tendrils of silver hair had come loose from his topknot, whipping about his face in agitation as he approached.

I wondered how he'd feel about being bald.

"Miss Embercrest." He smiled thinly at Dori. "I hear exercise is the perfect cure for constipation, and since you don't *give a shit*, you can give me ten laps. Now."

Dori's jaw tensed, and for a moment, I thought she'd argue, but she dropped a curt nod and jogged off toward the track.

"Miss Tavona, find a group to teach on defensive maneuvers. Ironhart, you can do the same but with offensive."

They hurried off, leaving me alone with Sterling. I fixed him with a blank look, waiting for instructions.

He looked me up and down, slowly and derisively, his gaze lingering on my bandaged hand before he turned to walk away.

What the fuck? "Hey! Damascus, what about me?"

He paused but didn't turn around. "What about you?"

"What do you want me to do?"

"You?" He threw a scathing look over his shoulder. "You can do the only thing that you're good for. Nothing." He walked off, leaving me standing on the outskirts of the arena with a hot coal of hatred burning a hole in my chest.

I couldn't kill him, but I'd find a way to make him hurt. To make him scream. "I guess we can't all be Daddy's little lapdog!"

He stopped, shoulders bunching beneath his black, fitted

shirt before reaching into his pocket to draw out a whistle.

He blasted it twice in short succession, and everyone stopped what they were doing. "Miss Onyx has kindly agreed to aid me in demonstrating the Hamlin maneuver."

The horror on my fellow Unwoven's faces, coupled with the grins on the younger students' faces, was enough to put me on edge. But I'd be damned if I showed him that I was concerned.

He turned, wearing a smile that didn't reach his eyes. "Miss Onyx, if you wouldn't mind joining me." He headed for the other side of the training arena, all sand and gravel.

I followed as Dori rushed to catch up. "What are you doing? The Hamlin is one of the most aggressive hand-to-hand techniques. It's meant for a piper-Horror. Only seasoned Hunters are allowed to demonstrate it on each other. There's a way to play the piper to avoid getting hurt, and you're already hurt."

I had no clue what a piper was, but if Sterling thought he could hurt me, he was going to be sorely disappointed. "I'll be fine." I broke away from her to join Sterling. "What do you need me to do?"

"Stay calm," he said. "Don't tense up. Don't fight me. And you'll be fine." That smile again, all deceit and jagged edges.

I shrugged, feigning indifference. "Let's do this."

I rolled my shoulders and ordered my body to relax—no easy feat in the presence of a male I wanted to stake then barbecue. The students gathered close, nudging one another and whispering. A boy with a silver buzz cut pushed his way to the front. His facial expression, the hair, and the sharp arch of his eyebrows were all similar to Sterling. He had to be his brother, Tyler.

"Do we get to try after?" he asked.

"No," Sterling said.

"Why not?"

"Because I said so."

"But—"

"Enough!" Sterling snapped. "One more word and you're off combat class for the month."

Tyler pressed his lips together, hands curling into fists at his side.

Sterling circled me. "There may come a time when you are without a weapon, a time when the Weave is out of touch, and you have only your body to rely on. One thing we have learned about pipers—their arms are thick and powerful, but their bones are not so strong." He stopped behind me, and my skin crawled with awareness. "In order to incapacitate a piper, you must get behind it and—"

He grabbed my elbows, yanked them back, and shoved his knee into my spine, forcing my body into a sudden arch before slamming me into the ground so hard that he knocked the breath from my lungs.

He knelt on me, pressing into my back and pulling on my arms in a way that would have had anyone else screaming.

"Then you yank," he continued, his tone conversational. "Sudden and hard to break the spine and dislocate the joints in the arm."

The pressure on my spine built, tendons in my shoulders straining. If he didn't stop soon, my arms would pop out of their sockets and my bones would snap.

I couldn't risk another injury.

There was only one thing to do.

Give him what he wanted.

I screamed, shrill and bloodcurdling.

Gasps of shock and cries of "Stop, you're hurting her!" filled the air.

Maybe I'd overdone it?

He leaned in, one knee still at my back, pinning me as his breath brushed my ear. "Accidents happen here all the time." His grip on me tightened, and in that moment, I knew for certain that he didn't plan to let me walk away from this demonstration unscathed. He was going to dislocate my shoulder.

He wrenched my arms again, but this time, I resisted. Tugging toward the ground to yank him forward, I dropped my head, then whipped it back in time to catch him in the face with a blow that slackened his grip enough for me to jerk free. I rolled out from under him and was about to pull myself up when he landed on top of me.

Straddling me, he slammed me to the ground by the throat. "And if the piper succeeds in slipping free and you get a chance to pin it—go for the throat and crush its windpipe."

Fuck he was strong. His grip like steel. I twisted and bucked, but he had me trapped.

Panic detonated inside me as he proceeded to squeeze, his attention on the students as he slowly cut off my breath. I clawed at his hand, eyes bugging. He couldn't do this. He couldn't kill me, the blood oath between his family and mine prevented that, didn't it?

Accidents happen here all the time...

No. This was no accident. There were witnesses, but Sterling didn't seem to care. The pressure on my throat increased. I choked, tears blurring my vision, as the other students' cries of alarm were muffled beneath the beating rush of blood in my ears.

Someone slammed into Sterling, knocking him off me and setting me free. I rolled onto my side, gagging and coughing as air found its way in and out of my lungs once more.

"Oh, Trinity, Ana!" Clary and Dori rushed to my side, helping me up.

It took a moment to regain mastery of my limbs—but the sight that awaited me made the last few minutes worth it.

Drayven straddled Sterling's back, one hand pressing the dhampir's head into the gravel, forcing him into submission.

It was a fucking vision. I took a mental picture and filed it away to examine later.

"Get off me," Sterling bit out.

Drayven pressed Sterling's head hard enough that the crunch of gravel against the Phage's alabaster cheek was a delicious melody. "What the fuck are you playing at?" he growled.

"Teaching," Sterling bit out. "You remember what that's like, don't you?"

"That was *not* teaching."

"If she can't handle a little pain, then she doesn't belong here."

Sterling was a lying piece of shit, but there was no way to prove that he'd planned to kill me. No way to prove that he wouldn't have stopped. Drayven must have realized it, too. He made a soft sound of disgust and with a final shove, climbed off the Phage.

"The Hamlin is *not* on the curriculum for Combat 101."

Sterling chuckled, the sound harsh and derisive. "You should know." He pulled himself up and dusted off his clothes. "*You're* the reason it was removed."

Drayven's jaw ticked, his fists bunching, and for a moment I thought he would hit Sterling. I *wanted* him to hit the bastard. To break his fucking face. But he didn't. Instead, he exhaled sharply through his nose and relaxed his stance. "Class is over." He strode toward me. "*You*—come with me. The rest of you get out of here."

"She's hurt," Dori said.

"I'll take care of her," Drayven replied.

That seemed to satisfy the Unwoven, and they backed off, allowing me to leave with the barghest, but not before I caught the malicious glint in Sterling's eye.

I gave him the finger with my good hand, then followed Drayven toward the gardens and through the gates, where he finally spun to face me, his attention dropping to my neck.

"How bad is it?" he asked. He gently nudged my chin up to examine my throat. "You're bruised. There'll be internal swelling." His jaw flexed. "That bastard."

"I'm fine," my voice came out a raspy croak.

"No, you're not. But you'll live." His shoulders dropped a little. "I've never seen Sterling behave like that toward a student before, so I need to know, what *is* going on between you two?"

"Nothing."

"You told me he was a murderer. He obviously hurt someone you care about, but what did *you* do to *him*?"

Heat gathered behind my eyes, and I gritted my teeth. "What

did *I* do to *him*? *Me*? A big fat nothing!" My throat pinched, warning me that I was hurt, in pain, even though I couldn't feel it. "And I regret that *nothing* every fucking day."

I'd been a child. A nobody, with no contacts, no power, and nothing to do but cry until my heart broke.

His shoulders slumped, and his tone softened. "Tell me what happened." I didn't want to talk about it, so I shook my head. "Listen to me. Sterling is a ruthless killer, and if he feels that you've wronged him, then you're in danger. I need to understand why he would want to hurt you."

It's not your fault. It was an accident. It wasn't your fault. But in the grand scheme of things, how much did the little details matter?

"Ana? Please tell me," Drayven said. "What did you do?"

I closed my eyes and took a breath, speaking the words I'd only ever said in my head. "I killed his sister."

Having been given centuries to wrestle control of the threat, we must now ask ourselves why the Imperium Alius refuses to allow members of the Custodes Hominum to survey their work. One must wonder what it is they are hiding...

Custodes Hominum Address, 285 A.O.

CHAPTER 21

We walked into the gardens and sat on the first bench we found. Telling this story hadn't been on my agenda, but now that Drayven had asked, I realized how much I *needed* to tell it.

Too long had it lived in my mind, unsaid, unspoken. Maybe giving it voice would make the soul-ache smaller somehow.

It was worth a try. My throat was tight, and I knew talking would only aggravate the swelling, so I kept my voice to a soft whisper. "Annabeth Damascus came to live in my village the summer I turned twelve. Although I didn't know who she was at first. She was just a girl who'd come to stay in the cottage at the end of the lane—a rental that had sat empty all year.

"I was excited—she was someone new, someone who didn't go to my school, didn't know who I was. To her, I was just Ana. Not Onyx. She told me she was there with an aunt but nothing more than that, and it honestly didn't matter that she didn't speak about her home life, because that meant I didn't have to speak about mine. We became friends, and that summer was the best of my life."

For a moment, I was back there, in a simpler time when the

summer stretched ahead of me, joyous and filled with endless possibility. For a moment, an echo of that joy swelled inside me. I allowed it to expand, breathing it in and closing my eyes to savor it before letting it go.

"We played in the forest and by the river almost every day, meeting at noon and staying out till dusk. There was a small, abandoned atrium close to the river. It had a dodgy door that tended to stick, but after we'd gotten trapped in there once, and had to use both our strength to get out, we'd kept it wedged open. The glass was some special, unbreakable material. We'd tried. That atrium became our haven. We planted flowers and herbs, spending hours in the warmth of the sun. Annabeth loved sunbathing. She always said she had to make the most of it while she could, that her turning could happen any day. I knew what she was—a pureblood vampire. That her summer in Pembrooke Village was her respite before her turning. I knew it, but I..." I lost my words for a moment, faced with the horror of what I was about to reveal.

"Go on," Drayven coaxed gently.

He had such kind eyes. Eyes that held no judgment. Not yet anyway. "I genuinely believed that I'd found a friend, that maybe I could tell her the truth of who I really was someday. But that choice was taken from me before summer's end. That fateful day, we met at the atrium as planned, but she was angry. So fucking angry, and I knew—before she said a word, I knew. It was in her eyes, you know? The look of disdain. The one I'd been subjected to all my life. She'd found out who I was. Someone had told her about the Onyx girl. The taint to be avoided. She called me a liar and a cheat, screaming that I'd tricked her into being my friend. How her father would be furious if he discovered the awful association. That I could have ruined her reputation.

"I screamed back, asking how, after everything we'd been through that summer, she could just turn her back on our friendship? She said she could never be friends with an Onyx. A murderous bloodline. I slammed the atrium doors in her face and ran.

"I locked myself in my room and cried for hours until exhaustion pulled me under. When I woke, the sun was setting, and there was an awful feeling in the pit of my belly, then I realized why. I'd slammed the door. The door that tended to stick." A lump formed in my throat, and I swallowed past it to continue. "I ran back as fast as I could. The door was still shut. I couldn't get it open. I cried out her name but got no answer, so I rounded the building, peering through the glass into the moonlit interior and...I saw her." The image flared in my mind now, as vivid as the day I'd seen it. "She was crouched on the ground, her arms up over her head. As if she'd been trying to protect herself...to shield herself. She was charred and blackened." I choked on a sob. "She was...dead."

"Her turning happened..."

I nodded, blinking back the heat gathering behind my eyes. "It happened while she was trapped beneath the sun, with no way to escape. I left her there to die. She burned to a crisp." I squeezed my eyes shut, dislodging tears. "I killed her."

"It was an accident," Drayven said—the same words everyone had repeated to me over and over in the hope that I'd believe them, and even though I knew it to be true, it didn't change the horror of the consequences.

I wiped my face. Crying wouldn't solve anything. "My father claimed the same thing when the Inquisitors came for me. They saw I was a minor and set a date for a blood trial, but two nights before the trial, hooded men came to our home. They came for me. Damascus's men. But my father begged them to take him instead. *His* blood instead of mine." I didn't want to relive this. Didn't want to see it in my mind, so I spoke fast, spilling words just to get it over with. "They dragged him into the street where a carriage waited. A man climbed out. Hooded and masked. He demanded to know where I was, and my father replied with, '*Her blood is mine, and mine is hers.*' The hooded figure drew his sword and said, '*Then I, Sterling Damascus, claim the debt,*' and cut off my father's head."

Silence stretched for several beats before Drayven spoke. "They bypassed a trial. A trial where the incident would have either been ruled an accident or a debt suitable for a minor would have been applied."

I squeezed my eyes closed. "I will never forgive myself for what happened to Annabeth. But I swear, it wasn't deliberate. I didn't want her dead. I just... I needed to get away from her. From her words and the pain that they caused. But because of that, because I'd been too weak to withstand them, she died in unimaginable agony, and my father was forced to give his life to protect me. But Sterling had no right to take it." Rage simmered in my chest. "He broke the law and suffered *no* consequences."

"It was your head he wanted," Drayven said. "But your father invoked the right of proxy. He had no choice but to accept because you were a minor."

"Are you defending him?"

"Of course not." He looked genuinely offended. "The fact he was there in the first place broke all the rules. He should have realized your family would protect you. In fact..." He trailed off, realization coloring his features.

"He knew what would happen. He didn't care—as long as he got blood vengeance, something he knew wouldn't happen if the case went to trial." He'd come to the same conclusion that I had over the years.

"And now you're here. No longer a child. Ana...you must stay away from him."

"He can't kill me, and as much as I want to kill him for what he did, I can't." An emotion I couldn't quite read sparked in his eyes. "My mother signed a blood contract. No retribution on either side. When he had me by the throat, I genuinely questioned whether he would break that oath, but...I think he simply wanted to frighten me." I drew a shuddering breath. "I have all these emotions and all this rage... Trust me, the only time I'll be spending around him will be mandated. Anna's death was an accident, something I will never forgive myself for. But what Sterling did to my father was straight-up murder, and for that... For that, he will one day pay."

We sat in companionable silence, something I hadn't done with anyone since...well, ever. Yet, I'd done it with the Unwoven and was now doing it with Drayven.

There was something undeniably and inexplicably soothing about sharing space this way.

But all good things had an end.

"Let me walk you back to Bramble Tower," he said.

"I'm sure you have better things to do than babysit me."

"I have things to do. Yes. But *better* things?" He leaned forward slightly, forearms braced on his thighs as his thoughtful gaze met mine. "No."

I chuckled. "I appreciate your help and...just you being here." Telling the story out loud had been cathartic. "So do you always take an interest in new arrivals, or do you have a thing for pariahs?"

His expression grew serious. "I don't think you're a pariah, Ana. In fact, I find you fascinating. You're here because you want to be. You're here because you survived out there." His gaze drifted over my head. "Nightsbridge is filled with Horrors for us, but you've been surrounded by horrors all your life. Horrors that wear human faces. I admire you, and I don't admire many people."

Heat bloomed in my cheeks and I ducked my head, not wanting him to see how his words affected me. Kind words were something only my mother had ever offered me, and with her gone, I'd given up hope of ever being on the receiving end of them again.

"Thank you." I took a beat to compose myself before lifting my gaze to his once more.

A soft breeze blew my hair forward, stray tendrils sweeping across my face. He gently brushed them aside, tucking them behind my ear. The contact sent a shiver down my neck, and his fingers lingered, warm and reassuring. I couldn't help but lean into his touch.

"Being the last of your bloodline doesn't mean you have to be alone," he said.

If only that were true. "Being alone is safe."

"Being alone is...lonely."

Was he counseling me or himself? "I like my own company."

He cracked a smile that made my insides gooey. "I like your company, too."

What was he doing to me? "Stop it."

A teasing smile lifted his lips. "What?"

"Saying all the nice things."

"I don't do it often, Ana, so take it while you can. If you make it onto my hunt team, you'll be treated just like everyone else." His fingers grazed my cheek before falling away. "But there is something else I wanted to talk to you about. It's why I came to find you at the training grounds in the first place."

"Oh?"

"Jay told me what happened with Tamina."

This again. "If you're going to try to talk me into breaking the deal, don't bother. Vitra already tried."

"He did?" Drayven frowned. "Did he tell you that two students have died trying to best her?"

He had not. "I can handle a little pain." I pointed to my throat, which, now that I focused on it, felt less constricted.

"What Tamina has to offer is more than pain. She'll get inside your head, find your worst fears, and use them against you."

"I'm not afraid of anything."

"Everyone fears something, even if they don't know what it is...yet. You don't have to prove anything to anyone by challenging her. There is still time to—"

"I'm not trying to *prove* anything. I want to help Ruspin." I lifted my chin and held his gaze, letting him know there was no budging on this.

Finally, he sighed. "Okay, okay. I'll drop the subject. Now, if you're sure you don't want me to walk you back, I have students to yell at."

"I'm sure."

He stood slowly, and a sudden sense of abandonment gripped me. "Will you be there tonight...on Coral Isle?"

"It's not my scene," he said. "But best of luck."

He left, taking his pleasant pine scent with him, and I ventured deeper into the gardens, hoping that the tranquil atmosphere would somehow soothe the tumultuousness inside me. Reliving my past, speaking it, had drained me, but nature was the perfect fuel to recharge. Not even the crisp bite in the air could deter the tiny purple blooms from flowering in the hedgerows. If only I were as resilient as nature.

I strolled down wide cobbled paths, past several benches and a lamppost hung with an old-fashioned lantern that would need a long match to light the thick candle tucked inside. Did someone come through here to light it?

I took a left at the next intersection and entered a gorgeous, wooded area that sported arches woven with ivy. Delicate stone figurines lined the path to a magnificent fountain with two winged horses rearing up nose to nose as the centerpiece. It was dry and dappled with moss but still a beautiful sight.

I parked my ass on the wooden bench closest to it and closed my eyes, breathing in the evergreen aroma of my surroundings. Long seconds passed, and I was beginning to relax, when my scalp prickled with the unmistakable sensation of being watched.

I snapped my eyes open to find the blond, spectacled guy from earlier sitting on the other end of my bench.

"How is Dori?" he asked bluntly.

O-kay... "You know it's customary to begin a conversation with an actual introduction, right?"

He smiled. "I suppose it is. Hello, I'm Timothy."

"Anamaya."

"How is Dori?"

Bloody hell. "You could ask her yourself."

"I could never bring myself to speak to her." He hugged his

book to his chest bashfully. "Well, except one time, but I ended up stuttering and ran away." He winced.

Aw, Dori had a secret admirer. "You've got it bad."

"Yes, I suppose I do."

"What are you afraid of? Just talk to her. The worst she can do is say she isn't interested."

He forced a smile, his gaze flicking over my shoulder. "But then hope would be gone." His brows knit into a frown. "I have to go."

"What are you looking at?" I followed his gaze, but there was no one there, and when I turned back to him, the bench was empty. I caught a glimpse of him down the path just before he rounded the corner.

Damn, he was fast. But he'd left his book. I grabbed it and ran after him, but by the time I got to the intersection, there was no sight of him.

A quick flip through revealed some kind of student roster. There were several image prints of students on each page, with their names printed beneath in neat script. The prints were sharp, the black and white images clear, not like the grainy image prints I was used to. They must have been taken by one of the more expensive Image Scribes. There was a magitech version in circulation right now called the Image Weaver. Did they have one of those here?

I shook off my thoughts and stood, tucking the book under my arm. I'd have to return it to Timothy. Maybe I'd see him at supper.

I retraced my steps out of the garden. I had work to do, like the reading for Mistress Selethis's class.

Maybe there was something in one of the textbooks about the library Dharma had mentioned in her journal.

Ugh. I'd forgotten how much I hated studying. Thank Trinity I had the challenge with Tamina to break up the evening's monotony. I was due a decent adrenaline spike.

Coral Isle couldn't come soon enough.

> One must ask: Why would the sea aid the land?
> After decades of humans using their waters as a waste
> ground, why come to our aid now? What has the Imperium
> Alius offered them?
>
> *Custodes Hominum Address, 145 A.O.*

CHAPTER 22

Despite my best intentions to research the library, I got caught up sketching in my cryptozoology journal. The dragon had been the most challenging one to get right. I was almost out of pages. I'd need to procure a new journal soon. I fell asleep while doing the required reading for Selethis, missed supper, and woke to Dori banging on my door—it was time to head to Coral Isle.

The sea between us and the island was like a smooth sheet of glass, gleaming with moonlight and the twinkle of stars. The line that waited for one of the two boats to ferry us across buzzed with excitement.

Frost crackled beneath my boots, and the air misted with each breath I took. It was freezing this close to the sea, despite there being no gusty wind.

I'd borrowed a large, fleece-lined coat from Benedict. It fell to mid-thigh, keeping the top half of my body nice and warm. But the chill still found my legs, creeping through the material of my trousers to kiss my skin. I tugged the knitted hat down over my ears—a bright pink loaner from Dori. Something I couldn't see her ever actually wearing.

She'd opted for a black knitted slouch cap and a fitted leather jacket, while Clary, wrapped in a wool coat and gloves, stamped her feet to stay warm. "It's a lot busier than usual."

"News of your match with Tamina has got around," Dori said.

"It's going to be a crush." Benedict frowned. "You should change your mind," he added wearily—we'd had this conversation several times on the way to the dock already.

I gave him a warning glance, answer enough, and he shook his head.

He'd tried to use my hand as an excuse to get me to back down. After all, how could I punch with a fractured hand? But I'd told him I had a mean left hook. Perks of being ambidextrous. Truth was, my hand felt fine. The bandage was just for show.

"The Hamlin was nothing compared to what Tamina can do," Dori said. "I'm with Benedict. I think you should reconsider and—"

"Guys, please. This is *my* choice."

"Well, in that case, it's lucky I brought you a change of clothes." Clary patted her bag.

"Change of clothes? For the blood?"

"No," Dori said. "For when you piss and shit yourself."

"Wow, thanks for the vote of confidence."

She winced. "No, I mean, it's happened before, so best to be prepared."

Doubt prickled my skin, but I shook it off. I could do this. I'd be fine. No fear. No pain. It would be a breeze.

With my curse letting up where pleasure was concerned, I'd been a little worried that the pain aspect might also be affected, but my throat hadn't hurt after Sterling's attack, and a few stabs with a needle earlier this evening double confirmed that the curse was still fully active where pain was concerned.

I spotted Tyler ahead with a few younger students from Combat 101. He met my gaze and dragged a finger across his throat.

"What is your problem, Tyler?" Benedict demanded.

Tyler ignored him, his gaze never leaving mine. "I hope Tamina makes your brain bleed, bitch." He shoved his way toward the front of the line despite several protests.

He must know what had happened to his older sister, but the Damascuses were prohibited from speaking of my involvement. My father's sacrifice had seen to that. Legally, the case was closed, and the culprit had been punished.

I *could* speak of it, though, if I wanted to. Although I'd told Drayven the truth, I didn't want to tell the Unwoven. Not yet, and maybe never.

We shuffled forward a couple of steps, and as if my thoughts had provoked it, Dori asked, "Is there something you're not telling us? About you and Sterling? It's just, the way he acted with you today...it felt a little too...personal."

"There's a lot I'm not telling you. We're just not there yet." They'd just have to speculate for now.

She nodded. "I can respect your candor. You'll tell us someday, right?"

I looked her in the eye and lied. "Of course."

Telling Drayven had felt natural. Maybe because he knew the kind of person Sterling was and had his own history with the Phage. But I wasn't sure if I'd ever feel comfortable telling the Unwoven.

The boat that had just arrived filled up, and we'd reached the end of the dock, now first in line for the next ride, as the current boat pushed off back to sea, taking Tyler with it.

"The other boat is almost back," Clary said.

"And there's still a line behind us," Dori muttered. "Entertainment is slim in Nightsbridge."

Entertainment. She meant me. At least for tonight.

That was fine. They wanted a show, I'd make sure they got one, while humiliating Tamina in the process.

It would be a win-win.

I hoped.

―✦―

Coral Isle earned its name from the coral reef that surrounded the whole isle. It was a place for the land folk and seafolk to mingle. The tower here, once belonging to the Blackthornes, now served as a base for the Ocean Guard. But the main attraction was a place called the Devil Fish.

The Unwoven had filled me in on the details, and mentally replaying them on the boat ride helped me ignore the whispers and pointed looks from other passengers.

Thankfully, the boat had an engine, so it didn't take long to reach the floating dock connected to the isle.

The sea on either side glowed pink and purple from the algae growing on the coral beneath the waves. I'd never seen anything so ethereal and beautiful, but the stunning sight did nothing to stem the tremor of anxiety building in my belly. Now that we were here, the enormity of what I was about to do hit me. I wasn't worried about going up against Tamina. I was confident in combat, and I didn't fear getting hurt. The factor that put me on edge was the thought of fighting for an audience. Being the center of attention wasn't something I enjoyed.

Benedict offered me a hand to help me disembark, his gaze probing.

"You okay?" he asked.

"Fine. Just want to get this over with."

He nodded. "Okay, we'll forgo the tour and get you straight to the Devil Fish."

The dock bobbed beneath our steps as we made our way across and onto the beach. We climbed a flight of steps that took us to a winding path that led to the center of the island.

Posts strung with flickering lanterns bordered a lively market square, dotted with stalls selling everything from shells and trinkets to gorgeously woven silk fabrics. Students milled about, browsing and chatting with vendors who had brightly colored hair spanning every color of the rainbow, hues shifting and shimmering in the lantern light. Their large, dark eyes and pale, poreless skin gave them an otherworldly air.

"Sea silk," Clary said, noticing me eyeing a turquoise scarf. "It's super resilient, and the dyes come from tiny flowers that bloom among the coral. I think they're called poppysalts."

The smell of smoked fish and barbecue drifted on the breeze, reminding me I'd missed supper, and my stomach growled in response.

"We can get a bite to eat if you want," Clary said.

I didn't think I'd be able to stomach anything until after the event. "Later, for sure."

We slipped past a group of giggling girls to a spot where the path opened, revealing the tower in the distance beyond the trees.

"That's the Devil Fish." Benedict pointed at a large brick building down the road.

We passed a couple more stalls, one selling jewelry made from coral and bone, another offering bowls of hot, aromatic soup, and one lined with leather-bound books with gilded script.

Clary let out a squeak and hurried over.

"We'll have to give her a minute," Benedict said with an indulgent smile. "Clary loves to read. Have you been in her room yet?"

I shook my head, curiosity piqued.

"Books from floor to ceiling against every wall. We had a clear-out a few months ago, but she already restocked."

"You can order stuff in from outside Nightsbridge?"

"Yep, once you've passed your grading, you'll get permission to place orders through the Border House."

Good to know. We headed after Clary and Dori.

Click. Clack. Click. Clack.

A woman sat in a rocking chair, knitting outside a shack on the opposite side of the road.

Click. Clack. Click. Clack.

She had no wares to sell, no stall; she was simply rocking and knitting.

Click, clack, click, clack.

"Well, hello there." She set her knitting on her lap. "It's a beautiful night, isn't it?"

Wait, when had I walked over here?

"It's all right," she said. "I won't keep you long. I was curious." She tipped her head to the side and ran her sharp gaze over me.

Her silver hair was neatly brushed and tied in a bun high on her head. Her face was smooth and youthful, but her eyes held the weight of ages.

My skin prickled and bloomed with goose bumps and the instinctual awareness that I was in the presence of something *other*. "Who are you?"

"An interested party. Maybe even a friend—depending on your actions."

"My actions?" I wasn't a fan of cryptic conversations.

"Yes, Anamaya. You have some important choices to make."

"You didn't answer my question. Who are you?"

"Someone who understands how lost you are."

Her intimate tone grated on me. "I'm not lost. I know exactly where I'm going."

"Do you?"

A cold finger of foreboding slid down my spine. "If you have something to tell me, then do it plainly. I don't have time for riddles."

"You're right. You don't. So I will speak as plainly as I am able. There is a storm on the horizon, and to weather it, you'll need to build a strong vessel of souls that touch you. You must find an anchor and a reliable compass, and you must ensure you surround yourself with wisdom and strength so that you can face the truth and turn the tide."

"The truth?" Was she talking about the book of truth?

"Ana? Ana!"

"What?" I looked over my shoulder at the Unwoven standing

a few feet away.

"What are you doing?" Clary asked.

"Talking. What does it look like?"

"Talking to who?" Benedict asked, frowning at the empty space behind me

"Talking to—" I turned back to the woman and found a run-down abandoned stall.

The woman and the shack were gone.

It is the nature of the Therianthrope to hunt the Haematophage. An instinct that dates back to the origins of their species. Two sides of a coin, spawned by gods at war to act as champions, they were created to annihilate each other. The gods are long gone, but the primal instinct to destroy remains...

The Evolution of the Supernal

CHAPTER 23

The Devil Fish stood two stories high, but the lower story had no windows, just a set of double doors open for admission. Several students lingered outside, plumes of purple smoke curling from their lips. The sweet, distinct aroma of pularia teased my nose. The herb was a mild aphrodisiac, mimicking the buzz that came from connecting with the Weave. It was safe in its natural form, but some bright spark had found a way to amplify its effects to create a substance called Pulse—a recreational drug for most supernals, but highly addictive to the Arcanus.

The group spotted me, nudged each other, then quickly headed inside. I was already on edge from the creepy encounter with the vanishing woman and her shack—something that the Unwoven couldn't explain. Now my stomach fluttered, reminding me that bravado didn't always lead to success.

"You okay?" Clary asked.

"If anyone asks me that again, I'm going to scream."

She held up her hands. "Noted."

I led the way into the building, shoulders pushed back to inject confidence into my stride, despite the knots forming in my stomach. The inside of the building was open-plan, with two floors separated by a wide balcony area. Ambient music filled the chamber and stark bulb lighting lit up the space, hung from the beams that crisscrossed overhead. There was a bar to our left, barely visible due to the crush of people surrounding it, and plenty of mismatched seating currently occupied by students.

"Let's grab drinks," Dori said, already headed toward the bar.

Our group followed but I faltered, my attention drawn to the sound of deep rumbling laughter across the room. The raucous sound came from a large, blue-haired male sprawled in an armchair, head tipped back as he let out another belly-rumbling laugh. His chest was bare and covered in ink, bronze skin gleaming as if dusted with gold. Several women stood around him, clutching their drinks and smiling coquettishly.

He dropped his chin, and our eyes locked across the room. His laughter stopped abruptly, and in the next moment, he was out of his seat, ambling toward me, leaving the simpering females behind.

O-kay...

He tilted his head, his smile returning as he came to stand in front of me. He was tall with a swimmer's build and carried the scent of the ocean.

"You look so much like her, it's uncanny," he said.

"I'm sorry?"

"Dharma. You have her eyes. You must be Anamaya Onyx."

He'd known my great-great-grandaunt? "I'm at a bit of a disadvantage, because I have no idea who *you* are."

"My name is Arnav. I heard you were fighting tonight. I came to watch."

"You're not the only one." I indicated the packed room. "But you didn't really answer my question."

He frowned slightly. "You weren't told of the Onyx connection to the seafolk?"

Dammit, I should have done my reading. Wait...seafolk? "You'll have to enlighten me."

He sighed, a flash of annoyance coloring his features. "Well, I can't say I'm surprised. The Coterie probably think it's redundant information."

I had no idea what he meant. "You're going to have to spell it out for me, Arnav."

He blinked sharply. "You have her blunt tongue too, I see." His gaze dropped to my mouth, lingering for a moment before flicking back up to meet my gaze. "Dharma and I were betrothed."

"Ana, we should go." Dori appeared beside me, tugging on my arm.

"Wait a second, I—"

"Now!" Dori dragged me back a step.

"Go," Arnav said, his gaze lingering. "We'll talk later."

He melted into the crowd, leaving me seething with questions—and more than a little annoyance with Dori.

I pulled my arm free. "What was that for?"

"He's dangerous."

"He was also once engaged to Dharma Onyx." He'd known her. Actually fucking known her. He might have vital information about what happened to her. Information that he might not even realize was important.

Dori's brows shot up. "Really?"

"Who's engaged to who?" Benedict asked, joining us.

"Arnav said he was engaged to Dharma Onyx," Dori said.

"The Land-Sea Pact..." Clary covered her mouth. "Oh... wow..."

I threw up my hands. "Will someone *please* tell me what that is?"

"You should read up on it," Clary said. "But in short, part of the agreement states that the land folk provide men and women to the seafolk for procreation."

"And how does that work?"

Benedict made a circle with his index finger and thumb of his left hand and poked his right index finger through it.

I rolled my eyes. "I mean, land and sea don't mix."

"There are ways," Dori replied.

"And Dharma was meant to procreate...with him?"

"It sounds like it, but it obviously never happened, and from the way Arnav was looking at you just now, I get the impression he wants a redo. With you."

Whoa. "Not happening."

"Arnav is a bit of a manwhore," Benedict explained. "He can get anyone he wants, and he takes advantage of the fact."

"*You* could get anyone you wanted too," Clary said.

Benedict snorted. "I have no interest in the stuck-up Arcanus females that go here."

Twin spots of color bloomed high on Clary's cheeks.

Was he really that clueless? "Clary and Dori aren't stuck-up."

"Dark skies, of course they're not. But they're like my sisters." He put an arm around each of them and hugged them to his sides. "I love these gals."

The devastation that washed over Clary's face was so obvious to me. How did *he* not see it?

"Just...steer clear," Dori warned. "Royal seafolk tend to be single-minded when they want something or...someone. But all you'll get is a broken heart."

Royal, eh? "Yeah, well, I'm no pushover, and when I say I'm not interested, I'm pretty single-minded about it too. If that's what you meant by dangerous, then trust me, I'm good."

Dori didn't look too convinced, but then, she didn't know me that well. No one did. I wasn't one to wear my heart on my sleeve, had never been in love, and had no plans to start now.

"Come on, this way." Dori wove through the masses, forging a path for us.

We went past the bar which was still heaving with people. The clink of glasses and the rise and fall of conversation melded to create a buzz in the air.

I could have done with a shot of something strong. "I guess we're not getting drinks then."

"It's too busy," Benedict said.

"I guess I'll grab a victory drink later."

I spotted several people with bright hair—pink, green, purple—but no blue. "Hey, is there a significance to the hair color? I assume they're all seafolk right?"

"Not sure about all the colors," Dori called over her shoulder, "but blue is the color of royal seafolk. This part of the sea is Arnav's domain. The Ocean Guard answers to him. They have done so for decades."

We passed shadowy booths draped in fabric, and the sounds coming from within made it obvious what was going on inside.

I was no prude but, seriously? "Can't they do that in their towers?"

"It's not what you think," Dori said.

I arched a brow. "They're *not* having sex?"

"The ones in the booth are because the feeding has escalated, but look over there." She gestured toward a candle-lit, incense-heavy area beyond the booths, where a woman knelt between a man's thighs, her mouth latched onto his wrist as she fed.

The man watched her with a small, satisfied smile, stroking her hair with his free hand.

This was nothing new. "A dhampir feeding on a human? So?"

"Nope," Dori said. "That is a *human* feeding on a dhampir."

"What the fuck?"

"Little-known fact," Benedict said. "Vampire blood is intoxicating to humans and can, in some cases, give them temporary supernal abilities. *Dhampir* blood has a similar effect—except dhampir blood is *addictive* to humans. So, some dhampirs use that to coerce humans into becoming free veins and playthings, since the addicted human will do anything for a fix."

"They call them blood whores," Dori said, her tone flat.

I knew about veins—humans employed by pureblood vampire houses to act as walking blood bags. They were kept in the lap of luxury and well taken care of, but they were still food. Expensive food. I guess trapping someone in addiction was the cheaper way to get what you wanted.

It was sick and twisted. It took everything I had to stop myself from marching across the room and wiping that shit-eating grin off that smarmy fucker's face. But I'd learned to pick my battles, and this was *not* one of them.

I gritted my teeth, turning away from the scene. "You guys actually enjoy coming here?"

"It's the only place we can go to let off steam," Dori said. "It's not all bad. The market is cool, and Cockle's Shack does the best seafood chowder. We'll go next time."

Static crackled, and the room fell silent as a voice blared across the building. "First fight of the night, people. Tyler Damascus versus Corrine Moon for control of two House Moon veins."

The arena loomed ahead, the wire mesh walls reaching for the ceiling, but that was all I could see beyond the gathered crowd.

"Come on," Benedict said. "Let's get up on the balcony."

We wove through the throng and up the stairs, which were already packed. It seemed everyone had the same idea to get to higher ground and a better view.

The seafolk stood out among the land folk with their vibrant hair, and it was easy to find Arnav among them. He stood a head above most everyone else.

He must have sensed me watching, because he glanced up the stairs and found me easily. His smile held emotions that seemed tied to memories of Dharma, not me.

"Excuse me. Out of the way." Benedict nudged and elbowed a path through for us.

No one gave me a second glance now. All attention was on the arena below.

We squeezed through to the barrier just as two figures entered the arena from opposite ends.

Tyler bounced on his feet, his silver buzzcut gleaming under the harsh overhead lights above the fighting ring. He'd stripped off his jacket and wore only a black undershirt and fitted black trousers. His feet were bare.

The woman across from him wore a ruby-red high-necked

blouse and black trousers. Her feet were also bare.

"Why aren't they wearing shoes?"

"You'll see," Benedict said, his eyes alight with excitement. "Thrope fights are all fur and fang. Vicious, of course, but Haematophage fights are brutal and terrifying because each party looks human, and yet...they're not."

Dori interjected. "What Benedict is—not so eloquently—trying to say is that Haematophage have a beast too; it just looks a lot like us."

"Two minutes," the voice on the intercoms bellowed. "Start the timer, hit the bell."

The bell rang, and Tyler threw back his head and roared. His eyes bled to black, and his mouth stretched wide, fangs lengthening as more teeth sprouted from his gums. Across from him, the female sith screamed, arching her back as her face morphed, jaw dropping and elongating. Her fingers grew long and tapered, tipped with black talons. Dark blue scales erupted across her shoulders, snaking down her arms, and the whites of her eyes turned red to match her blouse.

Their feet changed, growing long and wide. They used those mutated feet to launch into the air a moment later, pouncing at each other.

They clashed with bloodthirsty snarls, clawing and tearing at each other like rabid beasts. A mist of blood rose to surround them, swirling as if alive. It momentarily obscured our view, hiding them from sight. All we heard were the awful sounds of tearing flesh and the gurgle of a wet scream.

A few seconds later, Corrine shot out of the mist, hitting the mesh with a clang that shook the arena before dropping to the ground like a stone.

She lay on her back, eyes glassy and unseeing, skin as white as a sheet, cheeks sunken, lips pulled back from her teeth. She looked...dead.

Tyler landed on the ground a few feet away, taking half the mist with him. But it no longer hid him; it hovered over him like a red cloud. The other half drifted over to Corrine, pulsing erratically like an unsteady heartbeat.

Was she dead? She certainly looked dead. Not a twitch or a blink. No rise and fall of her chest. "Is she dead?"

"Fel, no," Dori said. "Sith are hardier than that."

"Not as hardy as dhampir," Clary said. "Dhampir are near impossible to kill—that's why the vampire houses keep producing them. Wait for it..."

Corrine's hand twitched, her arm rising as if reaching for the mist. It whooshed toward her, but Tyler struck first. He grabbed her by the throat, yanking her away and slamming her into the mesh. The crack and snap of bone filled the sudden silence. Corrine let out a high-pitched squeal, her body morphing back into its perfect, beautiful human form. Her skin began to glow silver, ethereal and breathtaking. My insides twisted with longing, and I gripped the rail harder, leaning over it, desperate to get to her.

"Careful!" Benedict's hand shot to my waist. "Don't look directly at her."

Tyler growled, shaking his head as the tension bled from his body.

"You don't want to hurt me," Corrine crooned, her voice like honey—warm, rich, and sweet. "Let me go." There was no tone of command in her words, only compulsion. It beat against my senses, the pin-drop silence confirming everyone else felt it too.

"Release me, Tyler," she crooned. "You want to let me go."

Tyler's shoulders heaved as he fought the compulsion. For a moment, I thought she had him—that he was going to back down. But then he slammed her against the mesh once more.

"Fuck you, Corrine!" He sank his teeth into her throat, ravaging and growling as her gurgling scream filled the room.

What the fuck? He was killing her!

The bell rang shrilly, ending the match.

Tyler dropped Corrine like a bag of trash and walked away, his body morphing back to his human form.

Corrine lay in an unmoving heap, her throat a masticated

maw, eyes glassy and unseeing.

"He killed her..." I turned to Benedict. "He fucking killed her."

"No, he didn't," Benedict said. "Look."

The mist sank into Corrine's skin, covering her completely. The wound in her neck began to knit, and life flickered in her eyes. She sucked in a ragged breath, then another, as the mist finally dissipated, leaving her healed and whole.

She sat up slowly, fixing Tyler with a murderous glare. "You're a bastard, Damascus!"

He spat blood. Her blood. Then wiped his mouth. "And you're a cunt. What of it?"

"You can't have them."

"You lost, so they belong to me. Have them delivered at sunset tomorrow." He strode to the exit but paused, looking up at me. His razor-sharp smile—so much like his brother's—made my soul quake. *You're next,* he mouthed. Then he ducked through the door and was gone.

"Next match," the arena master announced, "Tamina Vayne and Anamaya Onyx."

Voices and faces blurred as I descended into the arena. Students and seafolk parted, clearing a path for me. Jay and Brek stood on the opposite side of the cage, flanked by a couple of other bulky guys. More Thropes, no doubt. And standing on the other side of the arena was my opposition, the Phage of the hour, Tamina.

She'd dressed in tight red trousers and a red silk bodice. An ensemble that brought out the murder in her eyes and left nothing to the imagination.

She carried no weapons aside from her cherry-red nails, which were sharpened to points.

Maybe I was about to get clawed.

I could handle that.

But she was sith like Corrine. Could she use her glow and words to control me? Would she make me inflict damage on myself? I needed to be prepared to look away from her aura and resist. Drayven's warning came to mind about her ability to get into someone's head. Could she do that even if I wasn't looking at her? My skin prickled in awareness, everyone was watching me. If I failed, if I fell under Tamina's control, then my defeat and shame would be on full display. Had I taken on more than I could handle?

Ruspin sat behind the mesh, collar biting into his throat, warm brown eyes filled with shadows. Fresh welts decorated his flank. It was a message for me, and a panacea to my doubts. If I fell, I fucking fell, but like Tarrifel would I walk away without trying to save him.

Tamina followed my gaze and smiled. "You like it? I made a pretty pattern," she singsonged. "I plan to make more once we're done here. If you're still conscious, you're welcome to watch."

This bitch was going down. It'd been a while since my last fist fight—I was itching to break a nose, maybe dislocate a jaw. I flexed my fingers, registering the slight stiffness in my right hand. Fuck it, busting it again would be worth it to smash her nose in.

"Three minutes," the arena master said. "Let's bring the pain."

The crowd roared. Tamina raised her arms, urging them to cheer louder.

I looked up at the Unwoven. Clary gave me a thumbs up, Benedict dropped me a nod of encouragement, and Dori shouted, "Fuck her up, Onyx!"

"Boo!" the crowd yelled.

"Onyx bitch!" Someone shouted.

Great, Tamina went around beating her pet Thrope, yet I'm the villain? Twisted.

The crowd to the left of our cage parted, and Arnav stepped through. He crossed his arms, surveying the arena before locking his sharp emerald gaze on me. A small group of females surrounded him, preening even though he didn't spare them a glance.

Boy, did I feel special.

The bell rang, shrill and damning. Before I could act, pressure coiled around my shoulder, and an invisible force yanked hard at my arm.

My shoulder dislocated with a sharp pop.

"Fuck!" I clutched at my arm now dangling useless at my side, and Tamina grinned from ear to ear, her eyes alight with triumph.

"Is that all you've got?" I popped it back in, and her smug smile died. "My turn."

I closed the distance, fist connecting with her face, producing a satisfying crunch and gorgeous blood spray. She staggered back with a grunt, both hands covering her nose. I punched her in the head before she could recover.

She hit the ground, her shoulders shaking. Wait, was she... laughing?

Fuck, she was.

Her shoulders quaked with mirth, her laughter rising, annoyingly melodious as it echoed around us. She wiped at her bloody face and looked up at me with a perfectly healed nose.

What the fuck? How was I going to hurt her if she healed this fast? I shook off the doubt. I could do this. I'd hit harder, faster, not give her time to recover.

I threw another punch, but an invisible force grabbed my fist.

Tamina rose slowly, wiping her sleeve across her mouth to catch the last of the blood. "I let you have those two blows for free, Onyx. But now, it's time for you to kneel."

Pressure gripped my leg above the knee.

Crunch.

I buckled, hitting the ground, my palms scraping the stone floor.

Shit, she'd taken out my knee. I fake screamed a beat too late, mind whirring as to how I was going to kick her ass if I couldn't use my leg.

Tamina leaned down, her eyes glittering with realization. "You don't feel it, do you?" Shit. "*That's* your curse. No pain." She threw back her head and laughed. "Oh, this is perfect. I see now. I see why you agreed to this. How long has it been?"

"Fuck you."

"Do you miss it? Did you ever have it? Do you want to know what it feels like? Pain isn't just housed in our bodies, sweetie..." She tapped her temple with a cherry-red nail. "It's also housed in our minds. Let me show you." Her eyes narrowed as she focused on me and a band of pressure circled my head, blurring my vision. "This is what a dislocated arm feels like."

Fire burst across my shoulder, sinking claws into my skin so suddenly that my scream was nothing but a strangled gasp. "And your knee." Needles sank into my knee and my ears buzzed. "A broken wrist."

Ice-cold spread across my wrist before blazing with a fire that had my ears ringing and the edges of my vision darkening. This time, the scream that tore free from my throat was all too real. Shrill and awful. I couldn't breathe. Couldn't see. I was blinded by agony and crippled by pain. Pain hit in sharp, unforgiving waves—shoulder, knee, wrist—before finally sinking its claws into my abdomen.

I curled in on myself, body trembling, eyes rolling, and that's when I saw him...Drayven.

He crouched by the mesh, eyes on me, watching my pain with unblinking focus. Jay and Brek flanked him, along with the others.

The Thropes...

Agony tore through me in fresh waves, raw sobs clawing up my throat. But I kept my gaze locked with his, watching him through hot tears. He'd come for me. To bear witness to my pain, like they'd done for Ruspin.

Like they did in solidarity for all Thropes. But tonight... Tonight, they were here for me.

There was strength in that. Strength and beauty, just as there was in the pain, because for the first time in a long time, I wasn't numb.

I was a fountain of sensation. Rippling with it. Fire and ice, needles and blades, stabbing, burning, and pricking. I screamed again and again, venting until my cries morphed into laughter—because this wasn't real. This was temporary. This was her doing. And praise the Trinity—it was glorious, because pain was part of living.

And I finally felt alive.

I hauled myself to my feet, limping to favor my busted knee, riding the echo of pain she had given me,

"No..." Tamina said. "What is wrong with you?"

I laughed through tears, past the tightness in my throat. "You can't break me. I'm already broken, bitch."

The bell rang, and Tamina's hold on me snapped. Her eyes rounded in shock. "No..." She shook her head. "You can't... This can't be happening."

"But it is!" Drayven shouted over the clamoring crowd. "Ana won."

The silence was loud as everyone absorbed this truth.

Tamina looked across at Ruspin, then back to me. "You can't have him! I won't let him go!"

A sudden heat tore a path across my chest.

Drayven bellowed, grabbing the mesh and shaking it, his horrified gaze on my torso.

I looked down at the bubbling crimson stain seeping through my top. What... The edges of the world went gray. A scream pierced the air. Metal clanged, and the world swayed and tipped.

I hit the ground on my side, trembling as shock overtook me.

"No!" Drayven's shadow fell over me, snarls and growls erupting behind him.

Another scream echoed, but all I saw was him—warm moss-green eyes, hot breath against my cheek, my neck. Warm... My chest was warm, even though the world was darkening.

"I've got you," Drayven said. "Out of the way!"

I was floating. It was...nice.

"Stay awake, Ana. Stay—"

Darkness swallowed me.

Every species has a mating instinct, but for some, the instinct is more than biological. It's metaphysical. It's ethereal...

The Evolution of the Supernal

CHAPTER 24

I surfaced to the rumble of male voices, cracking open my eyelids to Vitra and Drayven standing at the foot of my bed.

Was I still dreaming? Some kind of kinky sex dream that... Oh... Oh shit...Tamina! The bitch.

I tried to sit up, but there was a boulder on my chest. "Ugh... how long have I been out?"

"A couple of hours," Vitra said.

I swallowed to moisten my throat and looked down at my chest where a bandage peeked out from beneath the loose sleep shirt someone had changed me into. Hopefully Darla. "How bad is it?"

They both took a step closer, shrinking the space with their muscular frames.

"You'll be fine," Vitra said tightly. "Mr. Thorn stopped the bleeding." His eyes narrowed at the words. "Darla applied a poultice to speed up healing."

"I did indeed," Darla said from somewhere beyond the guys. "Now, if you'll move."

The males parted, and Darla bustled in carrying a tray. "You need to eat, dear. You lost a lot of blood. Not as much as you could have, thanks to Mr. Thorn's quick thinking." Her tone suggested she was less than pleased.

I *did* feel weak and fuzzy-headed. Classic blood loss symptoms. My arms were tingly, too. The wound must have been deep to bleed so profusely before Drayven stopped it. "How *did* you stop the bleeding?"

Drayven fixed his gaze on the window, twin spots of color appearing high on his cheeks. "I licked your wound."

"*Licked?*"

"Yes." A muscle ticked in his jaw.

"As in licked with your *tongue* kind of licked?"

"Is there another kind?" Vitra asked, nostrils flaring. "Your shirt, however, is ruined—Mr. Thorn was forced to tear it off you."

"To get to the wound," Drayven bit out. He finally looked at me, dark eyes pleading for understanding. "My saliva has a clotting agent and...Ana, I'm sorry I—"

I was so confused. "Why are you sorry? You saved me from bleeding out."

He clenched his jaw before speaking. "I did, but I also exposed you. I stripped off your brassiere."

Seriously? He was worried about that? "Okay, so everyone got an eyeful of my boobs. So what? I don't care. I have nice boobs." I paused and reached for the bandage on my chest. "I *still* have nice boobs, right?"

Darla snort-laughed, and Drayven's mouth twitched, but Vitra remained still and serious as stone.

"Mr. Thorn, tell her, or I will," he ground out the words.

A low growl rumbled from Drayven's chest. "Dammit, Vitra, there's no need."

"Yes. Yes, there is. She *must* be made aware. You acted without her consent."

"I did what I had to," Drayven said, shooting Vitra a sharp look. "You would have done the same."

"No, Mr. Thorn, I would not."

"You'd have let her bleed out?" Drayven challenged.

Vitra opened his mouth, then snapped it shut, leaving me fascinated by the muscle that feathered along his jaw. He was furious.

But why? Because I was alive? Or because Drayven had licked me? Did Vitra want to lick me and see my boobs? Heat pooled low in my belly at the thought of his tongue on my skin. Of his hands on my body.

Both males broke their eye-off and slowly turned to look at me, nostrils flaring slightly.

Fuck, could they smell my arousal?

I filled my mind with images of dead critters and glared back at them. "What?"

Drayven quickly looked away, but Vitra held my gaze, a challenge in his topaz eyes.

Darla sighed heavily. "If neither of you will explain the significance of what's happened to Miss Onyx, then I will."

Twin spots of color stained the tops of Drayven's cheekbones. "No. I can do it." He cleared his throat. "A barghest marks his chosen mate with the scent carried in his saliva. A *healing* saliva, only to be used on a potential or *actual* mate."

My fuzzy brain took a moment to comprehend, and when it did, indignant heat gripped my throat. "You *mate* marked me?"

"No," Drayven said at the same time Vitra said, "Yes."

For fuck's sake. "Which one is it?"

"I need to mark you three times to claim you. This once won't matter."

I relaxed against the pillows. "Okay, so we're good. As long as you don't lick me again." Gosh, that sentence sounded odd.

"Then maybe don't get yourself injured," Vitra snapped. "You could have been killed tonight. It was foolish and stubborn to agree to battle a Baobhan Sith, especially without access to the Weave."

"But I won." I grinned up at him. "I beat her and... Shit." My smile dropped. "Is Ruspin okay?"

"He's fine," Drayven said. "He's in the barracks with the Thropes. I'm sure he'll want to thank you as soon as he's able to shift into his human form again. What she did to him over the years..." He shook his head, lip curling. "He's lost his beast voice and is trapped in his beast form. For now."

"As noble as your intentions were, Miss Onyx, they were still rash," Vitra continued. "If you're to survive at Nightsbridge, you must be more discerning in the battles you choose to fight."

"I chose to fight to save Ruspin, and I'd do it again."

"Because you feel no pain." Vitra arched a brow. "Yes, I understand why you thought you could best Miss Vayne, but a lack of pain doesn't exempt you from death. In fact, it makes death more likely, because you lack the basic biological system that warns you just how hurt you are."

"I know that. I've lived with the curse most of my life."

"And yet you chose to ignore it." Vitra exhaled sharply, as if he were done with this conversation. As if I were a child, not worth the effort of debate. As if my words—and I—were pointless.

Anger sparked behind my eyes, my nails biting into my palms. "I know exactly how much damage my body can take, with or without pain. Tamina lashed out *after* the bell. She broke the rules to try and break me. I was fine until then because I know my body, so back the fuck off."

His tawny gaze brightened with anger before going dull and flat. A look that was clearly a dismissal. "Very well. I shall see you in class tomorrow. Bright and early."

"Wait a second," Darla said. "She needs to rest and—"

"Actions have consequences," he said coolly. "Miss Onyx's injuries aren't my problem." He turned away. "Nine a.m. sharp. Be present or accept a failing grade." He strode off, leaving me with a stunned Darla and a seething Drayven.

"Well," Darla said. "I've never seen him behave that way before."

"You mean he's not always an asshole?"

"He's never an asshole," Darla said, looking perturbed.

"You're not going," Drayven said to me. "You need to rest. The poultice needs time to work. And without pain, you won't know if the wound has reopened."

"I thought you sealed it."

"I helped it clot, but it could still break open. The poultice needs time to work. One failed class won't matter."

But it did to me. Failing a class meant having the return of my power delayed. "I'll be fine. I want to go."

He looked set to argue, but a rap on the door interrupted him, and Clary stuck her head into the room.

"Hey..." She slipped inside. "We were so worried. How are you feeling?"

"Like I have a boulder resting on my chest."

"I'll leave you to it." Drayven ducked out before I could thank or reassure him any further.

"Get some rest and eat the food," Darla said before following Drayven out.

The Unwoven scattered around my room.

"You look like shit," Dori said.

"Thanks."

"No pain, huh?" Benedict said.

"Not a twinge."

Silence fell for several beats before Clary broke it. "I mean, when Drayven climbed the mesh and leapt into the arena to save you..." She clasped her hands to her chest with a dreamy sigh. "That was something."

He'd scaled the barrier. Leapt in to save me from bleeding out because... Because he cared. He cared about me. I wasn't sure how to feel about that. Attraction and banter were one thing, but emotions complicated everything. Drayven was a good guy, the kind of guy I could catch feelings for, and the fact that his touch seemed to bypass my curse was a bonus, but I wasn't here for romance. I couldn't allow it to distract me from my goal.

"You'll need a new bra," Dori said, biting back a smirk.

"And Tamina will need new pants," Benedict said. "She

almost shit herself when the Thropes descended on her."

I flopped back against my pillows. "I wish I'd seen that."

"What I don't understand is why the Weave didn't help you this time," Benedict said. "It defended you before."

"Good point," Clary said.

It *was* a good point, but not one I wanted to expend energy on at present. "I have no idea. Maybe it's just unpredictable right now."

"Well," Clary said. "You need to eat and sleep." She helped me sit forward and fluffed the pillows behind me. "Pass the tray, Dori."

Dori set the tray on my lap, and the place inside me that had been dead and cold for the longest time flickered with the first ribbons of warmth. This...them, surrounding me, checking up on me. They cared too. Genuinely cared. Panic squeezed my lungs.

I breathed through it. It was fine. I was fine. This was a means to an end. Their being here meant I was doing my job. Finding allies to reach my goal. They'd serve a purpose, and once I had what I needed, I was out of here.

The panic slowly subsided.

"I'll collect your notes from classes tomorrow," Dori said.

"No. It's fine. I'm going to class." I explained Vitra's terms.

"Wow, that does not sound like him at all," Benedict said. "He's usually so even-tempered and controlled."

The calm, collected Vitra seemed to have evaporated, leaving a domineering stick-up-the-ass eager to punish me for something that wasn't my fault. But if he thought I'd concede, then he was strongly mistaken.

There are places between waking and dreaming where messengers reside. It is here that we can often find the truth...

The Hidden World by Alfred Regent

CHAPTER 25

Mum sets a bowl of Onyx hot pot in front of me. "There you go, luv, just the way you like it."

"Thanks, Mum, but you didn't have to."

She strokes my hair and presses a kiss to my temple. "I wanted to."

This is my favorite time of day, when the late afternoon sun paints the kitchen in warm hues of copper and gold, and the world feels like a safe place.

But Mother looks tired and drawn. The pretty yellow-and-pink scarf covering her sparse, patchy hair looks stark against her waxy, sallow skin.

I want to wrap her in cotton wool and keep her forever. My eyes grow hot, and I drop my gaze to the food.

"It smells delicious." I eat, swallowing past the crush of emotion in my throat. "Are you having some?"

"Maybe later."

She pulls out a chair and joins me at the dining table. "You'll be all right, you know, Maya. You won't have to worry about a thing."

The food turns to ash in my mouth. "I don't care about money, Mum. I don't want it. I'd give up everything if it meant I could keep you."

Her sigh is filled with the weight of the world. "There are many things we can control, but death is not one of them. I'm tired, sweetheart. I'm ready. I need you to be, too."

She wants me to tell her it's okay. She wants me to say the words that will release her, but I can't. I can't let her go. Not yet. Not—

A shadow falls across the room, blocking out the sunlight streaming in from the windows. "What's happening?" I look to Mother, but she's gone. "Mother? Mother, where are you?" This isn't how it goes. This isn't right.

A huge bird flies into the room, inky black wings snapping closed as it lands on the table. A rook. I've seen them in the park, but this one is larger, and its beady eyes are filled with intelligence.

A man's voice invades my mind. *"You have to see. You have to know."*

"What? No. This is my dream. Bring her back! Bring my mother ba—"

My house vanishes, and I'm in a forest clearing, standing outside a circle made of flowers and toadstools that gleam in the moonlight.

What is this place?

The rook lands in the circle and caws loudly at me, calling me to join it, but an insistent tug in my chest takes me back to my room.

I'm by the window, looking out into the night.

Who is that in my bed? I tiptoe closer, then rear back at the sight of myself. I'm in the bed, but I'm also...not.

"See. You have to see. Keep going."

The bedroom vanishes and I'm outside, standing by the pavilion, where an awful sense of dread overcomes me.

I don't want to be here.

I want to wake up. Now!

The pavilion disappears, and I'm in an aisle of books. A library? The plaque on the bookcase says Botanics. Why am I here? A leather-bound book on the shelf opposite me begins to glow. Numbers flash in my mind. Classification numbers. A shadow falls over me again, its cold touch saturated with menace and malevolence. Someone is coming.

I have to run.

I have to run now!

But my feet are rooted to the ground as a hooded figure appears at the end of the aisle. I know instinctively that it means to harm me.

It drifts closer. Floating. Gliding. I'm trapped.

No. "NO!"

"Wake up!" Fingers bit into my skin, and I was shaken roughly. "Anamaya, wake up!"

Vitra had me by the shoulders, his wet face a mask of concern. His hair was plastered to his skull, soaked with rain. Ice-cold pellets beat against my skin.

"What..."

"You were sleepwalking," he said over the roar of the storm.

Words tumbled out of my mouth before I could stop them. "You're not supposed to wake a sleepwalker." Why had I said that? I was fucking sleepwalking, *and* I was outside in the rain.

"You were about to jump to your death." A crack of lightning lit the night, illuminating the port walkway attached to Bramble.

"Oh... Oh shit."

He hauled me to his warm, wet chest. "Let's get you inside."

I was numb, chilled to the bone, desperate for heat, so I clung to him as he led me through the halls, my mind attempting to grasp at the remnants of my dream, but it slipped away like mist through my fingers. I barely registered where we were headed until Vitra ushered me into a large room decorated in shades of brown with maroon accents. The details faded beneath the sensation of the plush carpet under my bare feet. He led me into a bedroom and attempted to pull away, but I reached for him, an involuntary sound of protest spilling from my lips. His tawny eyes brightened, nostrils flaring delicately.

"I'll be back with towels," he said.

I stood shivering and dripping on a patterned rug that looked expensive. This was his bedroom. This strange domed room with its minimalist décor, plain beige walls, no personal items on the dresser, and no tapestries or paintings on the wall. No clues about the man beneath the enigmatic mask. Nothing except the huge, round bed piled with pillows, dominating the space.

Vitra valued a comfortable night's sleep. Naked? No. No, do not think of that.

He returned with towels and wrapped the largest one around me, then covered my hair with the smaller one before patting and rubbing to dry it.

He was still beaded with rain, dark eyelashes wet and clinging together. "You're soaked too."

"I'm fine. *You* could catch a chill."

"And you won't?"

"I haven't been sick a day in my life."

"Naga power?"

One of his dark eyebrows lifted. "Something like that."

My teeth began to chatter, and he cursed softly under his breath. "We need to take your clothes off."

"We?" I tried for a teasing smile, but my chattering teeth ruined my effort.

He pursed his lips, eyes darkening slightly. "*You* need to take your clothes off." He broke away from me, and I bit back a sigh of protest as he ducked through a door to my left. He returned moments later with a bundle of clothes. "Put these on. I'll make you a hot drink." He left again through the main door, closing it firmly behind him.

My shorts and undershirt clung to my skin, the bandages

Darla had applied completely soaked. I peeled off my clothes and dried off quickly, careful to dab around my bruised knee. Whatever Darla had done seemed to have healed the worst of the damage, but I didn't want to aggravate it. I slipped on the clothes that Vitra had supplied—a loose shirt that came to mid-thigh and loose cotton trousers, which I rolled up so I wouldn't trip on the hem. There was also a knitted sweater that smelled of sandalwood. Had he worn it recently?

I inhaled the aroma greedily, then froze. What was I doing? This was so inappropriate. He had a girlfriend. Even though they might have some kind of open relationship thing going, I wasn't about to get involved. Not that he'd asked me to. Would I, though, if he asked?

Dammit. Stop this train of thought right now.

None of this mattered. I had to get back to my room and sort out my wet bandages. I lifted my shirt to check them. Shit, was that blood? Only a little. Thankfully, Darla had left me with a jar of healing magic stuff.

Vitra was waiting in the sitting room and, once again, the details of the room escaped me because all I saw was him—all long limbs and sex appeal, dominating the leather armchair facing me.

He'd dried off and changed into an elegant black silk robe over loose black pants. My gaze zeroed in on his bare chest, on the ink that licked over his taut muscle to vanish beneath the fabric. His hair was still damp, but he'd raked it back. He looked slick and sexy, all lean muscle and power.

He nodded toward the steaming mug on the coffee table in front of him. "Sit and drink that."

I parked myself on the sofa opposite him and picked up the drink. Tea. Strong. I took a sip. Sweet. Just the way I liked it.

"Do you sleepwalk often?" he asked.

"I've never sleepwalked before."

"Hmm..."

"But I'm fine. It won't happen again."

"You can't know that for sure."

He had a point. "I'll lock my door."

He frowned. "You're saying it *wasn't* locked?"

"No, it was." Dammit. "I guess sleepwalking me opened it."

He mulled this over for a moment. "This is worrying, Anamaya."

"Yeah, well, what can I do? Tie myself to the bed?"

Did his eyes light up at that, or was I imagining it?

"I have some cuffs I can loan you," he said casually, as if he'd offered me a cup of sugar.

"If I can unlock a door, then I can unlock cuffs. And why do you have cuffs?"

He tipped his head to one side, his penetrating gaze boring into me. "Why do you think I have them, Anamaya?"

The way he said my name, savoring each syllable, ignited something in me that I didn't want to address. "Oh...okay."

This time the silence between us was all kinds of awkward as I tried desperately not to imagine being handcuffed to a bed with Vitra looming over me.

"What are you thinking, Anamaya?"

He did *not* need to know. "I'm wondering why you have to say my name like that."

"Like what?"

Was he serious? The intense look on his face certainly was. "What are *you* thinking?"

"I'm thinking that I'll have Pip lock the doors to the Unwoven quarters when you're all asleep and unlock them for breakfast." But his gaze, locked on my mouth, spoke of other thoughts. Maybe *he* was imagining tying me to his bed. My cheeks warmed, and his eyes darkened, lifting to meet mine. The pulse in my throat throbbed thickly, making it suddenly a little harder to breathe. He slow-blinked, releasing me from whatever this strange spell was. "Let the other Unwoven know what's happened."

I sipped my tea to mask my fluster. "So you've decided to be nice to me now?"

He canted his head. "When was I *not* nice, Miss Onyx?"

Miss Onyx again now, was it? Good. This was safer. "Earlier, when you threatened to fail me."

"If I recall correctly, I also saved you from a water dragon." He tapped his fingers on his thigh as if considering something before continuing. "Why are you here, Miss Onyx? Here at Nightsbridge."

My pulse skipped, and his eyes narrowed as if he'd sensed it, and who knows, maybe he had. He was a naga, and they had abilities, abilities I hadn't read up on yet. Dammit, I had to do some reading and soon.

"Are you here to pick unnecessary fights or to become a part of something bigger?" he asked.

Neither, but he didn't need to know that. "To learn, of course."

"Then make better choices. Save your aggression for the hunt, where we can all benefit from it. If you get hurt out there, at least it will be for a worthy cause."

Annoyance flashed through me, and I sat up straighter. "Are you saying Ruspin *isn't* worthy?"

He exhaled and pinched the bridge of his nose, clearly exasperated with me. I didn't like how that made my stomach hollow. Didn't like how much it bothered me that I'd disappointed him in some way.

It was time to make an exit.

I set down my mug, and he stilled, sniffing the air.

"You're bleeding," he said.

"I'm fine. It's not too bad." I peered down my top to check if it had gotten worse. "I'll sort it out when I get to my room." When I looked up, he was gone.

When had he moved?

He returned a moment later carrying a roll of bandages and tape.

How had he moved so fast? "Are you sure you're not a vampire?"

"Take off the sweater and shirt."

The command in his tone had me reaching for the hem of my

sweater before I could check myself. "I'm not wearing a bra."

For a moment, I thought he'd insist I strip anyway—and Trinity help me, I might have done so—but instead he held out the bandages. "Go back into the bedroom and fix yourself up before you leave."

I stepped closer, fingers brushing his as I grasped the roll. The contact was slight but inexplicably intimate. He didn't release the bundle. Instead, he moved nearer, mere inches away now. His sandalwood scent spiked, saturating the air, leaving me no choice but to breathe it in. To breathe him in. A soft haze filled my mind, and the tension drained out of my limbs. I swayed toward him, suddenly lightheaded—like I'd had too much of the good stuff.

He grabbed my arms to steady me, and my skin came alive with awareness from his touch. The sensation was new and intense, and Trinity, I wanted more. I tipped my head back, failing to suppress a moan, because this man was a fucking aphrodisiac.

His gaze darkened, settling on my mouth with such focused intensity it made my chest ache with longing. I needed his lips on mine. Wanted him to kiss me. But all I got was his measured breath and his fingers digging into my arms, as if he, too, wanted more but was fighting it. I could break his resolve. Bridge the space between us and offer him my mouth. I could take what I wanted.

"You won't believe the weather out there," Selethis said as she entered the room.

Shit! I tore myself out of Vitra's grip, putting distance between us.

She froze, taking in the scene before fixing her gaze calmly on Vitra. "It's a little late for a conference, don't you think?"

My cheeks burned, and I was sure she could read the guilt on my face. This did not feel good.

"Miss Onyx sleepwalked onto the portway," Vitra said evenly. "She was drenched and shaken, but she's fine now. She was just leaving."

I clutched the bandages to my chest, my insides quaking. "Thanks for the help." I couldn't meet Mistress Selethis's eyes because even though I hadn't done anything, I'd wanted to, and that was bad enough.

I ducked past her, mumbling thanks again, and hurried out into the short hall, feeling like a dirty creeper for the thoughts that had just scrolled through my mind.

"Is it that time already?" Selethis asked him.

"No," Vitra said. "Not yet, and not her."

I paused, hand on the doorknob, interest piqued.

"It didn't look that way," Selethis countered.

"Drink?"

"Always."

Glass clinked on glass.

I should go now. I twisted the doorknob and cracked it open, but didn't step outside straight away.

"What are you playing at, Vitra?" Selethis said. "You know the rules."

"I don't play, Constance, *you* know that."

"But just now..." She trailed off. "Did she leave? I didn't hear the—"

Fuck. I quickly slipped out the door, closed it softly behind me, and hurried away from his quarters.

I had no idea what Vitra and Selethis's little exchange meant, but I was certain of one thing.

Vitra was off-limits. I was *not* that woman. *Never* the other woman, even if those two did have some kind of arrangement. No, this attraction would have to be buried. Deep. And the fact that he could make me *feel* couldn't matter.

I made it to the end of the corridor before realizing that I had no clue where in the tower I was.

Great. Fucking great.

I was shivering by the time I got back to the Unwoven quarters, but the fire in the hearth was nothing but embers. I fed it wood and then sat on the rug to change my bandages, sighing as my body warmed up.

The old bandage was dotted with more blood than before. I carefully peeled it off and threw it into the flames. They ate at it eagerly, flaring purple then blue, and as it turned to ash, a voice spoke from within. "Your offering is accepted."

What in the Trinity?

The flames settled into their usual hues of red and orange. "Solaris?"

Silence and the cheery crackle of kindling and wood were my only response. I hadn't imagined that, right? "Hello?"

The flames danced merrily, innocuously.

I was too tired for this shit.

I finished rebandaging my wound and headed to bed. If only I'd convinced Vitra to excuse me from class. Surely sleepwalking counted as a good excuse. It was too late now.

Tomorrow was going to be a long day.

Horror: A creature of an origin not of this world intent on doing harm to the indigenous population.

The Compendium of Horrors

CHAPTER 26

My joints were stiff in the morning, but my hand and throat were completely healed, and the bruising on my knee was all but gone. The chest wound, however, was another matter. It still looked raw—three claw marks that would most likely leave a scar. The angry red welts would no doubt take days to heal, even with the salve Darla had provided. I lathered up and refreshed the bandages before pulling on my uniform and grabbing the required text for Horror 101.

The student roster that Timothy had left behind sat on the desk next to Volume One of *History of Nightsbridge*. I needed to get it back to him. I popped it in my bag before heading for the door.

Clary stood outside, fist up, ready to knock. "Hey. You're really going?"

"Yep."

"Then I'm coming with you," she said. "I don't have any classes this morning, so I'll wait in the dining hall for you to finish up, and we can grab a late breakfast."

Why was she so nice? Why would she do that? Why did they all have to be so bloody caring? It made my skin crawl with unease and...guilt. Yeah, guilt seemed to want to be my best friend all of a sudden. "You don't have to do that."

"I want to." She smiled, all sunshine and light. "Benedict's coming too. He has a free period between nine and eleven, and he usually hangs out in the dining hall, downing several cups of coffee to wake up. He is *not* a morning person."

"Who's not a morning person?" Benedict mumbled from the sitting room behind her.

Clary winced. "No one."

Of course, she was coming with me so she could hang out with Benedict. That made sense. So why was I disappointed? "Where's Dori?"

"Trinity Tower. Heidi wanted to speak to her." Benedict yawned and stretched. His dark hair was mussed up, and his uniform looked rumpled. He personified the can't-be-bothered-vibe perfectly, while Clary, in her neatly pressed uniform, sleek hair, and bright, alert eyes, was the complete opposite.

But they say that opposites attract...

Clary wrinkled her nose at Benedict. "Did you sleep in that?"

He graced her with a lopsided grin. "Saves getting dressed in the morning."

"Ew," she said with a smile.

This girl had it bad.

"Hey, I bathed last night," he protested. "Smell me." He moved closer and lifted his chin, offering her his neck.

Her cheeks pinkened. "I believe you." She backed away, and he chuckled and hooked an arm around her neck, dragging her in for a hug.

She relaxed and closed her eyes, letting him hold her for a minute before pulling away. "Come on, we should get going, or Ana will be late for class."

I followed them out of the quarters. "Oh, by the way. I need to tell you guys what happened last night. Apparently, I sleepwalk now..."

Clary and Benedict walked me to class, and we made it there five minutes early. The doors were closed, and students waited outside. I recognized a couple from Selethis's class at the front of the line—the girl with the sleek bob and another with purple hair—Carter and Pouvoir if I wasn't mistaken.

It was almost nine, surely the doors should be open by now. "Why can't we go in?"

"Advanced Horror is in there," Clary said. "The students training to join the Carvers."

"The Carvers that made the ratakan?"

"They do more than that," Benedict said. "They dissect and study the Horrors that the hunt manages to capture alive."

"There are holding pens somewhere in Nightsbridge," Clary said. "But only the Carvers know the locations."

Interesting. "You can *choose* to be a Carver?"

"You can choose to study for it as early as seventeen, but there are tests and entrance exams and all sorts of requirements. The biology of Horrors is complex and evolving, and all the cutting and medical stuff that goes into it..." Benedict shuddered, but my interest was piqued.

Drayven had mentioned Carvers to me, of course, but I'd been a little out of sorts, what with being under the influence of ratakan toxin.

"The Carvers are bio-Horror-engineers," Benedict said.

"He made up that word," Clary added.

"It's a good word," he said proudly.

The CCC had a department for the study and classification of critters. I'd been thinking about applying before...everything. Honestly, this was the first time I'd felt a fission of excitement about learning anything since coming to Nightsbridge. Being a Carver would scratch an itch while I waited to get my power restored. I could apply the skills I'd learned working for the CCC. Surely some of the Horrors would have similarities to the critters outside the wards? Maybe I could help the Carvers using the knowledge I already had. At least until I found the *Libra Veritas* and exposed the Arcanum Imperium, of course.

I wanted to know more. "So how is Advanced Horror different from regular Horror? What does Vitra teach these potential Carvers?"

Clary answered, "101 is the basics. The five main types of Horrors that you might encounter as a Hunter. I'm not sure exactly what they do in Advanced Horror, but rumor is, they learn about the *hidden* Horrors and the new, evolving Horrors."

"Surely students planning to be Hunters need to learn about them, too?"

"They do, but only when they're seasoned," Clary said. "Regular Hunters don't go after the hidden Horrors."

And seasoned meant the Hunters had made at least twenty-five kills...

The doors opened, and the waiting students stepped back to allow the Carvers-in-training out. Students dressed in head-to-toe fitted black uniforms of trousers and scoop-necked tunics with a black shirt beneath. I counted eleven, all with studious expressions. They filed out silently and dispersed.

"Now that's not creepy at all," Clary said. "Men in leggings..." She shuddered.

"It takes a certain type to do what they do," Benedict said. "Dedication, too. They need twenty-five kills as part of the hunt while taking Advanced Horror and Carver 101. Then, several tests and a final exam administered by the Scentia Keepers in the Infra Sanctum."

I shook my head. "Slow down a moment. Scentia Keepers and what?"

"Infra Sanctum. It's a vault," Clary said. "Beneath Nightsbridge. A library of relics and books. The Scentia Keepers run it."

My pulse skipped. Could this Infra Sanctum be where the

Libra Veritas was kept? "I'd love to see it." Damn, I sounded a little too breathless and excited. "I mean...books and relics sound so cool."

"Oh, you can't see it," Clary said. "No one is allowed in except students taking the Carver exam, and I'm pretty sure they're restricted to a specific area."

Yep, this had to be the vault Dharma had been talking about in her journal.

Becoming a Carver would get me into the vault. This was my answer. The route to my goal.

The door swung open, and Vitra appeared, looking as classy and elegant as always. Half his hair was pulled back in a knot, accentuating his commanding features. A jacket hung loosely off his shoulders. Hands tucked in his pants pockets, he was a picture of sophisticated elegance.

I couldn't have this fine specimen of a man, but I could use him to get me closer to my goal.

Yep, Vitra was going to train me to become a Carver.

Vitra sat on the edge of his desk, mug in hand, his demeanor relaxed and easy, as if we'd gathered for a casual chat. "Horrors are elemental beings who took root in our world after The Overshadowing," he said. "They've made Nightsbridge their home—spawning, procreating, and populating—and it is only the efforts of this Academy, its Hunters, and Carvers that the threat remains contained. Locked away from the outside world." He sipped his beverage. "So, if you did your reading, then you'll know what the five main types of Horror are. Who would like to go first?" He scanned the room and pointed at a student in the back who I recognized from Combat 101.

"Mudarks," the boy said. "Tiny creatures that live in underground colonies. They're pests that keep growing in number. Oh, and they can band together to form one huge creature."

"Good. Pouvoir?"

"Wood weavers," she said. "They live inside trees, and some can disguise themselves *as* trees. They're carnivorous."

"Miss Clover?"

"Undines. Water Horrors that lay their eggs in the decaying bodies of their drowned prey." She shuddered.

"Good, very good. What else? Mr. Trent?"

The boy in question did his best deer-in-tramlights impression. "I... I didn't get a chance to do the reading."

Vitra tipped his head to the side. "Didn't get a chance or couldn't be bothered?"

The student looked trapped, eyes darting this way and that.

Vitra sipped his drink and sighed. "Get out."

"What?" Trent said.

"Don't make me repeat myself, Mr. Trent."

"Please, sir, I'll catch up."

"Yes, you will. You'll do the required reading and the next four chapters, and I'll be testing you on the content next class. If you fail, you'll be allocated to Domestic."

Trent looked about at his fellow classmates, as if expecting someone to stand up for him, but everyone was suddenly extremely interested in their notebooks. Vitra waited and watched, his body so still it was unnerving, until Trent gathered his things and quickly left the room.

"Miss Thistle, I hope *you* did the reading." He graced her with a smile of confidence, and she practically preened.

"I did." She glanced about, smug.

"Then please remind us of the last two main types of Horror."

"Sylphs and salamanders," she said quickly. "Sylphs will steal the oxygen from your lungs, suffocating you on dry land, and a salamander...well, it'll burn you up. Top tip: do not light campfires in the forest as these can spawn salamanders."

"The forest is alive," Vitra said with a nod. "A sentient entity that houses many more creatures than what we've learned. New Horrors are born every decade, and the old evolve and change.

What we know today is not necessarily what will be tomorrow. But we can learn a lot from the activities of the Horrors of today and maybe use that information to predict what might happen in the future."

Someone put up their hand, and Vitra lifted his chin in his direction.

"Is it true that mudark activity is increasing?" the student asked. "That their numbers have grown exponentially?"

Another student spoke up. "I heard there have been more proximity attacks on the boundaries the past few days."

"Are the Horrors getting bolder?" a third student asked.

Vitra's expression closed off. "That is a question for the hunt leaders and their teams. *This* is Horror 101, so open your books to Chapter Ten and read quietly."

I flipped open the book to the chapter titled "Origin of the Salamander" and set to reading.

I was so absorbed in the text that I barely registered everyone leaving, and when I looked up, I was one of the last students in the room.

Vitra stood with his back to me, fiddling with his satchel and some papers.

The jacket was off, leaving his pert ass, snug in his dark gray trousers, on view. I caught a couple of students checking him out as they slowly walked past.

Good to know I wasn't the only one lusting.

The door clicked shut behind the last student, leaving Vitra and me alone.

"Are you done looking, Miss Onyx?" Vitra asked.

Was I really that obvious? "Yeah, I'm done."

He turned to face me and leaned back against the desk. "You've probably heard that Constance and I are not exclusive in our relationship. Maybe that gave you certain…ideas and… expectations. But you should also know that I don't fuck my students. It is prohibited by the Coterie, but even if it weren't, I have a strict policy not to bring my work home with me."

The way he said *fuck*, with such intent, sent a stab of unwanted desire through me. Vitra was like blessed rain after a drought, and my body ached to satiate its thirst.

But like Fel would I let him see it. Last night in his quarters had been a moment of weakness that I couldn't repeat.

"You think I want to sleep with you?" Despite my resolve, the rasp in my voice betrayed me. I bit back a wince. "I don't."

"Liar."

He smiled thinly and crossed his arms, causing his shirt to stretch and smooth over his muscle-rounded shoulders. What would it feel like to dig my nails into him, to grip him hard as he thrust inside—

Whoa. No. Bad, Anamaya!

"I saw it in your eyes last night," he continued. "And I see it now."

Clearly, I'd have to work on my body language, but like Fel was I letting him put last night solely on me. "The look in *your* eyes wasn't exactly innocent either."

"A momentary lapse, because, you see, I have a weakness for women wearing my clothes." His tongue flicked out to lick at the corner of his mouth. "Makes me want to tear them off."

The breath exploded from my lips. What was he doing to me?

He inhaled and closed his eyes for a beat. "And there it is. The unmistakable scent of arousal."

Oh shit. "So what? You're attractive, and I have eyes and hormones. It's natural. It doesn't mean I want to *fuck* you." Yeah, I could use the 'F' word too. "Besides, I already told you, arrogance is a huge turnoff for me."

"Your scent says different."

"Whatever." I gathered my stuff, shoving it all hastily into my bag, and headed for the exit. "Bye."

I slammed the door behind me, wincing as his sexy chuckle followed me.

Whatever? Bye? Bye! That was the best I could do as a parting line? *Gah!*

Yash Vitra had a hard-on for me, despite his assertions otherwise. Student-teacher liaisons may be prohibited by the Coterie, but if I'd read him right, he'd toy with me like a mouse since he couldn't claim me.

People tended to get attached to their toys, so I'd let him play, and when the time came, I would use the connection to my advantage. No *fucking* required.

Perfect.

> **When the fabric between worlds thins, doorways can form in the unlikeliest of places.**
>
> *The Cosmologist*

CHAPTER 27

The bathrooms in the Main Building had marble-tiled floors and plush velvet benches. A bank of mirrors made up the wall above the fancy sinks with copper taps. I was supposed to meet the Unwoven in the dining hall, but I needed a moment to compose myself.

Damn Vitra and his sex appeal.

Maybe it was a naga thing.

I really needed to do some research about the supernal to figure out the full extent of his powers.

I splashed cool water on my face, then studied my reflection. Dammit, I still looked flushed.

My breath misted in front of me and goose bumps crawled up my arms.

What the—

The lights flickered, and a man appeared in the mirror behind me. His eyes were covered by a white blindfold, and his dark hair floated around his shoulders in a phantom breeze.

I was frozen. Unable to look over my shoulder as he approached. His reflection glided closer, his bare torso gleaming as if his skin were made of a billion diamonds.

He reached for me, and a scream bubbled up my throat.

I didn't want him to touch me.

I had to move.

I had to—

A door slammed.

The lights flickered again, and the man in the mirror was replaced by Clary.

"Ana?" She hurried toward me. "Ana, are you okay?"

A squeak fell from my lips—the remnant of the scream that had gathered there a moment ago.

Clary put her arm around me and drew me away from the mirror and toward the bench. "Sit. You look like you've seen a ghost. Like, a nasty evil ghost, not the Pip and his team kind."

I took a shuddering breath. "There was a man here. I saw him in the mirror." I described what I'd seen. "He was going to touch me." I sounded crazy, but there was no disbelief on Clary's face. "You don't look surprised."

"Well, you're not the first to see stuff in the mirrors," Clary said. "There have been rumors of specters living in the glass for decades. It's kind of a boast to say you've seen one." She leaned in conspiratorially. "But I'm sure most students make stuff up."

She made it sound so innocuous. "I'm not making this up."

"Oh, I believe you." There was a heaviness in her tone that pulled me out of my own head.

"Have *you* seen one?"

She smiled wryly. "No, it's not like that for me. I..." She sighed. "Sometimes when I look in the mirror, I'm certain it's not my reflection looking back at me."

"What do you mean?"

"Like...it's my face, but it's not me." She puffed out her cheeks and blew out a breath. "Okay, so I had a sister. A twin. She died before I came here, and sometimes... Sometimes I think I see her looking at me from the mirror." She let out an awkward laugh. "I know, it sounds crazy."

It sounded creepy. "How did she die? I mean, if you don't

mind me asking."

She shook her head. "It's fine. It was a carriage accident."

"I'm so sorry."

She smiled sadly. "Yeah, me too. Raina was a force of nature. It's hard to believe she could be snuffed out so easily. You know, we might have been identical in looks, but we were very different in personality. She was the smart, confident one who could light up a room with her presence, and her connection to the Weave was astounding. I used to be jealous of her sometimes, but it was impossible not to love her. I mean...she made everyone around her feel special. She should be here with me now."

"You were *both* meant to come here?"

"Trinity, no. It was meant to be just one of us, but Raina refused to let us be parted. She insisted they send us both, but a month before we were due to come here, she was killed." She tucked in her chin, fiddling with the leather bracelet on her wrist. "There was a party, and she begged me to go with her, but I was feeling off. My stomach hurt and... Anyway, I said no. So, she went alone and...well, she never came home." Her tone thickened with emotion. "A wheel came loose on the carriage, and she was thrown from the driver's seat."

"Oh...Clary..."

She sniffed and wiped at her eyes. "Raina wasn't the best driver. I knew that. Maybe if I'd insisted she take Percy, our driver. Maybe if I'd gone with her..." She exhaled heavily. "There's not a day that goes by that I don't wonder how different things might be if I'd gone with her."

She blamed herself. I could hear it in her voice and see it on her face. "Clary...you do know it wasn't your fault, right?"

She gave me a weak smile. "Our decisions have consequences, and mine killed my sister. I could have gone," she said in a rush. "My stomach ache was manageable, but what I *couldn't* stomach was being her shadow for the evening while everyone bathed in her light. My jealousy killed her." Her chest heaved and she blinked back tears. "There, I said it."

"Clary—"

"We had plans to be kick-ass Hunters together. To find hot Hunter boyfriends. We were going to rule, but... But deep down, I knew it would be Raina who ruled. Raina that shone. I didn't want to share the limelight with her, and it got her killed."

"Clary, you can't—"

"The energy we put out there has an impact, Ana," she said vehemently. "The negative thoughts I pushed into the world took my sister from me, and now... Now I have to live with that. But I vowed to do the right thing going forward, to never put my needs above those of others, and to set an example."

Is that why she'd refused to heal the student who got hurt attacking another student? She wanted them to suffer for what they'd done, even if it meant she was Unwoven?

"Clary, don't you think Raina would want you to be happy?"

"Of course she would," Clary said. "Because that's the kind of person she was. But I don't deserve it. At least not yet." She pressed her palm to her chest. "I don't feel it yet."

There was pain in this woman. Guilt and the belief that she wasn't good enough. It was a powerfully destructive combination that would eat her alive if not checked.

It wasn't my problem, but...I put my arm around her shoulder anyway. "I think Raina would be proud of you. Of the friend you've become to Dori, Benedict, now... Now to me."

She sniffed again. "You think?"

"Yeah, I really do."

She leaned her head against me. "I'm glad you came to Nightsbridge. I'm glad we're friends."

"Me too. Me too." And the fucked-up thing was, in that moment, I think I meant it.

Once a connection is formed, it cannot be undone, only monitored by boundaries. But if those boundaries fail, then there is chaos.

The Cosmologist

CHAPTER 28

The dining hall was nearly empty at this time of day, as most students were in class or still in bed. The busiest hours were between twelve and two, then five and eight. I made a note to avoid those. But with the morning sun streaming in through the newly fixed windows and only a handful of students scattered about—none of whom were throwing evil looks my way—it was almost pleasant in here.

"Not long left now!" Benedict held up his planner, flipping to the calendar page where each day was neatly crossed off. "Only three and a half weeks to the Restoration Ceremony."

"I miss Mr. Twiggins." Dori propped her elbows on the table and rested her face in her hands.

"I miss Mimi." Clary pouted. "She loves sleeping with me. The bed's been empty without her."

Of course. The block on their power would have cut them off from their familiars. It hit me how strange it must be for them not to have access to the Weave, considering that it had always been part of them. It was different for me, I had no real concept of what I was missing.

Clary confirmed my thoughts a moment later. "I'm sick of feeling empty, you know. I mean, I don't miss doing spells so much as feeling the buzz of the Weave like... Like a... A friend." She shook her head. "I can't explain it."

"I get it," Dori said. "It's like that feeling you get sometimes—you know, when you think you're forgetting something, or you go into a room and have this conviction that you were supposed to be somewhere else, doing something else. The absence of the Weave is that feeling, all the time."

I recalled the yearning that had sparked inside me beneath the wards at the Border House. The way a primal part of me had reacted to the power there. Ached for it. The Unwoven had always had it flowing through them. It was part of them, and the Academy was denying them that connection as punishment. It was a smart way to prevent further infractions.

"I don't mind," Benedict said. "Chaos Magic sucks."

My curiosity sparked. I'd heard Chaos Magic mentioned once during my studies with Mother, knew it was a specific thread in the Weave, but that was all. "What is it, exactly? The Chaos Magic?"

"They call it the outlier thread," Clary said, speaking for Benedict. "And it can be extremely powerful if the wielder learns to harness it." She nudged Benedict with her elbow. "I told you to get a better focus."

"I don't want a better focus. Can you imagine me having even more access to that damn thread's power? I'm struggling to control it as it is, and—" He snapped his mouth shut, his gaze flying up to meet mine.

Wait a second... "The fire you set...it wasn't deliberate?"

Clary and Dori exchanged wary glances.

Okay, it seemed like I'd stumbled on a delicate topic here. "Look, forget it. It's none of my business."

Benedict's shoulders slumped. He set down his ink pen and fixed me with a serious look. "The fire was an accident, but no one can know. If the covens find out I'm having problems controlling the thread, then... Just, please don't say anything."

"Of course. I won't say a word."

He dropped a nod, relaxing back into his seat as an awkward silence settled over us, leaving me itching to diffuse it. My gaze fell to my backpack where the corner of a book peeked out.

Timothy's book! The perfect change of topic.

I tugged it out and placed it on the table between us. "Okay, so I met this guy the other day after Sterling did the Hamlin maneuver on me."

"Oh? Do tell," Dori said, smiling suggestively.

"Not like that. He actually seems to have a thing for you."

"For me?"

"Yep." I filled her in on the encounter.

"Nope," Dori said once I was done. "I have no idea who this Timothy guy is."

I passed her Timothy's book. "He was carrying this. I was hoping to get it back to him."

"Looks like an annual student record," Benedict said. "There's an ASR for every year." He turned the book over and tapped the date on the spine. "This one's from last year. Claaary..." he singsonged.

She slapped her hand to her bangs. "Don't."

"What?" I looked between them.

"Last year, Clary decided to trim her own bangs," Dori said with an indulgent smile. "It did *not* go well, and there is image print evidence."

Clary groaned and dropped her forehead to the table. "I hate that print."

Benedict was already flicking through the book. "I love it. You look so freaking cute."

Clary's mouth turned down. "No one wants to be cute. I was going for sexy."

"Here!" Benedict turned the book around and tapped at the black-and-white print of a frowning Clary with bangs that were slightly wonky and a little too short. "You look so mad," he said. "I just want to squish you."

I looked between the three of them—a sorcerer and two witches, all from different bloodlines and covens. It was rare to see such a friendship. "How long *have* you three been friends?"

The trio exchanged fond smiles.

"Ever since the first day of Academy," Dori said. "I met Clary on the tram, and we ended up sharing a table with Benedict for supper that first night."

"I was getting my ass kicked by a couple of my brethren," Benedict said, his mouth twisting bitterly. "Being the runt of the Ironhart clan isn't always easy, despite the fact that my father is clan leader."

"Dori punched Randolf in the nuts," Clary said with delight.

"We've been friends ever since," Dori said.

A soft ache filled my chest. To have that...to be part of it...

"Show me this Timothy guy," Dori said suddenly.

I cleared my throat. "Good idea." I flipped through the book slowly, studying each page, searching for his face, until I came to a blurred photo. The name below was smudged. "That's weird." I flipped the next two pages and found another blurred image print, words smudged as well. A few pages later, I found a third.

"Let me see." Dori took the book. "That *is* weird."

"He has to be one of the blurred prints," Clary said.

"There is no way they would have published those like that," Benedict said. "They'd have gotten new image prints made. In fact, I'm not sure how Timothy checked this book out. It's a reference text."

A shadow fell over the book. "Hi..." Cami stood at our table. "I, uh... I wanted to thank you for the other day, for saving me when the water dragon attacked. I'm sorry I ran off and...yeah..."

I smiled up at her. "You did the right thing getting out of the way. Do you want to sit with us?"

"Oh..." She brightened at the offer. "I have class, but thank you. Next time?"

"Sure."

She hurried off, looking back over her shoulder a couple of times, all smiles.

"I think you made another friend there," Dori said.

Another friend...because they thought of me as a friend. To be part of their group for real...

My chest tightened, and I fixed my gaze on the windows, on the view of the sea and the calm way it moved, until the vise gripping my lungs melted away.

"Hey." Clary covered my hand with hers. "You okay?"

"Are you still spooked about the mirror guy?" Dori asked. "Whatever it was, it can't hurt you."

I'd filled them in on what I'd seen in the bathrooms earlier. "How can you be sure?"

"The rumors have been around for decades," Benedict said. "No one has been hurt by the shadows in the mirrors."

The man in the mirror had been more than a shadow. "But doesn't it bother you? Like...what are they?"

"Who knows," Dori said. "Mirrors are powerful tools used in scrying and as portals by the Arcanus for centuries. Nightsbridge is a magnet for *other* energy. But you can be certain that the Coterie has put precautions in place to stop any negative forces from getting in."

"Food's here!" Benedict rubbed his hands together as several trays floated toward us.

My stomach growled in appreciation.

Mirror men and shadows would have to wait.

I spent the afternoon catching up on my reading before heading back to the Main Building for my meeting with the resident counselor, Mandy Snap.

There was so much to learn about Nightsbridge—from The Overshadowing to the Land-Sea Pact to the histories of each bloodline that had stepped forward to bind themselves to keep the Horrors contained. I learned that not everyone was here because of that Covenant, though. Some families sent students here as punishment or to gain favor with other bloodlines or the Coterie. But every student had one thing in common—none of them wanted to be here.

They studied and worked hard because the alternative was becoming domestic staff, pandering to the whims of the Hunters and the Carvers. There was no leaving Nightsbridge if you failed, only drudgery, and in some cases, a trip to the catacombs to be consumed by the Weave Watchers.

Deep in thought, I drifted toward the Main Building in a daze. Only when I stepped out of the cliffside lift and onto the grounds did the howling wind and crashing waves register.

The sky hung low, dark clouds churning, warning of an approaching storm.

Hopefully, the meeting would be over before it broke. I hurried up the path, eager to get into the building, then yelped and leapt back as a huge shape darted in front of me.

Ruspin lowered his head and whined softly in apology.

It took a moment, my hand on my heart, for my pulse to steady. "It's okay. I'm okay. Are *you*? Okay?" He lifted his head in what I assumed was a nod. "Good. I'm glad you're free."

"Thank...you..." His voice was gritty and broken, sending a shudder up my spine.

"You've got your beast voice back."

"All...most...not...quite..."

"But you can't shift yet?"

He dipped his head, eyes taking on a dull sheen.

My nape prickled. "It'll happen. Just give it time. Look, I've got to go, but we'll talk again. Soon."

He took a step toward me, and I took an instinctive one back before I could check myself.

"Not...hurt...you."

"I know that." Of course I did. "Stay safe." I skirted around him and broke into a jog. Not because I wanted to get away from him. I needed to get to my session. But there was no denying the inexplicable unease that his presence had spawned in my belly.

~~~

Miss Snap's office was nothing more than a large broom closet on the first floor, with enough room for a desk, two chairs, and two shelves lined with crystals of all shapes and sizes. A single window behind her desk silhouetted her in sunlight, so that her frizzy blonde hair lit up like a halo. She had the kind of face that looked as if she were always listening, which, considering her profession, was fortunate. Or had she taken up the profession *because* of her face?

"Miss Onyx, you were saying?"

Shit, what had I been saying? "That I'm adjusting? I've made... friends." Thank Trinity the word didn't stick in my throat.

"Good. Good." She jotted down notes. On what, I wasn't quite sure, but whatever. "And how are you coping with your loss?"

I tensed. "Excuse me?"

"Your mother passed away a few weeks ago, didn't she?" She flipped through her notes. "I mean...it says here...am I right?"

"What does that have to do with anything?"

"Oh..." She sat back in her seat. "I'm sorry. I don't mean to pry, but it's my job to make sure you're okay. To provide any support you need through your time of grief."

"I'm done grieving."

She blinked sharply. "Right," she said, dragging the word out slowly as she scribbled more notes.

"What are you writing?"

"Just a few notes on our session."

The urge to get up and snatch the notepad from her surged through me. I curled my hands into fists in my lap. "What did you write just then?"

She pressed her lips together. "I wrote that *the student is in the denial phase of their grief.*"

Heat sparked in my chest. "Denial? That's bullshit. I know my mother is dead. I'm not *denying* that."

She set her pen down and laced her fingers together on the desk. "Denial is a complex emotion, Anamaya. We can choose *not* to grieve. To put the emotions aside. Maybe you think that it's better that way. That the grief will go away if you ignore it."

What the Fel was she talking about? "I didn't ignore it. I cried. I cried for fucking days."

"And then you stopped, and you did what? Applied to come here and put all your focus into admission?"

What was she getting at? "I decided to do something with my life."

"Uh-huh, and how often have you thought about your mother since coming here?"

My pulse raced, heat gathering behind my eyes. "I'm done." I pushed back my chair. "If you want to talk about classes or how I'm adjusting here, then fine, otherwise we're done."

She half stood, her expression earnest. "Please, Anamaya, sit down. We can talk about other things."

I didn't want to be here anymore. I didn't want to talk to her. A rainbow of colors washed over the crystals to my left as a beam of sunlight pierced through the window from a rare break in the cloud cover, bathing the room in vibrant shades of red, blue, and orange.

For a moment, I was back in the kitchen at home, the room filled with sunlight and my mother's warm laughter. A knot formed in my heart, twisting and tightening with a longing that echoed physical pain.

The color display faded, and I flopped back into my seat, deflated. "I'm fine." But I wasn't. I might never be.

"Okay," she said. "But I want you to know that if you ever need anything, you can come speak to me. Now...I heard you freed Ruspin? Tell me about that..."

We spoke for another thirty minutes before the session ended and I could escape the room. Despite the rocky start, I had to admit—Mandy Snap grew on me. There was something calm and patient about her. Sincere and soothing, but it was only when I got back to my room in Bramble that realization dawned...Mandy Snap reminded me of my mother.

I retrieved Mother's box from the bag I'd shoved into my wardrobe and took a seat at the dresser with it. How many times had she taken out these focuses and held them? Each focus must be saturated with her essence. Her imprint. I wished I could feel it. Feel her arms around me.

I gripped the box with trembling hands and squeezed my eyes shut tight against the tide of tears that wanted to break free. Ragged breaths tore at my lungs, leaving me hollow and full at the same time until I could take it no more. I broke, sobbing so hard I ate up all the oxygen in the room.

I missed her. I missed her so much it was like the world was gray and all the joy had been sucked from it. She'd been more than my mother. She'd been my best friend. My smile. My laughter. She'd made the shitty hand we'd been dealt worth playing.

I wiped at my face, wrangling my emotions into submission. I couldn't fall apart. Not now. Not yet. I had a job to do.

"I'm going to find the truth, Mum. And when I do, I'll be back to mark your grave with an Onyx headstone."

The Weave and Source are two different wells of power, and yet they can work in symbiosis through the right conductor.

The Secrets of the Arcane

CHAPTER 29

"Anamaya, wake up."

I jolted awake, facing the door, hands curled into claws, nails digging into wood. "Fucksake. Not again."

It had been three weeks since my first session with the counselor, and although I'd had a handful of episodes in the first two weeks after speaking with her, it had been a whole week since my last episode. I'd begun to think the sleepwalking was done with, but here I was again.

"Do you remember what you were dreaming about?" Clary asked.

"Not really. I think there was a forest and a rook. There's always a fucking rook."

She led me back to my room. "You want me to stay with you for a while?"

I did want the company, but it was probably some stupid hour. "What time is it?"

"Three a.m." She stifled a yawn.

"I'm sorry."

"It's not your fault that I'm a light sleeper."

I flopped back onto my rumpled bed. "Maybe I'm broken."

"You're not broken. You've been through a lot. Have you spoken to Mandy about your sleepwalking?"

"Yeah, she thinks it's the stress of...everything. Suppressed grief, blah, blah." I smiled. "I know she's trying but...nothing seems to be helping."

"Maybe this is an effect of having the mark removed, the whole connected to the Weave but not connected. Once you get part of your power next week, you might feel better."

The Restoration Ceremony, that had seemed so far away when I'd arrived at Nightsbridge, was now mere days away. Hard to believe I'd been here for more than five weeks.

Clary chewed on her cheeks, deep in thought.

"Clary, what is it?"

She sucked on her bottom lip for a moment then released it with a pop. "Okay, hear me out. I've been thinking that maybe your dream bird might be a portent."

I stared blankly at her. "A portent?"

"Yes. Rooks are messengers just like ravens."

"So, you think my sleepwalking is trying to, what? Warn me about something?"

"Maybe?" She shrugged. "Do you fight it? The dream. Do you try to get out of it?"

"Yeah. It feels...awful. Like I'm heading toward something bad."

"Okay, so try not to fight next time. Let the dream reach its conclusion, and maybe you'll remember it all."

I didn't like the sound of that. "I guess it's worth a try."

Benedict appeared in the doorway, rubbing his eyes. "What's going on?"

"Ana sleepwalked again," Clary said.

He yawned and scratched his chest through his undershirt. "You okay?"

"I'm fine. Go back to bed, both of you."

"Is this a private party, or can anyone join?" Dori said from behind them both. Her tousled halo of hair made her look much younger than her twenty-one years.

"I sleepwalked. I'm fine. Go to bed. We have Combat 101 first thing, and I don't know about you guys, but I need my sleep. Damascus will probably make me run a kazillion laps simply for existing."

The bastard hadn't allowed me to learn much of anything the past few weeks, making me run laps and play punching bag when he should have been training me with the others. Thank Trinity for the Unwoven, without them, I'd be clueless about the offensive maneuvers required to take down a basic Horror.

They'd taken turns staying back with me after class and going over the session's combat moves. I was getting handy with a wooden sword, and luckily, the grading wasn't happening for another week, so it would take place *after* I had more access to the Weave, which should provide me with some protection and—

Dori, Benedict, and Clary exchanged pointed looks in silent communication.

I sighed. "Care to clue me in?"

Dori spoke on their behalf. "You never did tell us why Damascus hates you."

"It's late," Clary said. "We understand if you don't want to talk about it, but—"

"We want to know," Benedict said bluntly.

The thought of telling them no longer felt overwhelming; in fact, I *wanted* to tell them. It was time they knew what happened, and if they thought I was a horrible person, then so be it. In fact... it might be best if they *did* think badly of me. It might slow the momentum of this burgeoning dynamic between us, which was becoming harder and harder to reconcile with my goal.

I blew out a breath. "Okay, so...he hates me because... Because I accidentally killed his sister."

Silence reigned for several seconds before Benedict broke it.

"And now I'm wide awake," he said.

The trio filed inside and closed the door, taking seats around the room.

I sat up against the headboard and crossed my legs. "It was the summer I turned twelve..."

I jogged past Clary and Dori for the umpteenth time. How many laps was that now? I'd lost track.

They waved as I whizzed past. I'd told them the truth about Sterling and me, and they didn't hate me. Just like Drayven didn't hate me. Drayven, who I'd barely seen the past few weeks. Glimpses here and there, but nothing more. Was he deliberately keeping his distance? Why couldn't he be the one teaching Combat 101?

No, it was fine. Once I passed this class, I'd be moved to Advanced Combat—away from Sterling. I'd be assigned a hunt leader. Every Hunter had one, even if they weren't on the active team. I just hoped I didn't get Sterling.

I focused on the slap of my sneakers on the wet ground, still slick from last night's storm, and breathed in the heavy, humid air. The weather here sucked. Running sucked, especially when someone was making you do it. Round and round—the same shitty view. Ugh.

The clang of metal on metal rang out in the training arena—today, the students were practicing with real swords.

I should've been with them, not running fucking laps, forcing my heavy limbs to keep moving, ragged breath pluming in front of me. *Slap. Slap. Slap*, against the wet ground I went, round and round while the asshole ruining my training watched from across the grounds, arms crossed, expression unreadable.

Bastard.

I hope he fell and impaled himself on an ashwood stake.

A hulking male figure loped across the grounds toward the training arena, mist rising off his muscle-packed frame. Drayven? Yes...yes it was. My pace slowed as the barghest joined Sterling. They spoke for a moment before Drayven looked across the field at me.

I raised a hand in greeting and picked up my pace, eager to get to his side of the field. He turned away, his back to me as he spoke to Sterling.

The dhampir glanced over at me, a cruel smile painting his lips.

My hatred for him was a physical ache in my soul.

Sterling blew his whistle, and everyone stopped what they were doing and veered toward him.

I hurried to join them, falling in step with the Unwoven along the way. "What's going on?"

"I don't know," Clary said, wiping sweat from her brow.

We joined the others surrounding Drayven and Sterling. The barghest's eyes softened when they settled on me, and the knots in my chest eased.

"I have news," Sterling said. "News about the grading. The date has changed. I feel that you're ready, so why wait?" The corner of his mouth turned up as his gaze slid my way. "I spoke to administration, and the grading will now take place in two days."

Gasps of excitement rippled through the students. Students who'd been training for months, but a heavy weight settled in my stomach—two days away was too soon. Two days away was *before* the ceremony to return some of my power, which meant I would be magically defenseless against the mystically generated Horrors.

"And there's more," Sterling continued. "This year's grading will be a truly unique experience because you won't be fighting illusory Horrors. The Carvers have created flesh-and-blood Horrors for you to face."

The excitement swelled.

I looked to Drayven, who had his head bowed, shoulders hunched.

"And it will take place *outside* the southern border," Sterling said. More gasps followed his statement. "Don't worry, you'll be monitored, and the Horrors are under Carver control. They will attack and maim, but they will *not* kill. And remember, you'll all have rift blades."

Rift blades were short swords powered by magitech, fuelled by the Weave. Their hilts were embedded with conduit stones, allowing any supernal to wield one—even those who couldn't use the Weave—because all supernals were created by the Source—a well of power considered to be a sister to the Weave. The stones gave supernals temporary access to the Weave's power or heightened their existing connections. The century-old block on my bloodlines' power disrupted the channeling power of the stones and prevented any connection from occurring.

I'd be defenseless out there.

"So we can be hurt?" Tyler asked.

"Yes. You could be seriously hurt." He smirked at me with a little too much relish. "This is a true test of a Hunter. Separating the wheat from the chaff. If you're meant to be a Hunter, you'll pass. And if you fail...well, best to learn now how *worthless* you truly are."

A tightness bloomed in my chest making it harder to breathe. He'd arranged this to ensure I got hurt. He must have. He wasn't allowed to hurt me directly, although he'd given it a good shot under the guise of training a few weeks ago. He hadn't touched me since, and now I understood why. He'd been planning for the grading to do his dirty work for him.

Oh, what I'd give to punch a fist through his brittle chest and yank out his cold, shriveled heart. But all I had was my resolve and my words. I lifted my chin and met his silvery, pale gaze with defiance. "I guess it'll also be a testament to your teaching ability."

Sterling's eyes narrowed to slits.

Drayven suppressed a smile. "Yes, Sterling. It certainly will."

Sterling ignored him and continued, "Get some rest and prepare, this grading will be watched by the whole Academy." He threw another lingering smirk my way.

The bastard expected me to fail in front of the whole Academy, and right now, with my connection to the Weave still blocked, it was highly likely that he'd get his wish. A sinking feeling bloomed in my stomach as I considered my chances.

"Class dismissed!" Sterling said.

He strode off, coat flapping around his calves, silvery hair rippling in the breeze, head held high like the fucker truly believed he was better than me. Better than us all.

The group dispersed, chattering eagerly among themselves. All except Tyler, who made it a point to lock eyes with me and drag a finger across his throat. Again. Seriously, the idiot needed to get some new material.

"Do you have a problem, Tyler?" Drayven asked, his tone low and edged with warning.

Tyler blinked sharply. "No."

"Good, then get the fuck out of here."

Tyler jogged off to catch up with his friends.

"I don't like this," Clary muttered.

"Me neither," Drayven said. "I tried to reason with the administration, reminded them that the Restoration Ceremony isn't until the weekend, but they were not receptive."

Hardly surprising. "They don't want me here. This way, they get to shove me into domestic and forget about me."

"You are not going into Domestic," Dori said. "We'll train with you. All day if we have to."

"No," Drayven said. "Ana will train with me. The grading will take place at sunset and go on till midnight. We'll train on the nights leading up to it. Meet me at the entrance to the gardens at sunset tonight. Dress in your training gear." The corner of his mouth curled up in a cold smile, an expression I hadn't seen on his face yet. "If Sterling thinks he can sabotage your chances of making the grade, he's sorely mistaken."

"The Grand Library is a masterpiece of architecture," Clary explained as we entered the vast chamber. I stopped to take it all in. Rosewood bookshelves climbed up to meet a ceiling so high it was hidden behind thick beams. A central staircase swept up and split into two balconies that spanned the circumference of the room. Smaller staircases branched off various points along the wraparound balcony, leading to a third level which was shrouded in shadows. But that wasn't the marvel here, oh no. There were entire bookcases hidden in the walls that could be drawn out with a lever mechanism and then locked into place. Rotating shelves were built into thick stone pillars that jutted up to meet a framework of rosewood beams. Beams that acted as walkways for students crossing the chamber.

I pointed up at the wooden bridges and whispered, "That's chaos."

Clary grinned, clearly pleased that I was picking up on the language used here. "It is. But it's for Advanced Academia students only." She peered up into the shadows with a wistful expression. "Once my power is restored, I'm taking the entrance exam."

"Wait, I thought you were qualified as a Hunter."

"I am, but hunting and Advanced Academia are two separate tracks. You can either work at being a Gold Stripe Hunter, or if you show promise academically, you can go on to the Advanced Academia program—which leads to working either in Border and Ward Management, teaching, or becoming a Carver."

"Wait...do you want to be a Carver?"

She shrugged. "I don't know yet. I just know that I don't want to hunt."

I toyed with sharing my plan to become a Carver with her but decided against it for now. I'd reveal it after the Restoration Ceremony. The Unwoven knew about my stint with the CCC, and I'd shown Clary my journal and all my sketches. There was no reason for anyone to suspect an ulterior motive in my decision to become a Carver, but the thought of revealing it made me uneasy.

A petite woman in a calf-length green dress and round silver-framed spectacles materialized beside us, making me jump. "Can I help you with anything, my dears?" She stood with her hands clasped in front of her.

"No, thank you, Mistress Smithers." Clary beamed at her. "I know where to find everything."

"Of course, you do." Her bright eyes found me. "A new student. How wonderful."

"This is Anamaya," Clary said to her, then turned to me, "Mistress Smithers is the head librarian."

"It is a pleasure to meet you," Mistress Smithers said. "I'm here to help if you—" Her chin jerked up. "Excuse me. I must go. Someone is eating on the premises." She hurried away.

"Smithers is a stickler for the no food and drink rule," Clary said. "Come on, this way." She beckoned me to follow, then hurried past the main staircase and into the aisles beyond.

It was my first time in this room, but it probably wouldn't be my last if the reading lists for study here were anything to go by.

Arcane Botany by Alberta Evergreen was on my reading list for next month's new schedule. It was required reading for the Arcane Herbology class with Portia Reign.

The thought of having to work with her triggered my gag reflex. No doubt she'd be a bitch to me, that's the kind of person she was, so I wasn't going to give her any ammunition by showing up unprepared for class. I'd do the reading and write the essays, whatever it took to pass with the grades I needed to join the Carvers.

Still, I couldn't fathom how someone like Portia could be related to someone like Kian. My stepbrother had been kind to me. A friend when I'd had none. He'd promised to come back for me when Daniel had forced him to leave.

He'd promised.

But he'd never returned.

I tried to hate him for a while, but the hate never stuck. Deep down, I knew that if he could have come back, he would have. Something had kept him away, and maybe one day I'd find out what.

"Here we are!" Clary dove into the book-lined shelves, index card held aloft like a dowsing stick.

I followed her down the sunlit aisle, where the air swam with golden dust motes and smelled of leather and parchment. Something in the back of my mind stirred. A sense of familiarity. I'd been here before. Right here, in this very spot.

There was something here... Something I needed to see.

Clary called my name, but her voice was a distant whisper, buried under the rushing of blood in my head as I reached for a slender green spine nestled between dark red ones. The classification numbers...I knew those numbers.

This book had been hidden here by...someone. A sharp throb lanced through my temple, and a memory hit me. I was standing here. Afraid. Someone was coming. I had to hide the book and then...the hooded figure.

I had to run.

I needed to run—

"Ana?"

The memory faded. But it wasn't a memory. "I think... I think I remember part of my dream." I slipped the book off the shelf and flipped it open to find rows of neat handwriting. Not a textbook. "This book was *in* my dreams." I looked up and met her stunned gaze. "I think you were right, Clary. I don't think my dreams are normal dreams. I think they're some kind of message."

"The name Selina Evergreen doesn't ring a bell," Dori said.

"Same," Benedict said. "But she's an Evergreen. One of the main bloodlines in the Evergreen Coven."

We huddled around the coffee table in our tower's sitting room. The journal opened between us.

"It must be old," Clary said. "There are no actual Evergreens that go here. Not that I'm aware of."

There were no year markings in the book, just month and day, which didn't help us in identifying when Selina had been here. The journal started out as an account of papers she had to write and books she needed to read. A few notes here and there about how homesick she felt, and how she wished she hadn't been chosen as the sacrificial lamb for her family. Then there was a month's gap, and the next entry was penned in an angry scrawl.

I didn't do it. It wasn't me but they don't believe me, and now I'm stuck in Bramble Tower for a whole month. Alone. I hate this place. I hate them all.

"She was Unwoven?" Clary asked.

I flipped the page. "Seems like it. Listen... 'They're all ignoring me. Like some kind of freeze-out. Even the teachers. What is this shit? I don't deserve this...'

"Then this... 'I can't take it anymore. I'm so lonely.'" I turned through pages filled with doodles until I reached the next passage, gooseflesh breaking out over my skin. "'Bramble is the best thing that's happened to me because of him. I'm staying here even after the Restoration Ceremony. It's crazy, or maybe I'm crazy, but I don't care. He's wonderful. I think I've finally found a friend. All I need to do is get him out, and he can help me. But I must act fast before they find out.'"

"What is she talking about?" Benedict asked.

"I don't know." I read the next entry. "'I've been dreaming about a hooded figure every night. I wake up soaked in sweat. He says that it means they're close. That they're almost ready to come for me. But I'm almost ready, too. If only I didn't have to do this alone. I'm scared. I'm so fucking scared.'"

"Go on," Dori urged.

But there was no more. "The rest is blank."

"What happened to her?" Benedict asked.

I closed the book. "I don't know, but I plan to find out. Is there a record with all the past students' names on it?"

"Annual Student Records for the past ten years are kept in the library," Clary said. "Anything older is in the vault."

"Okay, so we check the ASR's first, and if we have no luck, we speak to some of the teachers. They've been here a while, someone should remember her, right? I mean, she was Unwoven. There must be a record of those students."

"I don't have classes until the afternoon," Clary said. "I can start looking through the books in the morning."

"I'll help," Benedict said.

"But that's your caffeination time," Clary reminded him.

"I'll take a travel cup to the library."

"Smithers doesn't allow food and drink," Dori pointed out.

"She does for me." Benedict winked. "I'm her favorite."

Dori rolled her eyes. "Only you would dare flirt with a hag."

I'd seen Smithers. She was old, but sweet-looking, hardly a hag. "That's a little harsh."

Clary snort-laughed. "No, Smithers is an *actual* hag." She sobered when she caught the blank look on my face. "But I don't suppose you know what that is. She's a caster, but she uses blood, bone, and flesh in her spells. She's one of a kind, and rumor has it she came here from another world during The Overshadowing."

"And that form you see," Dori said. "That is *not* what she truly looks like."

"What does she look like?"

"No one knows..." Dori intoned, drawing out the words in an eerie whisper.

"Because there is no other form," Benedict said. "And this hag business is just a rumor started by some students a decade or so ago."

"Yeah? And how old is she?" Clary asked.

"You don't ask a lady her age," Benedict said primly.

Clary laughed.

We were getting off track. "Back to Selina's book."

"Who?" they said in unison.

"Selina Evergreen." I tapped the journal.

"Oh yeah," Clary said. "First thing tomorrow."

Finding out who Selina was would be the first step in understanding why I dreamed about her. What was the connection between us? It had to be more than the fact she'd been allocated a room in Bramble.

Wait...if she'd been in Bramble, then Vitra was bound to have known her. I made a mental note to ask him after class tomorrow.

I tucked the journal into my bag. It was almost sunset, and I had a meeting with a barghest.

> Forever storms and angry seas,
> A winter's kiss, a chilling breeze.
> The nights are long, the days are short,
> And magic struggles to be taught.
> As new dawn breaks, and time resets,
> Those that are gone we must forget.
>
> *Nursery Rhyme, 2034 P.O.*

CHAPTER 30

Drayven was waiting for me by the arch to the gardens that evening as promised. He was dressed in loose cotton pants and a cream tunic that clung to his solid frame with every gust of wind that hit him. It was chilly, but it didn't look like that bothered him. In fact, there was a soft mist rising off his body, just like it had on the training ground, as his heat fought the cold night air.

His throat bobbed as I approached. "I'm sorry I didn't come and see you sooner," he said. "I wanted to say that earlier, but—"

"It's fine." I shrugged. "Honestly, I didn't even notice your absence." I smiled to let him know I was joking—and hide how much his absence had actually bothered me.

"There was a reason," Drayven said. "I needed the scent mark to fade just in case I was tempted to mark you again."

"I do bathe, you know."

His eyes lit up with amusement. "Scent marks don't vanish when you wash. My pheromones sank into your skin. Into your blood. They became a part of you for a while. Another barghest would also be able to smell the mark. It would warn him away from you, but to me...it would be a beacon to get closer and..." He shook his head. "The temptation to reapply the mark might have been too much."

"You could have just explained that."

He looked sheepish. "It's been busy outside the borders of late. The hunt has been out almost every night."

Excuses, excuses. I knew enough to understand that if a guy wanted to speak to you, then he'd find a way to do so, despite how busy he might be. But I smiled and nodded and let him lie to me because he didn't owe me a damn thing.

"You don't have to explain yourself to me. You don't owe me anything. In fact, I owe you. You've saved my ass a couple of times now."

"Still, I should have sent a raven."

Fucksake. "Then why didn't you?"

He flinched and his shoulders dropped. "Ravens won't carry a lie."

"Wait...what? So your whole explanation to me just now was a lie? Wow. Okay." I turned to leave.

"Ana, wait." He grabbed my arm, his grip firm but gentle. "It wasn't a lie, but it wasn't the whole truth, and a raven would have picked up on that, so sending a message would have been... difficult. The wording of it all..." He released me but didn't step away. "The truth is, scent marks don't just simply happen. I was able to use it because my primal half wants you." My pulse spiked. He wanted me? "And that is something that cannot happen," he continued. "I can't permit it to happen."

Permission... He taught an advanced combat class, so he was technically a teacher. My heart sank, but I forced my lips to smile. "I get it. I know about the Coterie rule against teacher-student relationships."

He blinked sharply. "Right. That's good. Good that you already know." He cleared his throat. "But I can help you with the grading. I want to."

I wasn't here for romance, so a relationship with Drayven had never been on the table. But there was no denying the hollow space that opened inside me at having the option taken away.

"Will you let me help you, Ana? Please."

Only an idiot would turn down this quality of help. It had nothing to do with wanting to spend one-on-one time with him. "Fine." I rolled my eyes, injecting a little levity into the moment. "You can help me."

The tension left his shoulders. "Good."

He led me through the gardens and into the woodland beyond, saturated with starlight and the floral scent of night blooms. Wildrun Forest was a popular Thrope haunt—or so I'd been told—but it gathered silent and watchful around us tonight, and my instincts told me we were alone.

He stopped a little way in and unbuttoned the top buttons of his tunic.

My gaze dropped to the smooth expanse of silken skin being exposed, and my mouth went dry. "What are you doing?"

"Stripping," he said. "I'm going to shift and chase you."

The pulse in my throat throbbed. "Um...okay." I turned my back on him, face heating because he was getting naked, and I desperately wanted to see.

"You can look if you like," Drayven said. "Thropes are not ashamed of their bodies. If you make it onto my hunt, you'll often be surrounded by nakedness."

Sounded like bliss. I took a breath and faced him, exhaling sharply at the glorious sight before me. He was somehow even larger outside the cage of clothing, his skin a moonlit, silken landscape of muscle and sinew, hard planes and shadowy dips.

Don't look down. Don't look down.

Dark skies, I wanted to look down so badly it hurt, but kept my eyes on his face by sheer force of will.

He smiled knowingly. "Come here."

The rumbly command sent a bolt of heat straight to my core.

"What?" The word came out as a squeak.

A glint of amusement danced in his eyes. "I need to take in your scent."

"Oh...of course." I forced my feet forward, stepping into his warmth and breathing in his crisp pine scent. *Lickable* came to mind.

He leaned in a fraction, inhaling deeply, chest vibrating with a purr. "Mmm, vanilla and...berries and...there you are."

I swallowed to moisten my mouth. "Is that what I really smell like?" The words slipped out, barely a whisper.

"It's hard to describe what pheromones smell like. But yours have a sweet undertone." He pulled back a little, and I froze as his pupils dilated, elongated, then dilated again.

He blinked and took a step away from me, and once again, it took every ounce of willpower not to let my gaze drop to the spot below his Adonis belt.

He cleared his throat. "For the grading, they'll employ an offensive Horror, so most likely one that will want to hunt you. They may have already provided their constructs with your scent."

"Wait, how would they do that?"

"Domestic probably took a small item of your clothing, something you sent to laundry."

I was missing a sock, but didn't socks always go missing?

"Echoes and wood weavers are both fast on land," Drayven continued. "The Echo you will see coming. The wood weavers you won't. You're fast, but so am I. Outrun me, and you might have a chance to outrun the Horror and Echoes."

"Don't I have to fight them?"

"Without access to the Weave, you can't wield a rift blade like the others. It won't channel the power you need, so your only option is to survive. Your only defense will be evasion."

And Sterling knew this. He fucking knew and was probably already celebrating my potential humiliation and all the nasty injuries I'd come back with. I couldn't control what happened during the grading, but I could damn well make sure I walked out of it on my own two feet.

"Okay. Let's do this. Do I get a head start?"

"As long as it takes me to shift. Elude me and make it back

here to this log"—he pointed to where his clothes were neatly piled on a fallen tree—"and consider it a win."

His body rippled as he began to shift.

I turned and ran.

There was nothing quite like the freedom of running, but not so much while being chased, although, knowing that it was Drayven doing the chasing excited me. Minutes blurred together as I wove through the trees, putting distance between us.

His growls, the heavy thud of his paws against the earth behind me, and the rasp of his breath sent tingles through me.

This was new.

Exhilarating.

I wanted him to catch me. To pin me to the fragrant earth and—

My boot caught on a root. I stumbled and hit the ground, but managed to scramble up and dash—just in time to avoid being pinned by his bulk as he pounced onto the spot I'd been just a moment ago.

My pulse spiked, and his laughter rang out behind me. "That was close."

"Close isn't good enough!"

I dropped my chin and pushed harder. The sound of rushing water reached my ears. There was a river nearby. If I crossed it, then I'd throw him off my scent. I headed toward the sound and spotted the gleaming body of water through a break in the trees a moment later. It didn't look too wide, and hopefully wouldn't be too deep either.

I burst from the tree line and splashed straight into the river. Water climbed up my calves, but I was out before the icy temperature could make too much of an impact on my skin. I dashed into the trees ahead, veering left to circle back upriver.

The sounds of pursuit faded, and by the time I crossed

upriver, they'd stopped altogether.

Ha, he'd totally lost my scent.

I dropped from a sprint to a jog the closer I got to the edge of the woods, the garden coming into view. The log with Drayven's clothes piled on it sat ahead, and triumph bloomed in my chest—if I could outrun a barghest, then—

A large, shadowy form pounced at me from the right.

Drayven!

I froze for a fraction too long—just enough time for him to sweep me off my feet and roll with me in his arms.

His arms...

He'd shifted mid-air.

I landed hard on my back with him on top of me, his thick thigh between mine, his body caging me. Our breath mingled, hot and heavy as our gazes tangled—melting, molding. I wanted to taste his mouth. To devour it.

I reached up to touch him before I could stop myself, my fingers tracing the firm shape of his parted mouth, pressing down on his bottom lip until he exhaled a soft hiss. His tongue flicked over my finger, and a lash of heat licked at my core.

I pulled my hand away, breathing hard past the sudden constriction in my chest and the powerful urge to offer him my mouth.

"Ana..." His voice came out low and gruff, resonating with a purr that vibrated through me. I curled my hands into fists to stop myself from giving in to the impulse to touch him again. But this time, he touched me, caressing my cheek with his calloused fingertips, his gaze like molten lava as it tracked over my face, down my neck, to my heaving chest.

I wanted him to touch me there. To lick me there. I wanted to feel him with every inch of my body. Tears pricked the back of my eyes with the desperation of a need I didn't understand.

He met my gaze with a longing that echoed mine. "Fuck." He pushed himself off me and walked away, leaving me with a rock on my chest and a hollow pit in my belly.

I stared at the winking stars through the canopy above while my tumultuous emotions recalibrated before finally sitting up.

Drayven had pulled on his pants but stood a few feet away with his back to me.

I wanted to go to him. Wrap my arms around his waist and rest my cheek on his back, but I'd be crossing a boundary, just like I'd done by touching him. "I'm sorry. The run and the adrenaline...I shouldn't have touched you, and—"

"I want to mark you again," he blurted.

My stomach flipped. "Oh..."

"You should go. We'll train again tomorrow night."

I stood and took a step toward him. "Why?"

He turned his head, offering me his profile. "Why? Because you need the training, and—"

"No. Not that. Why do you want to mark me?"

His shoulders rose and fell. "I told you. It's a primal thing."

"Yes, but what does that mean exactly?"

"It means that you're attractive to my beast. It finds you compatible in some way."

Primal attraction related to procreation and the production of the strongest possible Therianthrope offspring. If a female Thrope took a male lover who wasn't a Thrope, their children would be Thropes, but if a Thrope male took a female lover who wasn't a Thrope, then there was no guarantee of that. So, his primal side wanting me made no sense. It wouldn't take that risk. But the primal was just as influenced by a Thrope's human instincts as the human was by the beast within. Drayven's desires could affect his beast just as strongly as his beast's desires affected him. Which meant...it wasn't the beast that wanted me, it was Drayven.

He was attracted to me. "Drayven..."

He must have seen the comprehension on my face. His chest vibrated with a rumble, and he looked away. "By the blood, you're too damn smart."

"Have you felt this way before?"

A look of pain ghosted across his beautiful face. "Once. A

long time ago."

My chest tightened. "Who was she?"

"Her name was Brenna, but she's gone now. She was killed." He cleared his throat. "I... Uh... I'll walk you back to Bramble."

He obviously didn't want to talk about it. "It's fine. I can go myself."

"Are you sure?"

The fact he didn't insist told me that he needed some space. "It's just across campus." I smiled, but he had his head bowed again and didn't see it. "I'll see you tomorrow night."

I left him to his thoughts because I had plenty of my own to occupy me now.

I was so deep in my own head about Drayven, about his mate and his unwanted attraction to me, that I failed to sense I was being followed until I was trapped in a cold iron grip and shoved into the arch beneath the barracks.

Sterling blocked my path, his body coiled with tension, like a cat preparing to strike.

Fear twisted in my belly before I reminded myself that he had no real power to hurt me. "What the Fel do you want?"

"I want you to die," he said.

My pulse fluttered hard in my throat. "Yeah, sorry, not happening." I made to push past him, but he slammed a fist into my chest, driving me into the wall. My head whipped back then forward, and my teeth caught my tongue. The tang of iron filled my mouth, breath rushing out of my lungs, as heat bloomed across my breastbone.

His nostrils flared. "You're bleeding."

I blinked back the black spots clouding my vision. "And you're an asshole."

He moved in closer, and I shrank back on instinct before I could stop myself.

"Good," he hissed. "You should be scared."

I dragged in a breath, forcing my pulse to steady. "I'm not scared of you."

He chuckled, mirthless and cold. "Yes, you are. And you should be." He braced a hand on the brick above my head, caging me in and clouding the air with his linen-fresh scent. "I've been restrained. Patient. Waiting for the grading to have you put in your place once and for all—because you're nothing but a stain on humanity, a murderer just like your ancestor. It should have been *your* head under my blade that night. *Your* blood on my hands."

My eyes burned with rage. "Yeah? But instead, you killed my father! You broke the law. There should have been a trial and—"

His hand was around my throat before I could react, squeezing tight enough to cut off my words.

"You think a few lessons with Thorn will help you?" He pressed me against the wall, my bones grinding against brick, his grip on my throat tightening enough to choke. Panic burst in my chest. I clawed at his hand, lungs desperate for breath.

Oh, Trinity, he was going to do it. He was going to break his oath and finish what he'd started on the training field. He was going to kill me.

His eye twitched, and he released me with a rough laugh that made the hairs on my nape quiver.

I sucked in air, chest heaving in blissful breaths, relief pumping so hard through my oxygen-starved veins that I almost didn't hear his next words.

"Fail the grading," he said.

"Fuck you."

"If you don't, there will be nothing but pain for you here. I promise you that."

I lifted my chin and sneered. "Haven't you heard? I don't feel pain."

Moonlight caught his pale eyes, pupils dilating to drink me in. "Oh, but you will, Anamaya. You will..."

A prickle of unease penetrated the haze of my ire. "What?"

He backed away, and I followed, pulse racing. "What do you mean?" Wait... "You think you can use Tamina against me? I beat her once. I can do it again and—"

"Tamina has nothing to do with this."

I wasn't going to bite. I wasn't... Fuck it. "Then what? Tell me!"

He smirked, already turning away. "Tell you and ruin the surprise? Not likely." He walked off whistling a light, happy tune that left me buried beneath a fresh wave of doubt.

But maybe that's what he wanted. To psyche me out.

My blood boiled. Who the fuck did he think he was? No one and nothing, that's who. Just like everyone else here. Discarded by his royal father. Dark skies, why hadn't I thrown that in his face? Ugh. Next time. I had no doubt he'd attack me again, but I wasn't going to sit around and wait for him to act. I was going to take a jab at him first. I wasn't sure how yet, but I'd come up with something.

For now, my focus had to remain on the grading. Retaliation on Sterling would have to wait.

Sylph: An elemental creature that can become invisible to the naked eye. Suffocates its prey by stealing the oxygen from its lungs. Soulless creatures, sylphs are said to sometimes slip into the skins of their victims, desperate to feed on the lingering vestiges of a soul.

The Compendium of Horrors

CHAPTER 31

My blood was still simmering by the time I got back to Bramble Tower. Dori, Clary, and Benedict were in the sitting room, gathered around the coffee table by the fire, a deck of cards spread between them. The chatter died when I entered, and they looked up at me with enquiring expressions.

"How did the training go?" Dori asked.

"Training was fine," I bit out.

"O-kay..." Dori shot Benedict a look.

I let out a frustrated growl, threw myself onto the sofa, grabbed a cushion, and screamed into it.

I resurfaced to three faces staring at me.

"That good, huh?" Benedict quipped.

I set the cushion down. "Sterling grabbed me on the way here."

"What?" they said in unison.

"He threatened me." I filled them in on the encounter, a prickly heat needling my cheeks at the memory of his hands on me. "I hate him. I fucking hate him so much."

"We have to report this," Clary said.

Dori rolled her eyes. "Yeah, because that'll make a difference."

She was right. "Reporting him won't help. I have to deal with him myself." I needed a weapon. Something small and easy to hide on my person. Something I could use to poke out his pretty eyes—and a glass jar filled with formalin to keep them in.

"Um. Ana..." Clary said. "Why are you smiling like that?"

Shit. I tucked away my murder smile. "I need a weapon. Something small."

"Only Hunters are allowed weapons on campus," Clary said. "Ours were taken when we were Unwoven, so we can't help you."

"Yes, but..." Benedict sat up. "If it doesn't look like a weapon..." He jumped up and hurried across the room.

I twisted on the sofa as he ducked into his room.

"I'm intrigued," Dori said. "Nut?" She held out a bowl of peanuts to me.

I took a handful and shoved them into my mouth, chewing out my frustration.

Benedict emerged a moment later, something clutched in his hand. "Here, you can borrow this." He handed me a hairpin with a shell design on the end. It was small and delicate, but the pin part was wicked sharp. "It belonged to my mother. It's one of the few items I have of hers."

I turned the pin over. I could coat the end in some of the toxin I had. It would only hurt someone if I jabbed it into them hard enough to draw blood. But...it was a keepsake. What if I lost it?

"I can't accept this." I tried to hand it back, but he gently covered my hand with his, curling my fingers over the offering.

"My mother is gone," Benedict said. "She didn't care enough to stay. If it can keep you safe, I want you to have it. So that you can stay. I want you to stay..."

A lump formed in my throat. "I... Thank you." I wanted to hug him. Instead, I dropped my gaze. Get a grip, Ana.

"Okay, now that's settled, how about we play some cards?" Dori said, breaking the strange tension.

"I'm in!" Clary said.

"Yep, me too." Benedict reclaimed his seat.

Once again, all eyes were on me. I couldn't allow myself to get too invested in these people. Nightsbridge wasn't my home, and this trio...I could never be a real friend to them, but there was no denying that in that moment, there was nowhere else I'd rather be.

"What are we playing?"

I had counseling with Miss Snap first thing the next day. We'd switched our biweekly sessions to the mornings so we could have breakfast together. Mandy made the best scones, and our sessions had become the highlight of my week. Sometimes we just chatted about random things, nothing to do with classes or my feelings, and I'd learned that Miss Snap was an orphan. Her parents had passed away when she was fourteen, and she'd been forced to live with her aunt, a cruel woman who'd made her life miserable.

Mandy had made it her mission to help other young women like herself. She worked with an orphanage for almost a decade after she turned eighteen, helping children to find new families, while studying to be a counselor. Eventually, she petitioned to be recruited to Nightsbridge.

I feel that the children forced to be here need someone they can talk to about their fears and their doubts. Someone who doesn't want anything from them. Someone who values them for who they are and not what they can do. I want to be a safe place.

Just like me, she'd chosen to come here. She'd explained that not all the staff here were conscripted. That some had volunteered to work here. Even though I was the only student here by choice, I wasn't the only supernal here because I wanted to be.

Mandy Snap was a genuinely sweet woman, and I enjoyed our time together. I was eager to get to our session, focused on the building looming ahead of me, so I didn't register the figures hurrying toward me until it was too late.

It was always quiet on the Main Building grounds before nine in the morning, so no one saw when I was grabbed and hauled off the path and into the bushes.

A hand covered my mouth. More hands on my body holding me tight as I thrashed and kicked—and then suddenly, I was free, crashing to the ground.

I scrambled up—but a blow to the head slammed me back to the earth. My ears rang, and the world swayed.

"Hello, Anamaya, I think it's time we had a little chat."

Tamina…

I slowly raised my throbbing head to look up at her and the three Phages surrounding me. I guess it had been too much to hope that she'd simply forget about Ruspin. But after three weeks of no contact, I could be excused for thinking that she had.

"Do your chats usually involve fists?"

Tamina shot one of her companions a glare. "Theo gets a little protective of me, don't you, love?" Theo bared his silver-capped teeth in a snarl. "But no. We're not going to hurt you. Consider this a warning."

"A warning for what? Ruspin? Kind of late for that, don't you think?"

Her eyes narrowed to slits. "You have no idea who you're messing with, Onyx."

My stomach grumbled. "Fine, hurry up and warn me so I can go get breakfast."

Her left eye twitched, and she clenched her jaw. "You think this is a joke? You think taking him from me is a fucking joke?"

"No. I think you're a fucking psycho bitch who belongs in a cage."

She sneered. "You have no idea!"

I slowly pushed myself up and dusted off my uniform. "I think I do."

A cacophony of emotions flitted across her face. "I want him back."

"Tough shit."

She took a step toward me. "You're going to get him back for me."

"Um...how about go fuck yourself."

"You're going to assert a claim on Ruspin. You made a deal to free him, and so he owes you a debt. You're going to cash it in by asking him to offer himself to me once more."

She was delusional. "Why in the world would I do that?"

"Because if you don't, everyone you care about will suffer."

Seriously? I laughed. "That's perfect because the only people I gave a shit about are dead. Everyone else is one-hundred-percent dispensable. So have fun with that."

A few weeks ago, those words might have been true. Now? A bald-faced lie. But Tamina could never know.

"You think you're stonehearted?" she hissed. "You think you're above feelings? Well, we'll see about that."

A shiver ran up my spine. "Get a life, Tamina. Better yet, get some psychiatric help."

I made to shove past her, but Theo grabbed hold of my arm and hauled me back. "You don't get to disrespect the princess and walk away."

"Theo?" Tamina said sharply. "What are you doing?"

"I'm going to teach this bitch a little humility. I'm going to break her."

I yanked at my arm, but his grip was steel. He threw me to the ground and covered me with his body.

"Theo!" Tamina cried.

"Get off me!" I bucked, trying to get in a position to roll him off, but he was too large—his limbs in all the wrong places for me to enact the move.

"Stop fighting, and you might even like it," he said, breath hot on my cheek.

Horrific realization flooded me. I twisted, yanking a hand free to reach for the pin in my hair—but he was knocked off me before I could use it.

I scrabbled to my feet. Tamina was on top of Theo, her fingers curled into claws as they swiped at his face over and over. "Never! Never, never, never!" she screeched, eyes wild, blood-spattered across her face.

"Tamina!" Her cronies tackled her, prying her off her minion.

What the actual fuck? I backed up. She was chaos. They all were chaos. I grabbed my backpack and ran.

I washed my face and straightened my clothes before seeing Mandy. My stomach quivered from Theo's attack—and the knowledge of his disgusting intention. I would have jabbed that pin into his throat. Would have killed him. He wouldn't have succeeded. Still, it took a few minutes for the horror of what could have happened to leave me.

It wasn't the first time I'd been attacked, and it wouldn't be the last, but the kind of violation Theo had intended might have broken me. Tamina had saved me.

I guess the crazy Phage had boundaries. I had to respect that, which left me feeling all kinds of conflicted. I left the bathroom and hurried to my session with Mandy, determined to put the incident out of my mind because I didn't want it to dominate my session. An hour and a half already felt too short.

I rapped on the door then slipped into the room. "Morning."

Mandy looked up from her desk with a smile that dropped when her eagle eyes zeroed in on the bruise on my jaw.

"What happened?" she asked.

"Tamina and her cronies happened, but I'm fine."

Her eyes flashed. "This is unacceptable."

"I can handle her. Don't worry. Now, please, can we eat? I'm starving."

She looked ready to argue, then sighed and nodded. "Fine. But we *will* talk about it."

I groaned. "Fine."

I filled her in on Tamina and her empty threats while we ate, leaving out the part about Theo. The blood spray from Tamina's attack was proof enough that he'd gotten his comeuppance, and honestly, I didn't want to dwell on it. Best to shove it into the box in the back of my mind with all my personal horrors.

I quickly moved on to Sterling and his assholery. "And he's moved the grading up to punish me." I toyed with one of the crystals on her desk. Mandy knew about my history with the Damascus family. Facts that had been in my file. The Academy was nothing but thorough.

"That doesn't sound ethical at all," she said.

"Tell me about it." I set the crystal down and flopped back into my chair.

"And how is the sleepwalking?"

"I had an episode a couple of nights ago. But yesterday, I remembered a little bit about my dream."

"That's good," she said. "It might help us figure out why it's happening." She poured more tea into my cup then topped up her own.

I filled her in on the library incident. "Selina Evergreen is the name of the girl in my dream. She hid her journal."

Mandy frowned. "That name doesn't ring a bell. Meetings with me are mandatory for all students under eighteen, and all new students for at least six months. But then, I've only been here for three years, she must be an older student."

"Yeah, we figured that."

"And this journal...what was in it?"

"I think she was being bullied. I think something happened to her."

Mandy sat forward in her seat. "Could I see it?"

"Sure." I reached into my bag for the journal, rooting around for the book. Where was it? Shit. "It's not in here."

"Are you sure you packed it?"

"Positive. But it's gone."

And there was only one person who could have taken it.

Tamina.

Vitra's gaze went immediately to the bruise on my face as I took my seat in class, but he didn't say a word. We'd barely spoken the past few weeks. Even though I'd seen him around the tower, our encounters had been brief and guarded on both sides. But despite the distance, the chemistry between us was still there, flaring every time we spoke or looked at one another for too long.

Frankly, it was annoying as Fel.

Today was quiz and essay day, so the hour passed quickly. I'd done the reading, so answering the many questions on wood weavers and writing an essay about salamanders didn't take long.

The fire-elementals were fascinating. Hailing from an elemental world occupied by beings called djinn. Salamanders were distant cousins to creatures called efreet. Not all salamanders were Horrors; some were benevolent, and both kinds occupied the forest. The only way to tell one from the other was if they attacked or not. They also had a hierarchy of their own, and according to ancient lore, you could make pacts with the higher-level salamanders by giving certain offerings.

Vitra ended the session with a clap of his hands and instructions for us to drop our papers on his desk on the way out. "Please stay behind a moment, Miss Onyx."

My stomach did a little flip that I studiously ignored. I needed to ask Vitra about Selina, so it was just as well he wanted to speak with me... But what did he want to speak with me about? My stomach quivered again. Dammit.

I waited in my seat while everyone filed out, noting a couple of side-eyes from some of the older female students. They probably thought there was something going on between me and Vitra.

The door closed behind the final student, and Vitra took his favored spot, leaning up against his desk, arms crossed. "How did you get the bruise, Ana?"

Of course, *that's* what he wanted to talk about.

Like Fel was I telling him about Tamina. He'd made it clear what he thought about me going up against her. "Combat class."

His jaw ticked. "Don't lie to me. That bruise wasn't there when you left for counseling this morning, and you don't have combat today. So tell me, how did it get there?"

"I ran into a fist. I'm fine." I shrugged.

The air was suddenly charged, pricking my skin. "Whose fist?" he bit out.

"It doesn't matter."

A strange tension in the air pressed against my skin for a beat before it vanished.

His eyes narrowed. "Then you won't mind telling me who put it there."

Dark skies, he was persistent. "Fine, one of Tamina's cronies."

"Which one?"

I threw up my hands. "I don't know. Now, can we drop it?" I held his gaze steadily and arched a brow.

He smiled coolly. "Consider it dropped."

Just like that? After he'd pushed so hard? Hard to believe, but I'd take the reprieve. I had more important things to worry about. "I actually wanted to ask you something. Do you know a Selina Evergreen?"

He shook his head. "No. Should I?"

"She was a student here. Maybe still is."

He smiled wryly. "There are and have been many students here."

"She was in Bramble at some point."

He frowned. "I would remember her if she'd been in Bramble."

"She definitely was."

"Like I said, I would remember."

"I found her journal." I filled him in on what I'd read and my sleepwalking dreams.

He leaned back against his desk, arms crossed, his attention focused on me as he listened. I stumbled through my account, hyper aware of every moment his gaze dropped to my lips. The heat of that awareness coiled low in my belly, a far contrast to the cool, collected figure that he presented.

"Where is the journal now?" he asked once I'd finished speaking.

"I think Tamina or one of her goons took it. But I'm going to get it back."

"No. You're not. Leave it with me."

Annoyance flared in my chest, because why did he have to be so... So helpful. "I can fight my own battles, Master Vitra."

He blinked sharply before a small smile curled his lips. "I'm sure you can," he said softly. "But you don't always have to."

I dropped my gaze to the floor, cheeks warm with an awareness of this male that I didn't need or want.

"Get some rest," he said, words coasting on a sigh. "You'll need to be sharp for the grading."

He was right. I was exhausted from the constant conflict, and I still had training tonight with Drayven, then the grading tomorrow... "You heard about the changes, huh?"

"I did. But I have faith that you won't let these changes affect your performance."

"What do *you* know about my performance?"

"I know that you stay back every class to work on the moves. I know that Mr. Thorn has been helping you prepare. I know that you want this, so I know enough."

"Well, that's not creepy at all."

He'd been keeping tabs on me. Watching me? No contact over the past few weeks hadn't meant he'd forgotten about me. Ah, my sexy naga stalker.

"It's my job to watch you, Ana. I'm your mentor."

His words were a cold reminder that he could never be more. "I should get going."

I gathered my things and moved toward the exit.

"Anamaya..."

I glanced over my shoulder. He was standing a mere foot away. He'd moved so fast and silently that I hadn't heard him.

I lifted my chin to drink him in, chest aching with an inexplicable longing that made me want to rub my face against his chest. "What?"

His gaze flicked to my white-knuckled grip on the door handle, his smile wry. "Good luck."

I slipped from the room, taking his scent with me, eager to put distance between us. The man was dangerous, the way he made me *feel* was addictive.

Fate certainly had a cruel sense of humor.

The dining hall was filling up by the time I finished telling the others about my encounter with Tamina and how she'd threatened to hurt people I cared about. Once again, I left out the part about Theo's attack. I wasn't ready to talk about it yet. Probably never. It had shaken me too much, and I couldn't afford to be shaken while here.

"I told Tamina there wasn't anyone I cared about here, but she's seen us together a lot, so just...be careful, okay?"

"That's bullshit," Dori said. "She can't touch us, not without breaking half a dozen treaties and contracts that exist between the covens and the Baobhan Sith houses."

"Then what was she talking about?"

"No idea. Blowing smoke, no doubt," Benedict said. "But it's sweet that you care."

"Even if you don't want to," Clary added.

I looked away, rubbing the back of my neck. "Am I that obvious?"

"Yep," they said in unison.

I ran a hand down my face. "Look, I don't do friendships."

"Good," Dori said, chewing her baguette. "Because this isn't a friendship. It's an alliance."

I couldn't help but grin at her attempt to make this easier on me. For a moment, I entertained the possibility of simply going with it. Of letting down my guard and letting them in, but then what? They'd find out why I was truly here and either hate me or end up getting hurt trying to help me. Which... Which was what I'd wanted from them to start with. A few weeks ago, they hadn't mattered, but now...

No, I couldn't tell them the truth. I couldn't risk them getting involved—getting hurt.

I'd have to do this myself. "Um, Clary, did you find anything in the student records?"

She blinked sharply, clearly confused. "Student records?"

"Yes. About Selina Evergreen?"

"Who?"

I turned to Dori and Benedict, but they looked just as confused as Clary.

"Seriously? Is this some kind of joke?"

"Ana, what are you talking about?" Dori asked.

A cold pit loomed in my belly. She looked and sounded deathly sincere.

I tried again. "The journal we found in the library yesterday? The one belonging to Selina Evergreen?" They stared blankly at me, and my stomach dropped. "You don't remember?"

"Don't remember what?" Clary said.

Something was very wrong here. I gathered my things. "I have to go. I'll see you guys later."

"Ana? Wait!"

But I couldn't wait. A theory had taken root in my mind, and I needed to test it.

I found Vitra in his classroom, marking papers. He looked up with a frown as I entered. "Miss Onyx?"

"We spoke earlier, right?"

"Yes. About the bruise on your face." His eyes narrowed. "Is there something else you wish to tell me about that encounter?"

"No, but...we talked about the journal belonging to Selina Evergreen, too."

He canted his head quizzically. "Who?"

Ice trickled through my veins. "You don't remember us talking about her?"

"Ana, are you feeling all right?" He made to stand, and I took a step back, blood thundering in my head. "Ana, what's going on?"

If I explained it to him, would he even remember? No. Something was seriously off here. The Weave Watchers' warning came back to me now. *Much is hidden in memories lost, but eyes born of ancient power can see... Be watchful, be wary, be vigilant.*

"Nothing. I... I have to go." I ducked out of the room before he could stop me and headed for the main entrance, eager to get back to my room.

If I was going to figure this out, then I'd have to do it alone.

Interviewer: And why create such a machine?
Prof. Brimstone: Why not?
Interviewer: Well, that's hardly an answer, is it?
Prof. Brimstone: Very well. I hope that through this we might be found.
Interviewer: Found? Are you saying that we're lost?
Prof. Brimstone: Aren't we? Aren't we all?

Extract from Interview, 2030 P.O. (Vault Archives)

CHAPTER 32

Without the journal to guide me, I didn't have much to go on. Just a fuzzy dream and the Weave Watchers' cryptic words. But this was all connected to my sleepwalking, I was certain about that much.

There was a force guiding me...somewhere. Some power reaching out, trying to connect. It had led me to Selina's journal and... Wait! I rushed to the windowsill, to the initials etched into the wood.

S.E. Selina Evergreen.

Oh Trinity. This had been her room.

That had to mean something.

Selina had been a student here, but no one remembered her. Even when I told them her name, they forgot.

There had to be a spell in place—one that, for some reason, wasn't affecting me. But if it was affecting everyone else, then who could help me figure this out? I'd need to be careful who I spoke to about this. Whoever cast the spell was most likely still at Nightsbridge. I couldn't risk tipping them off. But I couldn't do nothing either.

I was stumped.

For now.

But my brain worked best when I let a problem simmer in the background. I pulled out the book on arcane botany and parked my ass at my desk. I had tons of reading to do before my new classes next week, so the Selina problem would have to wait.

I was nearing the end of my chapter when a sketch of a circle of mushrooms caught my eye, the tops gleaming in the moonlight. I'd seen this before. But where? Oh, Trinity, I'd seen it in my dream.

I dropped my gaze to the caption beneath the image.

Custos Naturae is a powerful spell that takes weeks to prepare. The fungi must be planted and nurtured with dew water and moonlight, each cap sown with intention. Completed correctly, the circle will protect its creator and hold any force that wishes to harm him or her within its grasp.

A protection spell. If my dreams were about Selina, then the spell must have belonged to her, too. But what had she been trying to protect herself from? The hooded figure?

I glanced at the window, at a sky painted orange by the dying rays of a setting sun. Where had the time gone? I closed the book and quickly changed into my training gear. Drayven would be waiting for me, and it wouldn't do to be late.

Drayven didn't show. Instead, he sent Jay and Brek, and I couldn't even lie to myself—I was disappointed. They didn't offer an explanation as to why he hadn't come, and I didn't ask.

My ego was bruised enough as it was.

We ran wooden sword drills. I couldn't use a rift blade, but I'd still have a regular sword, and any blade was better than none. It could buy me time or cut me out of a tricky situation.

I sparred with the Thropes in their human form where they both attacked at the same time, shooting instructions and tips on where to stab and how to evade. Then Brek shifted and attacked me in his Thrope form while Jay taught me the best places to stab a beast like him.

I couldn't help but grumble, though. "How will this help? There are no Horrors that look like Thropes."

"Echoes can take a Thrope's form," Jay explained. "If they can get inside a Thrope's head."

"We haven't had any training on shielding an Echo attack, so I doubt they'll throw any at us."

"Never underestimate a grading situation," Jay said. "They could certainly throw in an Echo to test your natural mental shielding. But even if there are no Echoes, use this training to hone your reflexes and stamina. You're going to need both."

That shut me up, and we trained for another hour before I was too exhausted to continue.

They offered to walk me back to Bramble, and I accepted, not wanting another run-in with Sterling. I had my venom-coated hairpin in place just in case, but the thought of another scuffle made me want to weep with fatigue.

The chilly air was bliss on my overheated skin, and the night walk, flanked by two guys, allowed me to appreciate the nocturnal beauty of the Academy grounds.

This place was a work of art, from the neatly clipped and shaped bushes to the graceful sculptures and statues, down to the array of flora, planted in such a way that pastel and deeper hues worked together to brighten even the night.

We walked in companionable silence for a few minutes before it occurred to me how little I knew about these guys.

"So...I know that Drayven is a barghest, but what are you two?"

"Thought you'd never ask," Jay said with a cheeky grin.

"Shit, I'm sorry."

"He's joking," Brek said, shooting him a scathing look. "I'm a loup-garou and Jay is rakshasa."

"I've heard of loup, but not rakshasa."

"We're a rare breed," Jay said proudly. "Not many packs left. Mine is one of the largest."

"And how come you guys were sent here? Is there a way that your packs choose?"

"It's done by lottery to keep it fair," Brek said. "At least in my pack."

"Not for us," Jay replied. "My grandfather signed the Covenant, and so our specific bloodline is responsible for supplying Thropes to the Academy every few years."

"I know your cousin, Cami. She's sweet."

"Too sweet to be here," Jay said.

Brek made a sound of agreement.

"She's a twin," Jay said. "Her brother Raj is what we call a runt. They were set on sending him—they usually send a male—but Cami fought them. She demanded the right to take his place."

"Brave girl."

"She is," Jay said. "But I wish she didn't have to be here. She's much too smart to waste her life stuck in this place. But she says you've been hanging out with her?" He said it tentatively, as if he was worried it wasn't true.

"Yeah, I have. She's a good kid. I like her."

His smile bloomed. "Thank you."

"What for? My motives are completely selfish. She's one of the smartest students in my class." I winked. "She makes the best study partner."

Bramble came into view, the upper windows glowing with amber light. Was that the Unwoven floor?

"He wanted to come tonight," Jay blurted suddenly. "Drayven did."

"Jay," Brek warned.

My neck heated. "It's okay. You don't have to explain."

"Yes, Jay, you really don't," Brek bit out.

Jay puffed out a breath and nodded. "Just...don't give up on him if he pulls away."

"By the blood," Brek rolled his eyes. "You're such a meddler."

I didn't have the emotional energy to worry about Drayven right now. Yes, I was attracted to him, but attraction wouldn't get me through the grading. It wouldn't get me into the vault.

I was glad he'd backed off. Now I could focus solely on my goals without having my heartstrings played with.

We slipped under the arch that led to the quad surrounding Bramble, and from this angle, it was easy to determine which windows belonged to my floor and which specifically belonged to me. I'd left my lamp on, and the gentle glow was visible. The light stuttered and a moment later a shadowy figure appeared in my window. I was sure I'd locked my door. "What the fuck?"

"What is it?" Jay asked.

"There's someone in my room." I broke into a sprint across the quad.

The bodies of the dead littered the battlefield, rot and decay permeating the air. Pools of crimson dappled the earth as if the earth itself were bleeding. Nameless, faceless, the lost. There is no triumph in war.

Unknown Author (The Vault)

CHAPTER 33

My door was locked, which brought me up short. If it was locked, then how could anyone be inside?

Brek and Jay exchanged skeptical glances as I unlocked and pushed it open.

The room was empty. But Jay checked the washroom and under the bed anyway. He raked back his thick, dark hair. "All clear."

"You must have gotten the rooms mixed up," Brek said.

My scalp prickled, nape tightening. "Yeah. Must have. Sorry about that."

They wished me luck for the grading tomorrow, said their goodbyes, and left.

I closed the door and leaned against it, scanning my room once more, trying desperately to pinpoint the source of my unease.

I spotted it a moment later.

My mother's box was open on the dresser, Dharma's ruby amulet beside it.

I hadn't taken it out.

Someone *had* been in my room.

Clary climbed into bed beside me, and Benedict and Dori got comfortable in sleeping bags on the floor.

"Just let anyone try to come through that door now," Benedict said, plastering a menacing scowl on his face.

"Yeah, that face will totally scare them off," Dori drawled.

"Or you could just sing to them," Benedict shot back.

"Hey!" Dori pressed a hand to her chest. "That's just mean."

"Dori is tone deaf," Clary whispered to me.

"I heard that," Dori said.

None of them had questioned my suspicions when I explained why I thought someone had been in my room. They simply offered to sleep in here with me tonight.

"That bitch Tamina could have sent someone," Dori had said. "They might have bypassed the lock somehow."

Now I had three bodyguards. I'd have liked to say I didn't feel the need for the company, but I'd be lying.

I was spooked. By Selina, the missing memories, and now the person who'd snuck into my room simply to rifle through my mother's things.

Despite all those factors, sleep came surprisingly easy. I slipped into dreams of home and Mother. But the dreams soon turned sour, taking me into the forest once more. To the circle of mushrooms and then to the quad outside Bramble Tower.

A shadow circled overhead.

The rook.

"You have to see. You need to see so that others may see."

I didn't like this. I didn't want to look.

But my feet moved forward of their own accord, dragging me step by step toward the pavilion.

Every inch of me wanted to fight the pull, but even in my dream, Clary's advice came to mind.

"If you don't fight it, then maybe you'll remember."

If I wanted to solve Selina's mystery, I'd have to give in. To let the dream take its course, even though dread pooled in my belly.

The pavilion loomed, closer and closer. My heart swelled with impending doom. No. I didn't want to see. I didn't—

"Dammit, Onyx!"

I jolted awake in Vitra's arms, the wind howling and ripping at my nightshirt.

"What..." I was outside. How had I gotten outside?

"You're bleeding. Again." Vitra scooped me into his arms, his jaw tight with anger. "If you want my attention, there are better ways of getting it."

I was too shaken to take umbrage at his assumption. "I was locked in my room. The quarters. Pip..."

"Yes, yes. I'll be looking into that."

I clung to him, using his body heat to stave off the chill. "I was dreaming. I need to remember."

"You need to get warm and have your feet tended to. You've cut them on the gravel."

The soles of my feet began to throb as if on cue, a sure indication of an injury.

We slipped into the tower and up the stairs. "The others were in my room. They were sleeping in my room. I don't understand..."

The thud of boots echoed down the stairs, and Benedict and Dori appeared above us.

"Fuck!" Benedict came to a halt, raking a hand through his hair. "Ana, we don't know what happened."

"What happened is you slept through your friend getting up and sleepwalking," Vitra bit out.

"I'm a light sleeper," Clary said. "I felt you get out of bed—but I couldn't move."

"Same," Benedict said. "I heard you open the door, but I couldn't pull myself out of sleep."

"Something happened to us," Dori said.

Vitra's eyes narrowed as he studied me. "You'll stay with me for the rest of the night."

"What?" I tried to wriggle out of his arms, but he simply held me tighter.

"That is *not* an offer, Miss Onyx. It's an order."

"You can't order me."

"You'll find that I can." He continued up the stairs, past the others. "I'm your Tower Master, and it is my duty to keep you safe. Right now, the safest place for you is in my quarters. In my bed."

"Now, you wait a minute—"

"If a spell *was* used to incapacitate your friends, then they can't be trusted to watch over you. I, however, am immune to most magical influence."

"I'm *not* sleeping with you."

He let out a bark of laughter. "Really? That's where your mind goes? Don't worry, I'll be on the sofa."

My face burned as we crossed a hallway and climbed yet another flight of stairs.

"What if your dreams and your sleepwalking are some kind of spell?" Dori suggested.

"Oh shit," Clary said. "They could be."

"We get our power back in a few days," Benedict reminded us. "If we can keep you safe till then, we'll figure this out once we have access to the Weave."

"Good plan," Vitra said as we reached the Unwoven floor. "Now get some rest. You'll need your energy to cheer Miss Onyx on in the grading tomorrow." He didn't wait for their responses before continuing up the next flight of stairs to his floor.

There was no fighting this man, and frankly, I didn't want to. I relaxed in his arms, and his grip on me eased a little.

"What happened earlier today?" he asked. "When you came back to the classroom? You were stressed about something."

"There's no point telling you. You'll forget. Everyone I've told has forgotten."

"Forgotten what?"

What harm would it do to explain it to him? "There was a student who went here. But something happened to her, and now every time I tell anyone about her, they forget."

His body stiffened. "And you told me about her? You told me her name?"

"Yes. I had her journal, and I think Tamina took it. You were going to get it back for me. But you forgot. I guess you're not as immune to magical influence as you think."

He was silent for several beats. "Theo Moon is in the infirmary. Severe facial trauma. He refuses to name his attacker."

I felt his regard like a warm caress and looked up to meet it. "What?"

"Do you know who attacked him?"

Tamina was a crazy bitch. The things she'd done to Ruspin were despicable, but she'd jumped in to save me from Theo. I owed her for that.

"Ana?" Vitra probed.

"I have no idea. But he probably deserved it."

"He's the one responsible for the bruise on your face?"

"Maybe..."

He pushed open the door to his quarters and carried me into blessed warmth. "Then yes, he deserves it." He set me down on the sofa and knelt in front of me before gently lifting my bloody foot to examine the sole. "It's not too bad. Let's get you cleaned up." He went into the neighboring room, returning a few moments later with a bowl of warm water, a washcloth, and bandages.

I sat up and reached for the cloth, but he pulled his hand away. "Sit back."

"I can sort myself out."

The corner of his mouth lifted. "I'm sure you can."

If only he knew how often I didn't bother with...sorting myself out. It did very little for me unless I was already feeling emotionally and cognitively aroused over someone. But tonight, his touch evoked pleasant tingles that spread out over my foot and climbed my leg.

He glanced up. "Your pulse is racing. Since I know you can't feel pain, I can only assume that you're deriving pleasure from my touch."

"I don't feel that either." It was a lie when it came to him, but I didn't need him knowing how he affected me.

He stilled. "What?"

"Pleasure." I shrugged. "Pleasure and pain. Gone. It's my special curse."

He slowly lowered my foot. Then ran his hand from my ankle to my calf while maintaining eye contact. My pussy throbbed, and I pressed my thighs together to quell the sweet ache blooming there. I was dressed only in sleep shorts and a soft cotton shirt. Practically naked, and he was touching me. Oh, Trinity, I wanted him to continue to touch me.

"You can feel me?"

"Yes, obviously I feel it." I kept my tone neutral. "It just... It doesn't do anything for me."

He pushed up on his knees, leaning forward to brace himself on the arms of my chair, his body close, too close. My breath quickened.

He licked his lips. "So...when you fuck...do you come?"

My stomach quivered, the way he said that damn word... "This is hardly an appropriate conversation." I sounded like a prude, and I didn't even care.

He frowned, gaze dropping to my parted mouth. "I'm curious. Tell me."

I swallowed past the throb in my throat. "I've had orgasms, of course, but more because of what's up here." I tapped my temple. "Pleasure isn't only about physical sensation, you know."

He sat back on his heels with a look on his face that I couldn't decipher. "You're right. It isn't. With the right partner, you could feel all kinds of pleasure."

Was he offering? My mouth was suddenly dry as sandpaper. "I suppose so."

The look on his face intensified, gaze darkening, and for a moment, I thought he might offer to show me, but then he dropped his gaze and reached for my foot again. "It's late. Let's get you cleaned up and into bed."

The hollow place in my chest did *not* mean that I was disappointed.

He finished cleaning and bandaging my feet with slow, precise movements. He had nice hands, large hands. Strong hands with long fingers and manicured nails. Hands that would look good against my skin.

Nope. Do not go there, Ana.

I turned my musings to safer topics. What traits and powers did a naga have aside from the ability to command water? Did he shift into a snake?

"You're thinking hard," Vitra said, sitting back on his heels again. "Care to share?"

"Do you shift into a snake?"

His mouth twitched. "Are you afraid of snakes?"

"Not afraid, but...I'm not a fan."

"I'm not a snake, Miss Onyx. I'm a naga. There is a huge difference. Maybe I'll show you sometime..." His sandalwood scent sharpened, stabbing at my senses, and his pupils went from round to slitted, then back again in a heartbeat. My stomach knotted, but not in fear. No, these knots were something else entirely.

"Oh, Anamaya, Anamaya, what will I do with you?" he crooned under his breath.

Whatever you want was the answer I wanted to give, but I swallowed the words and dropped my chin. "I should...sleep."

"Yes, we both should."

He led me down a short corridor with metallic purple wallpaper and stopped at the door to his bedroom, stepping aside to let me through.

I lingered a step as I passed him, closing my eyes briefly to allow his body heat to caress my skin and the soft cotton of his shirt to brush my bare arm.

Then I was over the threshold with him on the other side.

We stood there face-to-face, the doorframe a sentry between us, the air thickening with intention and possibilities that couldn't be.

"Lock the door behind me," he said finally.

"Why? Do you think someone will try to break in?" I teased.

His tawny gaze darkened, his expression deathly serious. "Yes. I think I might."

My pulse stuttered at his admission, and for a moment, I was tempted to break our stalemate and step across the threshold toward him. If only he wasn't with Selethis... I sucked in a breath and dropped him a nod. "Okay. I'll lock it."

"Good girl." He closed the door, but not before I saw the gleam of disappointment in his eyes.

I stood with my hand on the key, torn between obeying and yanking open the door and throwing myself at him. What was wrong with me?

"Lock it, Anamaya." His voice was low and gruff through the wood. "Now."

There was a slight growl to his tone this time, prompting me to quickly turn the key. I pressed my ear to the door, listening. He was still there. Standing on the other side. I could hear him breathing. Heavy. Labored.

Heart racing, I pressed my palm to the cold oak. I could still open it. Let him in. I reached for the key with trembling fingers just as the sound of his retreat filtered through the wood. I dropped my hand, the decision made for me.

Danger over.

I climbed into his bed, slipping between silken sheets that smelled of him, and pressed my nose to his pillow. Warmth bloomed low in my belly as his scent filled me.

Maybe the danger *wasn't* over.

I stretched out, running my hands over the soft fabric that he'd slept on. Naked maybe? Yeah, he seemed like a sleep naked guy. So he'd been naked, touching himself, his body slick with perspiration, legs tangled in the sheets, hand wrapped around his cock—pumping slowly at first, then faster as his arousal grew. He'd moan softly, then groan deeper as he got closer to climax and... What if it wasn't *his* hand around his cock, but mine? What if I was straddling him and working him and... Oh...I could rise and press him to my entrance before slowly lowering myself onto him, taking him deep inside me. Fuck. Yes. Yes! I'd move with him. Oh Trinity. Deeper and harder, his hands on my body gripping and kneading. He'd growl and flip us so that he was on top, pushing me into the mattress, driving into me, eyes blazing like topaz jewels. Fuck.

My body shuddered, pussy clenching around air as I came. I slapped my hand over my mouth to stifle my cry, riding the wave of pleasure that came from within, thighs parted, hips rising to meet an invisible lover as I imagined him thrusting over and over, pushing my orgasm to the limit until I was spent and shaking.

I fell limp, limbs quivering, pussy soaked and stuck to my panties. Oh...wow...yes, I was definitely going to keep Vitra in my special-time memory banks.

But the high ebbed soon enough, leaving me with a hot face of shame and the gnawing bite of guilt. I shook it off. I was allowed a mental distraction. After all the shit that I'd been through and all the shit I was sure was waiting for me, I bloody deserved it.

Vitra was off-limits in real life, but I'd do what I liked to him in my head.

I wrapped myself in his aromatic sheets and rolled onto my side. My feet no longer throbbed, which was a good sign. I just hoped the injuries wouldn't slow me down tomorrow night.

The grading was the first step to getting into the hunt, and the hunt was my way into the Carvers and the vault.

Failure was not an option.

I was drifting into sleep when it hit me—Vitra hadn't asked me any more about the forgotten student, almost as if... As if he'd forgotten. Again.

The spell haunting Nightsbridge was more powerful than I'd anticipated. Meddling with it could prove dangerous. Maybe even derail my plans to find the book of truth.

Could I take such a risk?

That was a question for tomorrow.

> **They came out of nowhere. Landing from the sky like stray bullets. There was no time to think, to act. When they arrived, we knew it was over.**
>
> *Anonymous from Unknown Newspaper (Vault Archives)*

CHAPTER 34

The southern border had two wards, one that separated it from the Academy grounds, and another three miles from the first. The grading would take place between the two, an area dotted with woodland and valleys, with a mountain range to the west.

The field before the first ward had been turned into a spectator ground, sporting an arena bordered by seats that rose three levels, occupied by eager, excited faces.

There was an area in the middle of the arena for the administration—Coterie members, and a few faces I didn't recognize.

I searched the stands for Drayven and found him in the upper row with Brek, Jay, and the other Thropes. Cami was among them and waved when she spotted me. I waved back. She'd be taking her grading in a year, and hopefully, I'd be there to help her through it. My gaze tracked back to Drayven, hoping for a smile, but all I got was a dip of the chin.

Fine. If he wanted to act like we hadn't had a connection, then so be it.

I had Horrors to hunt.

If only they would let us out of the fucking wards. Around me, the other students from my Combat 101 class shifted from foot to foot, nervous and excited to begin. We were the first group to take the grading this way. The group to lead the charge of change, and I was certain the students from Sterling's other classes were keen to see what it was all about.

My stomach churned in a mixture of dread and excitement, an internal conflict that would only be resolved with action. I needed this test to begin already, but we wouldn't set off until sunset, and the sun was still making its descent.

I flexed my toes in my new boots—thick leather with steel caps at the toe—not broken in yet and waiting to give me blisters. My whole outfit felt stiff and new—from the linen shirt under my long-sleeved, fitted tunic, to the breeches hugging my thighs.

I scanned the crowd again, eager for a distraction, and found the Unwoven in the stands to my right, their faces pale smudges of anxiety, and our conversation on the way here scrolled through my mind.

"It'll be perfectly safe," Clary had said, her tone overly cheerful. "The Horrors are carver-made, so they won't kill you."

"But they will do serious damage," Benedict reminded me. "I spoke to one of the Carvers this morning. He was tight-lipped about the whole thing, but he said this grading was as close to a real hunt as you could get without...you know, going on a real hunt."

"You're making her nervous," Clary chided.

"She should be nervous," Dori said. "Nerves will keep her sharp."

Yes, nerves would keep me sharp.

The air crackled with static, and then a voice blared, "Welcome to the first True Grading." Walter Regent stood in the stands, a megaphone held to his lips. "Thanks to the hard work of the Carver Initiative, today, we will administer our first True Grading, where students will hunt real Horrors. These are Carver creations, designed to operate and function like any other Horror.

Combat students will be required to work together to hunt and subdue a Horror of their choosing to pass the grading. Active hunt teams will allocate marks based on your performance, which will be watched through our corvus speculum."

A shimmering wall shot up between us and the Coterie, and the next moment, a flock of ravens appeared overhead. The shimmering wall flickered, and an image of the arena appeared, shifting with the unnatural tilt and glide of the ravens' flight—watchful, tracking, capturing every movement below. The image zoomed in on Vitra's face—his mouth set in a firm line, gaze hooded—before shifting to Sterling, who looked bored out of his skull. Then it flashed over to Tamina and her Haematophage cronies. She looked bored, too, like she'd prefer to be anywhere else but here. The image panned away, settling on a tall, pale woman with inky eyes and dark hair streaked with gray.

She wore a high-necked coat, fitted to her upper body but flaring at the hips, falling loosely down to her calves.

"Hello, students." She did use a megaphone, but her voice carried regardless. She must be using magic. "For those of you who do not know me, my name is Helena Grimani, and I am Master Carver here at Nightsbridge. The Initiative has worked tirelessly to create accurate representations of what you will face outside the sanctity of our wards. Make no mistake, these Horrors will want to harm you, just as real Horrors will. Although they cannot kill you, they can maim and maul and bring you to the precipice of death. This grading is the closest representation to what you will face as a Hunter."

The image swung away from her and back to Walter. "Maddox, Murder, and their flock will keep watch as you progress through the hunt." The ravens cawed as if in confirmation. "The hunt will end at midnight, when the Horrors will be recalled by the Carvers, and you will be free to return to the Academy." The last rays of the sun died. "Make your way to the wards now."

The wards rippled, preparing to fall.

"Move!" A pair of older students, probably hunt members,

ushered us toward the wards.

Panic gripped me, digging its claws into my lungs. I was about to enter a hunt with people I didn't have any connection to, some of whom hated me and wanted me dead. Sterling had done his best to keep me separate, never allowing me to get to know the others. Never allowing me to build relationships.

Deliberate, no doubt.

But if I was going to pass this grading, I'd need to find a way to integrate and work with them.

My skin prickled as the ward dropped, and we stepped through. Moonlight spilled over the dense forestland waiting in the distance across the vast frosty plain.

We jogged across the frozen ground, ravens flying overhead, before the group slowed.

"If we're going to do this, we'll need a team leader," a student named Poppy said. Small and delicate looking, she was fearsome with a sword. I'd studied her form plenty of times. She was also the oldest in the class, aside from me, at nineteen. A late starter to Nightsbridge.

"You should do it, Poppy," Bryce, a short, stocky Thrope, said.

"Like Fel," Tyler snarled. "I'm not taking orders from a fucking kappa."

Poppy's eyes narrowed. "Then maybe you'd like to take a fist to the face instead."

"Stop it!" Bella, an Arcanus with Silverthorn Coven, stepped up. "You're a bully, Tyler, and if you think we're going to let *you* lead, then you're mistaken."

"Yeah, and exactly how are you going to stop me?" Tyler demanded. His three Phage friends stepped forward to flank him. Were they from the Damascus bloodline, or simply bloodlines affiliated to Damascus and here to garner favor? It didn't matter—they outnumbered the opposition. Even if I jumped in and backed Poppy, it would be four against four.

Above us, the ravens circled, and an idea struck me. "Nice, Damascus, show *everyone* what a bully you are." I glanced up at the birds.

Tyler followed my gaze, comprehension dawning before his expression closed off. "I'm simply saying that I'm better suited to leadership."

"And why is that?" I crossed my arms. "What qualities do *you* have that make you a better leader than Poppy?"

I had no idea if Poppy was a good leader, but I'd take her over Tyler any day.

His eyes narrowed to dangerous slits. "No one asked your opinion, Onyx." He spat out my name like it was a curse.

"I want to know," Bryce said.

"Me too," Bella added.

"You don't want to follow my lead, then fine. Catch your own Horror." He tipped his head up to the ravens. "We have two teams now." He dropped his chin and smirked. "Come on, boys, let's bag us a Horror." They broke away and began to run westward across the plain. The flock above us split into two, and half the birds followed them, while the rest remained circling us.

"Dark skies," Poppy said. "We could have done with muscle. I wish you'd stayed out of it."

Great. "You're welcome."

"No, Onyx is right," Bryce said. "Tyler's an asshole. We don't need him. We can do this."

"And we have one of the supply packs," Bella said.

Tyler had taken the other two with him, so we'd have to make do with whatever was in Poppy's.

Poppy exhaled. "Fine. Eyes peeled. Stick together." Her gaze slipped over my shoulder to the sword strapped on my back. "If we're attacked, run. Regular steel won't do a damn thing to a Horror."

"We should be fine till we cross the plain," Bella said. "It's the forest we have to worry about."

"True," Poppy said as we set off toward the forest at a steady jog. "We'll see any threat out in the open for miles."

It made sense.

We lost sight of Tyler and his team quickly as darkness swallowed them. We aimed for the eastern side of the forest, staying in tight formation as we ran.

Frost crunched underfoot, but at least there was no snow to deal with, and visibility was good except... "Is that mist ahead?"

"Yeah," Bella said. "It's come out of nowhere."

"Nothing comes from nowhere," Poppy said. "We should avoid it."

"Agreed," Bryce said.

We veered away from the mist, but it expanded, moving closer, aiming straight for us.

This had to be part of the Carver's plan. "I don't think we're going to be able to get away."

"Which means Horrors," Poppy said. "Be ready. Onyx, aim for the forest if we're attacked and wait on the outskirts."

I wasn't used to taking orders, especially not from someone younger than me, but her orders were sound, and she'd been here longer than me. "Okay."

The mist rushed forward to swallow us, reducing visibility to the extent that we could barely see each other.

"Stay close!" Poppy ordered. "The mist isn't natural. It smells off."

We kept moving in the direction we'd been going, but the mist was everywhere, disorienting and thickening by the minute.

"It's following us." Bella's voice pitched. "It has to be."

"What's that?" Bryce pointed at nothing. "There, again."

"I don't see anything," Bella said.

"Doesn't mean there's nothing there." Poppy drew her sword, and the others followed suit.

The muscles in my thighs bunched, ready to propel me into action at a moment's notice, as I scanned the mist, gaze snagging on a tall, elongated shadow before it melted into the fog. "I see something."

"Me too!" Bella called out.

"No!" Bryce cried. "No, get out. Get out of my head!" He fell to his knees, clutching his head. "They're in here. I can hear them."

Ice filled my veins. "An Echo?" We hadn't been trained to shield against echoes. Jay had warned that the Carvers might pit us against one to test our mental acuity, but I hadn't expected it to happen.

Bryce screamed, an awful, shrill sound that morphed into a roar as he burst from his skin in all his beastly glory—five feet of fur and claws, red eyes burning with hunger.

Several shapes coalesced around him—echoes imitating his form. Fuck, there was more than one?

"Run!" he roared.

We didn't need telling twice.

Echoes: The most terrifying of creatures. Origin unknown. Classification undetermined. Can take any form.

The Compendium of Horrors

CHAPTER 35

Bryce was feeding the echoes with his Thrope power, and five beasts were on our tail, including Bryce, who seemed to be under their control.

One echo, I could understand, but they'd sent four. It was overkill, considering our lack of training. Surely this wasn't right. Maybe someone had made a mistake in releasing too many?

"Why is Bryce helping them?" Bella huffed. "They should be attacking him. Breaking his mind."

Another piece that didn't fit.

"I don't know!" Poppy yelled back. "But I don't think we can outrun them. We'll have to fight."

"How the hex do we kill one?" Bella said.

My mind flashed back to the night I'd been attacked by echoes. Sterling had saved me. "Chop off their heads. That's what Sterling did when they attacked me."

"Good to know," Poppy said. "You keep going. Get to the forest."

"I can't fucking see the forest."

"You will once we engage them. The mist moves with them.

It'll be a distraction."

Bella and Poppy slowed, turning to face the threat, their blades glinting dully, then flaring bright as they channeled the Weave through the conduit stones in the hilts. I kept running, arms pumping, hoping to break cover.

Snarls and growls rose behind me, and then one of the girls screamed in agony.

Keep moving, Anamaya. You can't help. You can't channel.

Another scream followed, sharper and filled with desperation Shit!

I skidded to a halt and turned back, running full force toward the sounds of battle.

"Move, Bella, move!" Poppy yelled.

Bella screamed again.

Shadows shifted and formed into Bryce's beast form, surrounding the girls, eyes glowing yellow—all except one, whose eyes were red.

Bryce.

Even as I drew my sword, I knew it would be useless against the echoes...but maybe not against Bryce. He was the source of the Echoes' power right now, cutting him down was our best chance.

A beast pounced on Poppy and knocked her onto her back, pinning her sword arm to the ground with a huge paw.

"NO!" Bella struggled to her feet, clutching her abdomen.

The scent of blood saturated the air.

I had to act now!

With a battle cry, I charged past the beast that held Poppy down and launched myself at Bryce.

His eyes flared bright as I leapt onto his back, gripped his bulk with my knees, and grabbed a fistful of fur to anchor myself. He bucked and twisted, trying to throw me off, but I held fast, bringing the hilt of my sword down hard on his temple. Once. Twice. A third time. He swayed, then toppled to the ground, trapping me partially beneath him.

Around us, the other beasts howled as their bodies morphed

back to regular echoes.

Poppy, back on her feet, attacked. Taking one head then another. Bella managed to cut off a third. The fourth one ran at me. I wriggled and kicked, trying to break free of Bryce's unconscious bulk.

The echo leapt into the air, sailing toward me, clawed hands aimed for my head. I screamed, hands flying up in a futile attempt to shield myself. The air crackled and the echo twisted away from me, repelled by an unseen force, which sent it flying toward Poppy.

It slammed into the ground, hard, and Poppy lopped off its head before it could get back up.

With a final shove, I managed to push Bryce off me and hurried to join the girls. "We need to bag a head. Take it back as—"

The echoes disintegrated, and the mist sank into the earth.

The ravens overhead cawed, and a moment later, Walter's voice came through as they spoke in unison.

"There has been a slight technical problem. The echoes are not part of the test. Please disregard and proceed."

"What?" Poppy yelled. "But we bested them. It should count!"

"There has been a slight technical problem," the ravens repeated. "The echoes are not part of the test. Please disregard and proceed."

"This is bullshit!" Bella kicked at the ground, then sucked in a sharp breath and clutched her side.

"Let me see," Poppy said.

"It's fine. I'll dress it. It'll heal."

"What happened?" Bryce sat up, rubbing his head. He was back in human form and totally naked.

"Oh..." Bella pressed a hand to her mouth and quickly looked away.

His clothes were ruined. "You'll have to stay in beast form unless you want to freeze."

Without hesitation he shifted back to his Thrope form.

"Where's your rift blade?" Bella asked Bryce.

"I don't know. I... I must have dropped it."

"Shit." Poppy stood hand on hips, looking back the way we'd come.

"Should we go back and look for it?" Bella asked.

"No," Bryce said. "I can fight in Thrope form. It's what I'll be doing on a real hunt anyway."

It was true. Thropes didn't always wield blades, they fought alongside the blade-wielding Hunters to incapacitate and maul a Horror while the Hunter finished it off.

"Let's move," Poppy ordered. Then to the crows, "Let's hope you don't call our next catch a glitch."

In another time and place, Poppy and I could have been friends.

It was another half hour before we made it into the forest. It was dark beneath the thick canopy, but the nocturnal sounds of nature made it less ominous. We stuck to the trail that wove between the slender tree trunks, walking in pairs.

"We have three hours left till midnight," Bella said, looking up from the timekeeper on her wrist.

"Then we'd better catch a Horror," Poppy replied.

Timekeepers were expensive. Bella must come from money. Tyler Damascus probably had one too, which left me wondering how the heck the rest of us were meant to keep track of time.

My question was answered a moment later when Walter's voice drifted through the canopy above.

"You have three hours and ten minutes remaining until the conclusion of your grading."

We picked up the pace, and I took up the rear with Bryce. His large Thrope form emanated heat, which was the only thing keeping my circulation going. A soft haze surrounded Bella and Poppy, some kind of warming spell, no doubt.

"How did you do that, back there?" Poppy asked over her shoulder. "With the echo? How did you repel it? I thought you didn't have Weave access."

"I don't. The Weave Watchers removed my mark. But that's all they did. I think the Weave might be protecting me somehow."

"Why didn't you tell us that earlier?" Bella asked. "We'd have kept you with us."

"It doesn't always work."

But I had been running through the occasions when it *had* worked, and I was starting to believe it only worked on Horrors and Echoes, and *only* when I was in dire peril. But I wasn't sure yet.

"You did well, though," Poppy said. "Smart, taking out Bryce like that."

"My head still hurts," Bryce said. "But yeah, good call."

The trees thickened here, the trunks wider, the canopy denser, allowing only slivers of moonlight to make it through.

"Bella, can you light the way?" Poppy asked.

A small ball of light appeared a few feet ahead of us, hovering six feet above the ground, illuminating the path.

"Can you smell anything odd, Bryce?" Poppy asked him.

"Nothing but the forest," he said. "And Bella's blood."

"Is it still bleeding?" Poppy asked, her tone sharpening.

"No. I'm fine," Bella said.

Poppy and Bella were obviously close. I'd noticed them training together often, and the older girl was protective of the younger in a sisterly bond that was sweet.

"How long have you two been friends?"

Bella and Poppy exchanged glances before Poppy answered. "I was Bella's nanny for several years—until her family…released me."

My gaze bounced between them, coming to rest on Poppy. "Released you?"

"I was in servitude," Poppy said. "Always was. Young kappa are often reared for servitude by the sith and then sold to other houses."

"But she came here with me anyway," Bella said. "When she

found out they were sending me here, she came." She put her arm around Poppy's waist.

Poppy hugged her back. "Always, Bella. Always."

My knowledge of kappa was vague. They were considered elemental beings with an affinity for water. But some were also blood drinkers.

"Do you think the flock can see us?" Bella asked, peering up. "It's pretty dense up there."

The beat of wings was still audible on and off. "They're definitely tracking us from the canopy."

We walked for another minute, and it was only when my nape tightened that the silence registered. Deeply unnatural and ominous.

"I smell something...odd," Bryce said.

Bella's light glowed brighter, rising to cast a larger circumference of illumination, and hovering in place as we stepped into the circle.

"There's something out there," Poppy said. "I can feel it."

"Stay in the light," Bella said. "Most Horrors don't like bright light."

An insidious rustling tracked our movement from both sides, and my stomach clenched and knotted. It sounded like something was being dragged across the forest floor. The tree trunks that had felt like a protective barrier before now felt like shadowy wooden bars, forming a cage that was keeping us trapped on the path.

"Wood weavers," Poppy said. "It has to be."

"But where?" Bella said. "They could be any one of these trees."

"We need to drop the light," Bryce said. "So our eyes can get used to the gloom."

I didn't like the idea, but he was right. In the light like this, we were blind to what lay beyond.

And there was another fact we needed to consider. "Wood weavers aren't bothered by the light."

"No, they're not," Poppy said. "Which means they're playing

with us."

"Hush, what if they understand what we're saying?" Bella's voice trembled.

"There's nothing in the lore that says they do," Poppy said to reassure her.

"Nothing to say that they don't either," Bryce muttered.

I sifted through everything I'd learned about wood weavers. They were morphing Horrors who preferred to take the form of trees and other woodland flora. Their hearts turned to crystal upon their death. Their weakness was fire, and they didn't like crossing water, so rivers and streams were great if you wanted to lose them. "We need a body of water. If we can get to one, then we'll have a safe spot to build a fire."

"We don't want to risk spawning salamanders," Bella pointed out.

"We can take the risk if we have water on hand," Poppy said.

Bella's lips formed an O. "Of course."

"It's just as well that I smell water. Bella, dim the lights a little and push it ahead of us."

Bella did so, allowing our eyes to slowly adjust to the gloom again. I kept my head facing forward, but movement flickered at the periphery of my vision, shifting a foot at a time, smooth and almost silent as it tracked us.

"Trinity, it smells bad," Bryce said.

I could smell it too now, not as strongly as he could, but just a whiff, like rotten meat and death.

"Water isn't far," Poppy said, keeping her tone low but steady.

We kept our pace even as more weavers gathered, joining the first lot. "What are the Carvers playing at?" Bryce said. "Why so many?"

"I don't know. Maybe this was planned because they expected Tyler and the others to be with us."

"Do you think he's okay?" Bella said.

"I don't care," Poppy replied.

I did a surreptitious count. "There are six trailing us. Three on either side."

"Water is up ahead," Poppy said. "After a break in the trees to the left, which means we'll have to run right past some of the soil suckers. Bella, dim the light a little more." Bella complied.

Long seconds passed, tension coiling in my belly. My eyes adjusted to the gloom once more. "On my count, make a run for it. One. Two. Run!"

We broke into a sprint, cutting left, off the path and into the trees. Chilling moans, interspersed with the crack and pop of wood, shattered the silence.

I kept pace with Bryce even though I could have gone faster.

"Almost there!" Poppy yelled.

The moon was round and bright up ahead, spilling over a clearing that sat between us and the rush of water.

We were going to make it. Once we crossed the river, we could build a fire and—

Branches whipped into our path, forming long arms with hands that wrapped around Bella and yanked her off her feet. Her scream was cut off by vines whipping over her mouth as she was dragged toward the brush.

"Bella!" Poppy dove toward her, fingers grazing Bella's before she was swallowed by darkness. "NO!" Poppy ran into the trees. "Bella! Bell!"

Dark branches reached for her, blocking her from view.

"Anamaya, move!" Bryce body-slammed me out of the way as another set of branch hands made a grab at us. He snapped and snarled as it tried to get a hold of him, dragging its bulk onto the trail. A wet maw of pulsing flesh and jagged teeth surrounded by bark, the trunk moved on thick fleshy roots that spawned more roots to wrap around Bryce.

"Run!" he barked. "You have to run."

His scream broke my paralysis. I drew my sword and attacked the roots, cutting them away faster than they could grow back.

Bryce twisted and bucked as I chopped and stabbed, screaming at the top of my lungs, the only way to purge the terror trying to cloud my mind. There were more coming. Pressing in on us. Hungry for our flesh.

I ducked to avoid the swipe of a branch, my scream dying as I gagged on the awful, rotten meat stench coming off the creatures.

Bryce broke free. "Come on."

I swung my sword a final time, severing a few more roots, then ran for the river.

Lungs burning, throat dry and raw from screaming, I hit the icy water, splashing as my sprint turned into a wade. The water rose to my thighs, my hips, and finally my chest. My lungs hurt from the cold, shriveling in my chest until every breath was a struggle. I pushed past the discomfort, forcing my legs to move faster.

Bryce swam, sleek and fast, his bulk cutting through the water, reaching the other side before me.

I dragged myself out, fighting the chatter of teeth. Bryce stood at the shore, watching the trees we'd just abandoned. "They're leaving," he said. "They have Poppy and Bella." He paced back and forth, dripping water all over the earth.

"We're going to get them back." I started gathering wood to make a fire. Movement would help warm me up. Movement and a fire. "Poppy had the pack of supplies, so I need flint."

Bryce darted into the trees and returned with flint while I gathered dried bits of wood from the edge of the forest. I worked fast; every second that Poppy and Bella remained in the wood weavers' clutches was a second too much.

I built the fire as close to the river as possible but didn't light it straight away. First, I found a large stick that would work as a torch. The top of my shirt was dry, so I shrugged it off and pulled off a few strips to wrap around the stick and... Shit. "We need some kind of accelerant to keep the torch lit." I hadn't thought this through fully.

"Wait..." Bryce sniffed the air then bounded into the forest. "Over here."

I joined him by a slender tree. "There's sap in this one." He stabbed the trunk with his claws, and thick, dark sap bubbled out. Perfect.

I scooped it up and coated my makeshift torch with it. "Now to light the fire..."

"You've got this," Bryce said.

"Be ready to shake your fur and soak any salamanders that form."

Above us, wings flapped as I set to work with the flint. Come on. Come on. If I couldn't get this lit, then we were fucked. Fire was our best weapon against the wood weavers. The only way we'd be able to get Poppy and Bella out of their grasp.

One spark, then another—yes! The fire caught. I blew gently, coaxing it to life.

"You did it!" Bryce said, clearly impressed. "And no salamanders."

It was too soon for relief. I lit the torch and held it high. "We can't get it wet. Can you carry me back across?"

"Damn straight I can."

I grinned at him. "Let's go get the girls back and kill some Horrors."

> It shouldn't be possible, and yet it is. If the Arcanum
> Imperium find out, then we're doomed.
>
> *Extract from Missing Pages of Dharma Onyx's Journal (Vault Archives)*

CHAPTER 36

We moved stealthily in the direction the wood weavers had taken Bella. Not even the ravens made a sound as they tracked us. The torch burned bright, but for how much longer?

The forest was thick with flora here, no trail, nothing but dense canopy and the scent of rotting leaves and flowers.

"I smell Poppy," Bryce said. "Bella, too. Blood...fresh."

Shit. We picked up our pace.

Low moans of pain guided us, and then I spotted them. Both suspended four feet above the ground, their backs pressed to tree trunks that pulsed softly.

The Horrors were feeding. Why were they feeding? Surely the Carvers hadn't set them up to do that. The Horrors were meant to maim, not kill—and wood weaver feeding would kill.

Bella hung limp and unconscious, but Poppy was awake. She reached for us. "Help...her..."

An unconscious Bella would be no help to us. I had to get Poppy out first. I swung the torch at the wood weaver who had her captive. It screeched as the flames grazed its bark, releasing Poppy with a wet squelch. She hit the ground hard, catching herself on all fours, blood seeping from puncture wounds dotted across her back.

"Bella," She tried to stand but collapsed. "For the love of Trinity, help her!"

Bella was sinking into the Horror's body. It was swallowing her!

"No!" I thrust the torch at the branches holding her. The weaver screeched and spat her out.

Bryce shielded Bella with his body while I waved the torch at the wood weaver, forcing it back. Shadows moved around us—more wood weavers circling.

"Bella, please, wake up. Wake up." Poppy gathered her friend in her arms while Bryce prowled around us, his body whipping from side to side as he tried to keep all the threats in sight.

One torch wouldn't keep us safe. One fire wouldn't stop these bastards.

I needed more. I needed a barrier. I scanned the ground searching for inspiration, torch held aloft to ward off the weavers. Leaves crunched beneath my boots.

The ground was dry. Kindling all around. I darted forward, dragging my torch along the ground, lighting up bracken to create a fiery line between us and them. A circle to protect us.

"What the Fel are you doing?" Bryce demanded. "Salamanders will come!"

The wood weavers screeched and reared back.

"Fuck the salamanders. We can deal with them after these soil sucking bastards are gone," Poppy said, hauling Bella over her shoulders. "Worst case, I'll draw water from the air and hold them back while we make a run for it."

The wood weavers pressed in, testing the barrier, then retreated, only to test it again.

"The fire's dying," Poppy said.

The barrier fizzled, burning low in places with nothing to fuel it. "Shit."

My torch was almost dead too. "Come on! Come on, burn." I pressed the torch to the barrier flames. "I need you, please."

A root whipped out, slashing my hand. I pulled it back sharply, and a droplet of blood hit the flames with a sizzle. Another root tried to snag my wrist, and I dodged it, splashing more drops of blood into the fire.

The flames fizzed and flared—blue then purple, and a male voice spoke from within them. "Onyx blood spilled in offering is now ours to protect."

"Solaris?"

The flames flared higher, morphing into a large lizard-like beast, then into a humanoid form which split into several, until the fire itself became an army of burning figures.

The wood weavers attempted to retreat, but the fire men swept toward them, engulfing them in flames, and for the next few moments, the forest was filled with the shrill screams of dying Horrors.

When silence finally fell, and the flames winked out with a satisfied sigh, we were left with five blackened, crystallized hearts.

The hearts of wood weavers.

Bella regained consciousness once we were back on the plains, but she was pale and weak. Bryce offered to carry her now that she was able to hold on to him, and we picked up the pace.

No one asked me about the salamanders—or why they'd helped us. Just as well, because I didn't understand it myself.

The five wood weaver hearts were in Poppy's pack, tiny things for creatures that had looked so large.

The ravens tracked us from above, silent and watchful.

It's over, right?" Bella said, her face pressed to Bryce's back. "It's midnight."

"Yes," Poppy said. "We just have to get back now."

Figures sprinted toward us across the plain. Tyler and his

cronies. "Great."

Tyler had something dangling from his hand, and as he got closer, I made out the details—a disembodied head with long, dark hair and empty sockets where the eyes had been.

"They got an undine," Poppy said.

"One?" Bella scoffed. "Ha!"

Bryce chuckled.

"Heading back with your tails between your legs, eh?" Tyler gloated as he approached. "Oh, did you get hurt?" He pressed his hand to his chest, mock concern twisting his smirk.

"Fuck off, Damascus," Poppy said.

"Make me."

Poppy took a step toward him.

"Don't," Bella said. "He's not worth it. Besides, we got five wood weaver hearts, so he can suck a dick."

Tyler's smug smile faltered. "What? Bullshit!"

We ignored him and kept walking.

"Show me," he demanded.

"No," Poppy said.

"Because you're lying."

I was so fed up with the little shit. "Do you think any of us care what you think?"

He lunged at me, and I punched him in the mouth, hard enough to make him bleed.

"You bitch!" He charged, and I hit him again, blow after blow, one to the gut, one to the jaw, and one to the temple.

He hit the ground on his knees, wheezing hard, and I crouched down to his level. "Listen to me, you disgusting, arrogant, piece of shit. Your family name might get you special treatment outside of Nightsbridge, but here, within the wards, you're just like the rest of us. A fucking conscripted grunt who has no choice but to put his worthless life on the line. So get over yourself. All of you." I looked up at his cronies. "If you don't, then you're not going to make it here."

"This is perfect for you, isn't it?" Tyler snarled. "You get to matter here. To have a purpose when out there, you were nothing. No one. You think you can change that? You think we're going to forget what your murderous family did? And what you did..." His eyes narrowed to slits. "I bet your mother was glad to die—so she could stop pretending to love you after what you took from her." Blood rushed in my ears, heat flooding my veins as his words nudged every doubt, every insecurity, and every horrific fear inside me. "You ruined her life, and look at you now, playing hero."

My pulse thrummed in my throat and thudded in my head, something wild and untamed blooming inside me. I pressed my palms to the ground, bracing against the strange feeling rippling through me.

"Stop it!" Poppy said to Tyler. "Just back off."

"You have no idea what she is," Tyler said. "What she did."

Annabeth's blackened body filled my mind, followed by my father kneeling in the dark. The blade slicing. The thud of his head as it hit the ground. The blood and the screams. Mine and my mother's. Her tears, so many tears, and the silence for days, so many days.

My fault.

Mine.

The ground trembled.

"What—what is that?" Bella cried.

"Anamaya! Anamaya, we have to go!" Poppy yanked at my arm.

I snapped out of my daze, allowing Poppy to pull me up as the ground shook.

The ravens spoke in Walter's voice. "This is not us. Get to the main wards! Run!"

We ran while the world shook and groaned. The ground cracked and splintered, a mound of earth pushing up to our left and running alongside us.

There was something underneath.

Something huge.

"It's coming this way!" Tyler yelled. He shoulder-shoved me

toward the rapidly approaching furrow of earth.

The ground heaved, splitting apart with a scream that filled the air with the stench of sulfur and rotting flesh. And then, out of the aperture rose an impossibility. A creature so large it blocked out the moon with its massive body, all glistening dark scales and jagged ridges, maw large enough to swallow the stars.

The monstrous worm arched its armored body toward me, mouth yawning wide, ready to swallow me and the world. Its black eyes gleamed as they locked onto me. A shudder coursed through me, my mind screamed to run, even as my limbs locked in place. Move. Dammit, move! My muscles strained with effort, but my feet remained rooted to the spot.

The worm's maw hurtled toward me, and a scream lodged in my throat.

"Ana!" I was swept off my feet and bundled against taut muscle, enveloped in the scent of pine, and protected as we rolled.

Drayven.

My terror melted, limbs unlocking. I wrapped my arms around him as he hauled me to my feet.

Where was it? Where was the worm?

The ground furrowed to our right as the thing burrowed around, circling back toward us.

"You have to run," Drayven said. "Don't look in its eyes. Just run, and—"

The ground behind us erupted as the worm burst forth once more, blocking out the blanket of stars and casting us in its mammoth shadow. It screamed into the night—a horrific sound of triumph and domination.

The ground groaned and rumbled beneath the strain of expelling such an epic form.

Drayven grabbed my hand, and we ran.

"Move!" He ordered the others. But his command was lost beneath the roar of another tremor. Not that it mattered. The other students had the right idea, sprinting for the wards. Bryce and Poppy ran parallel to us, Bella clinging to the Thrope's back.

We could outrun the beast. It was huge, but it was slow. We could make it if we—

The world went dark beneath the shadow of the beast.

"Shit!" Drayven veered to the left, taking me with him.

The worm slammed into the ground, missing us by a mere foot. The earth crumbled as it burrowed, creating a landslide of soil. My boots slipped, the only thing saving me from falling into the pit after the beast was Drayven's grip on my hand.

"I'm going to shift. Get on!" Drayven cried.

He burst out of his clothes, morphing into his barghest form without breaking stride.

I stumbled, almost losing momentum, but managed to grab a handful of fur and haul myself onto his back. I locked my knees and pressed my body to his as the world rushed by.

Icy air tore at my face and ripped at my hair, burning my eyes and blurring my vision with hot tears.

I tucked my head, heart hammering against Drayven's back as I attempted to block out the sound of the world crumbling by focusing on the steady thud of Drayven's heartbeat.

"Wards incoming!" Drayven growled. "Hold on."

I risked lifting my head a fraction, searching for the shimmer of the wards—how close were we?—when movement in my periphery drew my attention.

A furrow of earth headed our way.

My heart leapt into my throat, momentarily stealing my voice.

"Drayven, watch out!"

A mountain of earth slammed into us. The impact—sudden and hard—knocked me loose and up toward the sky.

The stars winked at me, as if trying to send a message. I reached for them, but gravity had other plans, wrapping its jealous arms around me and tugging me back to earth.

The impact knocked the wind out of me, sending shockwaves through my bones. The metallic taste of blood filled my mouth as the world went strangely silent for a beat before a humming filled my head.

Move.

I needed to fucking move.

I rolled onto my side, and the world tipped beneath me.

"Ana! I'm coming!"

Drayven? I blinked to clear my vision as he bounded toward me.

I pushed up on my palms, arms trembling—a sure sign that my body was in shock. Wait, the tremble wasn't inside me, it was shooting *through* me from the ground.

The ground was shaking.

Shit!

I fell back on my ass as the earth split before me, cutting me off from Drayven. The worm shot into the air, its massive frame creating a wall between me and sanctuary.

Pressure filled my head, setting my teeth on edge as the beast arched its body, ready to slam down and swallow me.

There was no time to evade. No time to run, I waited for terror to claim me, but a cold, steel-edged conviction filled my veins instead.

As the worm hurtled toward me, horrific maw wide and pulsing with thousands of teeth, I stopped thinking and allowed instinct to guide me. Primal conviction snapped into place, bringing a surge of heat that spread across my chest, drawing from a place buried deep inside me.

"Stop!" I threw up my arms, body rocking as energy rushed through me and outward.

The worm halted mid-attack, its monolithic frame quivering as it fought my command.

Arms wrapped around my waist, and the scent of pine filled my head. "Fuck. Ana, how?"

I shook my head. Every ounce of will focused on the worm, afraid that if I took my eyes off it, I'd lose control.

My blood burned hot, then cold. I wasn't going to be able to hold the beast much longer.

A gust of air smacked me in the face, and a figure landed on the worm—silver hair flying like a flag behind him.

Sterling.

He climbed up the worm, using its scales as handholds.

"Hold it, Ana," Drayven said, "I don't know how you're doing this but don't fucking let go."

I blinked cold sweat from my eyes, gritting my teeth as my chest vibrated with power that seemed to come from everywhere at once, using my body as a conduit.

My stomach quaked. A warning that I was running out of time. My fear was confirmed a moment later when the worm jerked to the left, almost breaking free of my hold. Sterling cried out, barely holding on.

Heat sizzled behind my eyes, spread across my palms—then the worm went still once more.

Sterling reached the worm's head, clambering higher, until he balanced precariously atop the beast.

The edges of my vision darkened, and I pushed out one desperate plea. "Please..."

"Hurry!" Drayven bellowed. "She can't hold it much longer."

My gaze flicked up to the dhampir, locking with his cold and unreadable stare. He dropped his chin in a nod, then brought his sword down, impaling the beast's brain.

The worm toppled, and Sterling leapt off it, somersaulting in the air and landing on his feet, light as a cat.

The ground shook as the worm made impact, and I fell back against Drayven, free of the power that had saved me.

Other Hunters rushed onto the scene, yelling words that were swallowed by the thunder of blood in my ears.

"Ana?" Drayven's grip tightened. "Ana, can you hear me?"

But the world was getting dark.

It was time to sleep.

Landwyrm: Ancient Horror. Extinct. Able to paralyze its prey with a look. Origin unknown, classification draconic.

A History of Horrors

CHAPTER 37

"It was truly something to watch," Clary said. "When you stepped in front of Drayven, held up your hands, and the Wyrm just...stopped."

Late afternoon sun streamed into my room as I sipped the herbal concoction Darla had prepared. A restorative remedy that should recharge my depleted strength. Whatever I'd done to ward off what I now knew to be a Landwyrm had drained me. That, coupled with the aftereffects of terror—a condition the Landwyrm could inflict on anyone who looked into its eyes—meant I'd slept for a whole day and night.

But a little bit of food, a restorative herbal drink, and company were enough to set me to rights.

"You should have heard the silence, then the cheers," Benedict said. "It was like watching a moving picture."

"But it shouldn't have happened," Dori pointed out. "Not the Wyrm or the echoes. I heard the Carvers admitted that *their* echoes never left their holding pens."

I lowered my cup. "Wait...so the Echoes that attacked us—"

"Were from *outside* the wards," Dori finished. "Same as

the Wyrm. Ana, Landwyrms haven't been seen for decades. We thought they were extinct. They're the first Horror that entered our world during The Overshadowing. The Landwyrms are the reason so many of our cities were destroyed and had to be rebuilt. There isn't much information on how we were able to kill them back then, but I do know that there was no such thing as rift blades."

The question of how those mammoth Horrors had been brought down was buried in history somewhere. "But one survived. Where was it all this time? Dormant somewhere?"

"It would seem so," Dori said.

"Then why wake now?"

"The Hunters are looking into it," Benedict said. "And the ward keepers are getting some serious heat right now, too."

"And they should!" Clary said. "They have one job. Just one. And they get to just...relax the rest of the time."

"I think it's a little more than that," Dori said.

"Really? I saw Augustine Berrywinkle last week, and she hadn't left her tower room in three days. Three days!"

"Do you want to stay in your room for three days straight?" Dori asked.

Clary scowled. "I wish I had the option."

"I would," Benedict said with a cheeky smile. "Depending on who I was with." He gave an exaggerated, suggestive wink.

Dori groaned. "Lower the tone, why don't you."

"Always," Benedict said.

"But we're getting off topic," Dori said. "What you did, Ana... I did some research on Weave powers, and although there is a repelling spell and a shield spell, they don't work on Horrors. No one has *ever* repelled a Horror or held one at bay like you did with the Wyrm."

"I'm sure that'll have the Coterie in a spin," Benedict said. "Considering you haven't come into your full powers yet, they'll definitely have questions."

Great, just what I needed, another session in front of the

establishment to explain how I'd stopped the Wyrm. "If they have questions, they can ask the Weave Watchers, because I have no idea."

Silence fell for a few seconds as we retreated into our own thoughts.

Clary was the first to break it. "If there's one Landwyrm, there could be more. The ward keepers are going to have their work cut out for them."

"And the Hunters," Benedict added.

"I'm just glad everyone is okay." Poppy had come by earlier to thank me for saving her and Bella.

The Carvers had said no one would die, but after everything that happened, it was unlikely that they had as much control over their creations as they'd hoped.

The Initiative was now under administrative investigation.

"And when you beat Tyler up," Benedict punched the air, mimicking the shots I'd landed. "That was so satisfying to watch."

I dropped out of my thoughts. "I'm sure that'll come back to bite me in the ass at some point. Tyler will get revenge. Somehow."

"Just let him try," Dori said, mouth twisting in a sneer. "He's a bully who doesn't have much support here, despite what he might like you to believe. If he comes at you, we'll deal with him."

"I do have one question, though," Clary said. "The salamander thing...they helped you, and they said something about an offering?"

I'd forgotten about the salamanders, but my mind had been working on the problem subconsciously. Now that Clary brought it up, I had a possible explanation. "I changed my bloody bandage and threw it into the hearth in Bramble Tower a few weeks ago. Solaris's voice came through and said something about accepting my offering. At the time, I thought that maybe I imagined it, but I think... I think I accidentally *did* give him a blood offering. So, when I bled on the flame barrier in the woods, I must have summoned Solaris."

"That would make sense," Clary said, wide-eyed. "I've heard

of students trying to form bonds with Solaris and his salamander brethren, but never of anyone succeeding."

"I'm just glad you're safe," Dori said. "Everything else is icing."

The warm, safe feeling these three evoked, the feeling I'd been trying to deny for weeks, bloomed sudden and insistent inside me, and my eyes heated.

"Whoa, Onyx, are you... Are you crying?" Dori reached for me, but I waved her off.

"No. I'm fucking not. I have something in my eye."

"No, you don't," Clary said. "You're all emotional."

"Because you love us," Benedict said. "Or...is it that time of month?"

"Shut up!" I wiped at my eyes.

"It's all right," Clary said. "It's okay..." Her smile was filled with gentle understanding, and my heart ached—I wanted this. I wanted them as part of my life.

I wanted...friendship. With them. Real friendship. But how could I have that and complete my mission here?

Stealing from the vault was a crime punishable by death. If the three of them found out, I had no doubt that they'd agree to help me. But they'd be putting themselves in harm's way.

This is what I'd wanted, though. Friendship that I could leverage. But now... Now everything was different, because I cared. I fucking cared, and I couldn't let anything happen to them.

The only option was to keep silent and enjoy them while I could.

I deserved it.

After all this time, I bloody deserved it.

Drayven came to visit when I was starting to think he wouldn't, and my heart leapt at the sight of his large frame blocking the doorway.

"Hi..." I drank him in from the dark top knot on his head

down to the kick-the-shit-out-of-you boots on his feet. "Are you coming inside, or are you going to stand there all day?"

"Can I, uh...open a window?"

"Does it smell bad in here?" I resisted the urge to sniff myself.

A blush stained his cheekbones. "Not bad, just... May I?"

What the... "Of course."

He entered without closing the door behind him, cracked the window open, then pulled a chair to the bed. He sat with his forearms pressed to his thighs, head bowed. Silent.

A minute passed, long enough for my emotions to tie themselves into anxious knots. "Drayven, you're making me nervous."

"I can't allow myself to be around you." He blurted the words, then closed his eyes as if annoyed with himself. "Fuck..."

"Is this about the mate mark, scent thing?"

"Yes and...no. I thought I could control it. That once my scent on you faded, I'd be fine around you. But when you passed out in my arms after the Wyrm attack, I marked you again." He squeezed his eyes closed. "I'm so fucking sorry."

"But I wasn't physically hurt. I mean, my hand was, but it wasn't bad and—"

"I know."

But he'd done it anyway... Oh...

"I can't seem to stop myself from trying to claim you," he admitted.

I wasn't sure I wanted a relationship with him, and I certainly didn't want to be mated to him. So it hardly mattered that he was trying to stay away from me, but my curiosity was an insatiable beast, and I needed to know.

"Why are you fighting this thing between us?" Because despite my intentions, there was definitely a *thing* between us. An attraction, an inexplicable connection usually only born of long-term familiarity.

He looked up, stunned. "You *want* me to claim you?"

"I didn't say that. I just... I want to understand your reluctance, because my gut tells me it's about more than my consent."

He sighed. "You're too damn smart, too damn perceptive—"

"Yeah, yeah, I'm perfect, I get it. Now, please, tell me why."

He cracked a smile, and my heart melted a little. "You are all those things, Anamaya, and more. You're resilient and determined and loyal and I... I admire you, which is why I'm so drawn to you. But...I made a vow a long time ago that I wouldn't move on with my life, not until I ended the life of the male responsible for Brenna's death."

Brenna...the woman he'd loved. He'd mentioned that she was dead, but... "Someone *killed* her?"

His nostrils flared. "Yes." His hands curled into fists. "My kind, my pack, do not live together like most. We own vast territories in which we make our homes separate from each other, yet close by. We are solitary beasts until we take a mate and have our own families. Brenna was human, so she could never have a full mating because she had no beast—but she agreed to come live with me on pack land. We had a family. A boy and a girl. But six years ago, I was called away urgently, and in my absence, our territory was stolen. Set ablaze by the thieves who wanted to claim it." His throat bobbed. "Brenna and my children died in that fire." He swallowed hard again. "She couldn't shift and run like the barghest, so she perished. I found her corpse wrapped around our children. She'd shielded them with her body, protecting them for as long as she could with her flesh and bone."

Oh Trinity. "Who... Who did it? Who set the fire?"

"Our land stood in the way of a Damascus development project. My father, the alpha, refused to sell. We thought that was the end of it. After all, the Thorns and the Damascuses had been close friends for decades. I grew up with Sterling. He'd been like a brother to me. But it was Sterling who called me away that day. Summoned me to help him with some important business, and while I was with him, his father burned my land and killed my family."

My breath caught in my throat. "Oh, Drayven...I'm so fucking sorry."

He looked away. "I wanted to die too. But Brenna and I made a pact when we had our first child. We vowed that if anything should happen to either of us, the other would learn to go on with their lives. That we wouldn't mourn forever. She was sunshine and happiness, and I couldn't disappoint her. But I made another vow on her grave. I vowed not to move on with my life until the person responsible for taking my family and most of my pack was dead."

"Sterling?"

"Yes."

"Then why... Why haven't you—"

"Killed him already?" His mouth turned down. "Oh, believe me, I've tried, but I can't. When we were ten, we made a blood pact. A stupid oath that bound us to protect one another. I can't kill him, and he can't kill me."

Vampires and their fucking blood pacts. Wait... "Is that why you joined me when I was facing that Wyrm? To force him to protect you—and me by extension?"

"I would have been by your side regardless, but yes, it forced him to act. Forced him to bring down the Wyrm."

If it had been just me, Sterling would have let me die.

"I can't break the pact," Drayven continued. "But I've been told that with time, as long as we don't replenish it, it will weaken. So, I'm waiting. And in the meantime, I can be here, a constant reminder of what he did. I want him to see Brenna in my eyes every time he looks at me. To remember Tabitha and Troy, the children who once called him Uncle Sterling. I want him to know that there is no running away from me, and as soon as the bond breaks, I'll claw out his fucking heart." The pain dripping from his words echoed mine, resonating in a way that made me want to wrap my arms around him and cradle him to me.

I moved toward him, and he slid his chair back. "Don't. I can't." He swallowed hard. "You smell too good."

I relaxed back against the pillows. "I'm sorry."

He dropped his chin and took a couple of deep breaths before speaking again. "I wanted you to know. To understand why I'll have to keep a distance."

"I understand." Even though it left me feeling hollow and empty. "I just... I hope that in time we can be friends."

He lifted his head, a wry smile on his beautiful lips. "No. Ana. I can't be your friend. Not when all I can think about is pressing you into the mattress and marking you over and over until you're mine." His knuckles whitened and his thighs bunched, and for a moment I thought he'd leap onto the bed and act out his words, and my stomach warmed with need. But he reined in his emotions, standing slowly, fingers flexing. "I should go."

I nodded, lost for words.

He stopped in the doorway, his back to me. "You're in my Advanced Combat class next month. I won't see you outside of that, and when I do, things will be different. Goodbye, Anamaya."

He closed the door behind him. Closed it on any possibility of an us, and that was fine. It didn't matter.

Then why the fuck did it hurt?

I pulled up the sheets, snuggled down, and closed my eyes. I needed a reset, and sleep was the best way to do that.

I love bedtime stories with Father. He does all the voices, and he always allows one more chapter. I love how safe he makes me feel, and how his dark eyes light up with smiles when he looks at me. But tonight, we've come to the end of the book, and he closes it with a sigh. "The End."

"But is it?" I sit up straighter. "Won't Penelope have more adventures?"

"Maybe," he says with a secretive smile. "Maybe there is another book."

I let out a squeal. "Where? Where is it?"

He chuckles and ruffles my hair. "We can start it when I'm back from my trip."

I pout. "Do you have to go?"

"Yes, darling. I do. But it's the last trip, and then I'll be back, and I won't ever leave you again."

"You promise?"

He holds up his pinkie. "I promise."

"But he did leave you. He left forever," the rook says from the windowsill.

"Go away. I want to stay here."

"You can't. You know you can't. You have to move forward. You have a job to do, and I can help you. Let me show you. Let me show you so that we can begin."

My childhood bedroom melts away, and I'm outside Bramble Tower, looking at my window, lit softly by lamplight.

"This way." The rook flies over my head. *"Can you see?"*

A girl stands by the pavilion up ahead. Her dark hair falls over her shoulders, sleek and glossy, and her blue eyes are bright and eager.

"Hello?" I hurry closer. "Hello, who are you?"

"You know who she is," the rook says. *"You know..."*

Her form flickers, and she's no longer sleek-haired and bright-eyed, but gray-skinned with dark holes for eyes. Her head is tipped at an impossible angle, and her hair is a rat's nest of tangles.

"Find me..." she whispers.

I want to run away, but my feet carry me forward, toward her.

"Don't fight. You have to see. You must see!"

My blood burns, limbs screaming in protest even as I tell them that yes. Yes, I need to know. I need to see.

The woman vanishes, only to reappear inside the pavilion. I don't want to go inside the gloomy interior. Don't want to see what lurks in the dark, but I follow anyway, slipping past the ivy veil draped over the stone structure.

"Find me..." She points at the ground, at the planks, once white but now scuffed and speckled with moss. "Find...me..." The hollow sadness in her tone stokes a fire to life inside me.

I have to find her.

I drop to my knees and run my hands over the wood that fits so neatly together. "There's nothing here. Nothing—"

The rook lands on the balcony, wings flapping in agitation. "*Look and you will see.*"

But I *am* looking. I... Oh... Silver lines flicker to life across the wood to form a symbol that's arcane but unknown to me, and then another line blooms, moving across the wood to create a square. A seam...there's a seam cut into the wood, so slender anyone would miss it if not searching for it. Heart pounding, I trace it with my fingers until I come to a small gap. Too small to pry open with a finger. I push my nail into it and feel something click.

A soft whirr sounds, and the hatch slips down, then shifts sideways, revealing a space beneath occupied by a bundle of thick cloth.

A blanket?

I look up at the gray figure of the girl who my gut tells me is Selina, then down at the large bundle wrapped in the blanket.

"Find me..." A tear rolls down her cheek, and my chest aches.

"Selina?"

She nods. "Find me."

Oh Trinity. I take a breath, steeling myself before reaching into the hole to peel back the blanket. A face stares up at me, perfectly preserved and serene, as if only sleeping. "Oh... Oh, Selina..." There's something poking out from the blanket, pressed to her chest. I pull the fabric aside, revealing a crystalline gem.

"Find me," Selina says again, urgent now. Pushing me to act.

"I have, I... This i*s* you, isn't it? This dream. It's you. You're showing me where to find you. I've got to wake up and see, so—"

"Find me now!" She jabs a finger at the gem.

I reach for it, allowing her to guide me to take it. To remove it. But the gem seems to resist, fighting me as I tug, until finally, with a fizz and crackle, it comes free.

The body in the hole snaps open its eyes and screams.

I fall back, dropping the crystal. It shatters, and a shockwave of energy blasts me in the face, lifting my hair and stealing my breath. The stench of death fills my nose.

"Now you see..."

The rook flies at my face, and I fall back, head slamming against the pavilion floor.

"Anamaya? Can you hear me? Anamaya?"

Vitra appeared above me, his face a tight, unreadable mask. "Get up." He slips a hand under my shoulders, helping me sit up.

Oh Trinity. I remember. I remember it all. "I was dreaming. I saw her. I saw her body."

"I see it too," Vitra said, shifting slightly to allow me a view of my surroundings.

I was in the pavilion. Truly here, and the hole was here too. I scrambled toward it, gagging as the stench of decomposition hit me.

"Who is it?" Vitra asks. "Who's the girl?"

I peered into the hole, at the face with no eyes, head cocked to one side, neck snapped. "Selina Evergreen. The girl no one remembers."

His face drained of color and he exhaled sharply, "Selina... Yes. Yes, I remember her." His hand went to his temple. "If what I suspect is true, now that you've found her, everyone else will remember her too."

In dreams, nothing is forgotten.

Anonymous

CHAPTER 38

The tea did nothing to warm the cold place inside me. I huddled under a blanket on the sofa in the Unwoven quarters, surrounded by my friends and overlooked by a shaken Vitra.

Selina had lived in my room in Bramble Tower, not because she'd been Unwoven, but because she'd been unwanted. Bullied and shunned for being bright, she'd asked to continue to be housed in Bramble for solitude. Her parents were dead, and she'd been raised by an aunt on her father's side, who'd been happy to give her up to the Evergreen coven when they'd come looking for a conscript to save their pureblood children from having to attend Nightsbridge.

"Someone murdered that girl," Clary muttered. "Someone *here* at *this* Academy killed her, buried her, and made everyone forget."

"She was a quiet thing," Dori said. "Studious. I always thought she had so much potential."

"I spoke to her a few times," Clary added. "I should have asked her to hang out."

"But who killed her and why?" I couldn't stop thinking about it. "I saw a hooded figure in my dreams. I felt her fear."

"And why you?" Clary asked. "Why did you dream about her? Why could you remember her name?"

"I may be able to answer that," Vitra said. "Miss Onyx came to the Academy after the spell that wiped Miss Evergreen from collective memory was cast. Therefore, it didn't affect her. She was also staying in Miss Evergreen's former chambers. I believe the spirit of Miss Evergreen was able to reach out to her because of those reasons, and maybe... Maybe part of Miss Onyx's Weave abilities are necromantic."

"A Morbus Arcanus? No, thank you."

The Morbus Arcanus were rare. Their connection to the spirit thread of the Weave gave them not only necromantic abilities but also allowed them to walk through the land of the spirits. They often went mad, as the boundary between the living and the dead blurred.

"You can rest easy—this matter will be looked into as a priority," Vitra assured us.

A girl was dead. A girl who'd lived in my room.

Find me... Her tormented face filled my mind. Was she at peace now? If I were her, I wouldn't be. Not until my murderer was discovered and brought to justice. "You need to do more than look into it. You have to find the bastard who did this."

Vitra's jaw tensed. "The Coterie will ensure the safety of the students."

"Like you ensured Selina's?" Dori said.

"And what about the non-aggression wards?" Benedict asked. "How come someone was able to kill on campus?"

"I don't know," Vitra said. "But I will find out. The Coterie will meet with representatives of the Imperium Alius to discuss a way forward. New protocols will be put into place." He headed for the door and stopped. "Oh, and you should know—I spoke to Pip about why the doors to your quarters were left unlocked the other night. He claims he locked them. I believe him, which means someone else unlocked them. We think the culprit is Mr.

Raichand."

Raichand? "The radio guy?"

"Yes. He must have unlocked the doors again tonight."

Because he'd wanted me to get hurt sleepwalking. Bastard!

"That doesn't explain why we were incapacitated the other night," Benedict said. "He's an Embercrest, right? Does he have that spell?"

Dori shrugged. "No idea."

"I'll be speaking to Mr. Raichand tomorrow," Vitra said. "I *will* get answers before he is appropriately reprimanded. In the meantime, your doors will continue to be locked."

But I didn't think I'd be sleepwalking again. "I think Selina got what she needed. She's been remembered."

He pressed his lips together and sighed. "Yes. Tomorrow, Nightsbridge will wake to the memory of a girl long forgotten. Tomorrow, Nightsbridge will mourn."

Restoration Day dawned bright and sunny despite the chill. While Nightsbridge planned a memorial for the student they'd forgotten for the past eight months, my friends and I made our way into the atrium for the ceremony that would return their connection to the Weave and where, hopefully, my journey toward assimilation would begin.

The atrium was hidden inside a huge domed building that sat behind Trinity Tower. With its many tall windows and a partial glass roof, it was designed to let in both sun and moonlight, elements essential to many Arcanus spells and rituals.

I'd passed this building several times in the past few weeks, always pausing to admire the white stone statues that framed the doorway. Two women wearing flowing robes, arms outstretched toward a stone bust of another woman, which was set above the doors. All three looked upward, their faces serene and expressionless.

There was something compelling about the figures that had me stop and stare each time. So now, as Heidi Embercrest led us up the steps to the sanctum, I took a moment to get a closer look.

The statue to my left had something wrapped around her arm. A slender ribbon or thread? No irises had been etched into the stone for her eyes, but I got the impression they were still open. The one to the right had no irises either. Like the figure on the left, she reached up toward the bust above the door with one hand, her other held at her side, fingers folded so that only the index and middle finger were on display, as if she were indicating the number two.

The bust above the door had no arms, but it did have irises that stared upward. I'd asked Dori who the statues were, and she'd had no idea. *Just statues*, she'd said. But the tightening at my nape as I passed them now told me different.

Heidi pushed open the heavy wooden doors and strode into the building. "Come along," she said.

The room beyond was marble-tiled, filled with glass and sunlight, flowers, and fountains of running water. The air was thick with a floral aroma that struggled to mask the acrid scent of magic. Magic that hummed in the air in greeting. It pricked my skin in welcome, urging me to come forward.

My body reacted with yearning anticipation, just like it had to the wards at the Border House. Excitement and nerves held hands and danced in my belly.

Heidi led us to a beautifully carved rosewood wheel, balanced horizontally on a stone plinth in the center of the room. Arcane symbols and images I'd never seen before were etched into the wood. They seemed to shift and move beneath the buttery sunlight.

"Place your hands on the wheel," Heidi instructed. "It represents the eternal cycle of creation. The infinite power of the Weave."

Dori was the first to oblige, and we all followed suit. A gentle buzz kissed my fingers when I made contact, and my stomach contracted. I blew out a shaky breath and smiled across at Dori, who dropped me a reassuring wink.

"The Weave gives, and the Weave takes," Heidi said, her voice echoing eerily around us. "But here, at Nightsbridge, we do not tolerate the abuse of power. One infraction, and you may be marked and forgiven. Two, and you may be marked and forgiven. A third time and you *will* be Weaver-Marked. But abuse your power a fourth time, and you will be Unraveled."

My gaze flitted to Benedict, who'd gone decidedly pale. He was on his second infraction after all.

"Ironhart, you have been twice warned," Heidi confirmed. "Be wary." Benedict gulped and nodded. "And now, your marks will be taken, and your power returned. For you, Anamaya, this is the lifting of the veil. It may feel odd, but don't be afraid."

I nodded. "I'm ready."

She began to chant words in a tongue I didn't know. But the wood beneath my fingers warmed, and the symbols began to glow. The air at the center of the wheel rippled, and a sleek blue cat materialized. Clary's eyes lit up at the sight, her face breaking into a huge smile. "Mimi!"

A familiar? *Clary's* familiar.

Mimi leapt lightly off the wheel and onto Clary's shoulder, curling her small body around Clary's neck before nuzzling her face to her cheek. Clary giggled. "I missed you, too."

"You may step back, Tavona," Heidi said.

Clary released the wheel and took a step back.

Heidi began to chant again, and once more the wheel heated, symbols shifting and moving across its surface until the center shimmered and a white cat appeared. The black patches on its fur resembled a waistcoat and tie. Larger than the blue cat, it glared at everyone before padding over to Dori, bumping her arm with his head, then leaping off the wheel as if to say, *come on then*.

Dori rolled her eyes. "Someone is in a mood."

Heidi stopped chanting and nodded at Dori, who released the wheel and joined Clary a few feet away.

"Come on, Mr. Twiggins," Dori called.

Mr. Twiggins ignored her in favor of grooming his paws. This cat had attitude—much like his mistress.

Heidi started up her chant again, and this time my hand began to tingle.

A pricking sensation traveled up my arm, the pressure and sharpness almost...uncomfortable. A memory from a long time ago filled my mind, the feeling of a dead leg waking up. Pins and needles! Wait...what was happening? Was this real? Did I have pins and needles in my arm? I mean, I could *feel* them. The prick and stab and... Oh Trinity!

Panic warred with exhilaration, leaving me dizzy.

The center of the wheel shimmered, and a figure began to form.

"What is that?" Benedict said, frowning.

He was a sorcerer like me. We didn't get familiars...so what was manifesting?

The form solidified into a huge black bird with a thick, powerful beak, and my pulse quickened.

A rook.

Heidi gasped and stared at me wide-eyed.

The rook cocked its head and fixed a beady eye on me. "*Hello, Anamaya. It's good to finally meet you in the flesh.*"

I opened my mouth to speak, to ask what the fuck was going on, when the warmth in my arm turned to a searing heat.

It *burned*.

It *hurt*.

In the next moment, the heat shot up my arm and slammed into my chest.

My scream filled the world as the Weave blessed me with the return of pain.

VITRA

Purina glides into my chamber and slithers onto my bed, her sleek, scaly form gleaming in the overhead light.

"You called, Massssster?"

I finish binding my hair and pull on a shirt. "I did. I need you to deliver a message."

"Of coursssse." She lifts her serpentine head and inclines it in deference. "It will take time. A few dayssss, if not more."

"I know how long the journey is."

"Very well..."

She waits patiently as I craft the message that must be sent, then recite it for her. "The sage spoke true. I believe the key is among us."

Purina glides away, vanishing into the walls with my message. A message that should be so much more. But not yet. Not until I'm certain.

Because our only hope of salvation is also the key to our downfall.

"Anamaya, Anamaya, what *am* I to do with you?"

GLOSSARY

History & Religion

A.O.: After Overshadowing.
Apex Breach: The legendary site where the members of the Covenant stood as one to close the rift between realms.
Tariffel (fel): Supernal afterlife.
The Covenant: The agreement made by several bloodlines to work together to purge Nightsbridge of otherworld threats. The members of this pact vowed to provide adolescents from their own bloodlines to cull the threats spawned by The Overshadowing.
The Overshadowing: Occurred three hundred years ago and resulted in the barriers between worlds thinning, causing a merger of worlds, which allowed Horrors and Echoes into Nova Terra. The Overshadowing warped technology and mutated certain creatures and insects.
The Trinity: The three daughters of the ancient gods, born to manage and protect the Weave. Worshipped by the Arcanus.
P.O.: Pre-Overshadowing.

Bestiary

Arcanus: Magic users.
Barghest: A Therianthrope or shapeshifter. A Barghest's saliva has a clotting agent and healing properties, but it's only to be used on a potential or actual mate. A Barghest uses his scent to mark his chosen mate and must mark them three times to claim them.
Chamaeleontis Vermis: The chameleon worm. A species of critter. Can change color and texture to mimic aspects of other insects and critters.

Critters: The collective name given to all the mutated creatures that live beneath the cities and towns of Nova Terra.

Daeva: Beings from another world. Helped the humans and supernals of Nova Terra seal the breaches and restore balance during the Overshadowing.

Dhampir: Offspring of vampire and human procreation. Dhampir blood is addictive to humans. Dhampirs are unaffected by sunlight.

Echoes: A type of Horror. Mimic a person's personality and appearance because they have neither. They leave their victims faceless and forgotten.

Floramus Arachmus: A species of critter. Docile by nature. They mainly live off fungi and algae, with a little protein from rats, mice, and small insects. They are difficult to catch due to their nests being in the hardest-to-reach spots of the sewer system. Injects a psybond toxin when it bites, allowing the critter to telepathically communicate.

Haematophage: Classification for supernals that require a diet of blood to survive.

At the top of the haematophage pyramid are the Vayne and Damascus houses. Bonded through blood and marriage for centuries, these two houses are rooted in ancient traditions.

Horror: A creature originating from another world with the intent to harm the indigenous population.

Landwyrm: Ancient Horror. Extinct. Able to paralyze its prey with a look. Origin unknown, classification draconic.

Mudarks: A type of Horror. Elemental beings made of earth. Mudarks are tiny creatures that live in underground colonies. They can band together to form one huge creature.

Naga: A rare breed of snake shifters, about whom little is publicly known.

Obsidian Venenum: Commonly known as jet stingers. Highly sought after for the paralytic effect of their venom.

Pipers: A rare breed of horror known to occupy the marshlands of Nightsbridge. Pipers lure their prey in with high-frequency sound waves and incapacitate them with a neurotoxin to consume them alive.

Ratakan: Created to act as sentries to keep horrors from getting too close to the wards of Nightsbridge.

Salamanders: Fire elemental horrors. A salamander will burn you up. Bonfires in the forest can spawn Salamanders.

Sicut Mors: Large mosquito-like bugs found in the western forestlands on the outskirts of Carlston.

Sith: Full classification Baobhan sith, Haemotophage. Houses of Vayne and Moon. Known for their sexuality and lack of empathy, sith are hardy but not as hardy as Dhampirs. They can compel people with their ethereal glow.

Supernals: Beings that were created by the source. Not human.

Sylphs: Horrors that can steal oxygen from a victim's lungs, suffocating them on dry land. They can also become invisible.

The Shining Ones: An unknown species named for the ethereal glow emanating from their bodies. They occupied Nightsbridge between 1 A.O. and 10 A.O then vanished. The only evidence of their existence now is a halfling—a hybrid species that is hurtling toward extinction.

Supernals: Non-humans.

Therianthropes: Supernals that can shift fully into a beast form. Live in packs and have their own rituals, most related to nature and the lunar cycle.

Undines: Water horrors that lay their eggs in the decaying bodies of their drowned prey.

Wood Weavers: Horrors. They live inside trees, and some can disguise themselves *as* trees. Carnivorous.

Magic & Technology

Focuses: Objects that allow Sorcerers to control the level of power that flows through them from the weave. Focuses act as conduits, a central focus for power, and a way to direct the raw magic flowing through them without burning out.

Incantors: Magic users who harness the Weave through spells, potions, and other arcane methods. They draw and shape magic using incantations, rituals, and enchanted tools, channeling their power precisely. Each Incantor forms a deep bond with a familiar that enhances their connection to the Weave.

Magical Objects: Arcanus can create magical objects. Objects can be cursed and connected to the Weave, allowing humans to use them. Examples include glamour amulets and magical potions.

Magitech: Technology enhanced by magic.

Port: A magical means of long-distance travel. Ports disassemble the traveler at the point of departure and reassemble them at the chosen destination, bridging vast distances in moments.

Rift Blade: Short swords powered by magitech, fuelled by the Weave. The hilts are embedded with conduit stones, allowing any supernal to wield one, even those who could not use the Weave. The stones give supernals temporary access to the Weave's power or heighten their existing connection.

Sorcerers: Born with an innate connection to the Weave, sorcerers channel raw magic directly through themselves rather than relying on spells, potions, or external conduits. The Weave flows naturally through them, allowing them to manipulate magic instinctively. While they don't require focuses, some sorcerers use them to refine and control their power with greater precision.

The Source: The source of all magic. This well of power created supernals, gifting them their powers. Its nature is a mystery.

The Weave: The network of magic that exists in any particular world. The Source and the Weave are two distinct wells of power, but can work in symbiosis through the right conductor. Spawned from the essence of all gods.

Unwoven: Arcanus who have had their connection to the Weave blocked as a disciplinary action.

Government Bodies & Political Terminology

Arcanum Imperium: Governs the Arcanus and all Weave users.
Arcanum Lex: A book setting out the laws that all Arcanus must abide by.
Custodes Hominum: Governs humans.
Imperium Alius: The supernatural council that governs all supernal beings, even the Arcanum Imperium. Also referred to as "The High Supernal Council" or "The Otherworld Governing Body."
Infra Sanctum: A vault under Nightsbridge containing relics and books.
Libra Veritas: "The book of truth."
Scentia Keepers: The individuals responsible for running the Infra Sanctum.
Superna Coteri: Nightsbridge's governing body.
Perculiari Petitione: A petition to be admitted into Nightsbridge Academy.
Timor Exstinctionis: Fear of extermination. A law that prevents Arcanus bloodlines from being extinguished to prevent destabilization of the Weave.

Military

Carvers: Bio-horror engineers who create creatures such as the Ratakan. They run a program called The Initiative, which involves dissecting horrors to understand their mechanics.
Hunters: Fight Echoes and Horrors in the Nightsbridge region. Hunters are trained from age sixteen and up. Twenty-five kills designate a seasoned hunter.
Ocean Guard: A naval force.

ACKNOWLEDGEMENTS

Let's start by thanking coffee, because without it, there wouldn't have been a first draft. Okay, now that that's out of the way, let's get to it.

Andrea, you helped me knock that first, second, and third draft into shape. Your brutally honest feedback made me cry... I mean, it made me a better writer. Seriously. Thank you.

Nikki, this book would not have made it to submission without your support and encouragement. Thanks for kicking my butt when I faltered. You championed *Wicked Onyx* from the heart, and I'm so lucky to have you as my agent.

A huge thank you to Meredith for taking a chance and bringing me into the Page and Vine family. I vow to write amazing books and hopefully make you tons of money. Wait...am I allowed to say that?

Jordyn, Jordyn, Jordyn—you know what you did. You adopted *Wicked Onyx* as your baby, and you helped me polish the heck out of it, smoothing out the rough edges to get to the diamond beneath. I am so blessed to have you as my editor, and I can't wait to work on book two with you.

And finally, last but by no means least, thank you, with all my heart, to the team at Page and Vine. You guys rock!

ABOUT THE AUTHOR

Deviyanee Cassidy is a *USA Today* Bestselling Author of Paranormal and Fantasy Novels. She writes under the pen name Debbie Cassidy. Born in the UK, and raised in a small town, she spent most of her time reading and dreaming up stories. After studying psychology at university, she worked various jobs before finally pursuing her passion for writing full time.

Deviyanee has drawn upon her cultural experiences, and Indian Mythology when creating some of her worlds. Her books are filled with action, vivid descriptions, multi-layered plots, and heart stopping romance. They feature strong female protagonists who find themselves drawn into supernatural worlds filled with magic, danger, and romance.

Deviyanee explores themes of personal growth, redemption, and the struggle between good and evil. She's been praised for her engaging characters, intricate world building, and emotionally resonant storytelling.

Learn more at: debbiecassidyauthor.com

STORIES WITH IMPACT

WWW.PAGEANDVINE.COM